From #1 *New Y*
Carlan, discover The

You can now dive into the Kindle Vella phenomenon with over 2 MILLON READS. This saga has ranked #1 for over a full year and continues to break records each month as America's favorite serial. Each book contains more than 10% new content that includes two never before scenes from some of our favorite couples.

What would you do for three million dollars?

Four young women enter into a clandestine auction to be married to the highest bidders. For no less than a million dollars a year, for three years, each woman will do what it takes to secure her future. Entangled in a high-stakes game of money, lust, power, and the hope for absolution, this group of women becomes a sisterhood unlike any other.

Once chosen by a man she's never met and agrees to marry sight unseen...there is no going back. Hidden secrets, wicked desires, fiery couplings and intense family drama are all part of the deal when you willingly enter into The Marriage Auction.

You may now kiss the bride...

THE MARRIAGE
AUCTION

Also from Audrey Carlan

Montreal
London
Berlin
Washington, D.C.
Madrid
Rio
Los Angeles

Lotus House Series
Resisting Roots
Sacred Serenity
Divine Desire
Limitless Love
Silent Sins
Intimate Intuition
Enlightened End

Trinity Trilogy
Body
Mind
Soul
Life
Fate

Calendar Girl
January
February
March
April
May
June
July
August
September
October

November
December

Falling Series
Angel Falling
London Falling
Justice Falling

THE MARRIAGE
AUCTION

BOOK FOUR

By Audrey Carlan

The Marriage Auction: Book Four
By Audrey Carlan

Copyright 2021 Audrey Carlan
ISBN: 978-1-957568-53-9

Published by Blue Box Press, an imprint of Evil Eye Concepts, Incorporated

Editor: Jeanne De Vita
Cover design by Asha Hossain

Episode 95

Baby on Board

DAKOTA

I am going to be someone's mother.

I was pregnant.

With child.

The reality of what we'd just uncovered was a whirlpool swirling around like a vortex within the confines of my mind. My stomach twisted and churned as I breathed through the sudden onslaught of nausea. I stood completely still, desperate to stop the acid crawling up my throat so I wouldn't vomit all over the floor. I ground down on my teeth as I scanned the florist shop looking for a trash can I could use—just in case.

Savannah's movement caught my attention as she pointed to the palest peach carnation in the entire store and then to a baby-pink rose.

Baby.

I was having a baby.

"What do you think?" Savannah turned around, her face beaming with joy. She held a handful of carnations, roses, daises, and baby's breath all clutched together in a quasi-bouquet.

Baby's breath.

A living, breathing human was growing inside of me right now. One I was going to have to take care of. Teach about life. About how to be a good, kind, decent person.

Am I a good person?

I covered my flat belly, and my bottom lip trembled as wave after wave of anxiety and primal fear roared through my system, obliterating every inch of cautious excitement I'd had when Sutton and I found out we were about to be parents.

Savannah's gaze flicked to my hand, to where it rested over my stomach, and then back to my face, her expression shifting to one of concern.

"Can you excuse us for a bit, hun? I need a moment with my sister to talk this through." Savannah patted Nancy, the florist, on the shoulder. I didn't even realize Nancy had been standing there helping Savannah pick out flowers. The entire time I'd been lost within the turbulent mess that was my mind.

"Oh, of course. I'll just get started writing up this order and making sure we have the right number of carnations and roses for the event this weekend." Happiness exuded from Nancy, the only florist in our small town, as she bustled to the front of the store.

Savannah nodded. "Thank you. I'll be right over."

I stared numbly at the bouquet she was holding as I remembered the real reason we were here. My little sister was getting married this weekend. Not to her high school sweetheart but to a Viking of a man who planned to cart her off to Norway. I was now married to a man from a family we'd believed had been our arch nemesis. And was pregnant with said man's baby.

If someone had told me last year we'd be in this very position today, I'd have called bullshit. Except it was all true.

Our new reality.

In a single month, our lives had changed so drastically that

I barely recognized us. We had become completely different people. All while dealing with extreme tragedies like the barn burning down. The horses we'd lost in the fire. The insurmountable debt. Our father almost killing two men. And here we were, trying to eke out a tiny speck of happiness within all the muck that had stacked up ten feet high.

Oh, and I was pregnant. That little factoid plagued my every waking thought.

"Kota, talk to me," Savannah pleaded gently.

"I'm going to have a baby." I could hear the break in my voice, a crack that was splitting open the wall I'd built around my emotions. I'd been adding brick after brick to that wall of protection, and with each new realization, the barrier I'd built was weakening. Like a spiderweb of shattering brick and rock, it started to crumble, bit by bit falling away, leaving me exposed and vulnerable. Each new life-changing event added a new fracture to the framework.

Savannah's gaze flicked to the florist across the room and then back to me. "Yes, and?" she asked, lowering her voice.

"You're getting married this weekend," I stated flatly.

Savannah nodded. "I am. To a wonderful man."

"To a *stranger*," I hissed, clenching my teeth.

My sister reacted automatically, hooking her elbow with mine and tugging me straight out of the front door of the shop while calling out, "Be right back, Nancy."

Once we were outside, she spun us both around and placed one hand on her hip defensively, the other still clutching the pretty flowers she'd gathered.

"What in the heck is going on with you?" she snapped.

I slumped against the building and brought my hands in front of my face to rub at my forehead, trying to knead out the tension knotted there. "I don't know, it's...it's *everything*. Everything is changing."

"Yes, it is. We knew this when we signed up for you know what. When we stood on that stage. When we signed on the dotted line. We knew this when you married Sutton back in Vegas…"

I groaned loudly, like a horse being pushed too hard to ride when it didn't have much left in the tank. I let my frustration bleed out right there on Main Street as my stomach tightened and the telltale sour taste hit my tongue. I dashed over to the garbage can at the corner of the building and hurled my meager breakfast into its gaping maw.

Savannah was at my side holding my hair within a second, her hand rubbing up and down my back, always right there. That touch was a comfort and a curse as it worked double-time to not only soothe, but also to remind me of what I would lose after this weekend.

I heaved into the garbage and then pushed myself upright, sucking in a heaping breath of air.

Savannah handed me a wad of tissues she must have pulled from her purse. I wiped my mouth and then reached for the water bottle that she handed me. I swished and spat into the trash, then drank a few small gulps of water. The cool drink soothed the back of my throat which felt like I'd swallowed a series of razor blades. I'd tossed my cookies until my esophagus was painfully raw.

Savannah handed me a piece of unwrapped mint gum. I chewed it, taking the time to let my queasy stomach settle while sipping the water.

"You need to see Doc Blevins," she commanded, bending over and picking up the bouquet she'd dropped.

"You on Sutton's side now?" I glowered at her.

She tipped her head, and her eyebrows rose on her forehead. "If it's the side that gets you medical attention, then yeah, I am."

I snarled and drank more water, the minty gum helping tremendously with the icky tension coating my gut.

"Kota, I know all of this is a lot to take in. I'm dealing with it too. You're not alone. You have me. You have Sutton. And I have Erik. It's not just us anymore. We have support. Lean into it. Stop fearing it."

Her words were a balm and a punch to the chest at the same time. Mostly because she was right. We weren't alone anymore. Sutton had made it crystal clear that he was one hundred percent in this with me. Ready to take on my pa. Prepared to be a father to his child. *Our child.* And here I was, having a mental and physical meltdown in the middle of the goddamned street. I'd never been so weak in my life.

"I'm scared," I confessed.

Savannah let out a breath and nodded. "I am too. What are you most scared of? Let's tackle that first."

Hot damn. My sister was wise.

I licked my lips, inhaled sharply, and acknowledged the truth. "I'm afraid of being a mother," I croaked, pesky unwanted tears making my eyes glassy. It was as though I was seeing the world through a warped, dirty window.

My sister pressed her lips together and tipped her head to the side. "Okay. I can see that being pretty scary, but again, you have help. It's not like with Mom and our pa. Sutton is *elated* you are having his child. Ever since this morning, the man has been so puffed up with pride it's oozing out his fingertips. He's a peacock, full fan of feathers stretched wide for everyone to see."

I chuckled at the visual she presented and wiped away the tears. "You're right. He's acting like he battled a wild animal and came out the victor."

Savannah grinned wide. "I mean, if it walks like a duck…"

I narrowed my eyes. "You calling me a wild animal?"

She lifted her shoulders toward her ears. "You are a little wild."

Her response had me suddenly bursting into fits of laughter. So much so that I bent over with the need to let it out fully. Big heaping huffs spilled from my lungs right alongside the desperation and tension controlling me. When I got hold of it, I reached out and pulled her into a hug. "I missed this. I missed you."

Savannah held me just as tight. "Me too. But I'm here now. And even when I'm not here, you'll have Sutton and his family. Honestly, Kota, they seem like really good people. Nothing like what we had. Definitely not the horrible people our pa raised us to believe they were. Give them a chance. Let them in."

I nodded against her shoulder. "What if they don't like me?" I admitted a fear I'd had since Sutton brought me home. I was the descendant of a woman one of their elders had loved and lost. History repeated itself again when my father stole my mother away from Sutton's dad.

"If they didn't like you, do you think they'd be helping your sister plan a wedding on their property? Every last one of them offered to personally handle a specific aspect. Cook the food, get a band, decorate." She eased back but kept hold of my hand. Her other one still holding that damned flower arrangement.

"True."

Savannah sighed. "Kota, you need to get out of your head. Stop fearing what you've been taught and told about these people. Treat them like they are your family—because *news flash*—you are legally and biologically bound to these people."

I covered my lower abdomen protectively.

"Sutton is happy," I confided. "Ecstatic, really. He wants a family with me. A whole houseful of little ones. I can't imagine why."

"And that freaks you out?" she asked.

"What if I'm a bad mother? What if I lose my mind the way ours did?" My tone was sharp as a knife, cutting right through the heart of the issue.

Savannah shook her head. "Not possible."

"It is!" I fired back. "It is possible. Our mother was weak. Beaten down physically and emotionally. She had very little to give us, and what she did give wasn't enough to save us from our pa. And we weren't enough for her to save herself."

"Our mother was lost," she agreed. "She was knocked down for years and years and couldn't find her way to the light. And that seed of doubt grew within her until she believed we were better off without her. That the world would be better off if she didn't exist. That is not you." Savannah said the last with such conviction...I wanted to believe her.

"It could be," I whispered. We shared DNA with Carol McAllister. That part of her could very well live inside of us. Probably lived inside all the women in our family.

"No. It isn't within you because you've already proven to be a great mother," Savannah bit out.

I frowned, having no idea was she was referring to.

"To me, dummy!" she snapped. "It wasn't our momma who taught me about being a woman. About what to do when I got my cycle for the first time. That was you. Showing me what pads and tampons were—and cramps and cravings and mood swings. It wasn't our mother who went with me to get a training bra when I hit puberty. It wasn't our mother who went shopping with me for a prom dress. It wasn't our mother who I couldn't wait to talk to when I gave my virginity to Jarod," she spoke, emotion coating every word.

"*Savvy,*" I croaked, my heart in my throat at what she was confiding. At the gift she was laying at my feet.

"All of that was *you*, Kota. You were the mother I needed. You were the voice of reason during the hard times. The advisor I listened to when I chose to apply to college instead of staying here and working the land. It's always been you. So yes, it's scary as all get-out that you're bringing a life into the world...but look at me." She patted her chest with emphasis. "I'm who I am today because of you. And I like who I am, and the woman I've become."

My eyes filled with tears as I stared at my favorite person in the entire world. The love I felt for her was overwhelming in its glory. "You're the most beautiful woman I've ever known, inside and out," I breathed, wanting her to feel how impressed I was with who'd she become.

"And I learned all of that from you. My big sister. The woman who raised me."

I swallowed against the lump of cotton clogging my throat. "That was a pretty good speech." I sniffed and wiped my nose with the remaining tissue she'd given me.

"Yeah, I learned a few things about how to speak my mind from my big sister," she continued, grinning.

"Now you're just laying it on thick." I glared.

She snorted. "More importantly, did it work? Because it was nothin' but the truth."

I closed my eyes, took a deep breath, and thought about all she'd said. I did have a hand in raising her. Had devoted my life to her and the land we were born on. And that was with no help and a bastard of a father. But I had help now. People in my life who weren't opposed to working hard and living life to the fullest. People who lent a hand whenever it was needed simply because they were good.

I had Savannah.

I had Sutton.

I had his family, who I had a sneaky suspicion would be as happy as Sutton when they found out another Goodall was cooking in my womb.

"How do you always do that?" I asked, filled with awe. "Turn things around until all I can see is the good."

Savannah shrugged. "Must be something I learned standing alongside a strong-willed, hardworking, compassionate, land-loving woman."

Her words took a sledgehammer to the wall I'd built around my emotions and destroyed it completely.

I pulled her into another hug. "I love you, Savvy. Thank you for setting me straight. For dulling that razor's edge of my fear. I'm still nervous about being a mother, but you're right. I did help when you were growing up. And I have help now—more than I could have ever imagined."

Savannah put her hand over my stomach. "This baby will experience nothing but love. And that's all any of us really need. The rest will come with each new day, and I've no doubt that with you and Sutton it will come naturally. Have a little faith in the bond and union the two of you have built because it created something pretty special." She tapped my stomach once more and then removed her hand.

"We did create something that's wholly us. And I am happy about it. Scared, yes. Uncertain about everything else, hell yes. But I hear you, and I agree. I'm going to push the fear aside and focus on the blessing instead."

Savannah smiled huge. "And it is absolutely a blessing. Now I'm going to go in there and use the fancy-dancy black American Express card that Erik gave me to pay for my wedding flowers. Then we're getting you a dress."

"I'll be out here. I need a minute to settle." I leaned against the wall, taking a moment to simply breathe. Which was when my phone rang.

Sutton's name appeared on the display.

"Hey," I answered, the nerves still present but slowly easing as I mulled over everything Savannah had said.

"What's wrong?" he demanded instantly.

I chuckled. "Nothing. I just had a moment with Savvy, but she set my stubborn ass straight."

"Oh yeah? That's a miracle all on its own. I'll have to ask how she did it." He laughed. "What was it about?"

This was when I would usually lie, change the subject, and internally battle my feelings alone.

But I wasn't alone anymore.

"I, uh, I admitted how scared I am about becoming a mother."

He wanted to be a part of it all, which meant I needed to be honest when things weren't okay. Even if those things were imagined and in my own mind.

"Darlin'…" he murmured in that low rumbling way that

made my knees feel like jelly. If I'd been right in front of him, he'd have pulled me into his massive arms and plastered me to that warm chest I was becoming rather obsessed with.

"What Savannah reminded me was that I'm not alone. I've got you," I spoke with confidence.

"And you always will have me. We're going to learn how to be parents to our child together. Help one another through the good, bad, and the ugly. I've got a solid support system in my family. You have the same in your sister. We're not going to fuck this up. Have faith, baby."

Faith.

I huffed. "You sound like Savannah."

"Did I ever tell you how much I like your sister? Mighty fine woman," he rattled off playfully.

"Says the man who went into verbal battle with her just this morning," I reminded him.

"Bah! That's what families do. When you're passionate about something, you make your thoughts, feelings, and opinions known. You take in what your loved ones have to say and hash it out. You can talk to me about your fears. We'll resolve them together. I'm excited about this baby, Dakota. I'm happy I married you. I'm so damned thrilled about our future, you can't wipe the smile off my face just thinking about it. Darlin', it's all good. You, me, this baby…"

"It's all good," I repeated.

"That's right. I want you to be excited and enjoy this time. We only get to experience this first pregnancy once."

"First?" I blurted. If this man thought I was going to be pushing out another baby right after this one, he had a screw loose.

He chuckled. "I think barefoot and pregnant is going to be my favorite look on you," he teased.

"Are you serious?"

"As a heart attack," he joked. "Gonna fill you with so many babies we'll need a bigger house," he added with a sexy growl that flowed through my body like a sensual tidal wave.

Then what he said filtered through the arousal. Shock and irritation built up within my chest and shot out from my mouth like a garden hose set to full blast. "Sutton Goodall...you take that back!" I yelled into the phone.

"Fuck you so hard and so good you'll be begging for me to get you pregnant one after another." His voice took on that rumble that made me hot and bothered.

"You're a pig," I protested, but I genuinely enjoyed our little game of trying to get one another's goat.

"Oink, oink!" he spouted. "At least I'm your pig! And you're stuck with me. Having my piglets like a good little cowgirl," he taunted, stoking the fire within me to a blazing inferno.

The man loved riling me up, but what I realized was that I no longer felt as frightened about our situation. Between Savannah's reminder, Sutton's commitment, and of course, the sparring with him, I felt lighter. Less afraid of what the future held because I was entering it with people who loved me and cared about this baby.

I wouldn't fail at being a mother because I'd have help. And because I'd already had practice to some extent with Savannah.

Anticipation suddenly washed over me like a sweet-smelling breeze, covering the fear and anxiety with hope for the future.

"I love you, Sutton Goodall. You know that?" I whispered into the phone.

He was silent for a moment as though he was letting it sink in.

"I love you, too." My stomach fluttered every time he said those words. "Try to have a little fun with your sister. If you need me, I'm here."

"Okay. Oh, why did you call anyway?" I asked.

"Just wanted to check on my wife and child."

Such a good man.

"I'm glad you did. See you at home?" I added.

"Yeah, Dakota, I'll see you at home." I could practically visualize the smile on his face when he responded.

The phone went quiet right as Savannah came out of the store. "You ready?"

I let those two words roll around in my mind, clearing out all the emotional crap that had built up over the past month.

"I'm ready."

Episode 96

Bucket List

ERIK

I flipped the folded-up, ratty, yellow-lined paper between my fingers while I sat on the porch and viewed the land outside Savannah's childhood home. This single paper had held me together the past couple years. Had given me purpose.

Until I met her.

Seeing Savannah, my other half, on that stage had changed me. It cultivated a part of my soul that I didn't know had been lacking. I knew our coming together had changed her, too. Sitting here planning to take her away from this life was proof of that fact.

Savannah had chosen me.

I'd given her the space she needed over the past month to work through any reservations she might have had about marrying me. She'd stuck to her guns. And over the past month, we'd become connected. Closer than I'd ever been to any person in my life, including Jack. He'd been my constant support system for so long that it was odd to feel that shift within me. I knew Jack felt it too and was possibly wounded by it. Even though he was supportive and beyond thrilled that I'd found the person I wanted to share my life with, the woman who brought me out of the darkness, it was still hard. Change was always hard on those involved.

Regardless, Savannah was my ultimate priority. Before it had been work and family; now it was Savannah, family, and then work. I finally knew that I was on the right path.

I unfolded the heavily creased paper I'd used to pen my bucket list. I'd scribbled each item when I was at my absolute lowest. Laid up in that German hospital, grieving the loss of one of my best friends. Losing Troy in the helicopter accident had broken me. For years I'd felt as though it was my fault because I'd chosen to attend a meeting in Germany. Wanted so desperately to secure a multimillion-dollar account for Johansen Brewing that I didn't think twice about jetting off in my helicopter with my friend Troy in the cockpit.

Through years of pain, remorse, and guilt, I'd traveled the world and scratched off all but two things on the bucket list I'd created after the worst day of my life. It was somehow fitting that the last two items were now connected.

Visit Yellowstone National Park

Marry my soulmate

I was in Montana to marry Savannah, who I knew with my entire being was my soulmate. In two days, we'd be husband and wife. And yet, I couldn't shake the need to mark off that remaining item. However, the only way to get to Yellowstone National Park and back in a single day would mean placing myself in the one thing I'd vowed never to set foot in again.

A helicopter.

My hands shook as I folded up the piece of paper, swallowed down the goose egg of fear lodged in my throat, and pulled my phone from my back pocket. I scrolled through the display and clicked *call*.

Jack answered on the second ring. "Hey, brother, Henrik and I finished building the arbor last night. We're going to stain and lacquer it today, and tomorrow Alana and Christophe are going to decorate it with whatever flowers Savannah and Dakota pick out."

I cleared my throat. "Excellent. Thank you. I, uh, I need another favor. It's not going to be easy, but you're the only person I know who can make magic happen."

"This is true. I am not only your best mate, I'm also a wizard. I'll use my mighty powers of manipulation to secure anything!" he boasted playfully, changing his voice in a poor interpretation of a British accent. "On my steed with my trusty wand…"

"Okay, I get it. I get it." I chuckled.

"What do you need?" His tone was back to straightforward—no bullshit, professional Jack. "This about work?"

"I need a helicopter."

There was a long pause during which neither of us spoke. Sweat beaded at my hairline, and my palms became damp.

"I'm sorry… Did I hear you right? A helicopter? You mean one of those flying machines you swore to yourself, me, and your mother and father that you'd never ride in again?" Jack's tone was accusatory.

I nodded even though he couldn't see me. "Yes. How quickly can you secure one?"

He cleared his throat and sighed heavily. "I'd rather talk about why you want it," he countered.

"There are two more items on my list that I need to scratch off."

"*That fucking list!*" he barked instantly. "It's the bane of my existence. The reason for my nightmares these past years, and you want me to help you scratch off a couple of items. Absolutely not. Fuck no! Especially if it means you're putting yourself in danger."

"Jack, this is non-negotiable. I'm speaking to you not as my friend, but as your *boss*." I reminded him of a technicality. I was, in fact, the owner of Johansen Brewing. He was my CEO, second in command. Not to mention the twenty percent interest I'd given him when we hit it big many years ago. The man was rolling in money even without the CEO salary. He chose to work day in, day out because he got off on running the empire.

"Fuck that. I don't give a shit. Fire me!" he spat, knowing I never would.

"Jack," I sighed. Pulling the boss card was a low blow, but I needed to do this. "I need you to get me a helicopter for the day as my best friend, *my brother.* I want it ready and at the nearest landing pad by noon."

"Give me one good reason I should help you with this," he demanded.

I sighed deeply, letting him hear the war within me through that single breath. "I want to battle the demon with the woman I love by my side so that I can move forward in our life together. Unafraid. Healthy. But more importantly, I want to be *whole* when I marry Savannah. I have to do this. Please understand."

"*Faen i helvete!*" *The Devil in Hell,* he cursed in Norwegian.

"Will you help me, Jack?"

He groaned. "*Ja,* I'll help. I don't want to. I hate that you feel this is a necessary step toward healing, but I understand it. We have all seen the change in you since Savannah entered the picture. And if this step means you're that much closer to finding closure over Troy's death, I'll do whatever it takes to support you."

"*Tusen takk,*" I thanked him.

I gave him the details of what I wanted to do, and he said he'd call me back when the reservations were confirmed. I hung up with him just as Savannah exited the house, two large steaming cups in her hands.

"*God morgen,*" I stated on autopilot, taking in her pearly skin. Her cheeks tinged pink when she smiled sweetly. I loved watching her. The way she moved so gracefully. How her ample figure gifted me rounded curves to hold on to. I wanted to pick her up, take her back to bed, and worship her body until she begged me to stop.

"Good morning to you. I mean, *god morgen*. I need to continue my Norwegian practice with Irene when we get back home."

Home.

I watched as surprise flitted across her face as she realized what she'd just said.

"Huh." She handed me one of the mugs and was about to sit in the chair next to me when I hooked my arm around her hips and eased her onto my lap, one arm around her, the other holding the mug. "I just referred to Norway as my home," she observed while staring out at the land that she'd grown up on.

"You did," I agreed and sipped the coffee she'd made me.

"It seems like it should feel strange thinking of Norway as my home. But I don't know." She pursed her lips. "I'm looking out at a view I've seen my entire life, and it feels foreign to me somehow. Is that weird?"

I shook my head. "Sometimes when we find where we are supposed to be, it just clicks. Like a puzzle piece slipping right into place. It was always meant to be there; it just took trying all the other options until finding the right fit."

She hummed and leaned back against my chest, making herself comfortable. "I'll miss Dakota," she admitted. "Don't be surprised if when we're back in Norway, I get sad from time to time."

I nodded and rubbed my cheek against her soft hair. "You will have endless means to visit. We can even buy a home nearby, a place that's not this one, that we can make our own."

Savannah perked up, sitting straight as she turned toward me. "Really?"

"All I care about is whatever you need to be happy and whatever we need to have full lives. Dakota, Sutton, and the baby on the way are members of our family. We'll make sure they feel our presence regularly." And I meant it. I'd found a camaraderie with Sutton. He genuinely wanted to give Dakota a great life, as I did with Savannah. We had a common interest in the sisters.

She leaned forward, her pink lips brushing mine as she spoke. "That would make me very happy."

"Then it will be done." I cupped the back of her neck with my free hand and took her mouth in a long, leisurely kiss that tasted of coffee and vanilla creamer. "Mmm, you taste good."

When she pulled away, her eyes were alight with a hunger I recognized. Since we'd been in Montana, we hadn't continued our exploration of one another's bodies. So much had happened that intimacy hadn't felt right, but I knew with that single lust-filled look, she wanted to take that next step as much as I did.

"Soon," I promised on a whisper.

She pouted.

"I need to ask you for a favor." I changed the subject.

She sat up straight. "Anything."

"Have you ever been to Yellowstone National Park?"

"Does a bear shit in the woods?" she retorted instantly.

I frowned. "I assume so. Why would you ask that?"

She giggled for a full minute. "It's an expression. Of course, I have. I live in Montana."

"Would you like to see it with me? Today?" I licked my suddenly dry lips. "From within a…a, uh, helicopter?"

Her breath caught as her mouth dropped open and her free hand went to her throat. "Um, a helicopter… You're wanting to view the national park from a helicopter?"

I nodded.

She put her coffee on the small table next to our chair then did the same with mine. She pushed a lock of her brilliant red hair behind her ear. "Okay. May I ask what brought this on?"

I reached into my pocket and pulled out the yellow paper

that I always carried with me. The only people who had ever laid eyes on this list were Jack and my parents. The damn thing had become a talisman of sorts. Something to focus on while I attempted to keep the darkness from overriding everything the last couple of years.

Savannah unfolded it, and I watched her eyes as they scanned each item. "Toured Machu Picchu. Walked the Great Wall of China. Drove the Road to Hana. Snorkeled in Australia. Skied the Swiss Alps… You've done all of these things? Who are you?" she asked, awe taking over her tone and facial expressions.

"I was a very lost man for a long time." I tunneled my hand through her beautiful hair, watching the myriad strands of red, burnt orange, sienna, and gold sift through my fingers. "Then I met you, and my purpose changed."

Her lip wobbled as she read the last two items. "Marrying your soulmate is the last item on the list." She gulped, her breaths coming faster.

"That will be marked off on Sunday. The second to last I want to do with you while fighting my biggest fear."

"Riding in a helicopter," she surmised.

I nodded, emotion filling me with a nervous energy. Then my *elskede* surprised me for what felt like the hundredth time. She eased off my lap and extended her hand to me.

"Then let's go! If we drive fast, we can make it to Yellowstone in a couple hours. They have helicopter tours all the time. Offer a pretty penny and we'll get in even if it's booked up," she announced with certainty. "We're going to need to hurry, though, because we also have a wedding in two days." She grinned.

I took her hand and stood up, but instead of following her inside to get ready to go, I pulled her into a hug. I pressed my face to her neck where I could soak up the good that was Savannah. I breathed in her wild berry and sugar scent while pushing out the absolute terror that flooded my veins at the mere thought of willingly stepping into a helicopter again.

My phone ringing disrupted the moment.

Jack had come through. Like he always did.

"Are you going to throw up?" Savannah asked, her hand on my shoulder as I stared at the death machine before us. It was black as coal, its wildly spinning blades making a rumbling sound that I felt hammering in my chest.

I shook my head, but it was a lie. My stomach was so tied up in knots I hadn't a clue how to unravel the sickness twisting within.

Out of nowhere, Savannah handed me a couple antacids. "Eat these. They will help."

I tossed them into my mouth and started to chew, the chalky taste almost unnoticeable in my mouth as I stared at the beast before us.

Sweat beaded on my forehead and upper lip as I stared at the shiny black and chrome helicopter idling before us. Its massive blades continued to spin around, creating gusts of wind that slapped against our faces. My legs were stiff, and the constant ache I felt on the side I'd injured in the accident suddenly throbbed right along with my rapid heartbeat.

"You don't have to do this, Erik. No one is expecting this of you," Savannah noted gently.

I gritted my teeth and snarled at the offending contraption. "I can't let it beat me."

"It's an inanimate object. It holds no control over you, Erik." Her words were strong and just, but she was wrong.

All of it had control over me.

Fear. Sorrow. Grief. Sadness. And most importantly, loss.

Loss of Troy. Loss of my self-worth. Loss of my own life.

"I have to do this to be whole again," I confided, not needing to look into her compassionate and concerned eyes to know how my admission would steal across her face.

My beloved slid her small, cool hand into my clammy one, interlacing our fingers and squeezing with intent. As I'd hoped, Savannah was here. All in. Ready to give me her love and support.

That was all I needed.

Putting one foot in front of the other, hand in hand with the love of my life, we approached the helicopter.

The feeling of getting into the aircraft with her by my side was surreal. I listened intently as the pilot checked and rechecked all of his gauges and displays and spoke into his headset with the local airfield. Before I knew it, we'd lifted off and were in the air, my stomach clenched. I had to breathe through the terror.

Minutes or what could have been an hour went by. I didn't know, I was so focused on breathing and not vomiting or blacking out. Then all of a sudden we were flying directly over Yellowstone National Park. The view was magical as we saw the incredible Grand Prismatic Spring with its circular shape like a rainbow or multi-colored eye staring out at the sky. The blue of the center faded out into teal, green, yellow, orange, and finally a crimson so intense I didn't think I'd ever seen the color in nature before.

The pilot was speaking to us about the scientific properties of the heat-seeking bacteria that gave the hot spring its colors, but my focus was on the moment. The feel of Savannah's hand clinging to mine, her steady heartbeat paired with mine through our touch. The way her face lit up at each new discovery the pilot pointed out.

As we flew, peace blanketed over the panic that had flooded my system. Nothing was going to happen. It was all in my head. A dark memory of a tragic accident. Slowly, I focused my gaze on the view, actually starting to enjoy the ride. Before the accident, the helicopter had been my favorite mode of transportation. I didn't think I'd reach that level of satisfaction anytime soon, but with every minute that passed safely, another granule of fear left me.

Savannah, on the other hand, was having a blast. Nudging me in the shoulder to look at a certain mountain or geological feature. She practically bounced in her seat when we passed Old Faithful, the geyser that looked like a yellow and blue-green calcite slab from above. The water sank low in the center and then shot out in a sudden burst, the fountain reaching over a hundred feet into the air.

"Nature is so cool!" Savannah cheered, fist pumping the air, and still, despite her excitement, she never let go of my hand. Solid, unbending support the entire ride. Her commitment and support only two of the incredible blessings Savannah brought into my world.

After we'd been given our tour, the helicopter safely landed back in the same small airfield that wasn't far from Sandee.

I thanked the pilot and handed him a stack of hundreds. "Thank you for bringing us back safely." I smiled, and Savannah waved sweetly as I walked her back to our rented SUV.

Once we were on the road, Savannah clapped wildly. "You are a rock star for fighting that fear, baby! I'm so proud of you." She beamed, her smile infectious.

As I drove, my heart pounded and my cock hardened painfully behind my jeans. The rush was so extreme my hands shook. I couldn't help but pull off near a crop of shady trees at the side of the road. Once I did, I jumped out and stomped a good six meters away, my hands linked behind my head as I breathed. Huge breaths of air sawed in and out of my lungs as an overwhelming sense of pride and elation coated my nerve endings.

"Honey, what's wrong?" Savannah asked, following me out of the vehicle.

I unlaced my hands and then shook them. "I'm fine, I'm just…" I jumped up and down where I stood, trying to fling off the electricity shooting through my veins.

"High on adrenaline, I'll bet," she surmised correctly with a grin.

"Yeah, exactly. So much of everything that happened is powering through me. I feel like a live bolt of electricity ready to light up the fucking world!" I groaned and paced, my nerve endings sizzling with the need to move, to run, to act, to do *something.*

"What do you need?" She approached where I was circling like a wild animal and placed her hands to my chest, stopping me in my tracks.

Her touch felt like a brand against my skin. Intense lust bolted straight to my cock, my balls drawing up, ready for action.

"It's not what I need, it's what I want," I growled through clenched teeth.

She licked her lips, and I swear my cock beaded at the tip behind my jeans and briefs.

"Fuck," I hissed, grabbing her hips and pulling her body flush against mine, letting her feel my predicament as I lost control bit by bit.

Her hands slid up and dove into the lengths of my hair. "And what do you want?" she whispered.

"I want to fuck you. Hard. Right here. Right now." My nostrils flared as I cupped her plump ass and ground against her. *God damn.* She was perfection.

She gasped, then boldly rubbed her breasts against my chest as she got up onto her toes, her mouth hovering just out of reach before she handed me the key to certain ecstasy.

"I want that, too."

Episode 97

My Second Chance

JOEL

"She's gone!" I barked into my cell phone as I paced the suite where I'd made love to my wife just last night, fully expecting to wake and do it all over again with her beautiful, willing body. My Faith was as insatiable for my touch as I was for hers. We were one another's equal and yet opposite in every way. Meant to be. Last night cemented our forever commitment to one another.

Then came Aiden.

Ruining everything we'd built with a single act of viciousness.

My mind was spinning with pure rage. Aiden had found and kidnapped Faith's sister. Knowing my wife the way I did, she'd never let someone she loved be at risk when she could offer herself up in exchange. Aiden knew that fact all too well. My nemesis had had years to learn Faith's reactions to such trauma. She would do anything to protect Grace even though her sister did very little to deserve that type of loyalty.

I firmed my jaw and listened to Jonas, Bruno's second-in-command speak rapidly in a flurry of Greek. He was well-known for being a master at manipulating technology. He could do things with a snap of his fingers that could make world leaders cower in fear.

"Where in the hell is Bruno!" I roared.

My cousin, my friend, my *weapon* was missing in action.

"I don't know, sir. I've been trying to pinpoint his location since the minute you called," Jonas answered.

Pinpoint his location?

Those words reminded me that Bruno kept tracking devices in a variety of places on both my person and on Faith.

"Stop looking for Bruno. Pinpoint Faith's location from the tracker in her phone. And don't you dare tell me that Bruno wasn't tracking my wife," I scolded. "I'm not ignorant."

"Okay, okay," Jonas noted in a placating manner. "Yeah, let me just finagle this and…" He paused. I could hear his fingers tapping across a keyboard a mile a minute. "Her tracker is on the move. Looks like she's going forty-five miles an hour. So she's in a vehicle." I clenched my teeth. "It's really strange, though. It keeps taking random turns and speeding through alleys, backtracking, and doing it again. There's no rhyme or reason to it."

"She's being followed," I snapped. "My money is on the elusive Bruno. I swear that man has an uncanny ability to be in the right place at the right time." I prayed he was following my wife and not someone on Aiden's team.

"Yep, I can see Bruno," Jonas announced. "His phone is showing only three percent battery life, but his tracker is following Faith's at a reasonable distance. He's not in a car rented by us or I'd be able to trace the car."

"That's why he hasn't called," I gathered. "He's saving the battery power for the tracker." My nostrils flared as a minute amount of calm settled over me now that I knew Bruno had eyes on my wife. "Good job, my friend," I whispered out loud. "Where are they headed? I'll need a team with me to go after them."

"Mr. Castellanos, if Bruno didn't use that bit of battery to call, he has a damn good reason. It could be that they are being followed or watched by the perpetrator," Jonas supplied.

I gritted my teeth. "Can you pull up the calls and text messages my wife received in the past twenty-four hours?" I hated going through her personal information, but this was life and death. She'd forgive me.

"Absolutely. Give me a second."

"Read me the names and the highlights of the messages. We need more information." I inhaled a harsh breath and ran my fingers through my unruly hair as frustration sang in my veins. I should have been hand-feeding my new bride strawberries and champagne for breakfast, not tracking her phone and planning to save her from certain death.

"There's a group message. A person named Dakota McAllister and another McAllister, this one Savannah. There's mention of two men. Erik and Sutton."

"Yes, skip over those," I instructed.

"Several from someone listed as Madam Alana. She sent a few repeated requests for your wife to check in with her, otherwise she threatened to come after her. Do you think this Madam intervened, and…"

"No." I cut Jonas off. "I know exactly who and what that situation is. Next?"

"Uh, a, um…" He cleared his voice sounding uncomfortable. "A man. Name is displayed as Memphis Taylor. Talks about joining the candidate ranks, something about a sister going to Harvard. His family needs money."

I frowned and went through the people Faith had mentioned in the past month, not recalling a gentleman named Memphis Taylor.

"Pin his name and look him up in the system later. I want everything there is to know about the man. Are there any from Aiden Bradford?"

The line was quiet for a minute. "An unknown text was

deleted early this morning. Let me see if I can bring it back and view it." I heard Jonas typing frantically. "Fuck!" he cursed. "I'm forwarding an image and the text that came with it. You need to see this for yourself."

Terror filled my pores as I waited. My phone suddenly pinged, and I put him on speaker and went to the messages. I clicked on the link and read the text:

Meet me at our place. 8:00 a.m. You know where. If Castellanos or his men come with you, Grace dies. Do not test me, Faith. I've had enough of your games. Your time is up. Choose. Your life for your sister's.

I glanced at the digital clock across the room and noted it was exactly seven a.m. Then an image came through. I hovered over it, steeled my spine, and opened it.

It was a picture of a woman suspended in the air by her wrists. Her face was bruised, swollen, and bleeding from her nose and lip. The rest of her didn't look any better. Her skeletal frame was clad in ripped-up fishnet stockings, a painted-on black leather skirt, and a filthy purple crop top. The woman's stomach was concave, the bottom rung of her ribs clearly visible through her skin. It was obvious she hadn't eaten a decent meal in months, if not years.

I cringed at the image knowing full well that the minute my wife viewed it, her fate had been sealed. The monster wasn't stupid. Not only did he play dirtier than anyone I'd ever known—and there were some seriously ruthless rich criminals in the world I tended to avoid—but Aiden knew exactly how to play his cards. The man did not bluff. He didn't have to. Because Aiden ultimately didn't care whose lives he ruined or the carnage he left behind when chasing his goals. He only cared about the outcome. Which in this case was getting his disgusting hands on my wife.

Lord above, I prayed he wanted her alive more than he wanted to hurt her. I wouldn't be able to survive the loss of another woman I loved so deeply.

"Sir? Sir? Mr. Castellanos? Are you still there?" Jonas's

harried voice broke me from my reverie. I shoved the hopelessness I felt into the darkest recess of my mind in order to focus on the here and now.

Saving Faith.

She was all that mattered.

"I'm here," I croaked, emotion clogging my ability to speak clearly.

"How do you want to proceed, sir?" Jonas asked.

Just as I was about to respond, my phone beeped, alerting me there was an incoming call. This one from an unknown number.

"Track the call that just came in. I'll be in touch." I hung up and clicked over to answer. "Castellanos," I greeted with malice and fury.

"It's me," Bruno spoke.

"Tell me you have her," I growled through my teeth.

"I have *eyes* on her. I do not have her in my possession," he stated curtly.

"Where are you?"

"We just took a right off West Bonanza Road and are headed North on Rancho Drive. I have no idea what is ahead. We've been following at a discreet distance because when I caught her slipping into a taxi, it was clear she didn't want anyone to see her leave."

"Bradford has her sister. Looks like he's got her strung up and beaten. Threatened to kill her if she didn't trade herself."

"Give me permission to take his life the minute I lay eyes on that waste of space," Bruno seethed.

"As long as Faith and her sister come out of this alive, I don't care what you do to him. The time for us to be civil is over. He essentially stole my wife from her marital bed the night after I claimed her as my own. This ends here."

A demon I'd not known before clung to the frayed edges of my subconscious. Clawed at my insides until all I felt was mind-numbing rage.

Faith was mine.

Mine to love. Mine to protect. Mine to spend all the rest of my days worshipping. I'd lost Alexandra to a vicious stealth attack, her own body turning on her and taking her young life. I couldn't fight a danger I wasn't able to see, hear, or touch.

I would not lose my Faith to a villain I could cut off at the knees. Aiden's destiny was going to come in the form of a reckoning.

My wrath would show no mercy.

"Whatever it takes, I want my wife freed of this stain on her existence."

"It will be done. First, I need to assess the situation. I cannot go in guns blazing, cousin. Besides, I only have one gun on me, and that's without additional ammunition. I was lazing about outside smoking a cigarette after a fun night with a dancer when I happened on Mrs. Castellanos leaving through the spa's employee entrance."

"How are you even calling me and whose car do you have?" I asked, not wanting to hear the details of his debauchery.

"An innocent bystander was leaving for the airport when I enlisted his assistance in the chase. It's his phone and rented vehicle we're in. Program the number. His phone charger doesn't work on mine."

"You carjacked one of my guests?" I closed my eyes as I rubbed at my forehead, knowing if the media caught hold of such a scandal, we'd be in litigation for years to come. "Is he well?"

Bruno made a gurgling sound. "Of course, he's well. And very excited about being part of said chase. I did, however, promise him a free stay with all expenses paid at the Alexandra for his next leisure travel."

"He will be rewarded handsomely for his participation," I agreed. "I'm assuming you've come up with a plan?" I entered the closet, put the phone on speaker, and hurriedly pulled on a pair of black jeans and a simple long-sleeve white shirt. My gaze settled on Faith's suitcase, which had been haphazardly pawed through, her belongings scattered in piles. An elegant nightgown I'd hoped to see her in this evening hung over the edge of the case, tossed aside, never having graced her perfect body.

My heart squeezed, and my eyes glassed over. I needed to get her back. Faith was my second chance. My salvation. Proof that the world could be good, kind, and just. My daughter needed a mother. Eden needed her aunt. I needed *my wife*. I didn't want to live another lifetime alone. My heart beat again the day I met Faith, and it would forever beat as long as I had her by my side. Centering me to this life where things weren't always easy or fair, but where ultimately karma always came through.

More than anything, I believed after my time with Faith that second chances could be had. We were living proof of it.

"I think we need to get the authorities involved," Bruno said flatly, bringing my thoughts back to the matter at hand.

I tugged on socks and shoes and then went into the bedroom to locate my wallet.

"That's quite possibly the last thing I would have expected coming from you," I admitted.

"True, which means it's the one Aiden isn't banking on. But think about it. Diego's men were hurt in that raid. Lives were lost on all sides. We cannot bring Latin Mafia in. The Feds are now involved, and they have the tape we sent of Bradford and his man killing one of ours, knocking out Marino, and putting him in the trunk. The IRS is all over his casinos looking into the embezzlement and fraud. If he's caught having kidnapped a woman and tortured her…"

"He'd have no leverage." I inhaled sharply. "Which also means he'd be a man with nothing left to lose. He'll kill her out of spite." I gulped, sweat dampening my palms.

"Do you trust me?" Bruno asked the one question I didn't know how to answer. I trusted him with my safety every day. Trusted him to ensure me, Penny, and my mother were able to live our lives without fear of harm. Having the wealth I did came with just as many negatives as it did positives. Money made me and my family a target. Was this situation any different? Did I trust him to keep Faith alive? Could I trust anyone with such a task?

That answer was yes.

I knew Bruno would do whatever it took to return Faith to me alive. He'd risk his own life doing so. He'd never let me down in the past. And I had to trust someone. Had to put my faith in someone else. I hated every second of it, but there was no alternative.

"Do whatever it takes to bring Faith back to me alive."

"She just pulled into the West Wind Las Vegas Drive-In. We're driving past and going to circle back around to see where she ends up. Call the cops and report your wife missing. We have to play this smart."

"What about Diego?"

"He and his men are wildcards. They get the job done, but mess and carnage aren't what we need here. We need stealth, speed, and patience. Let's remember, Bradford has a twisted sick love for your wife. He believes she is his property to use and abuse at his discretion. If Faith is smart, she'll play into that while I get things into place. Head this direction but don't enter the drive-in. I'll call when it's time for you to make your presence known. Okay?"

I clenched my teeth so hard I thought I might crack a tooth. "Be safe, cousin."

"I'll bring her back or die trying," he said, and then hung up.

It was the "die trying" part I couldn't get out of my head.

Once more, I pushed everything I was feeling to that dark corner and focused on putting one foot in front of the other. I left the suite and snapped my fingers. Two guards followed me into the elevator. When I got to the first floor, two more guards flanked our sides. My driver and good friend, Carlo, opened the door for me, then promptly ran around the other side and got into the driver's seat while the rest of us folded into the blacked-out SUV.

"West Wind Las Vegas Drive-In, Carlo. As fast as you can without being pulled over."

In a moment, we were headed toward my wife and her captor. Never in a million years had I wanted to inflict pain and violence on another living person so completely. Thoughts of ripping off Aiden's nails one finger at a time suddenly became appealing. The idea of removing his eyes with a switchblade…downright cock-hardening. Watching his life bleed out onto the concrete while Faith and I looked on would be the opposite of nightmare-inducing. It would bring peace and harmony to our nights, because we'd share the knowledge that he could no longer hurt a single soul ever again.

I'd been in many battles through my lifetime. Most with ruthless businessmen who would lie, cheat, and steal to get what they coveted. I always came out on top of those situations because I didn't lead with my heart but with my head. Losing Alexandra to her battle with cancer was the only time I couldn't control the parties waging war. Neither of us came out the victor. I learned from that battle that I always played to win and only risked what I was willing to lose.

I lost my heart the day Alexandra died, and then found it once more, years later, in the hands of a woman who had been just as broken as I was. Together we'd mended those cracks, glued our hearts back together, and found our ability to love again.

Aiden Bradford was going to wish he'd never set eyes on the woman who was meant to hold my heart in her hand.

I just hoped I made it in time to hear hers still beating.

I pulled out my phone and pressed three numbers.

"9-1-1. What's your emergency?" the caller answered.

"My name is Joel Castellanos, and I'd like to report my wife missing."

Episode 98

Cash Money

FAITH

The taxi driver pulled into the West Wind Las Vegas Drive-In movie theatre lot twenty minutes early. It was empty at this time of day, and the snack shack was all locked up with no employees in sight. The blacked-out SUV that sat a football field's worth of parking spaces away was my ultimate target. I could practically feel evil incarnate polluting the dry desert air through my open window.

"Miss, I do not like the idea of dropping you here. It seems unsafe," the driver announced.

I gave the kind man a half-hearted smile. "It's okay. I'm meeting a friend."

"Based on the route you had us take, in and out of alleys, random turns for no reason, it feels as though you are trying to escape something or someone. Are you in trouble? I have a daughter half your age, but if she was in need of help, I would hope a kind soul would reach out. This is me reaching out. If you want to leave right now, I'll take you wherever you want to go free of charge."

I glanced at the mileage meter. The fare came to sixty-eight dollars. I pulled out my wallet and grabbed five twenties. "I'm fine. Really. Take care of your girl." I dropped the money through the small divider window and got out of the car.

He rolled down the window as I came around the front, my eyes set on the single vehicle in the distance.

"Are you sure? Maybe I could wait for you." He made a last-ditch offer.

I shook my head. "Thank you, truly. I'll be fine."

The man lifted his phone and brazenly took a photo of me.

"Just in case." He smiled, waved, and started his engine, then drove back the way we'd come.

It was times like these that I remembered that genuinely kind people did exist, and most people were in fact good, just jaded by life experiences.

I inhaled deeply, filling my lungs with the cool air that would burn off once the sun crested fully over the horizon.

By now, Joel had probably learned I'd left. Hopefully he understood what it took for me to leave him. That if there hadn't been a threat to a member of my family, my very flesh and blood, I wouldn't be here putting myself and our future happiness at risk. I'd be working with him to rid Aiden from our lives.

The truth was I'd never been lucky. My entire life had been a series of one bad decision after another. Proof of that was leaning against the back of an SUV, his long legs out in front of him, his brown hair shifting in the breeze. Once upon a time, I'd believed he was the very sun in the sky. He'd wooed me endlessly. Until I realized the darker side of his business and started to question things. Suddenly I'd become a liability. A pretty possession. Something he needed to keep in line *or else.*

It was the "or else" that had turned into black eyes, split lips, endless bruises all over my body, and later, sexual assault.

When Joel kissed me right after he'd won me at auction, I'd allowed a sliver of hope to warm the cold, bitter woman that I'd become. In Greece, we had made love and became a family, and

I'd believed my luck had changed.

That I'd found my person.

The man I was meant to share my life with.

I'd never been happier than when I was sitting poolside in Joel's home in Greece, the girls playing in the aqua-colored water, the man I loved making all of us smile endlessly. For a short time, I'd found my true self. The woman I wanted to be with every fiber of my being. A mother. A wife. A woman who was in charge of her own destiny.

Until we got the call that my father's restaurant had burned down.

Aiden had single-handedly ruined my entire life, over and over, for years. And what had I done? I'd run. Lived in the shadows. Existing but not living. Now, somehow, some way, I needed to get my sister and myself out of his clutches.

I watched as Aiden pushed off the back of the SUV and opened his arms wide as though greeting a long-lost lover after years apart. I was good at pretending, but not enough to willingly go into his arms. It would be a cold day in hell before that happened.

I stopped twenty feet from where he stood. "Where's Grace?"

"No hug for your one true love?" he responded, ignoring my question.

"I asked you a question. Where is Grace? You promised that if I turned myself over to you, you would let my sister go free. So where is she?"

He smiled widely, but it wasn't his patented, plastered-on grin that had my attention. It was his hazel eyes. Startlingly beautiful when backlit by the light of the sun rising. They were mesmerizing and as familiar as my own, because I looked into those same eyes almost every day.

"She's not here. You think I'd bring her right out in the open for you and whoever may have followed you to snatch up without me being the wiser? No, sweetheart. I planned ahead. If you want to see your sister alive, you'll get in the car." He pulled open the rear passenger door.

I fisted my hands, knowing he was going to pull a fast one. But I had no choice if I wanted to see Grace.

I approached the SUV with my chin lifted and my spine straight.

Before I got in, he held up a hand, palm facing out. Then he whistled loudly. The driver and another one of his goons exited the vehicle. One approached me, his hands already going to my shoulders. I shrugged and shifted my body from left to right in order to escape his touch.

"Back off, asshole." I snarled at the one I recognized as his long-time driver, Lenny.

Lenny scowled and pulled me toward him, then patted me down sloppily.

"I don't have any weapons if that's what you're looking for. I'm not into violence. Or have you forgotten the reason I kept running away?"

Aiden just chuckled and shook his head as if all this was some big joke to him. Probably because he lived in la-la land and not the real world where a person's actions had actual consequences.

"No weapons and no phone," Lenny rumbled after patting down each leg and my ass, his big paws lifting up my breasts and feeling between them over my clothing to make sure I wasn't hiding anything.

"No phone?" Aiden cocked a brow then made a tsking noise with his tongue against his teeth. The sound grated on my last nerve like nails on a chalkboard.

"A phone can be tracked. I'm not an idiot." What I had done was take the tracker from the back of my phone and shoved the damn thing against my scalp and tightened my ponytail over it. The physical phone I'd hidden in the hood of the zip-up. If they found it, I'd still have something that Joel and his team could track. I had to trust that my husband and his men knew what they were doing. If they couldn't locate me or if the tracker was found, eventually I'd find a way out like I always did. It would just take more time than I'd planned.

Aiden huffed. "Get in the car, Faith."

I got in the vehicle and put my hands in my lap, letting out a relieved breath when I felt the weight of my phone resting against my nape where the hood was bunched. It was hard to believe Lenny hadn't run his hands up toward my neck and found it. Maybe my luck had changed.

Within moments, Aiden jumped into the other side of the back seat, and we were off. He reached out and snatched my left hand with his, eyes boring holes into the large diamond wedding ring I still wore.

Okay, maybe I was an idiot. I should have left my ring with Joel for safe keeping, but I couldn't bear to part with it.

Stupid, stupid, stupid.

"Is this what I think it is?" he snapped, disbelief filling his voice.

"If you think it's an engagement ring, you'd be right," I lied through my teeth.

Only lies didn't often work with Aiden. He could see through most people, and everyone had a tell. He knew mine the second my eye started to twitch and my hand trembled.

"You married him," he snarled like a fire-breathing dragon. "You fucking bitch! How dare you!" Spittle flew from his mouth and landed on our hands in wet droplets. "I asked you hundreds of times to marry me. Begged you on my knees…"

I yanked my hand as hard as I could, but he wouldn't let go. "No, you *demanded* I marry you. And the only time you were on your knees begging was for forgiveness after you'd beaten me so badly I couldn't leave the bed for weeks! That is not love, Aiden."

"You're wrong. I have loved you from the minute I laid eyes on you standing at the snack shack, finger-pointing and yelling at a boy who tried to go to third base without your consent. You were the most beautiful creature I'd ever seen. Roaring mad, teeth bared, skin misted in your fury. I got involved, remember? Told the little prick to leave or I'd slit his throat. Showed him the knife I'd use to do it. Then I offered you a ride home."

"How could I forget?" I sneered. "It was the last time I felt safe."

"I'd never let anyone hurt you," he said softly, taking my response in the opposite way from which it was meant. I'd felt unsafe with *him* from that day on.

Correcting him would have only made things worse, so I kept my mouth shut and tried once again to remove my hand from his. Instead, he lifted my hand toward his face and enclosed my entire ring finger in the wet heat of his mouth.

I physically gagged at the sensation of his tongue whirling around my bare skin until he scraped his teeth harshly along my ring finger. I hissed and bit back the pain, not wanting him to have the benefit of seeing me hurt.

When he pulled back, my wedding ring was no longer on my throbbing finger but in between his teeth. "You won't be needing this." He dropped the ring into his hand and shoved it into his jeans pocket. Then he petted my ring finger as though he were captivated by the sight of it. Without so much as a word, he moved lightning fast and bent the finger all the way back until I heard it snap.

I screamed bloody murder at the explosion of pain that hit me like a grenade going off. Stars blinked across my vision as a halo of black pushed at the edges, threatening to take me under. I gritted my teeth and breathed through the excruciating pain while I cradled my hand to my chest. My finger swelled instantly and pulsated painfully along with my heartbeat. The last thing I needed was to pass out. Anything could happen if I didn't stay lucid.

"Let that be a small reminder of what happens when you give something away that's supposed to be mine," he grated, his voice low and menacing.

"You. Disgust. Me." I grunted through the agony, staring at

his once handsome face with a death glare. Fingers could be splinted and healed. I just needed to make it until either Joel and his team found me or until I could secure Grace and escape somehow.

"You'll get over that in time. You just need to be reminded of how good it can be between us. Just like old times." His expression warmed as though he hadn't just outrageously broken my finger in order to teach me a twisted lesson.

I kept breathing, my body trembling at the sudden shock and horror. I forced myself to focus on what was important. Getting my sister and getting as far away from him as possible.

"Are we almost there?" I grumbled. "I want to see Grace."

"Actually, we've arrived." The SUV pulled into what seemed to be a series of industrial warehouses in full working order. People were everywhere. Men in construction hats walked around, and cranes lifted shipping containers from semi-trucks and placed them in neat stacks, like multi-colored dominos all lined up. Work vehicles zoomed past us without a care in the world.

"What is this place?" I continued to scan the environment in the hope I would see something memorable in the event I was left alone long enough I could call for help.

"Side hustle," he answered, non-committal.

Aiden was known to have his finger in as many pies and women as he could claim, so a side business wasn't unusual. The fact that he'd brought me to such a busy location was surprising. He must truly have believed he'd gotten away with taking me. I hoped to ruin that sense of security soon.

I held back any possible facial expression as a triumphant sensation filled my chest. Joel would come for me. I just needed to bide my time until an out presented itself.

The SUV pulled into a large open metal door that was attached to a gigantic warehouse in the very back of the lot. The door came down the moment the vehicle cleared it, practically shaking the floor with the boom it made when the heavy material hit the concrete.

I cuddled my arm as Aiden turned to me. "Now you be a good girl and do what I say and no one else has to get hurt."

"You mean any more than my broken finger and my tortured sister?" I hissed with nothing but venom.

He cupped my cheek and I flinched away. His lips twisted into a menacing smile as I did so.

"This is fun. I love having you back. I can't wait until I can lay you out on my bed and fuck you into submission." He placed a finger on my knee and ran it up my thigh teasingly. "You always liked it when I took you so many times you passed out."

He was wrong. Those times were a nightmare I'd blocked out. I instantly curled into a ball against the door, trying to escape his touch. "Don't. Fucking. Touch. Me," I wheezed, the pain from my broken finger and the memories of the last time he'd hurt me spinning through my mind like a horror film on repeat.

As I pressed myself to the door, he dipped closer, his heated breath against my ear. "One day soon you'll welcome my touch. Beg for it, even." He pinned me to the door with his sick and twisted murmurs.

"I want to see Grace," I demanded.

He sighed dramatically. "Fine. Let's take you to the junkie. Though I must say, you definitely won the gene lottery. Grace used to be a tarnished version of you, but still pretty. Now... *Woof!*" he mimicked, barking like a dog.

I waited for him to exit the vehicle when he abruptly reached in, grabbed my wrist, and dragged me over the seat and through the opposite door. I fumbled out, my hand reaching to balance myself against the car window. The moment my broken digit touched a firm surface, the pain was once again blinding. I stumbled the remaining foot and fell to my knees directly on the hard concrete. My teeth clacked against one another as my knees ached from the blow. I'd have bruised kneecaps for sure.

Aiden hooked me under the armpit and hauled me up. "Well, come on now, dear. If you want to see the girl, you better get a move on. Plane leaves tonight. No time to waste," he blathered on.

I could hardly focus through the pain surrounding my knees and finger, not to mention the vise-like grip he had on my underarm, fingers digging into my soft flesh brutally. While I picked up the pace, I looked around. The space was filled with plastic-wrapped pallets, wall-to-wall and splitting down the center like bookcases in a library. It was hard to tell what they were at first, but once we got to the very back and I saw the lines of women standing in nothing but simple white, practically see-through panties and bras, it dawned on me what was happening. The women were using machines and stacking money into them. The money would flutter through the unit, counting it so it could be placed in neat little stacks.

All of it in cash.

Bills in different denominations were bundled together and wrapped in plastic before being loaded onto the pallets. They were then lifted by men behind forklifts where they'd drive them into one of the many colorful shipping containers.

Either Aiden was laundering money, creating counterfeit bills, or stealing it somehow. His criminal activities had obviously grown exponentially and were far larger than Joel, Bruno, or even Diego knew. This wasn't the type of secret he'd let his ex-girlfriend or her sister learn about without extreme repercussions.

I started to shiver from the tip of my toes to the top of my hair where my tracker was hidden. If Joel showed up here, they'd kill him on sight.

It was then that I realized that Aiden was never going to let Grace go.

He was never going to let *me* go.

How the hell was I going to warn Joel without being caught?

Episode 99

My One True Love

RUBY

I walked hand in hand with Nile out of his, rather, *our* room. He'd made sure all of my belongings were now in his suite. When we hit the landing of the staircase that separated the halves of the estate, he curled a hand around my nape and took my mouth in a soft kiss. I hummed against his lips, opening for more. He chuckled but played along, giving me what I wanted, his tongue in my mouth sliding delicately against my own. I sighed into his kiss and wrapped my arms around his neck.

Eventually he pulled back and smirked, then rubbed his nose against mine. "I have work to do, darling."

"Hmm," I teased, then pecked his lips, lifting up onto my toes to press more fully against his muscular frame. He wore a pristine suit, while I had on a simple black sundress that came to mid-thigh. I knew he loved seeing my legs, so when I'd chosen my outfit for the day, I made sure to taunt him with my lotion-coated, shiny, tanned limbs, in the hopes he'd cave and give me what I wanted. The one thing he would continue to deny me until our wedding night.

His cock.

I'd never been a woman who wanted sex. I didn't think about it. Didn't seek it out. For the most part, I was a stripper who lived a rather celibate lifestyle. After my upbringing, no one could blame me. However, with Nile, I was *ravenous*. Something about his flippant, teasing, carnal mannerisms and devotion to only me—especially as it pertained to intimacy between us—stoked my libido deliciously. I found myself eagerly desiring a man, and that feeling was so foreign that it boggled my mind.

Instead of analyzing it to death like Opal would surely have done, I chose to jump in with both feet and consume as much of the incredible experience as I could. Good things didn't tend to stick around when I was involved, and parts of me feared that no matter what Nile said, there was always a chance that it could all go up in flames at any time.

Until the second we said our "I do's" and became husband and wife, I'd hope for the best and assume the worst. And while that was my general philosophy, I couldn't help but touch, kiss, and want him regardless of what might happen. My husband-to-be nurtured a side of myself to come out into the open that had been in hiding. One I hadn't known was there. A sensual, sexual, feminine side that I liked. Getting to know the woman I was becoming was intriguing and exciting. But now that she was out of the box, she was ready to play, and Nile was her desired playmate.

"You are a sinfully decadent siren, you know that?" His hands curled into the long, flat sheets of my hair, cupping the back of my head.

"What's a siren?"

He pursed his lips. "A siren was a Greek mythological creature that lured sailors to their deaths with their enchanting songs and voices."

I scrunched up my nose and scowled. "That doesn't sound appealing."

"Oh, but their song and voices brought the sweetest death over a raging, unrelenting sea."

"Uh, still not liking the visual. I'd rather be seen as a sexy vixen." I batted my eyelashes for emphasis.

He chuckled and tipped his head down to press his forehead to mine. "Duly noted. However, as blissful as spending time with you is, I must go to work. I've missed several meetings this morning already as I devoted time and energy to my sexy vixen." He cocked a knowing brow.

I grinned widely. "Far be it from me to keep you from the daily grind. I need to check in with Opal anyway. What's on for tonight? Anything I need to be aware of?"

"I thought perhaps we could take a ride on the London Eye. You seemed interested in the activity," he offered.

"Really?" My heart started to pound as anticipation filled my chest. He'd not only listened when I spoke of my interest in the tourist attraction, but he genuinely wanted to share in the experience.

I jumped up and down on my bare feet. "Can we get fish and chips too? In all the movies where the characters are in England, they always order that dish," I breathed, my heart pumping and my belly fluttering.

He chuckled. "Absolutely. I know of a great pub that has excellent fish and chips and nice cold pints."

"A pub?" My eyes bugged as I smiled so widely I could hardly catch my breath. It was probably silly to get excited about something so small, but these were firsts I would cherish my entire life. Just thinking back to that scared little girl I had been in the Sunnyside Trailer Park who never believed she'd amount to anything... And here I was in England about to have a classic British meal with the most wonderful man who I would be marrying next week. It all seemed surreal.

"I'd love it." I swallowed the emotion trying to rise to the surface.

He gifted me a small smile, kissed my nose, and smacked

my ass before turning around and heading down the hallway that led to his studio.

"Hey!" I called out. "If I get bored and want to listen to you compose, am I allowed to come see you? Or would you prefer I leave you to your work?" I asked.

He tilted his head, pulled off his glasses, and reached inside his suit to grab a cloth. While he cleaned his glasses, he stared at me pointedly. "You'd want to sit with me while I work?"

I nodded and shrugged. "If it isn't too weird and it won't mess up, you know, your muse or whatever. I would be completely quiet."

"I'd like that very much, Ruby," he said with awe. "Very few women I've met have taken any interest in my work."

"Isn't it your passion?" I swished my dress from side to side, not wanting to be too inquisitive but loving learning every tidbit I could about the man I couldn't keep my hands off of.

He gave me a cocky smile. "Besides my passion for *you*, yes. I live to create musical scores."

"Well, if it feeds your soul, I want to be a part of it. Even if it's just to listen," I answered truthfully.

His eyes blazed with heated interest, then banked to a steely simmer as the seconds passed.

I shivered under his blatant scrutiny.

"You know where I'll be. Visit whenever you wish," he finally stated.

"Okay, I will. See you soon-ish."

He nodded, and then we both went our separate ways—him to his music studio, me to Opal's room.

The door was open when I got there. Opal was inside, carrying a stack of folded clothes and putting them into a small suitcase she had sitting open on the bed.

Panic the likes of a drowning victim rushed over me so quickly I broke out in a cold sweat.

"You're leaving?" I gasped, my hand at my heart, making sure the very important muscle didn't implode within the confines of my chest as fear burst through my veins.

"Not long term. I'm going on a trip with Noah to Denmark."

I shook my head. "Wait a minute. Back the truck up. Put that sucker deeply in reverse and start over. I'm confused."

"As you know, my birthday is Friday," she said as though I wasn't firmly aware of the fact.

I'd always been the one to celebrate it. Our mother never made a single cake for either of us. She didn't even tell us happy birthday on the day.

"Yes, and I fully expected to be celebrating it with you. Together here in London."

She nodded and pushed a lock of dark hair behind her ear but continued to pack her bag. My sister was an elegantly gorgeous woman, but she hadn't a clue of her own beauty. Part of why she was so endearing to both sexes. No one ever knew what Opal was thinking or where they stood with her.

"I understand that this comes as a surprise, me wanting to go out of town for a few days. But, Ruby, you need alone time with Nile. Time to really connect before the wedding next week. The big day is right around the corner, and you hardly know him. I don't want you to feel as though you're making a bad decision or doing it out of some type of obligation to give us a better life. You should be marrying for love and…"

"And?" I lifted my hand and rolled it in the air. "Go on. You seem to have a lot of thoughts about the decision I've made. One that has already gotten us both out of Mississippi, which was goal number one. And two: this will provide a future for us both monetarily. One that neither of us was capable of achieving otherwise," I snapped, feeling sensitive about her judgmental tone.

We'd never judged one another for the decisions we'd had to make in our lives. Together we simply accepted them and moved on.

Opal sighed and turned around, crossing her arms over her

chest. "Well, I'm worried about you. I want you to be sure that Nile's who you want to be with long term."

"There is no long term, Opal. I'm marrying Nile for a period of three years. Neither of us are in this for love."

"And yet you've made it clear you're compatible sexually," she added.

"Sex and love are not mutually exclusive. Or did you forget how we were raised?" I sneered, hating the direction she was taking this conversation.

Opal groaned and scrubbed her hands over her face. "All I'm saying is that you deserve the world. You deserve to choose the man you want to marry. You deserve love."

"I did choose the man I'm going to marry, and none of us know what the future holds. Could I fall in love with Nile? To be honest, yes, I probably could, but only time will tell. Right now, the two of us are entering into a mutually beneficial arrangement. One I'm not at all afraid to enter into. So please do not worry about me."

"Why? Because you're the big sister and it's your job to take care of little Opal?"

"What has gotten into you? You're combative and snarky this morning," I retorted, frustration filling the air between us.

Opal sat on the bed and looked down, seeming defeated. "I think after what Mom did, I need to get away."

"You're literally over four thousand miles away already!" I argued.

"Yeah, well, it's not enough. When Noah said he had to go pop in on a few of his businesses in Denmark and offered me the opportunity to tag along, I said yes." She looked at me pointedly. "Or do you have a problem with me hanging out with a man you were going to marry? Because as you know, you can't have them both."

The verbal arrow struck me right in the heart. "That was uncalled-for and super harsh, Opal. I've done nothing to earn your scorn. I don't know what's going on, but go, have fun with

Noah. I'm sure he'll take care of you and show you a damn good time. Just be careful." I turned and headed for the door to leave her and her attitude behind. I didn't know what was going on with her, but I wasn't going to allow her to use me as her punching bag either.

"Ruby…"

I stopped with my hand on the doorjamb, spun around, and focused on her face.

Opal's entire expression crumbled to one of misery. "I love you," she rushed to say. "I'm sorry I was short with you. I'm going through some difficult feelings, and I'm lashing out. I didn't mean any of it." She twiddled with her fingers in her lap, a nervous tick I knew well.

I walked back over to her and pulled her into a tight hug. "It's okay. If you have to be catty to someone, I'm your gal. It's me and you against the world, right?" I snuggled against her side.

"Always," she croaked, her face pressed to my neck.

I rocked her from side to side like I did when she was little. "Exactly. It's always me and you. But that doesn't mean we have to do everything together all the time," I begrudgingly stated. It was true, but I hated my own words so much they tasted like dirt.

"You sure?" She sighed and lifted her head, her dark gaze meeting mine.

I gave her a half-smile by pressing my lips together and rubbing her back. "Yes, I'm sure. Go with Noah, have fun, and score me a cool T-shirt or something. Just don't let him take you to anything called Eyes Wide Open, okay? As a matter of fact, I'll have a chat with him before you leave. You're to be taken to no sex clubs."

Opal chuckled and sniffed against my chest, tears tracking down her cheeks.

I eased away just enough to cradle her face and wipe her tears. "It's going to be okay. You know that, right? I'm going to change our lives for the better, and all of this…Mom, Mississippi, our childhood… everything will just be an ugly memory. A blink in the lives we're meant to have."

"I hate that you're constantly giving up everything for me. It's not fair to you," she whispered, her words fraught with sadness.

"It's my job as your big sister to take care of you. A job I take seriously. You're my one true love, Opal. The light at the end of every tunnel. When it was the darkest, you brought the glimmer of light. The hope that one day it would all be okay. Remember that."

"And you're my one true love too, Ruby-Roo." She smiled sadly. "I'd do anything for you."

"It's a good thing you don't have to because as of next week, everything we could ever want is coming to fruition. The minute I marry Nile Pennington, our lives change forever." An airy feeling filled my chest, pushing away any of the remaining ugliness from our chat.

She nodded. "Do you think you would have chosen Nile without the auction?"

I shook my head, remembering what it felt like to stand on that stage and pray for a bidder. Committing to the concept because of what it could do for me, not because I'd wanted to do it.

"Honestly, I probably would have never married or taken a man as my own. Our past messed my heart and emotions up pretty badly, but I'm on the mend. Every day I feel lighter and lighter." I didn't want to tell her that every day *Nile* was changing me for the better.

His attention. His hugs. His kisses. His words of praise and devotion.

Nile was rebuilding my belief in the opposite sex one day at a time, and I adored him for it. He was also helping me build up confidence in myself. Still, I didn't want to make Opal feel less than when she'd been my only support for so long. A role I knew she took intense pride in fulfilling.

We were each other's person.

Now it seemed I had two people. Opal and Nile. Maybe even Madam Alana, Noah, and the governess too. Then there was The Candidates Club: Dakota and Savannah, as well as Faith and Memphis. My cup was filling up with more good than bad, but I didn't want to jinx it by admitting how things were finally changing for me.

I had a life to live. I wasn't just existing anymore. Moving through the paces while shaking my ass on a stage in nothing but a thong. People liked me for me. They counted on me to take an active role in their lives too. It was a powerful feeling to be surrounded by people who genuinely cared about my well-being. I wanted that for Opal. And if Noah could befriend my sister, show her how to let go and live a little, I'd be in his debt.

I cupped Opal's face with both hands. "Stop worrying about me. I'm fine. Go with Noah and live a little. Get rid of the snarky, untrusting side of yourself for a whole weekend and live it up."

She smiled sadly. "Okay, I will. Be back Monday, though, and we'll give that old broad the governess a run for her money in the wedding planning department. We could tell her that we hate the flower choice or something equally devastating to someone who cares about those details. Set the old bag off while we drink champagne and watch her meltdown."

I burst into laughter. "Sounds like a plan. She could use a prank once in a while. She's so uptight," I agreed.

Opal hugged me once more. "Go on, get yourself some food. I know for a fact you missed breakfast and lunch banging your fiancé." She pretended to gag. "You must be famished," she teased.

"Actually, he wants us to save that last step for the wedding night," I shared.

"Shut up!" Her eyes widened.

"Surprised me too. He's demonstrative, sexy as hell, and I

want to jump him, Opal. I have never once wanted to bed the opposite sex so badly, but there it is." I sighed, the annoyance of not getting my way bugging me all over again.

She snorted. "Something to look forward to, I guess."

"Just wait, one day you'll find the right man for you, and you'll change how you feel about men and sex," I warned.

"Maybe," she responded dryly.

"Have fun in Denmark, and when you get back, our lives will surely change." I grinned, happy as a clam.

"Now *that* I'd be willing to bet on," she said cryptically, but I let it slide, content to go in search of sustenance before planning my next step toward getting Nile to bed me officially.

"Love you!" I waved and sauntered back to the door.

"Love you more," she hollered as I made my way down the hall.

I considered putting on the sexiest lingerie possible, wearing nothing but a trench coat to our date tonight, and dropping the entire thing on the floor while we were riding The London Eye. That would shock the hell out of Nile. No man could deny a scantily clad woman who was willing and ready. Especially my man. One who so obviously liked sexy time in public.

I grinned wickedly as I made my way to the kitchen. First, I'd appeal to him through his stomach by bringing him lunch— made by me—directly to his studio. Wasn't there something about a way to a man's heart being through food? I didn't care if I stole his heart... what I wanted was far lower on his incredible body.

With a wide smile, I set my plan in motion.

Episode 100

Happy Birthday Part 1

NOAH

"Do not under any circumstances take my sister to one of your tawdry clubs." Ruby prodded the center of my chest with her pointer finger and glared. She reminded me of a snarling baby kitten.

I grabbed her finger and made a cross sign over my heart. "I, Noah Pennington, will not take Ms. Opal Dawson to one of my gentlemen's clubs this weekend." I wouldn't say *never* because I planned on marrying the young woman. She'd eventually spend time at all of my clubs over the next three years. "There you have it," I announced. "I've sworn an oath, and I will protect your sister at all costs. Is that acceptable? Can we leave now?" I chuckled as Ruby squinted.

She shrugged a shoulder and then went over to Opal, who was waiting patiently by the door, her suitcase by her feet.

"Really? You had to make a scene? I'm not a child, Ruby. Please don't forget that," Opal grumbled.

Ruby pushed out her plump bottom lip, and it wobbled as though she was about to cry. "I know, I'm just... We've never been apart on your birthday. Are you sure you wouldn't rather leave tomorrow?" Opal's elder sister pushed.

Opal shook her head then pulled Ruby into her arms. "I'll be fine. Noah promised to show me around. While he's at work during the day, I'm going to the National Museum of Denmark where I understand there are incredible exhibitions featuring Danish historical art dating back 14,000 years! But I'm most excited about viewing The Holmegaard bows because they are the first of their kind and date back to the Mesolithic period. Isn't that just…" Her voice took on a whimsical tone that not only made my dick hard suddenly, it made my heart pound with the desire to hear that tone directed at *me*, but in a more private and intimate location. "Unbelievable?" she finished on a slight hum.

I gritted my teeth together, eager to get her out of Oxshott and onto our private plane. "We should be going, Opal." I tapped my Rolex pointedly.

Ruby hugged her sister once more as Nile entered the foyer, a small package in hand.

"Brother, this was sent over by your assistant. The courier was adamant that you had to receive it immediately." He offered a rare haughty chuckle before handing me the package, then looped Ruby around the waist. Nile tucked his fiancée to his side and kissed her temple. "Happy birthday, Opal," he stated good-naturedly while rubbing Ruby's arm.

"What's in the package?" Ruby asked, gesturing to the small box that I wished I'd tucked away before she could mention it.

"It's a gift for Opal's birthday," I lied. It was certainly not her birthday gift. It was an absurdly expensive vintage opal and diamond wedding ring I planned to give my intended at just the right moment. Which would ideally be when we were standing at the altar saying, "I do."

Ruby bounced up and down and clapped her hands. "Ooooh, great idea! Wait a minute, I have my present in the dining room. Be right back!" She set out at a dead run down the hall and disappeared around the corner.

"Quick, let's go!" I suggested to Opal, who started laughing and shook her head.

"We can't leave now. She'll lose her shit. Just give it a minute. Besides…" Her eyes lit up, and she smiled widely, making her face unearthly beautiful. "I love presents, and I rarely get them."

I fisted my free hand and bit my tongue, not wanting to ruin the moment for her with the flurry of complaints I wanted to spew on her behalf. Once she was married to me, I'd make buying her gifts a regular occurrence. I'd shower her with attention so she understood her importance in my life. I'd make sure Nile did the same with Ruby if they continued with the wedding after we returned from our elopement. These women had been through Hell and back. They were survivors who deserved far more than the rubbish they had waded through their entire lives.

Ruby ran back in, her bare feet slapping loudly against the floor, her long blonde hair flying like a golden cape behind her. I was surprised the governess hadn't chastised her regarding her penchant for bare feet. From as far back as I could remember, house rules stated the feet were covered at all times aside from one's personal bedchamber or the pool. Then again, Ruby naturally became the exception to every rule. Probably because she was so perfectly imperfect in a manner that was endearing to all who laid eyes on her.

She wore a simple blue spaghetti-strap dress, which seemed to be her preferred daily attire when inside. Opal, however, wore jeans, slip-on suede loafers, a white-and-black-striped shirt tucked into her jeans, and a black blazer that had beige patches at the elbows. Her hair was down around her shoulders in glorious dark waves. She looked exactly like what she was: a smart college student about to go on holiday. It was astonishing how different the sisters were from one another, not only in looks and attire choices, but also the manner in which they held themselves. Opal was leery of everyone and everything. Ruby was a vault. If she didn't want to share her feelings and opinions, there was no getting it out of her. She had softened over the past month while being around us, which I hoped would occur with Opal as well.

Ruby thrust a long, small pencil-shaped box in front of Opal's face.

"Happy birthday, Opal-Loo!" She beamed.

Opal smiled softly and took the package, pulled the pink ribbon, and slid open the box. Inside was a long, tarnished chain that looked worn by time. Dangling from it was a battered silver locket. The front was a cameo design that overlayed a baby blue stonelike background. It was reminiscent of something dated a couple hundred years ago with an ivory etched carving of a hummingbird and flowers on the front. Not being a jeweler myself, I could still tell that the item wasn't an original cameo and was definitely a reproduction, but it most certainly had been in someone's costume jewelry collection for decades.

"It's an old locket. Open it!" she urged eagerly, her body positively buzzing with unshed energy. My ever-present brother simply smirked at his fiancée's antics, clearly pleased with every new facet of the woman that was unfolding before us, as Ruby came out of her shell more and more with each day.

Opal flicked open the locket. Inside was a picture of Ruby smiling, and on the other side was a picture of Opal. She traced the edge of the locket tenderly. "It's us."

"Now we can always be together, even when we're not physically together." Ruby grinned. "And it's old-looking, which is so your style! Though it's not expensive. I ordered it off Etsy before..." She lifted her hands up to the house and then us brothers. "Before all of this. I guess I could probably get you something really fancy now." She frowned as though the idea had never occurred to her.

"It's incredible. I love it." She immediately put the locket around her neck and held the oval-shaped cameo in her hand. "It's perfect. Thank you, Ruby-Roo. I love it, and you."

Ruby pulled her sister into yet another hug. It was surprising how often women hugged.

Something good happened between them, they hugged.

They were mad at one another, they hugged it out.

Sad about something? Hugs healed all wounds.

They entered and exited a location, hugs all around.

It was fascinating and so far outside of our stodgy and proper British upbringing I didn't know exactly how to react every time Ruby randomly hugged me. Which she came in for at that very moment.

"Okay, bye, Noah. Be safe with my sister. She's my world, remember that. You hurt her in any way, you deal with me. And I can be super scrappy. Don't let this innocent look fool you."

Nile burst into laughter as he put his hands to Ruby's hips and tugged her back against his front. "Darling, there is absolutely nothing innocent about how you look." He growled against her skin and then bit down on the ball of her shoulder teasingly.

She giggled and instead of pushing him away, placed her arms over his and leaned into it, allowing him to cuddle her and be affectionate. A side to my brother I didn't think I'd ever witnessed outside of how he'd been with our mother when we were younger, and since then in rare moments with the governess.

"Astonishing," I blurted at the sight of the two. "I dare say, brother, Ruby has got you completely wrapped around her finger."

Nile placed another kiss on Ruby's shoulder. "Positively smitten with my fiancée. What can I say? She's an alluring temptress who's snared me in her net."

Her eyes got wide. "Ohhhh, a temptress! That's way better than a siren." She patted Nile's hand.

"That's debatable. Actually, a temptress and a siren aren't that far apart. In ancient folklore…" Opal immediately started to impart her wisdom on the historical facts of the subject matter. As much as I loved hearing her go into depth regarding something she was extremely knowledgeable and passionate about, we'd be late, and I had plans for us.

"This is all very interesting, indeed. However, I must insist we say our goodbyes or we're going to be late for our plans for the evening."

"Right." Opal nodded. "One last hug." This time Opal hugged Ruby and then stood silent for a moment, staring at her sister solemnly. "You know that you're the most important person in my life, right? That true joy comes to me when you're happiest? When you're free of obligation and just able to be yourself."

Ruby lovingly pushed a long swath of Opal's hair off her sister's shoulder. "Of course I do. I feel the same about you. I'd die for you, Opal."

Opal smiled. "And I for you. So don't worry about me. I'll be fine. Everything is going to work out as it should. Just you wait." She lifted her chin and stood tall as though she were about to head into battle. The exact opposite of what I'd hoped.

Was she genuinely not interested in marrying me? Would it be such a hardship?

"Well, that's rather ominous and mysterious, Opal. Why are you talking like this? You're just going away for a long weekend. I'll see you when you get back on Monday." Her big blue eyes widened and sparkled with excitement. "Unless of course you want to stay here and celebrate with us!" Ruby encouraged for the millionth time. The woman was tenacious, I'd give her that. But if Opal took the bait, that would mean all my plans to take over the family business would be flushed straight down the toilet.

"Don't worry about me, Ruby. I'm looking forward to this trip. There are so many things to see that I never thought I'd have the chance to experience." She squeezed Ruby's hands and let her go before she took the few steps toward Nile and hugged him quickly. She looked up into his face. "Take care of my sister, okay?"

"With my life," Nile responded automatically, a serious, emotional tone in his voice that I didn't expect from my normally stoic and often cold-tempered brother.

Could it be that Nile was falling for Ruby? The question hit me in the chest like a ton of bricks. Did he have genuine romantic *feelings* for her?

That could complicate things for him when Opal and I came back married. Then again, he would have done the same bloody thing under different circumstances. If he had been the man passed over to marry the lovely Ruby, would he have conceded defeat and walked away a gentleman? Or would he have found another way to win like I had?

These thoughts worried me as we finished our goodbyes, rode to the airport, and boarded the plane and continued all the way until we arrived at our hotel in Copenhagen, Denmark.

Was my brother actually in love with Ruby Dawson?

If I married her sister, Ruby would have no reason to marry him. The contract could be terminated since they hadn't married yet. The sisters would have all the money they needed. Ruby would have to return the deposit, but I'd cover that expense happily. And yet, when I'd made the deal with Opal, I had assumed Ruby and Nile were marrying only for convenience. He to win the interest in our family holdings, Ruby to earn the money she needed to gain a better situation for her and her sister.

What if that wasn't the case anymore?

Had things changed?

The unanswered questioned plagued my every thought. I shook my head, trying to clear it. Worrying was absurd. I knew my brother well. Nile was just taken with Ruby because she was a beautiful, sinfully sexy woman who had caught his eye for the time being. She served a purpose. He might be sore about losing interest in the family holdings, but perhaps he'd thank me for giving him a way out of the marriage. Things could go back to the way they were. Except I'd be the winner and the brother with a Dawson sister changing her name to Pennington.

The finish line was in sight; I just had to grab it with both hands.

I grinned as the sugary taste of victory coated my tongue. The win was just around the corner. Soon, I'd have a beautiful wife to whom I couldn't wait to teach the art of sex one delectable step at a time and the majority interest in my family's holdings. Not to mention, Nile's beloved Aston Martin.

Life could not have been any sweeter.

Episode 101

Happy Birthday Part 2

OPAL

Noah had acted weird all the way here. Was he regretting his decision to marry me? Maybe he wanted to bow out. If that was the case, he could have done so prior to us flying to another country. Not being one to make waves, especially when given the opportunity to sit back, watch, and listen before responding to a predicament, I stayed quiet.

When we arrived, Noah grabbed my hand and led me through an opulent hotel in the heart of Copenhagen. On the way there, I was astonished by how many people were on bikes. Not motorcycles, but actual bicycles. People on bikes outnumbered cars at least five to one, if not more, as far as I could tell. Another reminder that I was definitely not back in the States where trucks and SUVs reigned supreme on the roads, especially in the South.

I tried to gently remove my hand from Noah's as we stood in the elevator, but that plan backfired when he held my hand tighter.

Holding hands was new to me. Intimate in a way I

wouldn't have expected. It was nice to have someone to hold on to, a person who was always by my side, but how long would it last? Once Noah got his prize, would he truly continue to dote on me, or would he shove me aside for other interests? I posed the same question to myself. How close could two people from entirely different backgrounds become?

We entered the penthouse that seemed to span one half of the entire level. The floor-to-ceiling windows gave us an open view of the horizon. It was breathtaking. I stood silently, staring out at the landscape beyond.

Noah came up behind me and wrapped his arms around my form. I went completely still, not sure what to expect.

"Relax, poppet. This is part of our intimacy training. Throughout the years of our marriage, I'm going to be putting my hands on you quite a lot." He eased me back to rest against his chest the same way Nile had with Ruby. Though she had eagerly fallen into his embrace, while I stood ramrod straight as if a pole was between my shoulder blades preventing me from slouching.

"I don't know how to relax," I admitted. "This is new to me. Touching. Even the hand-holding was more than I've done with another person besides Ruby."

He hummed against the crook of my neck. His breath was warm along my skin, sending shivers racing up and down my spine.

"Does it feel good? To know that a man is standing behind you holding you...*desiring you*. Wanting to put his mouth all over you." His voice was a deep rumble I felt strum through my chest, making my nipples peak against the fabric of my bra. Then he pressed his lips to the column of my neck, and I closed my eyes. I focused on the featherlight press of his kiss and the prickly scratch of the five o'clock shadow he had grown since this morning rubbing along my sensitive skin.

"It does," I sighed, allowing myself to ease against Noah

fully. He was warm, so much warmer than me.

"You smell good enough to eat. I wonder how you taste..." He growled, licked my neck, and then sank his teeth into the tender flesh.

"Oh!" I shivered. Who knew there were erogenous zones all around the neck, shoulder, and ear? Well, technically my sexual education classes freshman year in college taught me there were, but I'd never felt them before.

A surprised squeal left my lungs as Noah slid his hands to my waist, his fingers tugging at my tucked shirt. The second he got the fabric free, his hands went directly to my bare abdomen.

I gasped as his large hand and fingers traced the skin around my naval in teasing circles. My heart rate kicked into high gear as I held my breath, not wanting to miss a single thing.

"Just as soft as I imagined." He nipped and kissed my neck, building me up from a scared little kitten to a ravenous lioness ready to pounce.

Was this lust and arousal? This achy, almost uncomfortable, twitchy feeling I wanted more of, not less?

I was completely out of my mind, focused entirely on what his hands and mouth were touching. Nothing else existed but the new and exciting feelings thrumming through every pore.

Noah ran his fingers around my navel, and I closed my eyes, hyper aware of the silky tips. They fluttered along my skin in a way that felt almost like a tickle but had more of a tingly effect. Gooseflesh rose on my skin, and the tension in my shoulders dropped as I relaxed more fully against him with a deep, pleasurable sigh.

"There you go." He ran his thumb along the waistband of my pants, and my mouth went bone dry.

Would he try to touch me lower? Did I want him to?

The single word entered my mind like a flashing green

light.

Yes.

I wanted his touch. I wanted to learn how he could make my body sing. I wanted to experience touching him and seeing how he'd respond.

Would his breath catch like mine? Would he break out in a sweat? Would his manhood become hard...*for me?*

My mind short-circuited at the image of me falling to my knees before him, his body bare... A cold burst of anxiety blasted me. But Noah was right there when I jerked back to attention. He eased me around, cupped my cheek, and took my lips in a searing hot kiss. He ravished my mouth, holding my jaw, tilting my head from side to side so he could sink his tongue deeper. I was a mess of skittering nerves when he pulled back and gave me the sexiest panty-dropping grin I'd ever seen.

"How was that?" He cocked a jaunty eyebrow and smirked.

The word passionate entered my mind first, followed quickly by confusing, that wove into heart-pounding, exciting, and bundled all together to land on surprising.

Mostly though, it was *magical.*

"Um...good?" I answered awkwardly as I opened my mouth and sucked in a breath, not exactly capable of an intellectual response. To be honest, I didn't know how the hell I felt, just that I wanted to feel more of it.

He traced my jawline. "I've had my personal shopper send over several options for dinner tonight and potential dresses for our wedding tomorrow. Feel free to try them all on and pick whatever you like. They are all yours to keep. You'll need a wide variety of outfits throughout the next few years. I'll connect you with my shopper so she can fit you with an entirely new wardrobe as well."

My eyebrows rose on my forehead of their own accord. "Uh...okay?" There was so much to decipher about what he'd shared that I was loathe to respond without having time to break it all down. Especially since my mind was still on his warm hand that had traced my stomach.

"You can get ready in there." He pointed to one side of the penthouse. "However, our room is over there."

"Ours?" I naturally assumed we'd have our own spaces.

"How else are you going to learn intimacy if you don't share a bed with your husband?" he asked flippantly, as if it was obvious.

"You're not my husband yet, and I'm not sure I'm comfortable sharing a bed with you." I finally found my voice. Turned out, when I was scared, it was a lot easier to battle this overbearing and often overwhelming man.

"Fair enough. We'll see how things go after dinner. Pick something sexy. I'm taking you out for a night on the town for your birthday." He winked.

I nodded, turned around, and beat feet to my room. Besides the fact that I needed to get ready, I needed a little time to decompress after that intimate encounter.

When I made it to the walk-in closet, I realized I was in way over my head. There were at least twenty or so dresses to choose from. Who needed that many dresses? Not to mention a walk-in closet in a hotel anyway?

Rich people, apparently.

And now I was one of them.

Deciding to take the 'fake it till you make it approach,' I grabbed the only dress I could see in my favorite color. A beautiful forest green V-neck with spaghetti straps and lace appliques intricately placed along the front, back, and down the sheer overlay on the bottom half. There was literally no back to speak of except a long tie that crisscrossed at my lower spine.

I took a shower, blew my hair dry, and then shimmied into the delicate fabric. It was absolutely the sexiest dress I'd ever worn, and also the most expensive. I'd glanced at several of the gowns, and each one cost a thousand or more dollars. Next, I dug through the boxes on the bottom shelf of the closet and found what I hoped were the right shoes for the dress. They were nude and gold with a strap that wrapped around the ankle and crossed over the top of my foot delicately. The gold details were the tiniest metal studs that I thought mimicked jewels. They certainly were gorgeous heels made by someone named Jimmy Choo. I'd never heard of the man, but he sure knew how to make sexy shoes.

I gulped and slid the insanely beautiful stilettos on, then went back into the bathroom to add a touch of bronzer, shadow, a black smoky eye, and lip gloss. I wasn't one for much makeup—that was definitely Ruby's department—but I did okay. If I was going to be a Pennington wife, though, I'd need to learn how to dress appropriately and do my makeup in whatever classy style that type of woman wore. I made a mental note to do some research online.

After taking one last glance at myself in the mirror, I thought I looked quite all right, but more than that, I looked expensive, which I was sure would make Noah happy. At least I hoped it did.

I made my way out of the bathroom to find Noah standing at the bar pouring two glasses of champagne. He turned his head when I approached and stared at me so long the champagne overflowed and spilled all over the counter.

"Bollocks!" he swore, and then set the champagne down, grabbed a towel, and put it over the mess.

I chuckled as I approached.

"Opal, by God, you are perfectly *effervescent* this evening," he gushed, his features showing true awe.

My cheeks heated as I smiled under his overt praise. "Thank you. And thank you for the clothing. Everything is beautiful."

"Not more so than my bride-to-be." He lifted a hand and gestured to my look while I beamed with satisfaction. "Turn around, my darling. I'd like to see the entire dress."

I slowly spun, glancing over my shoulder as I heard him making a groaning sound.

"Christ on high, poppet!" He cursed again, lifted his hand, and bit into his knuckles. "You should warn a man before showing that much skin," he said and then knocked back an entire glass of champagne as though he desperately needed a drink.

"You like?" I teased, knowing he did by his response.

"Like isn't the word I'd use." His gaze was intense as he stared into my eyes. "Frankly, Opal, I want to tug at those teasing ribbons of fabric at your spine with my teeth before hiking the dress up at the back, bending you over that table, and having my wicked way with you before we leave."

I lost my ability to breathe. He was so forward with his desires. I didn't even know how to accept that I had them in the first place, let alone respond accordingly.

I opened my mouth, then closed it, and then opened it again without any idea what to say.

He chuckled and passed me a glass of champagne. "Another time perhaps." He waggled his eyebrows.

I nodded primly while holding my glass.

He filled his own with more bubbly and then lifted it. "Happy birthday, Opal. May everything you could ever want in life be yours."

We clinked our glasses and then drank.

Once we'd finished our drinks and the silence had become stifling, Noah took my hand and led us out of the hotel.

"Off to party!" he exclaimed, dragging me straight through the hotel and into a waiting limo.

I now understood what Ruby meant when she claimed she was tipsy. It was a light, uninhibited feeling that made me feel loose all over. I hung on to Noah like a leech as he swayed me all over the dance floor. His body was so warm and hard I couldn't stop touching him.

"Are you having a good birthday?" he whispered in my ear.

I leaned back but continued to shimmy from side to side, his hands at my hips holding me close.

"Best birthday ever!" I squealed into the loud noise of the club.

Noah had taken me to dinner at a super fancy steakhouse where everything you ordered was an individual item that cost a bazillion dollars. Something he didn't seem at all concerned about, so I went with the flow and told him I preferred my steak medium well. A fact he cringed at but ordered on my behalf anyway, along with some side dishes to share. At the end of the dinner, the chef himself came out with a two-tiered birthday cake that had sparklers at the top.

I'd never had a fancy birthday cake. The best I'd ever had was store bought from the local Piggy Wiggly that Ruby had saved up to buy. She was eighteen, and I'd just turned sixteen. We'd sat in the hatchback of her beat-up car, just me and her, with two plastic forks and an airbrushed cake with big sugary frosting flowers on top and all around the circular edge. We'd had country music blaring on the radio while we dug into my cake. It was dinner, dessert, and all my presents combined. Back then, I thought having a cake was such an exorbitant luxury because to us, it was.

Noah and the chef sang *Happy Birthday* while one of the waiters took pictures for us. The only thing missing about the night was my sister, Ruby.

"I'm glad you're having fun," Noah said over the loud music. "Are you ready to go back to the hotel? We have our wedding to get ready for."

"Holy cow, we're getting married tomorrow!" I screeched. "And my fiancé is so hot and rich!" I cackled like a lunatic, pointing to Noah as the other girls dancing around us heard me. They high-fived me and fist-pumped the air in mutual celebration.

Noah laughed heartily. "I see my fiancée has had quite enough to drink. Let's head out, love."

I pouted. "Fine. Can we do this again sometime?"

He grinned. "Opal, I own more clubs than you have fingers and toes. I'd be happy to bring you to every single one of them."

I put my hands in the air and squealed. "Whoo-hoo!"

Time seemed to waver in and out as we left the club and made it back to the hotel. Noah led me to our room, where he tugged on the ties at the back of my dress, releasing them. "Okay, you should be able to get out of the dress now, poppet."

I frowned. "I thought you were going to pull them with your teeth. I feel cheated." I crossed my arms over one another and pouted deeply.

He shook his head, cupped my cheek, and rubbed his nose along mine. "Opal, I will not take advantage of a drunk woman."

"I'm tipsy at best. Besides, you've been drinking too," I snapped.

He shook his head. "I cut myself off hours ago so I could take care of you."

I looped my arms around his shoulder. "Aw, that is sooooo nice. You're nicer than you act," I stated, then became utterly fascinated by his hair. It was so soft as I twined my fingers through the longer layers at the back. Then I dipped my head and breathed in his manly scent, right at his neck. I sighed into the space and rubbed my body against his. "Smells yummy."

"Opal, I do not have much restraint left." His voice seemed pained and his body stiff as a board, while I was practically draped all over him.

Not wanting to stop the flushed, heated feeling inside me, I pushed at Noah's chest until he stepped back far enough that he ended up falling onto the bed.

"I want to practice intimacy with you," I breathed, then bent over and kissed along his neck. He tasted like the perfect combination of salt and booze, reminding me of a margarita Ruby once made me taste. Except instead of booze, this was salt and man.

Mmm, yum.

"Bloody hell," he blurted, then wrapped his arms around my form. Suddenly, he scooted all the way to the headboard, his back against it, while I straddled his lap. I yanked at the dress until it was loose around my hips and I was flush against him, my booty in his lap.

"Hi." I wiggled my fingers, then put them to the top buttons of his shirt, where I teased the pearly disc through the opening, gifting me more warm male skin to touch, kiss, and taste.

He groaned as I flicked my tongue against his Adam's apple. "What exactly do you want, Opal? You're going to have to ask me for it."

I shrugged. "I don't know. I want to feel good."

"Do you feel good now?" His voice was a sexy growl.

I nodded and finger-walked up his chest. "I want to feel more."

"Can I touch you?" he asked.

Feeling bold and still loose from the alcohol, I pushed the

spaghetti straps off one shoulder and then the other. I wasn't wearing anything underneath because the dress was backless and didn't call for an undergarment. I moved my arms and let the fabric pool at my waist, baring my breasts to his gaze.

"Fuck!" His hands came to my ribcage then slid up slowly, covering my breasts. Instinctively, I covered his hands with my own, feeling him touch me where no one had before. I moaned and arched, pressing into his palms, wanting more, not knowing what pleasure was still to come but desperate for it all the same.

He plumped my breasts and ran his thumbs over my nipples in dizzying circles that made me pant. The incredible pleasure sent a jolt of arousal straight between my legs, making a tiny part of me throb incessantly.

"You are so gorgeous, unfolding like a flower beneath my hands," he murmured, ducking his head and taking my nipple into his mouth.

I cried out at the acute sensation. Wet and warm. Like stepping into a natural hot spring for the first time. Not wanting to lose the feeling, I wrapped my hands around his head and held him while he sucked, kissed, and laved at the tender flesh.

"Oh my God. Oh my God," I cried out, the pleasure immeasurable. "I had no idea it could feel like this." I arched farther, shifting my hips and rubbing my lower half against his much harder bottom half. His manhood was swollen and erect behind his slacks, perfectly positioned right where I felt the ache. I rubbed along it.

"Noah!" I gasped.

"That's it, poppet. Rub yourself just like that against me. Find what you like. Find what feels good." He urged me on with his voice and then a hand as he curled his free one around my hip and thrust against me.

I keened at the sensation, my head dropping back as I stared at the ceiling and ground down over his hardness.

My entire body felt like a balloon filling with air. The weight and tension of something inside me about to burst at any moment.

I kept rubbing back and forth, chasing the peak.

It was too much and not enough at the same time.

I whimpered and cried out when he thrust his hips harder, rubbing exactly where I needed it most. Then Noah's head fell back against the headboard, and my hands went to his shoulders, where I started to ride the intense feeling of bliss, my hips undulating over him. I slid back and forth against him until everything started to turn hot, tingly, and a little blurry. I closed my eyes as my nerve endings sparked. Noah hissed, lifted both his hand back to my breasts, and shockingly pinched my nipples.

"Come, poppet," he demanded on a visceral snarl.

That was all it took.

The pleasure and twinge of pain shot me into the stratosphere. I ground as fast and hard as I dared, climbing that mountain and tumbling straight over the summit.

He groaned and shook, his body convulsing with beautiful release right along with mine, his face planting between my bare breasts.

We held one another in a vise grip until we both slowly came back to ourselves. He kissed my breasts and sucked my nipples until I couldn't take it and mewled in protest. He flicked his tongue teasingly over one and then gently kissed the other before sighing contentedly.

"I cannot wait to make you my wife."

His statement filled my heart to bursting.

I smiled shyly, feeling a little vulnerable and maybe a tad exposed since the top half of my dress was pooling at my waist between us. I tried to cover myself with my arms, but Noah wasn't having it. He swatted my hands away, lifted me up and off his lap, and set my feet to the floor. While I stood there covering myself awkwardly, he unbuttoned his dress shirt and removed it, placing it over my shoulders. He then buttoned it between my boobs, covering my nakedness.

The entire time I was silent, staring at his magnificent, toned chest. Good God, the man could have been an underwear model in one of those fancy magazines.

My cheeks went molten as he removed his pants. My gaze met his as we both stared at the dark wet spot on his gray boxer briefs.

"I'll be right back." He grinned boyishly.

I'd made him release in his pants. A weird sense of pride filled me, cooling the heat in my cheeks.

Within what felt like seconds, Noah was back in the room wearing a pair of clean black boxer briefs and nothing else. His entire body was on display aside from his manhood.

Noah Pennington was a handsome man and rather built. His muscular chest and abdomen proved that he indeed spent many hours in the gym working on his physique. His skin was that of someone who tanned regularly or was in the sun a lot. Seeing as England wasn't known for sunny days, I wondered if he used a tanning booth or maybe God had just been kinder to him than others.

I shimmied the rest of the way out of the dress, allowing it to gather against the floor at my feet before I bent over, picked the expensive item up, and laid it neatly across the chair in the corner. It was such a beautiful dress, and I'd had one of the best nights of my life in it. It deserved to be cherished and hung properly alongside the stunning shoes I'd worn.

When I turned around, I watched quietly as Noah pulled back the covers on the monster-sized bed, *my bed*, and promptly got into it.

"I thought we were sleeping separately?" I asked, still uncertain but feeling a little silly after what we'd just shared.

Noah yawned, ignored my question, and opened his arms. "Come here, poppet. It's time to sleep. We have a big day tomorrow."

I waited all of two seconds before I slipped into bed beside him, still unnerved but eager to experience a night of sleep next to a man. Well, not just any man—this man. Mostly because I'd already learned I could trust him. He wasn't going to take advantage of me and proved that tonight when I was throwing myself at him sexually. Instead of taking what was on offer, namely my virginity, he kept himself fully clothed and showed me an incredible experience that didn't cross a line I might not have been ready for.

Once I was in place, tucked to his front, Noah wrapped his arms around me, pressed his face against my neck, and hummed, "Happy birthday, Opal."

Happy birthday, indeed.

I wasn't lying when I said it was the best I'd had. Noah was not only fun, he doted on me. Made sure I had a great dinner, that my steak was cooked exactly as I ordered it. He'd splurged on all the expensive clothing and stayed right at my side all night. Even when we were at his club and scantily clad women tried to get his attention, he disregarded them, his entire focus on me. We danced, we drank, we practiced intimacy.

Maybe marrying him was going to be the best decision I'd ever made. It sure seemed that way after today. Not to mention that Noah had given me my very first orgasm that wasn't self-induced. And by golly, it was absolutely out of this world. Something I definitely wanted to experience again.

I thought about all the ways Noah would please me as his wife in the bedroom. I was sure this evening wouldn't even scratch the surface of what he could teach me. What he would do to me.

Would he be interested in cunnilingus? I trembled, unsure if I could open myself to such vulnerability. Then again, the way he used his mouth on my breasts...

I closed my eyes and was just about to fall asleep when Noah snuffled against my neck, his hand sliding up to cup my breast protectively. His hand molded to the globe, and he sighed happily.

I stayed completely still, not sure what I was supposed to do.

"Mmm, Opal," he murmured in his sleep. "My Opal," he mumbled softly, then pressed his mouth to the back of my neck and kissed me there. All while he was asleep.

It was my name Noah spoke in his sleep. Not my sister Ruby, not some ex-lover.

Me.

A smile stole across my lips, and instead of moving his hand, I pushed back deeper against Noah's body, allowing myself to be held by a man and taking the time to enjoy such a new feeling.

Tomorrow I'd become Mrs. Opal Pennington.

After tonight, I was no longer terrified about the prospect of having a husband or becoming sexually intimate with someone.

Frankly, I was looking forward to all of it.

Episode 101B

Show You the World (Bonus Content)

NILE

"Darling, if you don't get your arse in gear, we may not make it to our reservation on the London Eye," I called out to my fiancée and entered the walk-in closet where I figured she'd be since she had disappeared into it an hour ago.

I found Ruby sitting on the floor in nothing but her undergarments surrounded by what was quite possibly her entire wardrobe.

Her head lifted from the clothing items she held in her hands, and her eyes tracked up and down my form before they widened.

"You're wearing JEANS!" she snapped. Her tone was panicked and accusing as she glared at my dark denim.

"What would you have me wear to a pub and night of seeing the sights?"

She groaned and picked up her cell phone, tapping the screen with what seemed to be frustration.

"Madam Alana hasn't texted me back with what is

appropriate to wear tonight. And now I find you're wearing jeans of all things? I didn't even know you owned casual attire." Her pretty blue eyes squinted, and a cute little snarl made an appearance.

I pursed my lips and wisely held my tongue, waiting for her ire to burn out.

"Does that mean I can wear jeans instead of these fancy-dancy dress pants?" She held up a ball of black fabric.

"We call them trousers here, darling, and, yes, of course you can wear whatever you want. Why are you checking in with Madam Alana?" I asked, feeling confused.

She growled like an angry lioness under her breath. "Because she's been helping me choose my clothing every day. Nile, I can't be standing next to all that is you"—she gestured to my body from top to bottom—"and look like a *heathen*." Her Southern American accent came out loud and clear when she spouted that last bit.

"And when you're running around my house in those flirty little frocks and bare feet..." I crossed my arms over one another and smirked.

"When we're *hooooooome*..." She dragged the word home out so long it must have had a half dozen extra o's in it. "...I wear what's comfortable." She finished on a pout and I wanted to bite that pouty lip and tease her mercilessly until she smiled.

Instead, I chanced a couple steps closer, then put my hands out for her. She placed hers within mine, and I helped her up. Once she stood before me, I looped my arms around her body and dragged her flat against my chest. After I had her in my arms, I arched her back and kissed at her neck playfully in a series of sloppy, messy nips and pecks. She shrieked and giggled until the sourness lifted away from her mood and my sweet Ruby came back. I let her catch her breath, the wild layers of her hair falling around her bare shoulders, making her sunny effervescence shine with her joy.

"Ruby, you look magnificent in anything you wear...

especially your comfy frocks." I kissed her forehead and pulled back. "As the city gets quite cold this time of year, I'd suggest you dress a bit warmer than your lingerie. Though I will say the view is stellar." I grinned wickedly, my hand roaming down her sides to curl around her slightly rounded hips.

She chuckled and playfully slapped at my chest. "Fine. I'll be out in ten, but you better be ready for a long night because I've been cooped up in this mansion too long."

"Duly noted." I fingered a long-sleeve cashmere sweater in the deepest aubergine that would complement her coloring well. "This is lovely," I noted.

"You like that? Well halle-freakin'-lujah." She snatched the sweater off the hanger and pulled it over her head.

When she turned around and bent to dig through the pile of clothing on the floor, her perfectly heart-shaped arse was simply too tempting to ignore. I reached out and squeezed a cheek, getting a hearty grip on what I'd certainly be sampling later.

"Whoop!" She bolted upright and glared over her shoulder at me, but there was also a spark of lust I knew all too well in her gaze. "No touching the merchandise unless you're truly going to try it on for size." She wiggled her pretty arse as though she were waving a red flag to an angry bull.

I shook my head and grinned. "Not until the wedding." I tsked and then exited the closet. As I passed the bathroom heading out of the bedroom, I could hear her mumbling under her breath.

"He will cave one of these days."

She was not wrong. I was hanging on by the thinnest thread as we abstained from that final step before our pending nuptials. After the abuse Ruby had received, she deserved a man who would do everything possible to make her feel cherished. I could give her jewels, expensive clothing—any number of material things—and it wouldn't matter to her. Ruby needed a man to show her that she was valued. That connecting with her on that final intimate level was something special to be shared between man and wife, and I was determined to prove it to her.

Besides, tonight was all about truly wooing my bride-to-be and hopefully getting to know what made her tick. So far I was certain that fish, chips, a pint of beer, and a carousel ride would make my bride happy.

I wasn't sure who would be wooed tonight, me or her. Though I'd do my best to ensure it was the latter.

Ruby met me downstairs where I had a car waiting. Noah's car, to be specific. He'd lost Ms. Dawson's hand, and though I had every intention of finding a way to make the family holdings a fifty-fifty split in the future, the car, on the other hand, had been fairly won. I internally patted myself on the back as Ruby approached, looking every bit the American girl. She wore a pair of jeans so tight my fingers itched to run over the curve of her bum once more. Thankfully, I refrained, but only just. The aubergine sweater looked incredible, highlighting her tanned skin and piercing blue eyes, as I'd suspected it would. She had a scarf wrapped around her neck and a leather sportscoat over the curve of her arm.

"I'm ready. Oooh, this car is insane!" She stared at the red and black Ferrari with her mouth hanging open. "It looks like it might stand up and transform into a robot!" she exclaimed. "I'm here to defend the planet from sudden doom," she parroted, lifting her arms, her hands in fists as she moved from side to side as if she were a tough guy in a superhero movie.

I burst into laughter, watching her parade around, squatting and moving her limbs awkwardly to mimic a robot.

Only my Ruby would compare a child's toy to the artful machine that was a Ferrari.

"All right, Bumble Bee." I used the only Transformers name I could remember.

"Bumble Bee was yellow and black. Get your facts straight," she teased.

I put my hand over my chest and opened the passenger door. "Forgive me, madam. I stand corrected."

She approached, leaned against the door, and kissed me softly. She pulled back only a few inches. Her breath fanned against my face as she spoke. "Thank you for taking me out."

"Get in the car before I do more than chastely kiss you," I challenged, even though it was more like a promise.

She stared at me for a few seconds, the sexual tension and anticipation flying in the air around us. The pressure was so thick I could practically feel it pushing against my chest, demanding I pull her against me and never let her go.

I held my breath as she cocked an eyebrow and slowly smiled, then did as I asked and got in the car.

I shut the door and let the cool night air relax the tingling desire to ravage Ms. Dawson in my brother's car.

Well, technically my *car now,* I reminded myself.

Once I got in and we were on the road, I reached for Ruby's thigh and switched from copping a feel of her sexy leg to facilitating the stick shift all the way to London.

We started with the London Eye. I've never seen someone oooh and ahh so much or so loudly at literally every building and bridge. Thankfully I'd reserved a private viewing pod so I was the only one getting the Ruby show.

"Tell me more about your sister, Opal," I said, wanting to get to know more about her. Since she didn't prefer to talk about herself, I figured perhaps I could get her talking about the one person she loved most. Then that could lead to her sharing more about herself. In theory, anyway.

"What do you want to know?" Her tone was guarded—the opposite of what I was hoping to achieve.

I sat back, crossed my legs, and relaxed as Ruby went from window to window and back in a rather dizzying circle, but I wasn't about to stop her fun. She was in her element. Seeing something new, in awe of the beauty of her new home. I wanted her to feel at peace in England, and part of that meant experiencing our culture.

"You said she was studying art?" I asked.

"Yep. She wants to be a museum curator."

"A lofty goal. Not exactly the easiest position to get into, especially if she wants to work at a well-regarded museum."

"She'll do it. I have faith in her," Ruby replied. "Opal's mastered everything she's ever attempted to learn. I've never met a more intelligent person in my life. At least not book smart."

"And you? How were you in school?"

Her body went stiff for a moment, then she turned around, rested her back against the railing, and stared at me blankly as though waiting for me to say more.

"Ruby, I'm just trying to get you to open up. What you shared with me about your past, how you trusted me with the things that make you vulnerable... That meant a lot. More than you can imagine. I don't want to upset you by bringing up the past, but I'd like to learn about more than just the ugly parts of your life."

"I don't know what to tell you, Nile. I was below average at school. My mind, as you can imagine, was on escaping the abuse, not doing well in a math class. Most of my life has been filled with nothing but vile and ugly things. The only thing I can be proud of is that I did what I could to protect Opal from the worst of it so she could do more with her life. She wasn't assaulted as far as I know, but she heard and saw things no child should."

"And what about you? You suffered the most. Don't you deserve more?" I suggested.

She shrugged. "A lot of people are suffering, Nile. I'm just one of millions." She sighed and pushed her hand through her golden hair, her body language jerky and uncoordinated when before there had been a lightness to her. I shouldn't have brought up the past.

"Okay. Well, what is something you like to do? Something you enjoy or are good at?" I changed the subject.

"Like a hobby?" She perked up.

"Sure."

She bit into her bottom lip and then smiled. "You're gonna think it's stupid."

Now I wanted to know more than anything. "Hardly. I don't think anything about you is remotely stupid. I find you exceptionally fascinating."

"I like to sculpt," she blurted.

"Sculpt? In what medium?" I asked, genuinely curious about this new tidbit of information.

"Mostly clay. I had a work friend back in Mississippi who hosted a party in a warehouse that was connected to a small arts and crafts place. The party wasn't my scene so I snuck over to the store. There was a cool older man, maybe in his sixties, who wore tie-dye and a red bandana on his head. I learned later that he also drove a motorcycle. He was seated at a pottery wheel when I entered. We got to chatting about the various things he'd made and how much I liked it, and he offered to show me how to do it."

"And...? Keep going. I'm invested in this story."

She rubbed her hands up and down her thighs. "And I sat down and made the ugliest vase the world has ever seen." She laughed.

"No, really?" I chuckled.

"Yes. But I went back. Offered to help him in the shop if he would teach me more. So for a couple of years, I'd pop over after dropping Opal at high school. I'd sell things, clean up, do inventory, and he taught me how to make pottery. I got quite good at it."

"I'm buying a pottery wheel. I've got to see this," I announced.

"No! Don't waste your money." She shook her head, but her eyes were sparkling again.

I was buying the damn wheel if just talking about it made her face look so at peace.

"It's not wasted if my fiancée is going to make me something with her own hands. Did you paint them or leave them...raw?" I didn't know how else to describe it.

"Raw!" She cackled as she laughed. "Yes. We let them dry, painted them, fired them, and glazed them, then fired them again."

"So we need a kiln too. Noted." I made a mental checklist.

She came and sat next to me, reaching for my hand, her shoulder pressed to mine. "I miss Frank."

"Frank?"

"My tie-dye, bandana-wearing, motorcycle-riding pottery buddy. He and his wife were two of the good ones. He was the first male friend I had who didn't try to get into my pants."

God damn the bar was low for human decency in Ruby's past. But I'd be changing that. I closed my eyes and let the wave of sadness flood my system and seep out through my pores. I would give this woman the best life money could buy from this day forward. On my good name, I swore it to myself.

"Thank you for sharing that with me. I enjoyed your story, and I'm very much looking forward to seeing you create some pottery. I'm sure there is an empty space right on the mantel in the dining room that needs a little sprucing up."

She snort-laughed. "The governess would have your head if you put something handmade that wasn't worth a bazillion dollars on display. Your entire mansion is like a gallery filled with incredible art. I couldn't possibly create anything that would look good enough to showcase."

I turned in my seat to face her directly. "It doesn't matter whether the governess likes it or not. She is not the lady of the house, Ruby. That position, my darling, goes to *you*."

"I-I don't understand." Her voice shook.

"That means when we get married, you can redecorate the entire estate if you'd like. Alas, you may want to hold off, seeing as we have a home of our own here in London that could absolutely use a woman's touch," I amended.

"You're kidding. You have another house!" Her eyes widened.

I cupped her cheek. "Ruby, your husband-to-be is not only rich, he's obscenely wealthy. I have many properties across the globe. Property is an excellent investment. I will teach you how to invest your earnings from our marriage, too."

"Are you going to take me to all of your houses?" she breathed, excitement fueling her question. She ignored the investment discussion and moved right into the information I'd shared about the houses.

"If you'd like."

"I'd like!" she exclaimed. "I want to see everything, Nile. I never thought I'd have these opportunities. I don't want to take a single one of them for granted. Wherever you go, I'm happy to be at your side."

I stood up and held out my hand. The car stopped spinning. Our ride was over, but our time together had just begun.

"Then take my hand, darling. Let me show you the world."

Episode 102

Secrets All Around

SUTTON

Morning sickness was an evil bitch, I thought while I held my wife's hair back as she heaved over the porcelain bowl.

"It's okay, darlin', I'm here," I reminded her as she groaned and flushed the toilet.

I helped her stand and released her hair as she went straight to the sink, loaded up her toothbrush, and gagged through cleaning her teeth.

I leaned against the bathroom wall and stared at her image in the mirror, feeling completely helpless. "This shit normal? You being so sick all the time?"

Dakota shrugged then spit the foam and paste into the sink, finishing up. She washed her mouth and used a wet cloth to wipe down her face and neck. "I don't know. I haven't had a lot of experience around pregnant women. Pregnant horses, sure. Loads of those, but they don't seem to have this problem."

"I want to make you an appointment to see Doc Blevins." I used my take-no-shit tone in the hopes it might sway her my way.

She rolled her eyes, washed her hands, and then put a brush to her wild hair, smoothing out the tangles. "And I told *you* that I would go next week, after we get Savannah married off tomorrow." Her response was filled with annoyance, but I was used to that. If Dakota didn't want to do something, it was usually the end of the story. She didn't budge or cave because she was stubborn as a new horse before breaking. That stubbornness, however, was part of what made her so incredibly endearing and hot as fuck. My wife was an independent, smart-as-hell, driven woman. I loved that about her.

I growled low in my throat, the sound barreling from my chest as I stewed in my irritation. "He'd see you today if he knew how sick you've been," I added, wanting to drag her fine ass to the doctor right then.

Dakota ignored my suggestion, as expected, pushed past me, and headed to the closet. Once there, she pulled off my T-shirt that she'd worn to bed and stood in nothing but a pair of navy-blue bikini-cut panties. Her tits bounced delectably, a beacon to my eager gaze. If she hadn't just vomited her very soul from her body, I would have jumped my sexy wife quicker than shit, but I had a point to make, and I wanted her to hear it.

"Darlin', I don't like how sick you are. It would make me feel better if Doc gives us the all clear." I crossed my arms over my chest and waited for my request to sink in.

She sighed deeply, then turned fully to face me, giving me a better view of her perky pink tits. I clenched my teeth as my dick started to rise at the sight of her beautiful body. I couldn't help it. Everything about Dakota did it for me.

Her body. Her sass. Her convictions. All of it.

"And I promised I would make an appointment next week," she stated, exasperation making her shoulders tense up. "Sutton, honey, you have to let me deal with this change in my body in my own time. Right now, my focus needs to be on Savannah and Erik's wedding. There are a million things to do."

I shook my head. "Nothing is more important to me than

you and our baby."

Her shoulders slumped as she approached me and placed her hands on my waist, then pressed her amazing breasts right against my bare chest. I groaned and wrapped my arms around her, holding her close and glorying in the feeling of her skin against mine.

She lifted her head, peering up at me with those warm brown eyes.

"I know you're worried that I'm not getting enough nourishment for me and the baby. I'm concerned too. I will make a call to Doc first thing Monday morning. I promise," she added when I opened my mouth to interrupt. "But it's the weekend, and I truly need to focus on Savannah. My baby sister's getting married tomorrow. Before you and our little one on the way, she was the only important person in my life. I need to make sure everything goes well for her. I'm all she has, and this is a super life-changing event. I need to be fully present in this moment, okay?"

I sighed and wrapped my arms around her, enjoying my wife's body resting perfectly against my own as though she was always meant to be right there, in my arms, her head pressed to my chest.

I let her response roll around in my mind and came to the conclusion that she was right. A couple more days wasn't going to hurt her or the baby. Still, the nonstop sickness scared the bejesus out of me. I wanted answers, and I wanted them now. The fear was gnawing at my gut somethin' fierce. Then it dawned on me who would know exactly what we were dealing with. Someone who had been pregnant three times herself.

My mother.

"I'll let this go on one condition," I announced.

Dakota squeezed me and then looked up. "Which would be?"

"We talk to my mother about our concerns."

Her entire face went white, then she shook her head and

backed right out of my arms quicker than I could blink.

"Nuh-uh, no way. She's going to freak out! She wasn't exactly thrilled when you married me, lest you forgot what happened when you brought me home. Now I turn up preggers? She's going to be convinced I married you for your money. That I'm locking you down for good by getting knocked up." Her face twisted into a grimace.

"She will not. Ma apologized for the shit she spewed. She was just surprised at the time and reacting out of past hurts. Something you know a lot about." I reminded her of our own situation. Her family's history was dark, but once we'd gotten it all out in the open, Dakota and I had started to flourish. "And after getting to know you better, she's accepted you as my wife. Offered up the farm for your sister's wedding. If that isn't acceptance, I don't know what is."

Dakota rubbed her face and placed her hands on her hips.

"Besides, Ma knows we're a love match. We're settling in."

She smiled softly at that, her body language telling me she was warming to the idea. "She has been really nice to me since all the craziness started, and she is going above and beyond for Savannah and Erik. All the Goodalls are."

I let her have a couple minutes to roll the idea around within her mind as she focused on the clothing in front of her. When I heard her sigh, I stepped closer and wrapped my arms around her from behind this time, placing a hand over her stomach where our child was growing. I kissed the side of her neck and snuggled her there. An intimacy I knew she enjoyed when she leaned back, rested her head against my shoulder, and purred sweetly.

"I need to know if what you're going through is normal. I'm worried as all get-out, baby. My mother has had three children of her own. It would make me feel a thousand times better if we ran the situation by Ma and got her opinion. I'm not going to force you, but it's something I feel strongly about."

She slumped further in my arms, the bulk of her weight

transferring to me. "Fine. I'm sure everything is okay, but if it would relieve some of your fears, we can talk to her privately."

I smiled and placed several teasing kisses against her neck. "Thank you, baby." I slid my hand from her stomach and dipped straight into her panties.

Her breath caught as I cupped her sex possessively. "How's about I show my wife a little appreciation for working through a difficult request?" I swirled my thumb around her tender bundle of nerves and dipped two fingers into her slick heat.

She moaned and arched into my touch.

Dakota paced the kitchen, nibbling at her thumbnail as I sat at our table and sipped coffee. The two orgasms I'd given her in the closet, first with my hand and then with her bent over clinging to a shelf while I plowed her from behind, relaxed my wife only long enough to get ready for the day. Once we got down to the kitchen, I called Ma over. The minute I told Dakota my mother was on her way, she became a nervous Nellie.

I heard the unmistakable rumble of an ATV out back. The engine turned off, and then a knock came from the patio door at the same time as my mother let herself in.

"Yoo hoo!" she called out. "It's your mama!"

Dakota stopped mid-pace and leaned against the counter. She looked cute as hell and scared as a field mouse. She wore a pair of tight-fitting jeans that I already wanted to peel from her body, and I'd just had her not half an hour ago. On top, she'd donned a plain burgundy tank. But over that, she had on one of my flannels. The arms hung long, the fabric going well past her wrists, but it gave her something to grip in her hands, which she was doing now, much like a safety blanket. She had a penchant for stealing my clothes, but if I was being truthful, it made my heart beat hard as hell every time. Having Dakota wrapped in anything that was mine brought a smile to my face.

My wife was cute as a button, and it took everything I had not to demand that she come sit in my lap so I could kiss her silly and take away her nerves.

"Mornin'," Ma announced as she came through the back entrance. She went right to the coffee pot, grabbed a mug from the cupboard above, and poured herself a cup. "What's so hush-hush you needed me to come right over but not tell anyone where I was going or why?" She held the coffee in one hand as she braced her other on the counter.

I stared at Dakota, and she shook her head.

Nope. She wasn't going to spill. It was going to have to be me or not at all.

"Well, I ain't got all day. We're finishing up the details for the wedding, and I've got lots to do. Spit it out already," Ma demanded.

"Dakota's pregnant." I let it all hang out with those two words. Figured it was best not to pussyfoot around with it.

Ma slowly put her mug down on the counter, turned around, and braced her arms to the surface, her head lowered.

I looked at Dakota, whose eyes were practically bulging out of her skull. Fear evident in her expression.

Ma's shoulders started to shake. I got up and was about to go to my mother when Dakota yanked my arm and forced me to pivot in her direction. She stood behind me and clung to my waist, peeking around my side. First time I'd ever seen Dakota use me as a shield, and hot damn if it didn't make me love her more. I wanted her to see me as a source of not only comfort but also protection. Not that she couldn't handle herself, just that it made me feel good to be needed.

We both watched as Ma lifted her head to the ceiling, tears streaking down her rosy cheeks. "Praise Jesus!" she hollered, then brought her hands together in a prayer pose at her heart. "Praise the Lord above and all His blessings!" She whooped and bounced on her feet as though she were a much younger woman.

Dakota's nails dug into my sides.

Ma spun around, doing some type of awkward dance, her hands swaying, her hips shimmying. "God is good, God is great," she sang, tapping her feet.

"Ma?" I spoke and I swear it was as if she'd just realized we were there watching her happy dance.

When she looked at me, her eyes were brighter than they'd ever been. "My son," she gasped. "My daughter," she continued. "I'm gonna be a grandmama!" She squealed and continued her weird dance, whispering her thanks to the good Lord above.

"Ma!" I put more grit into my tone. "Hello?"

She stopped mid-dance and stood straight. "What? I'm celebrating over here. As should both of you!" She pointed and grinned. "A baby!" Her hand went to her chest. "I don't think I've ever been happier, son. Not ever." She beamed. "This is wonderful news. A blessing. I can't wait to tell your father. He's going to be beside himself. A little one running around the farm again," she gushed. "It's such a gift."

I nodded and maneuvered Dakota from where she was hiding behind me and tugged her to my side. She wrapped her arms around me in a vise grip, making it clear she was sticking to my side until she felt comfortable. I rubbed her shoulder, reminding her that it was all good. Ma had taken the news splendidly.

"Ma, we're keeping it a secret for a while, so you can't be spoutin' off to Dad or anyone else. The only reason we told you is because we need to discuss some concerns we have about the pregnancy."

My mother's eyes widened, and her mouth opened in an "O" before she covered it and nodded. "Are you okay, sweetheart?" she asked Dakota, then her gaze went to mine. "What's going on?"

"Well, Dakota here has been real sick. Not able to keep much of anythin' down," I started, but Ma cut me right off.

"You've been experiencing morning sickness?" she interrupted, focused on Dakota.

My wife nodded. "It's not only in the morning."

"Well, first of all, that's normal. Morning sickness doesn't just happen in the morning. It happens at all hours of the day and can come on for no reason at all. A scent. Food cooking. Too much sun. Working too hard. Pushing yourself when you need to be resting. Babies make it known exactly what they need from the get-go."

I nodded. "So you're saying we shouldn't be worried about it?"

Ma shook her head. "Not exactly. Are you losing weight? Can you keep anything down?"

"Not much. I wake up, open my eyes, and have to run to the bathroom. It's instant. Then when I come down, if I smell any meat cooking, I'm back in the bathroom. Randomly during the day, I'll get the sour taste in my mouth, and I'm rushing to the nearest trash can."

My mother nodded. "Sounds like you've got a bad case of it. I was lucky. Only had it bad with this one here." She pointed at me. "With the other two, I had light cases of morning sickness that disappeared after twelve weeks. How far along are you?"

"Oh, so it's my fault my wife is sick. Great. Add that to her list of complaints," I teased, trying to lighten the heavy mood.

"It's very early. At the most four weeks," Dakota answered.

"Okay. Well, we're going to start by figuring out what you can tolerate because you need calories and lots of fluids." She went to the fridge and pulled out a can of lemon-lime soda and popped the tab before handing it to Dakota. "Sip this," she instructed before rifling through our pantry. "Eureka!" she exclaimed, a box of crackers in her hands.

Ma unwrapped the crackers and handed those to Dakota. "Sit at the table and take small bites of crackers while sipping the drink. Those should help settle your stomach. I'll make a list of all the things I've tried and used in the past that helped me get through the tough times. Have you seen Doc Blevins yet?" she asked.

Dakota groaned and took a seat at the table.

"We're going to make an appointment on Monday after the festivities. Dakota wants this weekend to be about Savannah and Erik, not about the pregnancy."

"Makes sense. There's really nothing to worry about." She went over to my wife and ran her hand down her hair. "Morning sickness is tough, but you'll get through. If it gets to the point where you can't move around without vomiting or you can't keep small things down, then you may need to get some anti-nausea meds from Doc, but he can go over that with you next week when he checks everything out."

"Thanks, Ma." I sat next to Dakota and took her hand, interlacing our fingers. "I feel better. You?" I asked her.

"Actually…" She glanced at my mother. "I really do feel better. Thank you, Linda. And thank you for keeping our secret. We just want to make sure everything is okay with the baby before we make any announcements. I hope you understand."

Ma made a gesture of zipping up her lips and tossing the key over her shoulder. "Your secret is safe with me. But I will say I am so excited!!" She squealed like a young girl, which was very unlike my normally very put-together mother. "I hope it's a boy," she mused, then changed her mind immediately. "No! A girl. Sutton would be hilarious with a little princess to love and protect. My Duke was positively smitten with our Bonnie. Still is."

"Now that is the damn truth." I smacked the table for

emphasis. "Bonnie gets away with everything. Always has. All she had to do was bat her eyelashes and pout in my father's direction, and he'd move the moon and the stars to make her smile." I laughed, imagining having my own daughter to dote on.

"And you can continue the family name if it's a boy…" Ma hummed, whimsy in her tone as she grabbed her coffee.

Dakota made a stink face when Ma wasn't looking. "The name?" she whispered.

"Duke." I grinned.

She rolled her eyes and shook her head. "Not happening," she mouthed.

"We'll see," I taunted.

Dakota's eyes filled with mirth as she sipped the pop, then bit into a cracker.

"Everything's going to be perfect, darlin', just you wait," I said as my phone buzzed from my back pocket. I pulled it out and noted the display showed Sheriff Hammond was calling.

"What's the word, Sheriff?" I answered, frowning in my wife's direction.

"We've got a problem, Sutton." The Sheriff's response was all business.

"And that problem would be?"

"Brody's finally awake."

My heart filled with joy. "Good news, then. How can that be a problem?" I asked.

"The problem, son, is that Brody claims it wasn't old man McAllister who shot him," the Sheriff shared.

"What?" I stood up so fast my chair slammed to the floor behind me.

Dakota dropped her cracker and stood too. "What's wrong?"

I held up a finger. "If Everett McAllister wasn't the man who shot Brody, then who was?" I barked, the hair on the back of my neck rising.

"Brody claims it was Jarod Talley."

My mind stuttered, the information making no sense at all. "Jarod? He was one of the men being held at gunpoint." I reminded the Sheriff of what we rolled up on at the farm when it was all going down.

"Brody claims he walked up on Everett and Jarod in a standoff. Jarod turned around and pulled the trigger without saying a word. Just up and shot him."

Shock and confusion tore through my insides. "And what did Jarod say? I'm assuming you asked him."

"Couldn't," the Sheriff barked.

"And why the fuck not?" My voice crackled with anger.

"Because Jarod Talley left the hospital in the middle of the night, and no one has seen him since," the Sheriff stated bitterly.

"Are you fucking kidding me?" I asked.

"Nope, I wish I was. He's disappeared."

Episode 103

Brave New World

SAVANNAH

"And what do you want?" I whispered, my heart in my throat. A light breeze glided along the gooseflesh that had risen on my skin. The road we'd pulled off onto was quiet, a rarely used, off-the-beaten-path country road. Where Erik parked was a beautiful spot, and we huddled underneath the shade of several big trees.

I looked into Erik's swirling golden eyes, the sun creating a halo of light around his gorgeous face. My husband-to-be was incredibly handsome. Rugged and manly, a true outdoorsman, ready to take the world on with his bare hands.

We stared at one another, my fingers woven through the thick satin locks of his hair. It was smooth as silk and just as fine. Energy sizzled around the two of us, both waiting for the bubble to burst. I felt as though I'd been waiting a hundred years for this moment when really it had only been just under a month.

A month of kisses.

A month of caresses.

A month of attempting to quench the desire between us without taking that final step.

With our eyes locked, I could see his need for me within his gaze, just hanging by a single thread. All I had to do was snap it for him. Make the first move.

"I want to fuck you. Right here. Right now," he admitted. His nostrils flared as he cupped my booty and ground the delicious length of his erection against me. I gloried in every steely inch that he pressed to my form.

Wanting to be closer, I got up onto my toes, flattening my breasts to his chest.

I *needed* him. Needed him like I'd never needed anyone before.

My entire body tingled with arousal, the energy between us heavy and weighted. It was like jumping into the deep water of a crisp lake, the water pushing at all sides invading every inch of my body.

"I want that too," I agreed before I made my move and kissed him.

Our mouths crashed together like two atoms colliding, morphing and growing into something new, something insurmountable.

His tongue lashed at mine, his hands lifting me up until I wrapped my legs around his waist. Our kiss went wild, ravenous. Neither of us could get enough. I bit down on his bottom lip because I couldn't stop myself. He groaned and walked us forward. I didn't care where he was going as long as we landed with him deep within me, easing the ache between my thighs that would not be denied.

I whimpered when my back suddenly hit a hard, scratchy surface, then moaned when he pressed the full length of his body to mine.

"*Faen!*" *Fuck,* he cursed as he ripped his mouth from me on a sharp inhalation. He wedged his body tighter to mine, his head dipping down to watch my chest heave.

I'd worn a deep scoop-neck blouse, but Erik proved that wasn't a problem for him. He curled his fingers around the edge of my top and tugged it down until my boobs were exposed to the cool breeze. He cupped my aching breasts with his warm hands before undoing the front clasp of my bra. My large bosom fell perfectly into his hold.

"I have never seen more beautiful breasts in my life," he said, awe in his voice.

His thumbs rubbed along the sensitive peaks in dizzying circles until I moaned and arched my back, resting my head against the tree behind me. Then the inescapable heat of his mouth covered one nipple, and I was lost.

Lost to every flick of his tongue, nip of his teeth, and suck from his talented mouth.

I was burning alive, the sensation so great I felt I could orgasm from this act alone.

"Please." I thrust my hips forward, trying to ease the throbbing ache between us. "Please, Erik. I need you," I groaned, my mind filled entirely with the desperate demand to have him inside me as quickly as possible.

His nostrils flared, and his eyes blazed with desire. He brought his face to my neck, layering my skin with gentle, teasing presses of his lips. I trembled in his arms, the sensation of his wet tongue and quick little bites flooding my body with arousal.

"Our first time should be sweet and in a bed," he murmured softly against my flesh, his accent filling me with insane lust.

I shook my head and squeezed my legs. "Our first time should be out in nature, under these trees, after we shared something beautiful," I countered, tightening my grip on his hair.

He groaned deep and low in his throat as he bit into the sensitive space where my neck and shoulder met.

"*Elskede*, I am too far gone. I can't think. I am too…*hungry* for you," he growled, his arms shaking where he held me pressed against the tree. His jaw was tense, a muscle in his cheek ticking along with his restraint. The veins in his neck became visible as sweat misted over his skin.

Not one to be denied, I let my feet drop to the ground, my hands going to the button at his waist.

He panted in and out like a fire-breathing dragon, his eyes dark and intense while I worked. Once I got his pants unzipped, I reached inside and wrapped my hand around him.

"*For helvete,*" he cursed in Norwegian, which I'd learned was something akin to *damn it to hell.* "You undo me, Savannah." His voice was gritty and raw.

I watched as he licked his lips and reached for my jeans.

I grinned wickedly, circling the tip of his cock with my thumb, spreading the moisture I found there and teasing the sensitive underside.

He was quick to get my jeans undone.

While I stroked him, his chest rose and fell. He tunneled one of his hands into my hair and lifted my chin with his thumb. He dipped his head, letting me see what my touch was doing to him.

"I am desperate for you, Savannah." He breathed against my lips, his nose sliding along mine. I flicked my tongue out to taste his words. He tasted of salt, mint, and man. I sucked in his bottom lip and gripped tightly around his cock, stroking up and down.

"Not as desperate as I am to have you fuck me against this tree," I fired back.

He made a strangled noise as he pressed his forehead to mine.

"Turn around, *wife,*" he growled.

The word *wife* made my clit throb double-time as arousal flowed freely through my veins. Even though I wouldn't become his wife until tomorrow, the word still fanned my desire.

I spun around and faced the tree, my fingers dipping into the crevices in the bark to hold on to.

Erik's hands curled around my hips as he fell to his knees in the grass behind me. He tugged my jeans and panties down to my shins, not leaving me much space to move.

"You're gonna want to hold on, *elskede*" was the only warning I got before he spread my cheeks and his mouth landed on my sex in a lush, wet kiss.

I cried out, gripping the tree and bending as far as my body would allow in this position. He was voracious, insatiable in his need for me. His tongue dipped inside as one of his hands came up to play. He teased that pearl of nerves with his fingers while he fucked me with his mouth.

An embarrassingly short few minutes later, I was howling through an orgasm. His fingers sank deep inside as he stood up and pressed his mouth to my neck.

"I love when you come. Love feeling your insides tightening around me. Let's see if we can do it again when we become one," he rasped against my heated skin.

"God, yes!" I begged.

Erik bent me farther, yanking my hips back with purpose. His fingers spread my cheeks, and I could feel his gaze on my most forbidden and private body part. Then he brought the wide head of his cock to my entrance.

"*Faen!*" he hissed as though in pain and pulled back suddenly. "I do not have protection," he rumbled.

"It's fine, it's fine. I'm on the pill. And I'm safe. If you're safe, we're good," I rasped, my breath sawing in and out of my lungs.

"I would never endanger you." He kissed my back. "Not ever." He placed another soft, worshipful kiss to my skin.

I didn't want soft, and I didn't want him to stop. I wiggled my hips, his hard cock resting against my bum.

"Erik, baby, come inside. Please." I was beyond ready, primed and wet. Everything had led up to this very moment, and I wanted to experience it all. I wanted to be one with this man I had come to care for beyond any other.

"*Jeg elsker deg...*" Erik whispered with devotion and thrust slowly inside.

I held my breath. The intrusion of his body into mine so huge, so monumental I didn't know what to think, to say, to feel.

I gasped. It was too much and not enough at the same time.

"*Jeg elsker deg,*" he said again with such heart, I felt the words were being ripped from his soul. He gripped my hips tight, eased out, and then pressed back inside, going even deeper than before.

I cried out, sucking in air like a vacuum as the tension between us broke, splitting our worlds in two.

There was everything else: the road, the trees, the SUV, the wedding on the horizon, the move to Norway, my sister, even the auction to worry about.

Then there was us. Our world. Where we were one. The place where nothing else existed but Erik and Savannah. Peace and harmony filled the air as he pushed in and out of me. Working his hips in the most beautifully mesmerizing, deeply satisfying way, making the rest disappear.

Everything just fell away as Erik and I moved in tandem, him thrusting, me pushing back for more. He touched me everywhere he could reach while I arched and bent, lost to the pleasure between us.

When we were close, our bodies working rapidly to reach the same goal, he brought a hand down between my thighs, his fingers finding their target perfectly. He pressed and twirled his fingers around that aching bundle, and I let go.

I let go of all the fear. All the worry about what we were to one another and how we'd come to be in this position. I let go of the past hurts that plagued me and gave them all to him. To Erik. To the man who would protect me in all things. Give me whatever he could to make me as happy as I was in this very moment.

Erik swallowed all of my concerns whole as we came together in a fiery burst of passion. He roared his release, pumping into me as I cried out, the two of us open and free as we found nirvana together.

We finally were one. And tomorrow, we'd become one legally.

I smiled as a startling realization soaked straight into my soul.

I'd fallen in love with this man.

And it was so far beyond anything I'd ever felt before, it was astonishing.

Erik's breaths came fast and warm against my neck. "Are you well, *elskede?*" he asked, his cock still throbbing hotly inside me.

It took a full minute for me to respond, I was so shocked at the revelation I'd just had.

I loved Erik Johansen.

I was in love with him.

Everything that came before no longer mattered as long as I was connected to this man.

"More than well. I'm perfect. I'm in love." I whispered the truth, letting those words seep into Erik's mind.

He slid out of me, bent over, and eased up my panties and jeans. I buttoned them up while I could hear him doing the same from behind me. I tucked my boobs back into my bra and adjusted my top.

I took a full breath as he placed his hands to my biceps and physically turned me around.

I laid my palms flat against his chest as he looped his arms around my waist.

"You are in love?" he asked, not waiting a single minute to clarify what my words meant.

I nodded shyly. My heart beat a million miles an hour

within my chest as nervous tingles rippled down my spine.

Erik's cheeks pinked before my eyes, and he cupped my jaw. He traced my lips with his thumb. "Say it again, *elskede*. I want to feel your words against my fingertips when you say them to me, so that I may remember this moment for the rest of our lives."

I trembled in his embrace, but when I focused on his eyes, I found strength. I wasn't alone in this feeling. It was clear as day for all to see. Maybe his love for me had been visible all along, but I hadn't been ready to see it.

"I love you, Erik," I whispered, the sound of the wind trying to steal the admission from my lips. But he felt them. He felt them through his touch and from the undeniable energy sifting between us. It was confirmed when he smiled so widely any lingering doubts I could have had slipped away. With strength in my heart and the love I could see beaming from him, lifting me up, I raised my voice. "I'm in love with you."

He pressed our foreheads together, both his hands now cupping my face, his fingers trailing along my skin with reverence. Almost as if he didn't believe I was real.

"Jeg elsker deg," he said in his native tongue.

"What does that mean?" I remembered him saying that to me while we made love.

"It means *I love you*, but in my country, it is not as simple. It means far more than love. It means you are my life. You are my reason for existing."

I pressed my lips to his, and for several long moments, we kissed gently, connecting with one another in this brave new world where it was just the two of us. I wanted to stay here forever.

Unfortunately, it was not meant to be because both of our phones started to ring.

"Ignore it," he mumbled, sucking on my top lip.

I sighed into his kiss, doing exactly that. But the second our phones stopped ringing and the kissing ramped up again, the phones went off once more.

I chuckled. "We need to get back anyway. We have a wedding tomorrow, you know." I smiled and slid my hand down his arm, interlacing our fingers.

My phone blared again. Thankfully it hadn't fallen out of my pants when we'd been going at it against the tree. I used my free hand to pull it out of my pocket while Erik was content to keep ignoring his.

"How do you do that? Just pretend it's not ringing?" I smirked.

He shrugged. "The only person I want to talk to is right here. Anyone else can wait."

I rolled my eyes and nudged him playfully as I looked at the screen. It was Dakota, and this was her third call in a row.

I pressed the button to answer and held the phone to my ear. "Hello?"

"Oh, thank God! You freaked me way the fuck out!" My sister's voice sounded scared. "What are you doing? Where the hell are you? Why are you not at the ranch?" she hollered into the phone as though she were chastising an errant child.

"Jeez Louise, hold on a minute, Kota." I stopped at the truck as Erik finally pulled his ringing phone out of his pocket. He showed me the display that said *Jack Larsen*. He lifted it to his ear and stepped a few feet away.

"I have been worried sick. Literally. Tossing my cookies sick! Where have you been?" she demanded, as only my big sister could while also laying on the guilt thick as molasses.

"First of all, you're sick because of the baby, so don't try and pull that card on me. I know the truth. Second, Erik and I had to make a day trip. We had to do something important before we got married. Why do you sound frightened? What's the matter?"

"Fuck a duck! You went on a day trip? Without telling me!" she groaned.

"Last I checked, I'm an adult and can do what I want when

I want to do it, Kota. What is going on that has you so pissed or scared or whatever?"

"Sheriff called. Brody is awake. And you're never going to believe who he said shot him." She huffed as though she were pacing the floor like a maniac.

"Our pa shot him. We already knew that," I answered.

"Well, we were all wrong. Brody claims it was Jarod who shot him. Not our pa."

"Jarod?! No. That can't be. I'm sure you can clear it up with him and iron it all out."

"We would if we could find him. He up and disappeared from the hospital overnight. His family has been interviewed, and they haven't seen him. Sheriff searched their home, the bunkhouse, everything. Called all his friends. No one knows where he is. But the Sheriff is mostly worried about you and Erik."

"What? Why?"

"Because when Sheriff Hammond went to the Talley farm and broke the lock on the shed Jarod kept, they found everything they needed to convict him of the barn fire, not to mention a journal where he planned it out in perfect detail. Also included in the journal were multiple threats that he would kill any man that came between you and him."

"My God!" I gasped, utterly shocked.

"Savvy, you've got to get home. Erik's life is at risk, and we have no idea when Jarod will strike next."

Episode 104

The Queen of Las Vegas

FAITH

Aiden lifted his chin to one of his guards when we made it
through the heavily protected warehouse and to a nondescript
door in the back. From the outside, it had looked like any other
worksite. Inside the metal doors, though, was an entirely
different world. There were men standing along every inch,
holding guns that were clearly locked and loaded. It reminded
me of what I would imagine an army base looked like, only
these guys weren't wearing fatigues, nor were they guarding
American interests. Seeing all that cash they were counting and
loading into shipping containers proved how little I knew about
Aiden's illegal dealings.

Lenny pulled out a set of keys and unlocked two different
deadbolts that secured the metal door. The room was pitch
black as I was ushered inside. Once the door slammed shut, the
lights flickered on.

I blinked against the sudden piercing brightness, my gaze
instantly going to the lone, unmoving figure hanging in the
center of the room.

"Grace!" I screamed as I pushed past the guards' hold and ran to where my sister dangled at least two feet in the air. Her wrists were tied together, a big, rusted hook holding the rope that suspended her from the rafters of the windowless room.

I cupped her cheek as her head lolled forward. Her chin rested on her chest, unresponsive to my touch. She'd been beaten, and one eye was swollen completely shut. Dried blood crusted under her nose and down the side of her mouth where a nasty split in her lip had clotted. My heart pounded, and my mouth went dry as my hands shook where they hovered in front of her battered body.

"Grace, honey," I whispered, my voice shaking as tears flowed down my cheeks. "Wake up. I'm here. I'm here."

Her good eye fluttered open as her brow furrowed in pain.

"F-Faith," she spoke brokenly. I shivered at the agonized sound.

"Yes, it's me. It's okay. I'm going to help you." My heart cracked in half as I pushed a stringy lock of hair out of her face.

"And how do you propose you're going to help her, hmm?" Aiden's voice bounced and echoed off the walls.

I turned around and faced my nemesis, my hands in fists at my sides, my muscles straining to lash out. The hatred in my soul was so overwhelming I could hardly breathe through it as I imagined jumping on him and scratching his eyes out while I screamed with fury.

"You promised you'd let her go if I came to you," I grated through my teeth. "I'm right here, as you wanted. Let her go. Drop her at the entrance to a hospital, and I'll willingly go anywhere and do whatever you want," I sneered.

Aiden laughed heartily as he walked the perimeter of the room. Stacked along the edges were tightly wrapped bricks of something that looked like flour. I knew it wasn't flour. I wasn't sure what illegal substance was inside those packages, but I had a pretty good guess. Cocaine being the top contender.

"What have you gotten yourself into, Aiden? Drugs?

Endless cash?" I shook my head and wiped a hand across my face to disperse the tears. "This wasn't you," I stated, thinking back to the years we were together. I'd known he was into some illegal stuff, but I'd always thought it had to do with loan sharking, not drugs.

Aiden tsked as he ran a hand across his stacks. "Oh, this is very much me, my dearest. You just liked to look the other way. Pretending you were a goody two-shoes who didn't love riding the dick of the kingpin in town."

Bile rose up my throat. "I had no idea you were in this deep…" I spat.

"We're going to have to agree to disagree, my love." He smiled maniacally. It was as if all of this was some big game. He didn't see how vile and disgusting the way he'd treated me was. Probably because it was the same way he'd shown affection to every woman he'd been with.

Grace groaned, her body convulsing where she hung.

I wrapped my arm around her ribcage thinking I could help ease her pain, maybe take the weight off her arms when she screeched violently. I stepped back, my hands hovering near my tortured sister. Her ribs had been pummeled and were likely broken. Aiden liked to break ribs, if my memory served. He'd taken to mine many times when we were together.

"Let Grace go. Please," I begged.

"In good time," he stated with a flippant wave of his hand as if my terror and Grace's torture was just another day at the office. "I want you to settle into this experience," he continued. "To truly understand what it is I will do in order to keep you, Faith. There is nothing I wouldn't do, no person I wouldn't destroy to ensure you will always be by my side." He walked around Grace and me with his hands behind his back, a master inspecting his rowdy pets.

"Why?" I yelled, not being able to contain my emotions anymore. "Why me? What did I do to you that was so horrible that you continue to hurt me and those I love?" My body was wracked with fear and hate, and most of all…guilt.

Guilt that I'd gotten my father hurt, my sister tortured, Eden kidnapped, and Joel entangled with such a monster. I'd brought the nightmare right to my family's doors. It was me. I was the catalyst for everything Aiden had done to them. But I didn't know why.

Aiden stormed over to me, taking both of my hands in his. I cried out when he forced my broken finger against the others, but I clamped my mouth shut and breathed through my nose, holding the pain in.

"Faith, don't you see? We're soulmates," he gushed, his tone filled with awe. "I knew you were the girl for me when you were tearing that man down back when we first met at a dusty drive-in. Back then you were fierce, confident, and so beautiful I could hardly look at you. And you were only just a teenager. Then you flourished at my side. Became a woman right before my eyes. My queen. The Queen of Las Vegas. And I'm your king." He touched my face almost reverently. He believed his own lies.

"No." I pushed away from his touch. He was not my soulmate. I'd married mine just last night under a pristine, starry Vegas sky. Cemented my love for Joel and our girls before God Himself. I'd never felt more blessed than I did when the officiant announced us husband and wife. Aiden would not sully that moment with his disgusting illusions.

Aiden gritted his teeth and snarled. "It seems as though you're going to need a bit more convincing." He snapped his fingers and pointed to a wooden chair. "Tie her up, Lenny," he instructed his goon.

"No! Please. Aiden, I'm not running. I'm not going to try and escape!" I backed up and away from his men but was quickly outmaneuvered and manhandled until I was shoved into the high-backed chair. My wrists were tied down to the arms, my finger swollen and slanted out of place, already purple around the knuckles. My ankles were next, tied quickly to the legs of the chair.

As I struggled against the bonds holding me in place, Aiden came over to see if there was any give at my wrists. There wasn't enough to worry him.

"I've got business to tend to. We'll be leaving at midnight, eventually flying to a private island in the Maldives. You'll adore the beach house. You loved that Hawaiian vacation we took together," he spoke with a hint of whimsy.

I did remember that trip. Kauai was a beautiful place. He'd taken me there early in our relationship when I was still besotted with him. Believing he was a good man who was going to love me forever.

He cupped my cheek. "That vacation was when you told me you loved me for the first time. Do you remember?"

I clenched my teeth and snarled as he petted my face almost tenderly.

"It was the first time a woman said 'I love you' to me, and I believed it. You had no idea the depths of my empire then. No clue who the man behind the mask was. But you *loved* me anyway. It almost made me want to be good. Instead, I realized that love is blind. You were so clearly taken by your love for me that you couldn't see the monster underneath. It was beautiful to witness. So much so that I fell in love with you, with your innocence. With the way you viewed the world and the people in it as good. Innocent until proven guilty. I wanted to see the world through your eyes, keep the devil at bay... And I think with you by my side, I did more often than not."

"You're delusional," I mocked. Tears and snot streaked down my face as his twisted beliefs spilled from his curled lips, clogging the air with his darkness.

He cupped my chin and cleared away the mess with his thumb, wiping his hand against his pants after. "Your love makes me a better person, Faith. I've been lost without it," he murmured compassionately.

I closed my eyes, no longer able to look into his face and

see that stunning hazel gaze any further. It was too similar to the eyes I longed for. The ones I missed desperately. My Eden's. She'd be fully awake now, having breakfast with her new sister and grandmother. Joel would be a wreck. He'd have found the note and made every call under the sun to send his people looking for me. My stomach clenched, and sorrow filled my chest, making it feel tight. Then I thought about his eyes as he'd looked at me when I walked down the aisle, filled with so much love and devotion it was life-altering.

"Are you remembering how we made love on the beach under the stars?" Aiden rumbled. "Your expression is so soft and gentle now, the same I recall you having that night." He leaned forward and inhaled against my hair, pressing a kiss to my temple. "Christ, you smell good. I missed you, Faith." He ran his jaw and then his teeth over the rounded edge of my cheek, nipping at the tender skin there. "I could eat you up right now," he growled, a scary neediness in his tone.

I shivered, disgust making my mouth water and my skin feel clammy as sweat soaked my neck and trickled down my back where I remembered my phone sat hidden in my hood. An idea formed right then.

"I-I..I need a little time. To think. To breathe. To...remember what it was like," I lied and forced myself to look into his face. I kept my head dipped low and peeked through my lashes, playing up the idea that he might be getting through to me.

He smiled widely, his bright white teeth glaringly iridescent, much like a wolf's snarl before he struck his prey with a killing bite to the jugular.

"That's it, my love. Think back. Ponder what we had and could have again. Only now it will be more. My empire has grown a hundredfold in the years since you escaped my hold."

I swallowed and nodded shyly. "What about the cops?"

He laughed dryly and curled his hand behind my neck. "I have more cops and judges in my back pocket than a card deck has face cards. Don't you worry your pretty little head about anything from here on out. Once we get to the private island, it will be smooth sailing. Maybe that's what we'll do next. Sail the world. You'd like that, wouldn't you? Seeing the world?"

I forced myself to nod.

Grace moaned, and his head snapped to her, an ugly expression contorting his features. "Looks like I need to take out the trash. Give you some space to think while I finalize our plans." His lips curved into a snarl as he stood abruptly, his face twisted into one of malice as he stared at my sister's slumped and hanging form.

"No!" I called out. "Leave me with her. Let me say goodbye. She's my family," I said gently, wanting to remind him of the things I valued and found important, especially if he believed I was the only good in his life.

A muscle in Aiden's jaw ticked as he scowled at her. Then, right before my eyes, his features softened, and he transformed back into the happy-go-lucky, smiling male he presented to most people. He could turn on the charm like flicking a light switch. Placing that mask on so quickly that if you weren't paying close attention, you might miss it altogether.

He compressed his lips, then turned back to me. "So be it. You've got an hour."

"Thank you," I said.

Aiden came back to me, curled his hand around my neck, and I swore for a second he may have felt the weight of the phone.

"Kiss me!" I rushed to say, panic filling my veins. If he found the phone, I'd be lost forever, and Grace would have no chance of escape.

A wicked, shocked smile poured over his features.

"Remind me," I requested, my voice a sultry timbre that sickened even my own ears.

His hand slid from my neck to my cheek. Relief rushed through me instantly.

I closed my eyes and imagined Joel the second Aiden's lips touched mine. I sighed into the kiss, opening my mouth. When Aiden's salty, coffee-coated tongue touched mine, I forced myself to hum, desperately trying to trick my mind into believing I was kissing my husband. The love of my life. My true soulmate.

Aiden forcefully shoved his tongue deep into my mouth and groaned, taking charge of the kiss, sucking and biting in a way that was more painful than pleasant. It also made it impossible to envision Joel's kiss, because my husband would never harm while showing his affection.

I pulled back, gasping for breath while Aiden slid his tongue along my lips and chin, slicking down my sweaty neck as he moaned. "You taste exactly how I remembered. Like salty-sweet caramel corn." He licked his lips graphically. "My favorite."

It took Herculean effort to breathe through my nose in order not to gag and vomit, his taste coating my mouth.

"Boss," Lenny called out. "One of our friends at the police department called. Said Castellanos reported his wife missing."

Aiden grinned and stood. "Fantastic. If he's calling the authorities to report you missing, it means he doesn't know where you are. Well done, Faith. You are a woman of your word," he commented offhandedly.

"Yes, I am. And you promised you'd let Grace go in return for my adherence to your demands. I kept up my side of the bargain, Aiden. Please drop her at a hospital. I'll do whatever you say. I'll comply to anything. I thought…I thought you wanted me to be happy," I added with a practiced shudder. "The man I *loved* wouldn't hurt my family. You always swore you'd protect them."

He turned around abruptly, a wild look in his eyes. "And then you left!" he roared, suddenly spitting mad. "No, you need more time to understand what's at stake. To understand the consequences of your actions. You have the hour," he barked before moving to the door, his goons at his back.

The heavy door slammed shut, and then I heard the two locks being engaged, one after the other.

I went to work immediately at my bindings. I'd practiced getting out of ties like this while on the run. I'd had nothing better to do sitting in a hotel in the middle of nowhere, so I'd sit in a chair, tie one hand down and work to get out of it. I'd have to use the hand that didn't have a broken finger because the swelling and pain that came with moving it might make me faint.

One trick I'd learned was to place my hands into fists and hold my wrists sideways while being tied down. If my captor didn't tie my hand flat to the wood, there was a bit of space to work with, which was what I did now as I tugged and yanked at the ties.

Lenny was an idiot. He also didn't realize that tying my ankles to the legs of the chair and not using the foot brace was child's play.

Tipping my chair back slowly, leaning precariously on two of the legs, I pressed my toes to the floor and wiggled one rope down the leg of the chair until it broke loose, freeing my leg. I repeated the process on the other leg, now having full use of my lower body. Pushing backward and up, over and over, I rubbed my wrist raw in order to loosen the ties.

I hissed through the pain but kept going.

"Faith," Grace mumbled. "Don't come," my sister whispered in her delirium. Her good eye slitted open. She saw me tied to the chair, and her face crumpled even more. "Faith, no," she croaked and then passed out again.

I doubled my efforts, needing to get help. If the pain was so intense that she couldn't stay awake, she likely had internal injuries.

I counted the minutes while I worked, ripping and tearing at the bindings. It had been about forty minutes when the blood from my torn wrist saturated the rope and the wood, making them slicker.

Finally, my wrist slid free of the ties.

I had to hold back the yelp of pain mixed with glee as I reached over my head and into my hood. Blood smeared along the surface of the phone, and I wiped it down my chest, clearing the wet smudges the best I could. I found recent calls and clicked on the name Joel Castellanos. My heart squeezed when I saw he'd called over twenty times. More than anything, I knew I had to warn him.

He answered on the first ring.

"Faith, my God! Are you okay?"

Episode 105

A Life for a Life

JOEL

Thirty minutes earlier…

The drive-in movie theatre Carlo slowly drove past looked completely desolate. There wasn't a car in sight.

"Where the fuck are they?" I growled, my nose almost pressed to the window. I searched the area and saw absolutely nothing.

My cell phone rang, and I answered it before it could ring again. "Speak to me."

"I'm sending Carlo new coordinates," Bruno stated. "He's taken her to the industrial side of town, an area well used by businesses. It doesn't make any sense." I could hear Bruno speaking under his breath. "Go park over there, hidden behind that bush," he instructed someone not on the phone.

Carlo took the next right turn sharply and hammered the gas. "We'll be there in twenty-five minutes," he stated.

Twenty-five fucking minutes.

I breathed harshly in and out of my nose, my hand

clenched so tightly around the door handle it ached. "I swear to God, Bruno, I don't know what I'll do if he hurts her."

"Don't think about it, Joel. I'm here." Bruno reminded me of his position. "His SUV pulled into the back section of a bustling industrial park. There are construction guys with cranes and bulldozers everywhere. He can't do anything too crazy or someone might hear."

Might hear what? Her screams as he violated her. Her sister's screams while he tortured the poor woman in front of my wife.

All manner of frightening things filled my imagination. I clenched my teeth and stared unseeing out the window. "What's the next step? I called the authorities and reported her missing. They aren't going to do anything until she's been missing forty-eight hours. Apparently, lots of women disappear after their wedding night, most of those willingly because the next day after getting married in Vegas they realize the mistake they'd drunkenly made. Unless I receive a ransom demand or something that proves she was taken for nefarious purposes, we're on our own. I could forward the texts to the detective I demanded to speak to if you think it will provide us with the assistance we need."

"I'm not sure yet. I need to get closer, find out what's going on. The best-case scenario is we figure out the perfect moment to swipe her right out from under his nose, then report his location to the feds."

"And if you get caught? Two of the most important people in my life will be gone. You don't think he'd kill you on sight? He knows you were the one who escaped with Faith's father in the warehouse deal gone bad. I can't risk another member of my family to this cretin."

"I'm sorry, Joel. I need to see this through." He huffed angrily. "You have to trust my skills. I'm trained for this…"

"You're trained, yes, but you also were shot in the leg twice! Your body hasn't even had a chance to heal! How are you, one man, going to go against Aiden and whatever force he has at his back?" I bit into the phone.

"Just meet me at the location I gave Carlo. And be careful. Don't be seen," he snapped and then hung up.

"FUCK!" I roared and slammed my fist into the leather seat repeatedly until I'd burned an ounce of the fiery anger overtaking my every thought.

I was done.

Done allowing Aiden Bradford to hurt Faith.

Done allowing him to hurt my family.

Done allowing the bastard the ability to breathe.

I scrolled through my phone, my nostrils flaring and sweat beading at my forehead when I pressed the number for the one person who could live up to the inferno scoring its poison-tipped claws through my soul.

Diego Salazar.

"Where do you need me?" He spoke without a greeting. I'd seen the man just last night. Under far better circumstances, and yet somehow he knew. Maybe he really did have eyes everywhere.

"I don't know yet," I admitted.

"Last night after the festivities, I assigned my men to watch every entrance and exit to your resort. Hoping that our man would strike, and I'd get to him first." His response had a violent edge to it I wasn't surprised to hear. "Imagine my surprise when one of them called to inform me that the new Mrs. Castellanos had alighted from a back exit and jumped into a cab. Quickly followed by one of your own. I instructed my man to follow them."

"Then you already know where they are?" I surmised.

"*Sí, amigo*, but I promised no blowback to you or your pretty wife. And when I make a promise, it has teeth, *sí?*"

"My man is getting more information. When I have it, you'll have it," I vowed.

"I see you are done being the good guy. It is no worry,

amigo. You will stay clean. I, however, make no such deals. If you call again, I will do as I should have done when he stole the child." He was not lying. I heard it clear as day in what he didn't say.

"I no longer care how dirty or clean you have to be to get your vengeance, Diego. I want this man gone from my wife's life. From mine. Wiped off the face of the fucking earth!" I said, low and menacing.

I'd hit my threshold. When my new bride snuck out of our warm marital bed with the sole purpose of saving her sister's life, endangering her own, I'd had it.

"I see. I will eagerly await your call. *Ve con Dios.*" *Go with God*, he finished and hung up.

It took another twenty excruciating minutes to reach Bruno. We parked off the beaten path, which was rather far from the warehouse, but we could still see it. Each of my men took different positions as I located Bruno's hiding place.

Bruno waved me over, and I crouched down and crawled through the brambles to get to him.

"This is what we know so far. According to her tracker, she's not in the primary warehouse where they drove in. She's far off to the side. Jonas got the building specs and figures she's in a section of the building that doesn't have any windows. It's used only for storage. The entire place is one enormous warehouse with approximately six shipping doors at the back. There are two drive-through doors in the front, two entrance doors, and one exit at the rear. All of these doors are guarded by men with assault rifles."

"Jesus. What does he have in there?" I asked.

"To start, I think this is where he's hiding the bulk of the cash he washes through his casino. If he was trying to embezzle money, he'd allow his men to win at the tables. Since we found out those individuals we watched were bringing money in and losing it every day, it's gotta be coming from somewhere. I thought perhaps it was just the strip clubs. Not so. He's in deeper. My best guess is drugs."

"Drugs?" The word came out of my mouth in a hoarse burst of air.

"Cocaine, to be exact. Diego's lead mentioned Bradford had entered the drug business and pissed off a whole lot of entrepreneurs in the States, the biggest being Diego himself," Bruno cautioned.

"What's our move?" I firmed my jaw and stared at the building in the distance, willing myself to calm down.

Bruno shook his head. "You're not going to like it."

"Try me," I grated.

"We need to be patient. Wait until dark. The regular day job men who seem to be doing legitimate business alongside that warehouse..." He pointed to the one in question. "They'll be going home. And in the meantime, if he moves her, we'll be able to follow."

"I hate this plan." There were too many holes in it. Not enough certainty for my liking.

"It's not my favorite either, Joel, but we don't have an army at our backs, nor do we want Faith or her sister taking a bullet in the crossfire if we call in the authorities. Remember what happened in the other warehouse? It was a fucking bloodbath."

I closed my eyes and breathed through the pain, knowing he was right. Which was when my phone vibrated in my back pocket. I pulled it out and saw Faith's name, and I answered the call before it could ring again.

"Faith, my God! Are you okay?" I practically yelled into the phone.

Bruno's gaze went wild, and he put his finger to his lips to shush me.

"Joel, I'm okay. I'm in a warehouse outside of Vegas, but Aiden's going to take me away on an airplane. To the Maldives at midnight tonight."

"Okay, calm down. Where is he now?" My heart beat double time being able to hear my beloved's voice, even though it was panicked and scared.

"He's going to come back any minute. He left me in a locked room with no windows. Joel, he hurt Grace so bad," she cried.

"I know, honey. Be calm. Tell me everything you can."

Her breathing became ragged. "Grace won't wake up. I don't think he's going to let her go," she said brokenly. "He's going to kill my sister," she whispered through what I could tell was a deeply frightened admission.

"I'm not going to let that happen, Faith. I'm with Bruno. He followed you. We're right outside the warehouse waiting for the perfect time to reach you."

She choked on a sob. "I knew you'd find me."

"Faith, stay strong. We're going to figure this out." I used every ounce of confidence I had left within me to make her feel more secure in such an aberrant situation.

"No, no, no, he's back. They're coming," she said suddenly. "Joel, I love you so much. I don't regret anything. I'd be with you, marry you all over again. Please take care of Eden. Please give her a good life. And if I don't make it out of this, I'll love you from beyond this world," she croaked and then the sound went muffled but didn't stop.

I could hear the distinct noise of something large and made of metal creaking and scraping along concrete.

"Hello again, Faith." I heard Aiden's voice, though it was lower than Faith's had been.

She'd left the phone on.

Oh, my beloved wife was a smart woman indeed.

"Have you said your goodbye to the junkie?" Aiden asked rather jovially for someone who had kidnapped two women and was on the run from the feds.

"She hasn't woken up. Her injuries must be too severe," Faith answered.

"Hmm," he hummed, and I strained to hear anything. "Yep, this ought to do it," Aiden announced.

A groan-like moaning sound came through the connection, and I almost stood up from our hiding spot and stormed right into the damn place myself. I wanted him to deal with me directly. Bruno put a hand to my forearm to keep me still and tilted his head to listen. I shared the phone with him, not risking our hiding spot by putting it on speaker.

"Ammonia," Aiden said. "Wakey wakey, Gracey-Gracey!" Aiden taunted Faith's sister. I could only imagine how upset Faith was watching her sister being tormented by this vile creature.

Another painful moan could be heard.

"Leave her alone, Aiden!" Faith shouted, and I clenched my fist. Whatever Diego did to this man wouldn't be enough. He deserved to be tortured by the Devil himself.

Next came a slapping noise. "Wake up, you stupid bitch, or I'll kill your sister!" Aiden threatened, obviously referencing Faith.

My nostrils flared, and I shook where I knelt.

"Keep your cool, cousin. You have to. For Faith," Bruno whispered, reminding me of what was at stake.

"Don't...Don't hurt Faith." I heard an unfamiliar voice respond, but then quickly a sharp cry split the air.

"Please, please, Aiden, don't! Think of the child!" Faith begged, referencing little Eden, her niece.

"Oh, right. The little girl I took a beating for," he sneered as Grace screamed again.

Her screams were so loud they made my ears ache and my teeth hurt from clenching them so hard.

"You're hurting her! Stop! Please! Just leave her there. Take me. Let's go! I'll go!" Faith cried and pleaded.

"This filth doesn't deserve to go home to her daughter." Aiden's tone was filled with rage.

"Daughter? W-what d-daughter?" Grace mumbled incoherently.

"You can't even remember your own fucking child. You're so lucky I didn't kill your father when I had the chance. At least he can give your spawn a better life than you ever could. Killing you would be doing that girl a favor."

"I don't have a child!" Grace's voice rose over his disgusting jabs almost pleadingly. He must have been physically hurting her at the same time.

"Shut up, Grace! Keep quiet. Save your strength. You don't know what you're saying." Faith tried to hush her sister as the hair on my arms started to rise. That tone my wife used. She only used that tone when she wasn't telling the truth. But why?

"You don't have a child? You worthless junkie whore. You can't even remember giving birth to your daughter." He laughed, and the phone went quiet for a bit. "Look here," he said, but we had no idea what he was showing her. "I said look at this picture on my phone, you stupid bitch! You trying to tell me that this girl isn't yours! My people have a birth certificate that says otherwise, you cunt!"

Oh no.

No. It couldn't be.

My stomach dropped, and my heart was in my throat. I could scarcely breathe as I put the pieces together. The half-truths. The way Faith was with Eden. How even Robert Marino deferred to Faith when it came to Eden.

"I've never seen that girl in my life. I swear. I swear!" Her voice rose as though she were being threatened. "She looks like you, though! She does! Same eyes." Grace choked and started to cough, a gurgling sound following it.

A full thirty seconds of silence practically stopped my heart where I crouched.

"*Faith*," Aiden snarled her name with such menace gooseflesh rose on my arms. "Tell me. Who is the mother of this child? Better yet, tell me who the father is?" He rumbled the same way a lion would before he was about to pounce.

Fear swirled in my gut.

Grace was not Eden's mother.

I closed my eyes and let the truth sink in. How much Faith doted on the girl. How she never referred to Grace in Eden's presence. Why would an aunt not talk about her niece's mother? Not ever. How Eden called her Mimi. A scant few vowels from *Mommy*.

The truth was right in front of me, but there were enough subtle differences in the way Eden looked that I'd never questioned it. And why would I? I'd trusted Faith to be honest with me in all things.

Images of Eden were flooding across my mind's eye when Aiden yelled, "Whose daughter is she, Faith!"

The sound of Faith choking had me standing up, the phone pressed to my ear.

Bruno immediately and forcibly led me away from our spot and back to the car around the side of a building.

"Tell me or I swear to God, I'll strangle you dead right now!" he bellowed.

"NO!" I screamed as loud as I could. "Get your hands off her!" I yelled straight into the receiver.

"What was that? Who the fuck was that?" Aiden roared.

There was a commotion and Faith screeching, "No!" over and over again as my fear hit unbearable heights.

"A phone! Who did you call? Huh, Faith?" I heard a smacking sound that told me he'd hit her, but at least that meant he was no longer strangling her. A small relief.

Then suddenly a cold and cruel, "Hello, Joel. Welcome to the party," came through the phone.

"Keep your hands off her," I said with pure malice.

Aiden laughed. "Keep your hands off her," he mocked in a shitty high timbre that sounded nothing like my accent. "Did you know the woman you married has been lying her ass off? Pawning that sweet little angel off as her sister's. Bet you didn't know that."

"I don't care about the parentage of the child. I only care that she sees her mother again."

"Her mother," he scoffed. "Right. And what about the father? She's about what? Four or five? Tell me, Faith! Who is the child's father? Hmmm?"

"I don't know his name," she boldly lied again.

"Wrong!" he bit out. "The girl is mine, isn't she? She's the reason you left me the last time."

"No, I left you because you raped me!" Faith lashed out.

Aiden made a tsking sound. "You can't rape the willing, Faith. You were my woman. Maybe you weren't exactly in the mood that night, but you loved taking my cock. Every. Single. Time."

For the first time in my life, I wanted to murder a human being with my bare hands. I wouldn't even flinch. Wouldn't care if I spent the rest of my life imprisoned for it. Wiping this filth off the face of the earth would be worth it.

"I told you no over and over. You beat me, then you raped me!" she shrieked.

"Potato, poh-tah-toe," he responded. "Who would believe a nasty child-stealing liar like you? I can't believe you took my daughter from me! My own flesh and blood. You know I don't have any family. That all I've ever wanted was a child. A tiny human I could leave everything I've built. Lenny!" He hollered abruptly. "Find the child. Start with The Alexandra. That's where Joel keeps his treasures, isn't it, Joel?" He directed that last part to me. "You will bring me my daughter."

"Over my dead body," I swore with nothing but violence in every word.

"So be it. Ta-ta for now!" he said before cutting the

connection.

I'd lost contact.

The only contact I had with my wife.

Feeling completely enraged, I dialed one number.

Diego.

The second he answered, I started speaking. "We ambush at midnight." I spoke distinctly and slowly into the phone, pushing my emotions to the back of my mind. Faith needed her husband to be levelheaded and smart about how to save her.

"He's headed to the Maldives with my wife, and he's coming after Eden first. I'll have my family airlifted by helicopter and taken to a safe location. My men will find out what airstrip he plans on using. I'll call with exact coordinates soon." I barked the orders.

"I'll be ready. Leave the bloodshed up to me," Diego offered.

"I want him dead, Diego. *Not breathing.* Can you give me that?" I hissed through my teeth.

"A life for a life, *amigo.*" He reminded me of the last marker I still had with him. I'd used one when Aiden kidnapped Eden, and another when he'd taken her father.

"A life for a life," I repeated.

Episode 106

Shotgun Wedding Part 1

OPAL

When I woke up the next day, Noah was already gone from my bed. I tiptoed into the main room with the hotel robe over the dress shirt he'd given me last night. I expected to find Noah drinking coffee in the living space with a filthy contented smirk on his handsome face but was surprised to find a woman in his stead. She was a petite pixie with platinum-blonde cropped hair dressed completely in black from head to toe. She had a matching black apron around her waist with a variety of makeup tools and brushes sticking from the pockets.

"Thank God you finally woke up! We have such little time to get you ready!" she blustered, approaching me at a quick pace. "Wow. You are a beauty, that's for sure," she added.

I stepped back and held the robe tightly to my chest, focusing on her warily.

"Where's Noah?" I asked.

"Getting everything ready for your wedding, of course," she prattled, grabbing the handle of a large, boxy case and dragging it toward my bedroom.

"And who are you?"

"I'm Liza, Noah's personal assistant and your beauty consultant for today. He flew me in to help with the process. I'll be doing your hair and makeup. And ensuring the dress you chose looks perfect for the wedding." Her dark blue eyes were shrewd as she seemed to assess me where I stood, calculating the things she'd need to make me the perfect bride.

"I thought we were just going to the justice of the peace." I frowned.

"Noah never does anything by halves." She grinned. "Believe me, I've been working with him for years, and a surprise wedding isn't even the most shocking thing he's had me manage. Finding costumes for a pair of twin females who were about to wrestle in a vat of mud on a moment's notice was a far harder task than this." She laughed. "I am shocked that he's actually going to take the plunge into marital bliss, though, having always been the extreme bachelor. But with Noah, I never know what I'm going to get." She smiled sweetly then gestured toward the bedroom door. "Chop, chop. You need to shower and shave while I set everything up? We haven't any time to waste."

"Um, okay. I'm Opal by the way." I put out my hand.

When she smiled next, she showed all her teeth. "I know. I love it. Unique name for such a young little thing."

"I turned twenty yesterday." I lifted my chin, trying to show this woman who couldn't have been more than ten years my senior that I was, in fact, very much an adult.

"Happy late birthday!" Liza responded. "Do you want me to make you some tea? Or coffee, rather? I know Americans tend to prefer coffee."

I nodded. "That would be lovely, thank you. And maybe I can order something to eat. I need to settle my stomach."

"Nerves?" She tipped her head, and her all-business expression softened.

I gave a half-shrug. "Maybe a little."

"I'll have something brought right up. We have a few hours before we need to be at the chapel. Go on and get showered and put on something that buttons up the front so that you can easily remove it when your hair and makeup are done without needing to pull it over your head."

"Got it. Thank you, Liza. I appreciate your help. Do you know when I'll be seeing Noah today?"

"Not until the ceremony. Something about the American tradition of not seeing the bride the day of the wedding prior to the big event? He wanted to respect your privacy. Though he did leave that on the table there when he left."

Liza pointed to a brilliant bouquet of no fewer than two dozen white and pale pink roses that were sitting inside an empty glass vase. The bottom half of the arrangement was wrapped tightly around the stems with satin ribbons. There was a card tilted against the vase with my name on it. I pulled a white card with gold trim out of the envelope to see he'd written the note himself. His penmanship was really quite refined and lovely for a bold and brash type of man.

Opal,

I look forward to watching you walk down the aisle toward me. It will be one of the highlights of my life. Thank you for agreeing to become Mrs. Pennington. I promise to do my best to make you happy in all things. See you soon.

Noah

P.S. Last night was only a taste, poppet. The things I plan to do to you as your husband would make a priest blush…

I shivered where I stood, a flush stealing across my neck and cheeks as I remembered the way I'd wantonly ground against him fully clothed, his mouth sucking and teasing my breasts until I felt like I couldn't breathe. The pleasure was so intense. I'd soared higher than I'd ever taken myself with my fingers before.

If that was just a *taste* of what I would be getting as his wife, I had a lot more to be excited about than a simple exchange of legally binding words and phrases. With thoughts of what more Noah could give me on our wedding night, I took a shower, shaved, brushed my teeth, and finished by lotioning my entire body. As it turned out, I felt excited to be getting married today. It seemed forbidden and a bit taboo, especially since no one in our lives was the wiser. Just Noah and me coming together in a mutual agreement that would provide us both with what we wanted most. All while taking advantage of the natural sexual chemistry between us.

It made sense when I thought about it.

Still, I worried about the aftermath when we returned home and told Ruby and Nile what we had done.

Would Ruby feel relief or regret?

I was hoping for the former and dreading the latter.

I gritted my teeth and stared at myself in the mirror. My long dark hair was still wet while my face was clean and ready to be molded into something befitting a Pennington bride.

"You can do this," I coached my image in the mirror. "Everything is working out exactly how it's supposed to," I reminded myself. "The next three years are going to be fast-paced, filled with Noah's smiling, gorgeous face, tons of non-self-induced orgasms, college, and a whole lot of monetary security."

"Amen to that!" Liza interrupted as she bustled inside without even knocking. "Have you picked out one of the dresses?" she asked.

I shook my head, my cheeks heating with the knowledge that she'd heard my pep talk.

"Seriously, you have ten possible wedding frocks in there, each valued between ten and fifty thousand, and you didn't even try them on?" She blinked at me accusingly while my eyes felt like they were going to pop out of my head hearing the ridiculous prices of the garments Noah had provided.

"Um, can we just pick the cheapest? I'm sure it will be fine." I swallowed against the sudden dryness in my throat.

Liza looked at me as though I'd just transformed into an alien before her eyes. "No, we don't start with the cheapest one first." She made a gagging sound. "I've got some work to do with you, love. Always start with the most expensive. It's your wedding day, for goodness' sake."

I definitely wasn't going to tell her I'd planned on wearing a simple white flowy spaghetti strap sundress today that I'd balled up and tossed into my suitcase at the last minute. That would surely earn me no points with the spirited assistant.

Following direct orders from Lieutenant Liza, I entered the walk-in closet, found a skimpy pair of silky white underwear, and shoved them on. I'd forego the bra because I wasn't sure what type of lingerie on top would work at this time. Then I grabbed the first white dress I saw and put it over my head. It was definitely not my taste, but I gave it a gander in the full-length mirror.

"Nope, that's not it." She eased me aside and went through the rack before separating out one dress that was still in a black bag. I could see the satin through a peek-a-boo cut out.

"What's that one?" I asked.

She gave me a coy smile. "It's the dress Noah liked best for you from the images I sent him before I brought them here. He didn't want you to feel swayed to choose the one he liked best, so I left it in the bag."

"That's interesting. Well, hand me the next one," I instructed gamely, wanting to get through this part quickly. My mind was full of the pros and cons of today's nuptials, and I wanted desperately to spend some time in my own mind working through them while she took care of my makeup and hair.

We went through all of the gowns with the maybes hanging on the left and the ones we didn't like on the right side of the closet.

"That seemed like a lot of work," she huffed, hanging a super heavy princess-style dress on the "no" side. "Last we have the one he picked. Which one are you leaning toward of these three?" she asked.

"They're all pretty. I'm not exactly picky, nor did I have some grand idea in my mind of what I would wear on my wedding day." Mostly because I hadn't planned on getting married any time soon or perhaps ever, but I kept that last thought to myself.

She frowned. "You're supposed to feel like the most beautiful woman alive on your wedding day." Her shoulders slumped as she unzipped the last bag. The bag had the words *Phillipa Lepley* in cursive on the back.

"This one is from an amazing English bridal designer," she touted.

When she pulled out the elegant satin gown, my heart stopped, and I gasped. The dress was out-of-this-world stunning. It was a simple cut with sumptuous, buttery-looking cream-colored satin. The dress had wide draping that ran delicately along the neckline just above the bust. The fabric drew the eye up to the collarbone and face. It had a somewhat hidden corseted bodice with bow straps at the biceps creating an off-the shoulder neckline. The design sleekly nipped in at the waist and fell all the way to the floor in perfect sheets of silky satin.

When I put it on, tears pricked at my eyes as I stared at myself in the mirror. I not only looked like the perfect English bride, I *felt* like one. I was beautiful in a way I'd never imagined seeing myself.

"I should have known Noah would choose the most romantic and fitting dress of the bunch. And if that tear you wiped away is any indication, you seem to like it too," Liza noted gently.

I nodded, breathing through the sudden overwhelming feeling that I was actually getting married. Many women spent their entire lives dreaming of this moment. Usually, though, they'd be surrounded by all the people they loved to stand by and cheer. I only had Ruby, and she had no idea I was taking this enormous step alone.

I held back the tears I wanted to shed, not because I wasn't genuinely happy, but because my heart was cracking with the knowledge that Ruby would not be standing next to me.

I missed her presence.

I missed her support.

I missed *her*.

By the end of the day, I'd be Mrs. Opal Pennington.

I fanned my heated face and took several calming breaths.

"You okay, love?" Liza's expression was soft and her tone full of compassion.

"Mmm-hmm. Just a lot to take in." Especially without my safety blanket, otherwise known as Ruby. Doing something this life-altering without my sister would be unheard of under normal circumstances, but these weren't the everyday challenges we normally faced together. This was me taking the brunt of our situation and letting Ruby off the hook for the first time ever.

My sister, who had worked her body and fingers to the bone, would finally have the time and resources to figure out what it was she wanted to do with her life without the burden of taking care of me. Marrying Noah would provide us both with the financial security we needed. And in exchange, Ruby would be free.

Free to do whatever the hell she wanted.

That was the ultimate goal.

"This is most definitely the dress I want to marry Noah in." I refocused my attention on the here and now and swished the opulent fabric from side to side, then spun around to see it sway. It kept its form beautifully.

"I'm thinking with this dress we have to go hair up. With soft eyeshadow in shimmery tones. Then we'll glow out your skin to the max and add a pale pink glossy lip. What do you think?"

I smiled wide at myself in the mirror. "It sounds excellent. Let's do it."

With one last look at myself in the mirror, I smiled at my reflection, knowing that what I was about to do would change everything. I just hoped it was for the better.

"I'm ready to become Mrs. Opal Pennington."

Episode 107

Shotgun Wedding Part 2

NOAH

I stood at the end of the aisle waiting for her to appear. My palms were slightly damp as I clutched my wrists behind my back and pressed my toes into the plush carpet in order to keep my balance. The bespoke suit I wore was a cool soft gray in color with a white dress shirt and matching vest and tie. I had a single pink rose pinned to my lapel that had come from the bouquet of flowers I'd left Opal this morning.

Did she like them?

Which dress would she chose?

Would she show?

My mind was a tumultuous frenzy of nervous activity as I waited impatiently for the two doors at the end of the chapel to open and reveal her. I'd wanted to give Opal the time to prepare for our ceremony in the manner I understood Americans preferred, including the tradition of not seeing the bride prior to the ceremony. My loyal assistant Liza had texted an hour ago stating they were on their way to the church, but I hadn't heard from either of them since.

I inhaled sharply as the sound of the organ playing filtered through the room with its melodic, reassuring tones, announcing her presence.

The doors creaked open, and there she stood, backlit by the light streaming in from behind her.

She was an angel come to life.

My angel.

Her head was tipped down as she ran her hand down her dress as though she was straightening any wrinkles. The flower bouquet I'd left her was proudly displayed in front of her abdomen, making her even more picturesque.

It felt like I'd waited a lifetime for her to arrive, and now that she was here, I needed to make eye contact. To ensure through her gaze that she was willing and ready to change her entire life by standing at my side.

Look at me, Opal. Please show me your eyes, I chanted internally while nervous energy licked at my senses, making me jittery. I was a living, breathing bundle of tension. A ship's captain lost at sea, looking for an opening in the storm that raged all around me.

And then she lifted her head, and her gaze met mine.

Two dark pools of hope, fear, and excitement swirled and coalesced in a single moment. A tether reached out from the center of her chest and punched straight into mine. I gasped as relief poured through my veins and filled me with joy and contentment.

She smiled, and my heart settled. The heavy, frightened rhythm of a man waiting for his bride at the altar relaxed at the mere sight of her.

She was a vision. A dream I didn't know I'd had until it presented itself in the form of a beautiful woman standing at the end of the aisle about to become my other half.

For a few seconds, I allowed myself to imagine that this was what my father felt when my mother was about to become his wife. A soul tied to me, not by blood or familial obligation, but by *choice.*

The choice made all the difference.

Opal started to walk slowly toward me as the music lifted and flowed along with her steps.

She wore the dress I'd thought would suit her best, and, boy, had I been right. I'd not seen a more beautiful bride in my entire life, and I'd attended dozens of weddings. The cream-colored satin hugged her slight curves and seemed to glow against her toasted skin tone. Every inch of her was covered except her neck, shoulders, face, and arms, and yet she was the sexiest thing I'd ever laid eyes on.

Opal's cheeks were a stunning rosy pink, but her glossy lips held a hint of a playful smirk. Even now, she was determined and resplendent in her confidence, knowing her goals and giving them her all. This was not a woman afraid of the colossal step before her. Her head was high and her back straight, looking like a true Queen about to wed her King.

She continued forward, her steps even and sure, until she reached the altar where I stood along with the clergyman.

I wiped my clammy hand on my pant leg and held it out, palm facing the sky. My breath caught in my throat as she placed her cool, smaller one within mine. Warmth spread through our palms the moment they touched, filling the energy in the air around us with a golden comforting hue of peace and serenity.

"I am in awe of your beauty," I whispered, feeling the need to speak low to not break the incredible bubble of rightness that surrounded us. I dipped my head forward and kissed the top of her hand, taking in her unique scent of brown sugar and spice. It reminded me of the ginger biscuits my mother used to make when I was a child. An additional comfort.

"You look unearthly handsome," she said as a pretty flush stole across her neckline and cheeks.

The lighting above caught on the brushed silver chain she wore around her neck, the hummingbird cameo locket Ruby had given her for her birthday lying perfectly against her skin in clear view. A talisman of the one person I knew she loved above all others. Perhaps in the future, that love would shift from Ruby to me. I wasn't sure if I could handle that type of devotion, but only time would tell.

I smiled at the sight of her sister's love and couldn't help but lift a finger to touch the locket, openly recognizing its value and importance to Opal.

"I wanted her with me, even though she can't be here." Her voice caught for a moment, her eyes becoming glassy.

I removed my touch and nodded, squeezing her hand as we turned to face the officiant. In my peripheral view, Liza stood off to the side, phone in hand, taking photos. She would also act as our witness.

For the first time, I felt a sense of sadness at the thought that I was forcing Opal to do this without anyone she loved around—especially Ruby. Not to mention the fact that I'd never believed I'd take such a massive step forward in my life without my twin, *my brother*, at my side. We were both making a sacrifice for this union, and that made it easier somehow.

Opal squeezed my hand and smiled at me. "Ready?" she asked gently.

I dove into her gaze, drowning in the beauty I found there, allowing her calming nature to soothe the confused feelings I had and making them disappear altogether.

Today was about Opal and me becoming one.

Bound together for a similar purpose.

We were a team.

After today, it would no longer be Noah and Nile, twin brothers taking the business world by storm. It would be Noah and Opal, paving a new path toward a future filled with endless new possibilities.

When the clergyman asked me if I would take Opal Dawson as my lawfully wedded wife, I responded with certainty. I truly believed this was the path I was meant to take.

"I do," I said with pride.

Each moment of the ceremony came to me in a flash of

light, like capturing an image on film.

Opal saying her vows.

Me saying mine.

Her sliding the simple band I'd given the officiant prior to her arrival on my ring finger.

Me slipping on the enormous vintage Australian fire opal I'd purchased just for her on hers. The brilliant center stone had three diamond baguettes on each side of it, set into the finest platinum.

At the sight of the ring, she gasped, her mouth falling open delicately in a small O shape as I ran my thumb across the oval stone in the center. It sparkled and reflected a rainbow of colors that I too became mesmerized by. It was almost as beautiful as she was.

Then we kissed primly when instructed—nothing like how I wanted to kiss the woman who'd become my wife.

Finally, we were announced as husband and wife to an empty little church in the middle of the Danish countryside.

Walking hand in hand with Opal back down the aisle was surreal.

I was a married man.

When we got to the end, I scooped her into my arms and spun her in a wide circle. She laughed and arched into the dizzying feeling. When her feet touched the ground, her arms came around my neck, and she lifted to her toes and pressed her mouth to mine.

A kiss meant just for us.

I slicked my tongue across her glossy lips and drank deep of my wife's taste. It was nothing like the chaste peck after our vows. This was me and Opal.

Fire and ice.

Two very different people coming together in a burst of affection and sexual chemistry that could fuel a rocket to the moon.

The kiss went on and on, she just as ravenous as I. When we both finally pulled away, we simply stared at one another. Two suddenly shy, endorphin-fueled people desperate to be alone.

I grabbed her hand and practically dragged her out of the church. Only to be thwarted by Liza.

My little ball-busting pixie of an executive assistant shook her head and pointed at the stairs leading out of the church.

"You're not going anywhere until I get an official wedding photo of the two of you. You will thank me later," she added.

I snarled, wanting to get my bride to a place where I could have her all to myself.

Opal chuckled, cuddled against my side, and placed her hand to my chest. She leaned her head against my shoulder and smiled.

Liza lifted her phone and took several photos. I covered Opal's hand over my chest and looked down at the woman I'd married. I'd never felt truly connected to a woman until right then.

Her head lifted, and she grinned so widely that I couldn't help but kiss her sweet lips once more.

This was us. The us I wanted to be. Free to hold one another. Free to smile. To kiss. To just be together.

It was a new experience, but one I found appealed to me far more than I'd thought it could.

When Opal wrapped her arms around my neck and stared into my eyes, I was a goner.

Liza said something, but I was no longer paying attention to my demanding assistant. My full focus was on Opal.

"Kiss me, husband," Opal murmured and smiled softly.

I cupped her cheek, brushed her nose with my own, and whispered against her succulent lips, "With pleasure, wife."

I kissed her soft.

I kissed her slow.

I kissed her with my whole heart.

And I kissed her with my soul.

Eventually Liza cleared her throat, reminding us that we still had an audience. I pulled away, and Liza handed us some paperwork. We signed where she pointed and then she did the same on the witness line. Once completed, she took a photo of the marriage certificate.

"Congratulations. Everything is as you requested back at the hotel. Have a wonderful night, Mr. and Mrs. Pennington." She winked and then entered the church once more, I assumed to give the document to the officiant so they could take care of the remainder of the process.

I looped my arm around Opal's waist and crushed her body to mine.

She giggled playfully.

"All I can think about is getting you back to our hotel and our marital bed," I admitted, my voice rough.

Her eyes heated with desire, and she wantonly licked her lips, likely tasting hints of me there from our kisses. The thought alone made my dick harden painfully behind my trousers.

"No reception?" she teased.

I clenched my teeth and pursed my lips. "Oh, I will feed my wife. You will need sustenance in order to keep up with how much and how often I will ravish your gorgeous body." I gripped her hips and pressed her against my hard length.

Her eyes widened, and she bit into her bottom lip.

I ground against her brazenly, wanting to see her catch fire before my eyes, standing on the very steps of the church I'd just married her in.

She made a whimpering mewl sound that went straight to my cock. Which was when I grabbed her hand and dragged her to the waiting limo. Opal laughed the entire way until we both got in. The second she was inside, I reached for her, tugging her sideways over my lap.

My mouth was on her neck before the driver could even start the car. At least he had the good grace to raise the privacy screen.

"You make me insane with need, Opal." I slid my hand from her hip to palm her satin covered breasts, where I squeezed with intent.

She moaned and arched into my palm, pressing her flesh harder into my hold.

"Touch me," she begged, then put her mouth on mine.

Who was I to deny my bride her every wish?

As I kissed her, I tugged at the long satin fabric covering her bottom half until I was able to place my hand exactly where I wanted.

On silky bare flesh.

Her thigh was warm as I ran my hand up to where I knew she wanted me most.

"Open your legs, poppet," I requested, then sucked on her bottom lip.

She let one of her legs fall open, widening the space I had to work with.

"Good girl," I cooed, then went right for the heat between her thighs, cupping her sex possessively.

"Oh my," she choked out, her surprised response pushing my own desire beyond the breaking point.

"This is mine now," I growled. "Isn't it, my love?" I rubbed along the damp, lacy fabric.

"God, yes!" she gasped.

"You want me to touch you inside, poppet?" I flicked my tongue against her neck just below her ear and gloried in her corresponding moan. "Do you want me to insert my fingers deep into you? Fuck my wife until she comes all over my fingers?"

"Noah!" she breathed as though it was an ache. I responded by dipping my hand inside her panties and finding her slick and hot against my fingertips.

"Jesus! You are so wet for me, darling, you're positively dripping with need," I murmured and bit down on her neck. She jolted at the sharp nip to her skin.

She thrust her hips as I caressed her slit up and down, teasing her mercilessly. She tried to force my fingers to go inside by lifting her pelvis, but I knew better. This wasn't my first time playing in the sandbox, but it was hers, and I wanted her mindless for me.

"Should I fuck my wife with these?" I spun two fingers around her clit, using her arousal to ease the way.

"Noah, please. Oh my God." She gulped air into her lungs, and right as she was letting it out, I slid two fingers inside.

Her hands tightened against my shoulders, and her entire body went stiff at the intrusion.

"Relax, poppet. I'll never hurt you." I eased my fingers out slowly and then back in, lubricating them with her essence. She was incredibly tight, and I couldn't wait to feel her heat wrapped around my cock for the first time.

With each plunge, her breath hitched as if she was studying her own body's response.

It was hot as fuck.

I wanted to lay her out on the limo seat and cover her with my form and thrust something much larger between her thighs, rutting like an animal and taking her cherry in the process. But that wasn't us. That wasn't this. Not yet. We had years to *fuck*. Tonight was about showing her the beauty of true pleasure and sex when you trusted the person you were with.

Her body started to move with my fingers, and little moans escaped her throat. I ate those sounds with my kiss, swirling my tongue around hers and distracting her from processing what was going on in her body so she could simply feel what was happening to her by my hand.

I eased out of her and spun my fingers around that knot of nerves until she convulsed in my arms, her bodying stringing tight as a drum.

"I'm going to…" She closed her eyes as I plunged those fingers back into her wet heat, hooked them deep, and rubbed along the walls of her sex.

Her eyes opened wide as I found what I needed within her and manipulated it repeatedly. Her mouth went slack as her head bolted back, and she cried out.

I doubled my efforts, rubbing, fucking, then swirling around her clit as her body shook. She was so beautiful when she came. Her entire face lit up, mouth glistening and swollen from my kisses. Eyes endless pools of lust that I could look into forever.

She slowly came down from her release, her body trembling in my arms as she slumped against me.

I removed my hand from the plethora of satin. As she watched, I lifted the two wet fingers I'd had deep within her and put them straight into my mouth. I hummed at the salty-sweet taste of her on my tongue.

Within seconds, she surprised me by reaching up, curling her hand around my neck, and kissing me heatedly, stealing the taste of herself from my very tongue.

Then she groaned, yanked up the fabric covering her legs, and maneuvered herself upright on my lap.

"Make love to me," she requested.

I shook my head. "Not in a car. I will have you laid out naked so I can taste, kiss, suck, and fuck every inch of you until you're begging me to stop."

"I won't ask you to stop. Not if it feels like this," she breathed against my lips.

I smiled devilishly. "We shall see."

Episode 108

The Woman of the House

RUBY

A few days earlier…

I spun around in a flirty circle on my bare feet when I hit the second level of the staircase. The marble floors were cool against my toes, but the rest of me was nice and warm. I'd just awakened from another wonderful night's sleep. Since Opal left, we'd hit downtown London, ridden the Eye, and had a brilliant drunken evening in Nile's favorite pub—which I'd found out was one of Noah's establishments. Then last night we'd stayed in as he'd had a ton of work to catch up on. I spent the evening on his laptop looking into a variety of extracurricular activities such as jewelry-making, painting, and most importantly, a sculpting class. I planned to sign up for that class once the wedding and honeymoon were behind us and we'd settled into our lives. I also reviewed all the information I could find on Pennington Enterprises and the charities they supported. Turned out, Nile and Noah—well, their family, at least—were behind a lot of philanthropic endeavors. *Philanthropic* being a word I'd recently learned by the ever-present, ever-helpful governess.

Speaking of the devil, she waited at the end of the staircase, arms crossed, head tilted to the side in a stuffy pose that couldn't have been comfortable. Though her sleek pale-lavender suit rocked. How a woman could wear full-body pastel colors and look amazing was surprising, but somehow she made it look good. The governess was class from head to toe, and I wanted to learn all the things from her, even though I was finding that Nile enjoyed me just as I was.

"And the lady finally graces us with her presence," she stated coolly, her gaze running up and down the simple ribbed cotton tank dress I wore. It was neon pink and formed to my body like a second skin. Usually, I paired it with a pair of white tennis shoes and a baseball cap with my hair in a ponytail out the back. It was the perfect, comfy running errands look. And when you lived in the South where it was humid and sticky as a popsicle melting in a toddler's hand, the less clothing that touched your actual skin, the better.

"Good morning to you too, governess." I smiled, battling her natural grump with some sunshine.

"It *was* a good morning. One you missed as it's already 11:15. Practically time for lunch."

I shrugged. "I'm a night owl. If you want me to rise and shine with the sun, you need to tell your beloved Nile that he can't keep me out and awake all hours of the night." I winked and made a tsking sound with my tongue.

"Oh good heavens," she blurted. "A proper lady does not boast about, nor does she discuss the inner workings of her relationship. Especially with respect to matters that should be kept private."

"Got it." I tapped at my temple. "Where's Nile this morning?" I asked, my heart all aflutter.

"He had business in the city. You are to work with me today planning the wedding."

My shoulders fell. "I thought you had it all under control."

"Of course I have things under control, but your intended wants you to feel like this is your day."

I sighed heavily. "Fine. Can we do it over breakfast?"

Her gaze narrowed.

"I mean brunch!" I corrected while holding back a snicker. The governess was so uptight, but it was kind of fun to get her riled up.

"I suppose so. I'll meet you in the dining room with the planners."

The planners. As in, more than one.

I rolled my eyes.

"A Pennington woman does not roll her eyes, Ms. Dawson. It's uncouth."

I didn't even know what uncouth meant, but I could guess. Instead of responding, I just nodded and made my way to the dining room. There was a coffee and tea station. The coffee had been added when I arrived in England, and as far as I could tell, Opal and I were the only ones who drank it. Another sweet thing Nile must have added to ensure I enjoyed what I preferred.

He was so thoughtful. And sexy. And just everything I could have ever dreamed up in a fairy tale. Our time together was making me smitten with my fiancé. Smitten being a word I'd also recently learned.

Like last night when he'd teased and taunted me in bed for an hour before going down on me until I had two back-to-back orgasms. He then took himself in hand while hovering over my naked form and spent his release all over my chest, rubbing it along my breasts and sex as if he were marking me in a primal, hedonistic way. Promptly after he'd made his mess, he went to the bathroom and came back with a warm cloth. He cleaned me of his release in worshipful strokes, getting every nook and cranny until I closed my eyes and fell asleep.

I got my coffee, and when I sat, one of the kitchen staff came out with a plate of pastries and jams.

"What would you like for brunch, madam?" Eloise, the sweet young woman, asked. She was maybe eighteen and the only staff member who smiled regularly.

"Scrambled eggs with cheddar cheese and bacon, please. And can you ask the chef to overcook them?" I'd learned that the English preferred runny eggs and undercooked bacon. At least that's what the chef here seemed to prefer. "Thank you, Eloise."

"Of course, ma'am. Please let me know if you wish for anything else."

"I wish for you to call me Ruby," I added with a smile.

"Of course, Ruby," she reiterated and then promptly left to complete her task.

The governess smoothly entered at a brisk pace with another attendant carrying three binder-sized portfolios.

"Place them there." She pointed to the space next to me.

I tried not to groan at the ridiculousness of having three giant planner books for a wedding that would be attended by guests I didn't know. But if this was what Nile wanted, I'd give him that. I didn't care either way. I was marrying him, not the pomp and circumstance. Yes, it was originally for money, but the more I spent time being an actual couple with Nile, the more I dove deeper into having real feelings for him. And I knew he had them for me.

Already we were more than friends. Confidants definitely. I shared things with him about my past that I had promised myself I'd keep locked up in the back of my mind to never see the light of day. He'd shared his experience losing his parents at a young age and then later his grandfather. Explained how he believed his success was a direct reflection of his parents' reputations and memory, which was why it was so important he secure the governing interest in their holdings. It was a lot of pressure he'd placed on himself. I hoped that during our time together, I could be a source of comfort and help take some of that load off his shoulders.

The governess sat down, reached for the first book, and opened it to a page with wedding dresses.

My heart caught in my throat at the design being worn by a model. Since I'd arrived, Ms. Bancroft had peppered me with constant questions about what I wanted. The dress was the only thing I'd paid close attention to. Of all the designers she'd shown me, I had chosen one from a designer called Temperley London. This designer's clothing had been all over British *Vogue* and was worn by celebrities across the globe. I cared about none of that. Of all the wedding imagery the governess had shared, this particular designer had a unique style of pairing old and new. And after a lengthy chat with the design team and my always-present sidekick, we'd come to a design that I absolutely adored.

"Is that it?" I gulped, pointing at the image. Tears pricked at the corner of my eyes as I took in every meticulous detail. It was magnificent.

"It is." She gifted me a small smile and pushed the binder closer to me.

I traced the details with my finger. The front had a beaded lace sweetheart neckline that cut across the arms to an off-the-shoulder half-sleeve. There was a thin line of lace detailing that graced the base of the neck and ran across the clavicle to the shoulders. There were peek-a-boo cut-outs on both sides of the ribcage and down to the hip with the palest see-through fabric over it to hint at the skin underneath. The lace and beading clung to the front of the bodice in delicate swooping patterns that added to the regal, royal bride aesthetic. The details flowed to about three inches past my lady bits, where the fabric once again turned see-through, gliding all the way to the floor. The back was a unique open cutout that framed the body in the sultriest, yet most elegant way.

"It's the most beautiful thing I've ever seen," I whispered in awe.

"You chose well, I will give you that. It will be here tonight for a final fitting."

Excitement poured into my chest as Eloise brought my breakfast and placed it in front of me. The governess side-eyed my food choices and turned to the section regarding table seating.

I listened to her go on and on about every detail, agreeing with everything she wanted. It truly didn't matter to me where people sat, who was attending, what the flowers were, or what food was served. I was marrying Nile, and that's all I wanted to focus on.

"You're very accommodating," she finally stated, closing two of the books. "This is a positive trait of yours that I appreciate." She complimented me for the first time, well, ever.

"Were you expecting me to be difficult?" I rested my elbow on the table and placed my head in my hand as I focused on her.

"Your elbows never belong on a dining table, dearest," she chastised, but then her eyes widened at the same time mine did.

"Dearest?" I reiterated, my mouth falling open in shock. Was that a term of endearment coming from the stodgy, prim, and proper governess?

"I misspoke, *Ms. Dawson.*" She tried to change her tone and lifted her head and her chin in her normal stuffy position.

"You like me!" I teased. "*Dearest,*" I repeated. "You *really* like me. You do! Admit it," I taunted playfully.

"Don't be absurd. You are to be a member of my family. And if Nile chose you, he did so for a reason. That means you have redeeming qualities. I have found your eagerness and flexibility as it pertains to the wedding planning a welcome surprise. Also, I will admit to finding it endearing how much you aim to please my boy," she admitted.

I grinned widely. "Mmm-hmm which means...you like me!" I continued to tease.

She ignored my statement and asked a question of her own. "One thing we didn't discuss is your guest list. Each time I bring it up, you change the subject." She reached for the notepad and a pen. "Whom should I add on your behalf? Parents?"

Instantly a wave of nausea rolled through me, tightening my gut, threatening to make the eggs and bacon make a second appearance. I gritted my teeth and breathed through the discomfort. "No one on my side besides my sister, Opal."

"I was told when Opal arrived that a situation had occurred with your mother. Is she unwell?" Her tone was rather soft and compassionate, something I wasn't used to when communicating with the governess.

"My mother is a horrible human being who Opal and I no longer have a connection with. Can we leave it at that?" My voice shook, and I looked away, not wanting her to grill me further.

She nodded curtly. "And your father? Will he be in attendance?"

I licked my lips as my stomach clenched even tighter. "No." I offered no explanation as she made a note. I didn't know who my father was. Opal didn't know who hers was. Frankly, it could have been anyone back in Glory Springs. My mother opened her legs to any Tom, Dick, and Harry who could pay her meager fees.

"And friends? You don't have a single friend you'd like to send an invitation to?" the governess pressed.

I swallowed down the dryness in my throat and reached for my water glass, downing several gulps. The word friend bounced around in my mind, and I realized I actually did have friends now.

"Um, I do have a few."

The governess perked up with a hint of exuberance. She held her pen to the notepad. "The names?"

"Mr. and Mrs. Toussaint."

"Is she French?" she asked. "I've heard that name before."

"I think so." I remembered that her accent sounded French. "I don't know if she will be able to come...or any of my friends, for that matter."

She nodded and waited patiently for me to continue, and I felt weird not giving her a huge list of names, so I started rattling off The Candidates Club members.

"Sutton and Dakota Goodall. They are in the cattle business," I added, trying to share anything that might make the governess find me more endearing. Even if it was my new friends and their mates who were the interesting subjects.

"Noted." She scratched the names on her list. "Next?"

"Um, you could add Joel and Faith Castellanos? They just got married themselves, so they may be on their honeymoon right now."

"Castellanos? As in the Greek resort owner?" She sounded surprised and maybe even impressed.

"Yep, that's the one."

"I believe he and his new wife are already on the list of invites, as Joel is a friend of both my boys," she said.

"Oh, okay. Um, you could add Erik Johansen and his fiancée, Savannah McAllister?"

"Mr. Johansen is engaged?" She scoffed. "Last I heard about the ale entrepreneur, he was traveling the world." Her brow furrowed.

I shrugged. "I know his fiancée, Savannah, better than him."

"He is also on the list, as is his CEO, Jack Larsen," she responded.

"I don't know the Jack fella."

"Anyone else?" She scribbled down information on her

notepad.

"Two more. Memphis Taylor and Jade Lee."

"Jade Lee. Of Lee International Imports?" Her mouth fell open in a sudden, unladylike snort. She lifted her hand to cover her response and cleared her throat.

"Yeah, Jade's family is well-known if I remember correctly." I distinctly recalled when Faith put her foot in her mouth back at Madam Alana's conference room when we all met. Faith had made an insulting comment about Jade not needing to be there because of her family's wealth.

"Well, these additions are lovely. I'll have their addresses found and invitations forwarded." She snapped the last book closed and set the note and pen on top of it. Then she waved her hand in the air nonchalantly and nodded at the staff member who had been waiting across the room rather patiently for us over the last few hours while we worked on the wedding stuff. The attendant came over and removed the books.

"Place these in my office, please," the governess instructed.

I frowned. "You have an office here?"

The governess sighed, and then her gaze darted to me. "Have you not toured the estate?"

I shook my head. "I've been to the main living spaces, Opal's room, Nile's office and music studio, and my room. I mean, Nile's room." My cheeks heated.

"Yes, well, there is a lot more, including a full library, an indoor pool, a steam room, exercise room, guest houses, garage, the staff quarters, the atrium, gardens, the stables."

"Stables? You have horses here?" I breathed with excitement.

"But of course." She stood.

"I've never seen a horse in person before. Do you think it would be okay if I poked around?" I twiddled my thumbs as I held my hands clasped together in front of me.

"You can go wherever you please, Ms. Dawson. You live here and are soon to become the lady of the house."

My eyes widened at the thought that based on what she was saying, the governess herself would technically answer to me when Nile and I married.

I grinned wickedly. "I'll bet that freaks you way out," I chuckled.

"You have no idea," she stated flatly, but there was a tiny curve to her lips as though she was purposely preventing a smile.

I'd win her over yet.

I skipped to the entry that would lead me back upstairs where I could put some shoes on. "Real-life horses," I murmured. I couldn't wait to see and pet one. We didn't have horses around our small area. Only rich farmers had those types of animals.

Before I could exit, a man in a pristine suit came bustling in clutching a newspaper to his chest, almost mowing me down. I stepped back and flattened myself to the wall.

"What is it, Mr. Landry?" the governess asked. "I'm surprised to see you here."

Mr. Landry was one of Nile's attorneys. We'd met with him when we signed the documents to start the process for our marriage in the United Kingdom.

"We need to talk," he stated gruffly, then handed the newspaper to the governess.

"Well, I'm going to let you two talk. I'm going to see a man about a horse," I chuckled, laughing at my own joke.

The governess put up her hand to stop me as her entire face paled. "Not so fast, Ms. Dawson." Her voice was as strong as steel. "I'm afraid you're not going anywhere."

I frowned as the hairs on the back of my neck rose. "What is it?"

Her expression lacked any emotion when she tossed the paper down on the table.

There in black and white was a picture of me wearing nothing but pasties and a thong, my body hanging upside down, my legs locked in an acrobatic position on the silver stripper pole keeping me aloft. I remembered that pose and that image. It was a picture the club I worked at used in marketing materials to gain new customers.

My heart sank as the one skeleton left in my closet stared me straight in the face in horrifying detail for all to see.

I glanced up, my ability to speak completely gone.

The governess looked at me with a shrewd, disappointed gaze. "The wedding is off."

Episode 109

A Pennington to Wed a Stripper

NILE

I stared quietly at the front page of the society section of the newspaper, a million feelings and thoughts cascading through my mind like a rapid waterfall barreling down a cliffside. Right in the center of the page was my fiancée, her succulent curves and beautiful body on full display for the entire world to view and judge.

And good God, she was a true beauty.

I hadn't the slightest clue my Ruby had worked as a stripper back in the small town she grew up in. Though it wasn't a far reach after knowing her backstory. A woman abused from a young age using the very tool people wanted from her in order to gain her freedom. I commended Ruby silently for being able to switch the narrative on her situation in her favor.

My cell phone buzzed against my glass desktop for the tenth time today.

I glanced at the screen and noted the governess was calling again.

She'd most likely seen the papers, as I knew she read them

with her afternoon tea and would have a great deal of opinions and thoughts on how to best manage damage control. The first order of business would be to cancel the wedding. Throw Ruby right under the bus and play the woe-is-me card as the unknowing rich businessman who had been taken advantage of. Show the world how wronged I'd been by her deceit. Save my reputation and that of the family's good name.

I had to bite my tongue in order to not roll my eyes at the absurdity.

A Pennington to Wed a Stripper.

That was the headline.

My Ruby wasn't a stripper. Perhaps that was the job she'd had in the past in order to survive and provide for her kin, but that wasn't who she was. Not the woman I'd seen unfolding like a flower from within the safety and privacy of our bedroom at my home estate. Sharing her true nature with me under the quiet darkness of the night while we held one another close.

No, the woman I was marrying was sweet. Fiercely loyal. Protective. Curious. Intelligent in a way I was not. She felt things *deeply*, making her able to connect to people through her sincerity and genuine compassion. Ruby was a woman who had been given nothing but rubbish and had lived through unspeakable acts of abuse. A survivor through and through. And yet every day she woke with a bright smile and excitement for the possible adventures to come.

She was everything I could ever want and need in my life.

I continued to scan the article which detailed where Ruby had worked and for how long. Customers of the club had been interviewed, including the owner. I made note of the man's name as I had every intention of making business harder for him after speaking out against the woman I...

My chest tightened suddenly, stealing my breath. My heart beat fast against my ribcage.

Did I love Ruby?

Even thinking the phrase created a physical reaction within

my body.

Besides my chest and heart beating rapidly, my cock hardened at the memory of my bride waiting patiently for me to get home from work. Excited to see me. Ready to spend time together doing anything or nothing at all. I found that when I left her for any length of time I hungered to see her again. Desperate to see her face light up just because I'd entered a room.

Was that love?

Sweat beaded at my hairline and underarms as I inhaled sharply, trying to pull as much air into my lungs as I could in order to quiet the panicked, strained sensation clawing at my insides.

Could I have fallen in love with Ruby?

No…

Maybe?

It was hard to tell what I felt romantically as I'd never been in love. Never searched it out. Never thought I'd care one way or the other about it. My parents were the only two people I'd known and trusted who had an everlasting love connection. Experiencing them dying at the same time was brutal, the hardest days of my life, but somehow knowing they had been together felt right. One should not have existed without the other. Their love was that transcendent.

I sat back and let the feelings sweep over me, trying to understand and decipher what had plagued me most from the minute my assistant brought me this morning's paper.

Anger was high on the list. I wanted to burn the world down on Ruby's behalf. Destroy every single individual who was involved in printing this filth.

They didn't know my intended. Had no idea how much this would hurt her. It made my skin crawl knowing there was some arsehole out there getting off on the fact that he'd pulled one over on a Pennington. Without regard for the woman he'd exposed in the process.

I pressed a button on my phone, and my assistant answered

immediately.

"Sir?" she asked.

"Katherine, get my private investigator to find more information about the man who wrote this article about Ms. Dawson and any others who were named. I want the works. No expense spared."

"Yes, Mr. Pennington. Will that be all?"

"For now, yes." I stood up and tucked the paper under my arm. "I'll be heading home for the remainder of the day. I do not want to be interrupted. Please reschedule any meetings for today and tomorrow."

"Um, sir, Ms. Bancroft has called every thirty minutes for the past two hours."

I groaned out loud. "I'll handle her."

"Okay, but she's on the other line, and she says that if I don't transfer her to you, she's going to ensure I lose my job." Her breath hitched at the end of her comment.

"That woman," I growled. "Katherine, you work for me, not for Ms. Bancroft."

"I do. But…" Her voice dipped. "She's scary, and I know she's important to you."

"I'll deal with Ms. Bancroft. As a matter of fact, once you reschedule my meetings, I want you to take the rest of today and tomorrow off as well. I've got some personal matters to attend to, and I'm certain your husband and children would love to have some free time with you."

"Really? That would be lovely."

"Then it's settled. We'll both take a bit of time off. I'll see you in a couple of days."

"Thank you. And my husband and I are greatly looking forward to your wedding…I mean, I'm sorry. If there is still to be a wedding." She made a sound like she was chewing on her nails.

"Oh, there will be a wedding, I can promise you that. Take care, Katherine." I ended the call.

I grabbed my cell phone, ignored the calls from the

governess, and clicked on Ruby's contact number for the third time today. As I expected, it went straight to voice mail.

I could only imagine what I would find when I got home.

Provided Ruby was there when I arrived.

The very second I entered the garage, the governess was waiting at the entrance to the mudroom. As usual, she was dressed to impress, but her coloring was pale and her hair tousled as though she'd run her fingers through it repeatedly.

"Why have you been ignoring my calls?" she snapped when I reached her.

"Because I know exactly what you are going to say." I pushed past her and entered the house.

"If we are to cancel this wedding and get our side of the story printed in tomorrow's paper, we need to act fast." She was all business, but this wasn't a professional situation. What was taking place was likely affecting my dear Ruby's soft heart in a manner I would not tolerate. I knew deep inside that my intended was crushed and broken that her past had been painted across the newspapers.

"And therein lies the problem." I sighed as I placed my briefcase on the kitchen counter.

"The problem is that you must make a statement as soon as possible. One that absolves you of her lies regarding her past. We need the masses to know that you were unaware of her history and therefore will be cancelling any involvement. Otherwise..." Ms. Bancroft trailed off.

"Otherwise what?" I blurted, my tone rising. Irritation fueling my response.

The governess took a step back, her hand going to cover the skin of her throat. "Otherwise, your reputation and the family name will suffer."

"Bollocks! What will I, one of the most eligible and desirable bachelors in the United Kingdom, lose because of this article?"

"Status." She lifted her chin stoically.

"I don't give a rat's arse about status. My reputation speaks for itself. Iconic composer, giving philanthropist, winemaker, loving brother, son, and grandson. Who I choose to marry and take to my bed is my own personal business," I reminded her.

"In our circles, your reputation and achievements aren't enough. You know I tell the truth. Who you have by your side matters." Her words were soft, likely an attempt to deescalate my rising frustration.

"Well, it fucking should be enough. More than that, Ruby is enough for *me*. She is what I want," I grated.

"Please...*son*," her voice shook, using an endearment she rarely called me. Mostly because she understood how important our mother had been to us, even though she'd served in that role for years. The governess was undone. Worried about me, about the family, about how it would look to everyone else.

I reached for her and pulled her into a hug. Her body trembled in my arms as she held on tighter than she had in a long time.

"I don't care what other people think. I don't care about my reputation being marred by the woman I choose to share my life with. I will not allow anyone to sway my choices. I know what's best for me. For my career. For my future."

"But what if you make a mistake?" she whispered while clinging to my shoulders.

"The only mistake I could ever make would be letting Ruby go. I can't explain it. I'm not sure I have the words to express exactly how she makes me feel or what she brings to my existence, but it's becoming more than I could ever live without."

The governess leaned back and cupped my cheeks in her

cool hands. "Oh, my boy. You're besotted with her."

I nodded. "More than besotted."

Her eyes widened. "Love?"

I tilted my head and shrugged. "Maybe. All I know is that I'm not letting her go. We will be getting married next weekend as planned. I'd like you to work with my publicity team in order to spin this information to our favor."

"You want me to figure out a way to make you marrying an American stripper acceptable in your societal circles?" she scoffed.

I grinned and dipped my chin. "Are you saying you're incapable of such a feat?"

Her head jerked back, and she glared. "I'm capable of anything," she boasted.

"Then it sounds like you have work to do. Where's Ruby?"

"She's been hiding in your room since I told her the wedding was off." She stood there waiting for me to explode.

I ground down on my teeth so hard my gums ached.

"Eudora, I love you. Have always loved you. You are the closest thing to a mother Noah and I have. I don't want that relationship strained. However, this is your one and only warning. Ruby will become my wife. She will very likely bear my children one day. If you plan to continue here as our governess and run this estate, you will need to come to terms with that fact. And you will need to do so immediately." I leaned forward and kissed her cheek before giving her a small smile. "Think on it."

I walked away and headed to my bedroom to find my bride.

I found her sitting cross-legged in the center of our bed. She was wearing the dress shirt I'd worn yesterday. The sleeves went past her hands and flopped forward and back as she rubbed her nose with a tissue. There were wads of rumpled-up tissues surrounding her like newly fallen snow.

Her head lifted when I entered, and I watched with my heart in my throat as her gaze met mine. Her lips trembled, tears slid down her cheeks, and her entire face crumbled straight into a pit of despair.

"Darling," I whispered, removing my jacket and tossing it on a chair. I removed my shoes without losing her gaze.

"Do you hate me?" she rasped, her voice obliterated by her emotional turmoil.

I shook my head and crawled across the bed. "Not even a little."

She swallowed. "Then you haven't seen the paper." She tore at the tissue in her hand, making a bigger mess.

"I have seen it." I lifted my hand and pushed aside a stubborn lock of golden hair so I could see her pretty, reddened face.

"I'm sorry I didn't tell you. I…I honestly didn't think it would ever come out. I guess it was stupid to think it wouldn't."

I gripped her chin between my thumb and forefinger. "You're not stupid. You worked a job that provided for you and your family. No one can fault you for that."

"You make it sound like I was a receptionist or a teacher. Those are respectable jobs. I was a stripper. Let men watch me dance naked for money. Rubbed my ass all over their gross laps in order to get a big payout."

"The entertainment industry is not for the meek. At least that's what Noah tells me." I hummed in agreement.

"Wait. You're genuinely not mad?" Hope filled her tone.

I reached for her hands and tugged until she crawled up and into my lap, her legs wrapping around my waist, her chest pressed flat to mine—just where I wanted her.

Bloody hell. The feeling of having her wrapped around me, safely tucked in my arms as the world raged around us was exactly what I needed.

"No, I'm not mad." I pressed my face to her neck and inhaled her scent for a full thirty seconds, calming my nerves. "I thought you might have left. I worried when you didn't answer my calls that I'd come home and find you gone. It terrified me."

Her arms tightened around my shoulders. "I was going to

leave, but I just couldn't. Not without saying goodbye. Not without apologizing."

"You have nothing to apologize for." I eased back and stared directly into her stunning clear blue eyes. "Your past does not define you, my love. Sometimes we do things because we have to, not because we want to."

She nodded somberly. "You know, I don't regret it. Without stripping, I wouldn't have been able to provide a roof over my head or one for my sister. I wouldn't have been able to eat regularly or pay for Opal's schooling. It is a part of me. I may not be proud of the type of job I did, but I'm proud of doing it anyway. And ultimately, stripping is what got us away from the abuse. It gave Opal and me a new perspective on what we wanted to achieve. And in the end…it's what led me to you," she whispered softly.

"Explain?" I asked.

"A random businessman was doing some land research in the area. He came to the strip club because it was one of maybe three things people could do for fun in the town. He saw me and asked for a lap dance. When I went to give him one in the private room, he asked me to sit down next to him and talk. I shared some of my story, and he shared some of his. He explained I was too good for the life, too beautiful… His words, not mine. Then he gave me Madam Alana's card and told me I could get out of Glory Springs and stop stripping forever by marrying a millionaire. And here I am."

"Here you are. Sitting in my lap, wearing my clothes." I used a finger to peek beneath the loose shirt and was delighted to find Ruby bare underneath. "Wonderfully naked, and about to marry me."

Her bottom lip quivered. "You still want to marry me? For real?"

"Yes, Ruby. My team will handle any fallout from today's article. We will be wed next weekend as planned."

The sadness in her expression had not lifted as her next

question tore a hole right through my heart.

"Are you just doing this because it would be too hard for you to get a new woman to marry?" Her voice was clogged with tension.

I clenched my teeth and narrowed my gaze, my hands tightening reflexively around her. If I could imprint her into my skin, I surely would have.

"What do I have to do in order to make you believe I want to marry you? You. Ms. Ruby Dawson of Glory Springs, Mississippi. Stripper extraordinaire, protective sister, incredible lover, at least what I've sampled to date, and all-around incredibly kind and giving woman."

She swallowed and licked her bottom lip while in thought. I wanted to suck on that lip so badly, but more than that I needed her to believe how very much I wanted her to be mine.

"I keep thinking that any moment this is all going to go downhill. Today proved that theory. Ms. Bancroft said the wedding was off. My heart...it was *broken*. Thinking you'd let me go... Or worse, the fear that you might come home and make me leave. I just... I want to marry you. I want to start my new life with you. When that happens, I know it will all be okay."

A brilliant idea came to me as if carried on the wings of angels. Hell, maybe it was my mother and father blessing our union from the great beyond.

"I have an idea, but you'll have to keep it a very big secret." I leaned forward and whispered the plan against her ear.

Her eyes widened, and she gifted me the most beautiful smile. "Let's do it!"

Episode 110

One Time Offer

DAKOTA

Sutton held my hand as we trekked up the stairs to the Mountain Creek County Sheriff's Department located just outside of Sandee, Montana. We didn't have a local police department, but the sheriff and his deputies did a pretty good job of keeping the peace throughout the small cities they served within the county.

"I'm glad Savannah won't be here for another hour," I said as Sutton moved in front of me and held the door open so I could enter.

"Why's that?" Sutton asked.

I shook my head. "Even though our pa is a bastard, he's still our father. Savannah has a heart of pure gold."

"And you don't?" Sutton scoffed, then smiled.

I narrowed my eyes and glared. "I'll have you know most people think I'm a badass cattle rancher who takes no shit from anyone." I lifted my chin with purpose.

My husband looped his arm around my shoulders and snuggled my neck, kissing me there while he chuckled against my skin. "I know firsthand you're a ball-bustin' female who runs a ranch and has a good heart. You don't fool me, wife. I know better." He ran his nose up the side of my face and kissed my temple, rubbing his scruffy chin against my hair to get me riled up. "And I hope our child is just like her momma."

"Her?" It was the first time either of us had made any reference to the possible sex of the baby I carried.

Sutton grinned. "Wishful thinkin'."

"Mmm-hmm. I got my eye on you, mister." I pointed at him and grinned.

"Evening, Goodalls." Sheriff Hammond approached the long desk-like divider that separated the entire room from anyone entering off the street.

I went stiff against Sutton's side and realized what he'd been doing. Teasing me sweetly, which had calmed me down before the storm hit.

Sutton squeezed the ball of my shoulder in what felt like solidarity. "Sheriff, I believe we have some discussing to do about old man McAllister."

"Come with me to my office." The Sheriff opened the half-door that separated the front entrance from the bullpen. There were desks facing one another throughout the open room. Some had deputies working who we recognized, others were empty.

Once we got to the Sheriff's office, we sat in the two chairs in front of his desk. Sutton grabbed my hand and held it as the Sheriff took his seat and sighed.

"I'm going to get straight to it. We can't charge Everett McAllister for the fire or the shooting seeing as Brody's witness statement confirmed that Jarod Talley was in fact the man who shot him. Not to mention the heap of evidence we found regarding the fire. I've discussed the situation with McAllister. He claims that Jarod contacted him while he was hiding out with friends in another town, healing from the beatin' Sutton gave him. Everett knew if he stepped foot on the farm, he'd be arrested on assault charges, which is exactly what we planned to do when the hospital released him. But he skipped out of the hospital before we could arrest him, as you know."

"Sounds like you need to have men assigned to the hospital when you've got a threat like McAllister or Talley in custody."

"First off, Sutton, Jarod Talley wasn't even on our radar. I've known that boy and his family my entire life. No one suspected the horrifying things we found. I would have bet against him shooting a fly, let alone a human being."

Sutton grunted and tightened his hold on my hand.

The Sheriff wasn't wrong. Not a single soul in Sandee would have believed kind and quiet Jarod Talley could have a dark side, but the proof was in the pudding, and the Sheriff claimed to have evidence beyond a shadow of doubt.

"What can we do?" I asked, getting back to the point of us being there and not back at the farm preparing the final details for the wedding tomorrow.

"Your father is being charged with misdemeanor domestic assault and a felony assault charge for threatening your life by strangulation. That last charge could be fought in court, but since we have several witnesses claiming to have seen him attack and strangle you, your case against him is strong."

"What is the sentence for something like that?" Sutton asked, while I held back the sudden desire to vomit.

I side-eyed the trash can next to the Sheriff's desk just in case. Talking about my father was not helping my all-day morning sickness.

"He's looking at a $50,000 fine and up to ten years in state prison. This being a first offense and the fact that you are alive and well will likely reduce the sentence. My guess, knowing the judges, he'll get the fine and around seven years with the possibility of parole for good behavior."

"My father hasn't behaved a day in his life," I sneered. "What about the farm?"

The Sheriff sighed. "Sorry to say, but ownership of land

doesn't change when you're in prison."

"We'll have to get him to sign it over to you prior to his sentencing," Sutton stated.

Sheriff Hammond nodded. "Exactly. You can work with your lawyers to suggest a lower charge to the DA as a bargaining chip to secure the land. We've already arrested him for domestic assault and felony assault, so the rest is up to the legal system."

"You're in between a rock and a hard place, darlin'," Sutton accurately surmised.

"Can I see him?" I asked.

The Sheriff nodded. "He's actually already in a private room with his lawyer now. Should I ask if we can intervene to open up discussion?"

I nodded as my stomach clenched. I covered my belly with my hand, caressing the space lightly on instinct.

Sutton instantly clocked my discomfort and protective response. "We don't have to do this. We can just as easily discuss our terms with our lawyer, who will then relay the information."

I shook my head and stood up. "No. I have to do this in person. I have to stick up for myself and my sister. Hell, for my mother, and my grandmother before her. This is the first McAllister who will be given time in prison for the atrocities he's committed during his miserable life. I want to look him in the eye when we share our offer."

The three of us entered the bland room, Sutton's lawyer on the way with the paperwork we'd asked him to draw up days ago.

When Savannah made it clear she wanted no part of the land we'd been raised on, I'd had to find a way to get our pa to sign it over to me. Sutton and I discussed the best deal we could offer and worked with his attorney to put it all in writing. This would be a one-time offer. He either took it or we'd deal with him several years down the road when he got out of prison.

Sutton pulled out the chair directly across from my father, and I placed my butt in it. Once I was seated, Sutton dragged my chair a good foot away from the man who'd raised me, putting more distance between us. Then he moved the second empty chair next to mine and sat. He put a hand to my thigh, grounding me in his support.

My pa glared at Sutton and then looked at me with pure hate in his eyes. "So the rumors you married a Goodall are true," he sneered.

"They are, but that's not what we're here to discuss now, is it?" My voice was firm and direct. I was proud that I didn't waver in my strength as I stared into the face of the man who had abused every woman in my family and gotten away with it…until now.

"You want the land." His lip curled, showing his nasty yellowed teeth. His hair was greasy and slicked back over his scalp, reminding me of dirty oil that came out of old rusted up vehicles that had been left to age over time.

That's what he was. A dirty, rusted old gambling drunkard who had nothing to offer society.

"Look, Pa, Sheriff tells us that you're looking at up to ten years in prison and a fine of $50,000." I chanced a glance at his lawyer, who my pa turned to.

The man nodded curtly. He didn't seem all that thrilled to be representing my father, based on the fine suit he wore and the distance from which he sat from his client.

"The farm is in debt up to your eyeballs. Debt you yourself put us in." He didn't need to know I'd been working with the bank and had already paid the liens using both Savannah's and my marriage deposits. We were slowly getting caught up on the debt. Now that we had a clear determination of arson for the fire, the insurance company would pay to replace the barn, the horses lost, and all the equipment, but I wasn't about to share that information.

"I just needed a few more wins at the track and we'd have been home free." He spat, drops of spittle landing on the metal table before us.

Sutton inhaled deeply through his nose, his nostrils flaring, his expression set at disgust.

"Those times are over, Pa. By the time you get out of prison, the land would have already been repossessed by the bank and sold off at auction. Something I'm happy to allow to happen because then I can just buy it back free and clear, sans the debt," I boasted, even though that process could take eons, and I wasn't about to let my land be scooped up by a stranger with more money than me.

"Then why are you here? To poke and prod at your old man? To kick a man when he's down?" His voice rose to an unnecessarily accusatory volume.

"No, I'm here to make you a once in a lifetime offer."

"You think I want anything from you?" More saliva drops landed on the table before us. "You're crazier than your mother was."

I gritted my teeth at the mere mention of my mother. She may have been weakened by his constant abuse over the years and lost her way, but I wouldn't stand for him soiling her memory. I stood up, bent over the table, and brought my face closer to his, pointing a finger directly at him. "You leave my momma out of this! She's dead because of you!"

That was when Sutton grabbed my hips and bodily sat me in the chair and dragged my seat another foot away from my pa.

I could feel my protective husband about to go ape-shit nutso if my pa didn't tone his crap down.

"Weak, sappy women, every last one of you. Just a waste of

space. If I'd have had boys, I could have raised real men to work by my side."

I ground down on my molars and spoke through the tension tightening every muscle in my body. "If you'd have had sons, they would have ditched you long ago."

"This is going nowhere," Sutton announced. "I think a deal is off the table. Come on, Dakota. Let's leave this miserable piece of shit to the judge's whims. I'll have my family buy the land at auction."

"You'll do no such thing!" my father roared in anger.

Sutton stood and stepped in front of me. "You don't deserve a deal. I'd rather see them throw the book at you and watch you lose everything you've ever had. Maybe prison will give you the time to think about your actions and the lives you've destroyed." Sutton put his hand out, ready to leave. "Come on, darlin'. You don't need this stress in your condition."

"Condition? You having this man's kin?" My father gaped, his maw falling open in shock.

I covered my belly, ignoring my father's question, and answered my husband. "You're right, honey. Let's go. He's not smart enough to take the deal." I stood up and interlaced my fingers with Sutton's, presenting my back to my father.

Sutton started to move to the door with me in tow.

"Wait! Stop," my father growled. "I want to hear the offer."

Sutton looked at me, his pretty eyes filled with compassion even though his jaw was hard as steel. The rest of his body seemed agitated, poised to strike and defend me at all costs. "It's up to you, darlin'. This is your horse and pony show."

I inhaled deeply, taking in Sutton's earthy, freshly cut grass and country scent, allowing it to calm my nerves before I turned around. I leaned against my husband's chest for support, his hand coming around me fully to rest right over my abdomen where our baby grew.

"I'm going to make this short and sweet. You plead guilty and we'll have our lawyers suggest a reduced sentence of five years, no chance for early parole for good behavior. You sign over the land to me. When you get out of jail, you'll have a total of $250,000 in your bank account. You can pay your court fine and start your life over with a couple hundred thousand anywhere you want, provided it is outside of the state of Montana. Savannah and I don't want to ever see your face again. This is the only time you'll be able to receive this offer. Our lawyer should be here shortly with all of the paperwork."

On that note, I turned back around, opened the door, and walked through it, Sutton at my heels, my father's voice calling out for me to wait and discuss further.

There was to be no further discussion. He either took the deal or he didn't. As Sutton said, I wanted my land desperately but not enough to continue to lower myself or listen to that man break me down more than he already had in my lifetime.

Sutton pulled me into his arms the moment we were outside in the hall alone. "I'm so proud of you, baby. Taking on that demon. You were so strong. Your momma and grandmomma are smiling down from Heaven above, congratulating you right now."

I pressed my head to the center of his chest, clinging to his trim hips. "You think so?"

One of his hands threaded through the back of my hair, cupping my head and rubbing at the tension there. "I know so. You were amazing. My badass rancher wife who takes shit from no man," he murmured at the crown of my head while he continued his massage. "Exactly what I want you teachin' our daughter."

I chuckled through the tears threatening to fall. My emotions were all over the place, but at least I wasn't about to hurl.

"You don't know it's going to be a girl," I reminded him.

"We'll see." He kissed the crown of my head and forced

me to lift my chin with his other hand. "You okay?" he asked.

"Yeah. Thank you for being here. I don't think I could have done it without you."

He smiled, dipped his head, and stroked his nose along mine. "Yes, you could have, but I'm happy you didn't have to. I always want to be there for you. I love you. I want the best for my wife, our baby, and our future." He moved his hand to cover my stomach. "What's done is done. Now we wait."

I nodded, wrapped my hands around his waist, and hugged him until I heard my sister's voice in the distance.

"Savvy's finally here. Let's go give her the update." I sighed.

"Then I'm getting you home, and you're going to attempt food and rest. Tomorrow's another big day, but I think you've had enough."

For the first time since we met, I didn't argue with him. I was exhausted. Drained physically and emotionally. Honestly, I needed him to take care of me. Needed *someone* to put my best interests first.

We entered the bullpen, and Savannah waved when she caught sight of us. She was standing at the desk waiting for the Sheriff regarding Jarod's case. God, my family had been through too damn much in the past few weeks. Heck, the last decade.

"I just had a run-in with our pa," I said when we met up. "I made the offer of the shortened time in prison and the money."

"And if he doesn't take the deal?" Savvy asked, while Erik kept her curled against his side rather protectively.

Something was different about them, but I couldn't put my finger on it.

"If he's stupid enough to pass on the deal, we'll buy the land at auction," Sutton stated flatly, his tone belying his desire to get me as far away from my pa as possible.

"Let me know if that occurs, and we'll contribute half of the price of the land," Erik offered.

"That's mighty kind of you, but if Savannah isn't interested in owning half the land, I'd rather all of it be in Dakota's name. We'll pay Savannah what her half is worth and make things even," Sutton corrected.

"Makes perfect sense, but the money isn't necessary," Savannah agreed as she rubbed her hand up and down Erik's chest in an intimate manner. It seemed their relationship had grown even closer. My heart swelled on their behalf. My baby sister was falling for the man she'd been auctioned to, the same way I had. And with the news about Jarod and the threats against them, I wanted her protected by someone who felt deeply enough to put her safety first.

Erik was definitely that man.

Now we just needed to get her married off without any further tragedies. I silently prayed they'd find Jarod and lock him up before the wedding.

Episode 111

A Wolf in Sheep's Clothing

SAVANNAH

After I'd hugged Dakota one last time and was about to tell her I'd see her tomorrow, Sheriff Hammond entered the bullpen and made his way over to us.

"McAllister is going to take the deal. His lawyer made it clear that if his land goes to auction, he'd come out of prison with absolutely nothing to his name. He encouraged your pa to jump at the chance of not going to trial because anything can happen when you've got a jury of your peers evaluating your misdeeds. He's a good public defender. This is in the hands of the lawyers now, but I feel confident saying you can move forward with your lives." He nodded to my sister and her husband.

"Once we get this other situation figured out," I grumbled and clung to Erik, who kept me glued to his side. Since our impromptu lovemaking after our helicopter ride and our admissions about our true feelings only a couple hours ago, Erik had not seemed keen to spend the evening at the local law enforcement agency. It was the night before our wedding, and here we were, about to be questioned by the Sheriff regarding the frightening actions involving my missing ex.

"Looks like good news for once," Sutton said dryly.

"Yeah, I guess." Dakota's shoulders slumped, and she rubbed at her eyes.

"Take my sister home and get her to bed. She needs to be bright and beautiful as my matron of honor tomorrow." I moved out of Erik's arms and hugged Sutton. "Thanks for being the best thing that ever happened to my sister."

Sutton stared at me, a shocked expression marring his handsome face until it morphed into one of joy and gratitude. "Things you never think you're going to hear…" he said softly, shaking his head. "A McAllister thanking a Goodall."

Dakota bumped his chest with her shoulder. "Come on, big guy, don't let the compliment go to your head. You won't be able to fit out the door if you do," she teased.

"Love you, Kota." I winked in her direction. "I'll see you tomorrow. I'll be the one in white."

She snorted, then yawned. "Goodness me. Sorry, Savvy. I love you, too. I'll be there with bells on. Good night."

She waved awkwardly, yawning for the second time as Sutton ushered her out of the station.

The three of us watched them leave.

"They actually look really good together. Never thought I'd see the Goodalls and the McAllisters making nice, but it seems a lot is changing in this town. Some good…" The Sheriff lifted his chin in Sutton and Dakota's direction as he helped her into a truck, and then looked back at us. "…Some bad. Which leads us to why you're here."

"I understand you want me to look at the evidence you found and see if I can provide any clues to Jarod's whereabouts or next steps." I let out a tired, ragged breath. It had already been a long day filled with many highs. We should have been celebrating his achievement of fighting his deepest fear. Perhaps even having a rehearsal dinner with friends and family like normal people did the night before a wedding.

The absolute last thing I wanted to do was delve into Jarod's twisted fantasies. I wanted to remember my first love as something sweet and beautiful, but it didn't seem like that was going to be possible anymore. Not after what we'd learned so far.

"Lead the way." I gestured with a wave of my hand.

The Sheriff led us to a big conference room. There was a whiteboard on the wall and a few deputies poring over evidence while sitting at the large table. There were pictures of me, Erik, Jarod, and both farms taped to the board with notes next to the images.

I stood still and stared at what I had inadvertently become involved in.

"This is insane," Erik murmured against my hair. "Are you sure you want to do this? No one is requiring anything from you at this point."

I shook my head. "No. If anything, I want to make sure Brody gets justice. He almost died, Erik. And the horses…" My breath caught. "Some of them I raised as foals right alongside their mamas. They deserve justice as much as a human does." I straightened my spine and cleared my throat. "Sheriff, what do you want to show me?"

The Sheriff directed us to a pair of empty seats. On the table in front of one of those seats was a journal.

"I'd like to get your opinion on some of the things he wrote. It's sporadic and so far outside of the Jarod we all knew, I want to be sure this was in fact his writing. He details events that occurred that no one here knows anything about. Perhaps you can read the pages and share any impressions or thoughts that come to you?"

I shrugged. "I'll try. Can Erik stay?" I asked.

"I'm not leaving," was his automatic and firm reply.

The Sheriff smiled softly. "Yes, he can stay. Just make sure you both wear gloves so we don't contaminate any of the evidence with your fingerprints and such."

I nodded, and both Erik and I took a seat and put on a pair of latex gloves. The Sheriff pushed a black journal before me. "Start there," he instructed, then handed me a legal yellow notepad and a pen. "For notes, if you'd like."

"Thank you." I half-smiled, not capable of more than that.

Erik put his arm around the back of my chair, caging me in his embrace without being intrusive. I put my hand to his thigh and rubbed back and forth. "Thank you for this."

He dipped his head and kissed the tip of my nose. "What happens to you happens to me. We're a team. We go through hard things together. Like the helicopter. I could never have been brave enough to do that alone, but with you there, I felt safe. I can't exactly explain it."

I cupped his cheek and gazed into his eyes. "I get it. I feel it too. I only feel safe when you're close because I know you'd never let anything happen to me." I pecked his lips, then sighed and turned back to the journal. "Let's get this over with," I said out loud, more for myself than anyone else.

Opening the book, the first thing I noticed was the date. It was the first time we'd kissed. I remembered it clearly because I'd been so excited, I couldn't wait to run home and tell Dakota I'd had my first kiss. Jarod detailed how happy he was and how hopeful he felt for the future. But what was strange was the darker thoughts he added.

She's going to be mine forever.

I'm never going to let anyone get between us.

I will marry her one day, just like my mama wants.

I traced over the last line and frowned. "He never told me that his parents wanted us to be together," I said to Erik.

"Write that down. We can reference anything odd," Erik suggested, tapping the yellow pad.

"Yeah, like the creepy 'she's going to be mine forever' and 'I'm never going to let anyone get between us,' even when we'd simply kissed for the first time. We were so young for him to have these feelings..." My voice rose as a niggle of fear wove through my thoughts.

"You're going to need to detach yourself from some of these things in order to help, *elskede*. Try and think of yourself as a detective," he supplied helpfully. "What would they want to know about these entries that only you could surmise as someone who was close to him and who was the object of his obsession?"

"Obsession?" I gulped.

"Affection..." He tried to cover his word choice, but he was right. According to what I'd already been told, Jarod had made me his obsession and had hoped to make me his *possession*. That was not the frame of mind of a healthy man in love with his high school sweetheart.

I huffed and pushed my hair behind my ear, then turned to the next page.

For over an hour, I relived events in my past life with Jarod, only it felt as though I was looking at our relationship through a grimy, filthy window. He remembered men who had looked at me a certain way and threatened them in his journal. Wrote about fighting guys behind the school who'd claimed to have an interest in me. But more than that, the tone in his entries got angrier as we got older. A part of himself he'd never showed me.

One passage was so shocking I had to push the book away for a minute.

"What is it?" the Sheriff asked.

I pointed at the entry. It was dated two days before I left for college. The night before I gave him my virginity.

She's leaving me.

I hate her for it. I want to break her legs so she can't go away. Force her to stay with me here forever. She should be moving into a little place with me, starting our adult lives together, but nooooooo.

I'm not enough.

I've never been enough for anyone.

Not her. Not my parents.

Not even McAllister. I wish I could slit his throat. Smother him in his sleep. Then I'd be Savannah's savior, wouldn't I? She'd never leave me then.

But no. College is Savannah's dream. Becoming a fancy veterinarian is the only thing that will make her happy. Not marrying a poor ranch hand who's been mucking out stalls of horseshit for her father in the hopes that one day I could marry her and take over the ranch myself.

She's such a prude she hasn't even let me fuck her yet. Years I've devoted to her, and nothing.

I protected her from horrible men who only want to dirty her up. Me, I want to marry her. Have children with her. Take over her family's land and grow it into something bigger than my family has ever dreamed of.

Then everyone would see.

They would finally see me.

Erik read the passage too, his nostrils flaring and his breath coming in short bursts of air. His hand was clenched into a tight fist on top of the table as his mouth turned into a scowl.

What came after in the journal was so far outside of the reality I lived in that it was hard to read. There were several passages devoted to him fucking women in other cities while I attended college, blissfully ignorant. I started to skim those sections as anger and embarrassment pounded against my psyche.

Erik rubbed my back as we read together. Eventually we came to another passage about my father.

Old man McAllister punched Dakota today. Stupid bitch deserved it. She was yelling at her father for being drunk and blowing a load of cash on sick horses. I could have stopped him from beating her, but it was more fun watching him hurt her. She's always been indifferent to me. Giving the important jobs on the ranch to other men she claimed were more experienced. Never giving me the opportunity to shine. I was her baby sister's sweet boyfriend. Nothing more.

Little did she know I was the furthest thing from sweet one could get.

It was fun making them believe one thing but doing the exact opposite. Everyone in town thought I was such a pushover lovesick fool. That's exactly what I want them to see. And when I marry Savannah, I'll be stealing the land right from under the noses of all of those idiots. I'll get rid of McAllister and Dakota. Maybe I could come up with a plan to off both of them in an 'accident' at the same time.

I covered my mouth as tears slid down my cheeks.

"I'm sorry, Savannah," Sheriff Hammond cooed. "Some of the things he said and claimed to have done are twisted and dark. Clearly the rambling thoughts of a very sick individual."

"Jesus, Mary, and Joseph!" I stood up, shoved my hands into my hair and gripped the roots until I felt that prickle of pain, bringing me back to the moment at hand. "I didn't know him at all! And I was going to marry him. Love and honor him until the day I died! He probably would have killed me first to get the land!" I gasped, my hand going to my throat as my vision wavered in and out. Stars started to prickle at the edges of my eyes, and dizziness plowed through my head.

Erik caught me before I fell and put me back in the chair. "Breathe, *elskede*. Just breathe through it. You're panicking."

I stared into his beautiful eyes and mimicked his overexaggerated breaths in through my nose and out through my mouth. After a few rounds of breathing with him, my heartbeat calmed, and the prickly sensation dissipated.

"He's a monster," I whispered. "I was in love with a horrible man." I gulped back the tears and sniffled, trying to make sense of everything I was being shown.

"You didn't know. You couldn't have. Men like this are very good at keeping their dark side hidden from the light. And you're the brightest light I've ever seen." Erik kissed my forehead and brought me close.

I hugged my fiancé, keeping my face tucked to his neck. I needed to find a way to get through this because I was crumbling with every new passage.

"Gentlemen, I'm not sure any of this is helping you, but it's definitely hurting Savannah." He clutched me closer.

I pushed back and wiped my tears. "No. I can handle it. Whatever it takes to find him and put him in prison for life. It's the least he deserves. My sister deserves justice for what he did to our farm. Brody deserves justice for being shot and almost dying. And I deserve fucking justice for his lies and betrayal!" I croaked as I reached over and grabbed the book, determined to do whatever I could to help.

We both sat down, and I pushed all the feelings and emotions to the back of my mind. This wasn't Jarod Talley, the man I'd once loved. This was a suspect in multiple crimes where a despicable human being had preyed on others. With that new frame of mind, I got back to work.

Another hour went by, and I made a page full of notes to discuss with the team. I read every detail about how Jarod had planned and carried out burning the barn down and exactly how much he despised Erik for being the new man in my life.

I will gut him with my father's fishing knife, then drop him in the lake with concrete tied to his body. The water is so deep he'll never be found.

I shivered when I read Jarod's musings but continued on. Toward the end of the journal, he described how he planned to kill my father in cold blood but make it look like self-defense. Hence the reason he had his pistol that day they met up on the ranch and all hell broke loose.

The last entry Jarod wrote was scribbled on a blank page as if he was in a hurry. There was no long passage or detailed experience he'd shared like the others. Just a single sentence. It would give me nightmares for years to come.

I'll kill every last one of them before Savannah marries another man.

I whimpered as I read the line over and over again, my heart pounding a wild beat against my chest. I swallowed down the sour taste coating my tongue and closed the book.

"You don't need to look for him. He's going to come to us," I said numbly and stood up. "Erik, we can go now."

Sheriff Hammond stood and walked over to me. "Why do you say we don't have to look for him anymore? Do you have an idea where he's hiding based on what you read?"

I shook my head. "No, but it's obvious. Have you all been hiding under a rock? The entire town is abuzz about what's happening tomorrow."

"Tomorrow? Savannah, me and my men haven't left this station unless it's to chase a lead on one of the many cases we've got on our plate due to this individual. Can you explain how you came to this conclusion that Mr. Talley is going to come to us?" Sheriff Hammond asked.

"My wedding to Erik is tomorrow at the Goodall ranch."

Sheriff Hammond's eyes widened as the other men in the room gasped, likely coming to the same conclusion I had.

"He's going to try and stop the wedding."

Episode 112

Lost Cause

FAITH

Aiden paced in front of where I sat, one wrist still tied to the chair. I had steadily worked my wrist raw, shifting it back and forth, trying desperately to get free of the last tie before Aiden realized I was mostly loose.

He pulled a gun from the back of his pants and waved it around before tapping his forehead with it. I wished he'd accidentally discharge the gun and shoot himself. Unfortunately, I wasn't a lucky woman. Not until Joel chose me in auction and changed everything I'd known about myself. He made me believe life could in fact be beautiful if you shared it with the right people. Convinced me I was worthy of his brand of earth-changing love.

"You stole my own daughter from me," Aiden snarled, shooting daggers at me with his wild gaze.

I swallowed and tried to calm down even though tears were sliding down my cheeks. "I'm sorry. I was scared. That last time we were together was bad, and you know it."

He stomped over to me, bent over, and put his face right in

front of mine. "You kept my daughter from me!" he roared, and his nostrils flared, spittle flying onto my face along with his heated, sour breath.

I closed my eyes and turned my head to the left. "I'm sorry. I'm sorry, Aiden. What can I do to make it up to you?"

He ignored me, stood up, and glared silently. His gaze slid down my form. "How you'd get the phone, Faith?"

My bottom lip trembled, but I knew honesty was the only thing that could potentially win me some time. Maybe enough for Joel to put a plan into action and save me and Grace. "I hid it in my hood, and Lenny missed it when he patted me down."

"Stupid fucker," he sneered while his gaze traveled to my wrists, his brow furrowing at the sight of my free hand before shifting to my feet. "Apparently he needs lessons on how to keep a captive tied down." He shook his head and stood up. "It doesn't matter. You aren't going anywhere. Even if you'd managed to get out of here before we left, you'd have walked into a room of armed men," he reminded me.

"Aiden, please let Grace go," I begged.

It was as if I hadn't spoken. "Tell me about my daughter," he snapped.

I closed my eyes, her beautiful little face instantly coming to mind, but I didn't respond.

"Tell me about my daughter!" he bellowed, his anger piercing me straight through the heart and sending chills down my spine.

"Her name is Eden," I whispered.

"I know her name, Faith. I have a copy of her bullshit birth certificate. I want to know more about *her*. What is her favorite fucking color? What cartoons does she like? Her favorite foods, things that a father normally learns because he has access to her since birth," he grated. "The things you took from me! Years," he growled and went back to pacing. "Years I've missed because of you. And you are going to pay, Faith. You are going to pay for every last fucking minute I missed! Starting with your sister." He lifted the gun and pointed it where Grace hung limply.

"No, no, no, no, no!" I hollered breathlessly. "Eden likes purple! Her favorite color is purple!" I screeched. "She loves pasta. Any kind. Marinara, Alfredo, pesto, it doesn't matter."

"I love pasta. She must have gotten that from me." He grinned, forgetting that I was not only Italian, but my father was too, and had owned a traditional Italian restaurant until Aiden burned it down.

"More!" He readjusted the gun in Grace's direction.

"Um, she loves to sing. Turns everything into a song."

Aiden tilted his head and smiled boyishly. The same smile that had hooked me when I was eighteen and too young to realize it was a mask. One he hid his dark side behind in order to prey on unsuspecting souls.

"And she has Type 1 Diabetes. Is insulin dependent," I added.

He frowned and swirled the gun in the air. "What does this mean? She's sick?"

"Not exactly sick, but she needs regular medical attention and insulin injections in order to keep her healthy and living a normal life." I spoke slowly, wanting him to understand the severity of her condition if for some god-awful reason his men did in fact invade The Alexandra and kidnap my baby again.

Joel will never let that happen, I reminded myself. He loved Eden and would go to the ends of the Earth to keep her safe. I knew that bone deep.

"Then we'll get her a doctor on the islands. I'll make sure she has whatever she needs."

Before I could respond, Grace moaned, her head wobbling from side to side before she eventually lifted it and opened her one good eye. The other one was swollen shut. She turned her head, and her gaze met mine.

Her expression crumbled. "No." She wiggled her body and cried out in pain. "No, not Faith."

"Looks like someone's awake." Aiden prowled over to Grace, then used the barrel of his gun to tip her chin up.

My entire body seized with fear, and I held my breath. "Aiden, please…please don't," I begged.

Grace's good eye widened, and her busted lips quivered. "Kill me. But let Faith go," she mumbled.

"No!" I sobbed. "Grace, shut up!" I warned. "Aiden, look at me," I pleaded.

Aiden ignored me, gripping the back of Grace's ratty hair and pulling her head all the way back so her neck arched. He pressed the gun right under her chin. She whimpered as her body shook, likely going into survival mode mixed with shock.

"Aiden!" I screeched. "Aiden, please!" I continued. "I'll do anything you want."

He titled his head and ran his nose along the side of Grace's face. "It would be so easy to pull this trigger," he taunted. "So easy to make your pathetic life disappear. All I'd have to do is squeeze this tiny little trigger." He pressed the gun more forcefully under her chin, the skin bulging around the pressure of the metal. "Who would miss you, Grace? Who would miss a miserable bag of bones?" He moved the gun from under her chin down between her breasts. "Barely any tits to speak of." He kept going until he got to the hollow of her waist. "Sunken-in stomach." He continued until he was hovering over the apex of her thighs. "And a nasty snatch."

"Aiden," I called, wanting his attention on me and not my sister.

He was so intent on terrorizing Grace he didn't so much as flick his gaze to mine.

He shook his head. "You don't deserve to live, do you, Grace? A junkie who would do anything for her next fix, am I right? Yeah, I'm right. You should be begging me to end your misery. You didn't even know your sister had a child years ago and pawned it off as yours on the birth certificate. Years she and your father have been keeping a blood relative from you.

Why do you think that is, hmm, Grace?"

Her gaze came to mine, terror having been replaced with anguish. "I'm sorry, Faith."

Sorry. Why was she saying sorry?

With whatever strength she had left, she pulled back one of her dangling legs and struck Aiden straight in the balls.

"Fuck!" he cried out and fell to the floor.

I knew this was the only moment I was going to have. I stood up, the chair awkwardly tied to my wrist. Even with my broken finger, I curled my hand around the armrest the best I could and hefted the chair in the air. Pain seized my breath, but I ignored it, adrenaline pumping through my veins as I raced over to Aiden. With all my might, I slammed the chair against his fallen form several times, hitting my target. He dropped the gun, screaming and kicking out. Instinctively, I booted the gun across the concrete floor, where it slid right under a tall stack of pallets.

All too soon, Aiden got his hands on the legs of the chair and with what seemed like superhuman strength, punted me and the chair several feet to the side. The wrist that was attached to the chair twisted in the opposite direction, and I heard the sickening crunch of my wrist bones snapping.

An explosion of agony flooded my system as my hip and shoulder crashed to the concrete only a second before my head did.

Then it was lights out.

"Faith."

"Wake up, Faith."

I heard a whispering feminine voice calling my name and asking me to wake up. But I didn't want to wake up. I was comfy here. Safe in the dark.

"Faith! Please. Wake up now!" That time the voice was more firm, threaded with fear.

I blinked against the intense drowsiness. My cheek was ice cold for some reason. My teeth chattered uncontrollably. I was freezing. My entire body frozen where I lay on my side. I kept blinking against the overwhelming urge to go back to sleep where it was warm and safe.

"Faith! Get up!" the voice said, and this time I recognized it.

Grace.

That voice belonged to my sister.

"Please, Faith. Please, please, please, wake up," came the terrified voice from somewhere behind me.

I opened my eyes more fully and saw a wall of concrete. My face was level with the ground. The chill from the floor had seeped into my cheek and jaw. I moved to sit up and was blasted with pain so intense it reminded me of when I was fully in labor with Eden and chose not to get the epidural. I wished I could get one of those right about now.

Everything hurt.

I wiggled my toes and tried to move my legs but found that my ankles had been tied together.

"Yes! Faith. It's me. Grace. Wake up!" My sister's voice was panicked.

Trying to sit up, I rolled back a bit, and my hands connected with the concrete. Stars bolted through my vision as I almost blacked out.

Pure agony poured through my every nerve ending like red-hot lava.

I breathed harshly through my mouth, my eyes tearing as I finally figured out that my hands were tied behind my back and my wrist was most definitely broken. At least it was the same hand that had the broken finger. For a full two minutes I did nothing but breathe through the pain, calming my mind and heart while trying not to vomit or pass out.

"Faith..." Grace whispered. "I'm sorry, Faith," my sister sobbed.

Wiggling my lower half, I kicked and scooched, using my toes to spin my body along the concrete so I could face my sister. She still hung in the air, though Aiden was gone.

"Where is he?" I asked.

"He left. I-I think maybe a few...uh, hours ago. I counted the minutes for, um, about two hours before I passed out." She kicked her feet to twist my direction. "I woke and...and counted again." She hissed and took a few breaths before continuing. "Counted for another hour. I don't, I don't..." She swallowed and moaned. "I don't know how long I was out."

"Joel's going to save us," I promised, knowing my husband would do anything and everything to get me back.

"Who's Joel?"

"My husband." Tears pricked at the back of my eyes when I thought about the fact that I'd had only one day. One incredible, life-changing, magical day with Joel as husband and wife before I ruined it all.

"He knows where you are?" she asked.

I nodded. "I have a tracker. In my hair."

Her one eye widened at that.

"Long story. I'll tell you when we get out of here."

Grace shook her head. "You do whatever you n-need. Save yourself," she croaked.

"Don't do anything to piss him off, Grace. Joel will come for me, and when he does, we'll get you help. I swear."

She licked her cracked lips. "Lost cause. Save yourself and your daughter." A tear slid down my sister's battered, swollen cheek. "I wish I could have known her," she whispered and dipped her head down.

"You will know her. We'll g-g-get through t-this." My teeth

clacked together, the rest of me shivering as though we were in an ice box. My body was catching up with the trauma, adrenaline leaking out, stealing the pain-numbing blessing with it.

"I'm a lost cause, Faith."

"Don't s-s-say th-th-that. I'm gon-gonna s-save ya-you." I couldn't stop the shivers or the constant chattering. "So c-cold." I closed my eyes.

"No, Faith. Don't close your eyes," Grace begged.

I blinked against the weight of my heavy eyelids, which was also when the door flew open and banged against the wall.

"Wakey wakey, ladies! It's time to fly the friendly skies," Aiden boasted as he entered the room with four guards this time. "Grab her." He pointed to me. Two of his goons approached, each of them taking one of my arms and yanking me up.

The second my wrists pulled against the ties at my back, I screamed. Stars popped against my vision, and the edges started to blur. "Grace!" I tried to yell, but it came out sounding drugged and slurred.

"What do you want us to do with this one, boss?" Lenny asked, pointing to Grace.

Aiden looked me directly in the face, his eyes vile black pits filled with pure hate and malice. "Tie Grace up and drop her in the middle of the desert. The wildlife will take care of her. And if she's still alive by morning, the desert sun will do the rest."

"No!" I tried to yell, but it came out sounding garbled and unidentifiable.

"I love you, Faith. Tell Dad I love him and I'm sorry," she whispered as Lenny ripped her off the hook. She fell the couple feet, her body not able to withstand her weight as her knees smacked against the concrete. Her hands splayed out at the last moment, stabilizing her before her face found the same fate.

"You promised," I finally mumbled clearly.

Aiden tsked as he cupped my face. "That was before I

found out I had a child you stole from me. Now I'm going to steal your sister from you. Eye for an eye, baby. What's fair is fair."

"Please," I tried once more. "Please, Aiden. For me."

Aiden chuckled. The man fucking laughed.

"Maybe next time you think to steal from me and run away, you won't. Or I'll kill your father, too." He lifted his chin to the two men holding me aloft. "Take her to the car. The flight leaves promptly at midnight, and I want her and my daughter on that plane."

Episode 113

Man on a Mission

JOEL

"They're on the move!" Bruno's voice crackled through the electronic ear communication device he'd given all of us. I pulled out my cell phone and texted Diego the same message. His response was instant.

We are in place at the hangar.

Bruno's tech wizard had done some poking around the local airstrips' computer databases. He'd found a small private airfield that had a plane leaving at midnight with the final destination recorded as the Maldives. The location was perfect for an ambush. Which was exactly what Diego and his men planned to do.

After the call with Faith, when I screamed into the phone to get Aiden's attention on me instead of on strangling my wife, I was a man on a mission. The goal was to free Faith and Grace, whatever the cost. I no longer cared what happened to Aiden or the men who were loyal to him. He'd proven he would do and say anything to get Faith under his thumb, regardless of the collateral damage. And he had been true to his threats.

Not more than two hours ago, men with rifles stormed into The Alexandra on the hunt for my stepdaughter. Fortunately, I'd known it was coming. After my call with Faith, I reached out to Diego to put the new plan in motion. After that, I called my hotel manager. I had them pull the fire alarms and evacuate the building. All while Faith's father, my mother, daughter, and stepdaughter were airlifted to a luxury estate in California that belonged to a trusted friend. My last call was to the authorities to inform them of the raid that was planned on my establishment.

The men Aiden sent were picked up by none other than the FBI, who'd been lying in wait. His entire team was either taken out or fell to their knees in surrender and had been carted off to jail.

Now I waited for Aiden to move Faith and Grace from the warehouse to the airstrip so we could put our final plan into action.

"Shit!" Bruno cursed, his voice bringing me back into the moment. "They've got Faith dangling over the shoulder of one of his men. Her hands are tied behind her back."

"Fuck!" I growled, rage swirling in my chest. If they hurt her, I didn't know what I would do.

"She's alive, which is good, but they have another woman. I'm assuming it's her sister. She's not fighting her guard. And they're putting her in a different car. Hold," Bruno's voice demanded through the line as I gritted my teeth, hands on the wheel of my vehicle, ready to drive to my assigned location at the airstrip.

Earlier, we'd agreed to divide and conquer. Bruno and a few of his men watched the warehouse. My driver Carlo and I were halfway between the warehouse and the airstrip in case they made a detour. We also had men in all directions ready at a halfway point, just to be safe. We mapped out every single route so we were ready regardless of which direction they took. Diego assured me he had the airstrip situation on lock. I assumed "on lock" meant he had it covered. What exactly that would entail, I didn't know. What I did know was he had his fingers in a lot of pies across Vegas, and a privately owned airstrip apparently wouldn't be hard to infiltrate. I simply had to trust Diego's desire to get revenge on Aiden. And with Diego being the head of this region of the Latin Mafia, I was confident his word was solid. He hadn't let me down yet.

"Grace is being taken in a different direction than the airstrip. One of my men is following her. Team 4 is waiting at the halfway point east and will intercept. I don't know if she's alive." His voice was solemn, and my gut tightened. Faith would be devastated if Grace had died, but I'd help her through that pain if that's what our men found. Either way, we would stay the course as planned and hope our team could handle whatever situation they came upon.

Faith was our primary objective.

I didn't want to live in a world that she didn't exist in. Not after I'd had her such a short time. There weren't enough memories to hold on to. We still had so much to do and share. I'd already lost a woman I loved. It had destroyed me for years. I was not about to lose Faith.

I shook my head. There was no way I would allow myself to believe all was lost. We were close to ending this. I felt it in the blood that coursed through my veins.

"Team 1 has eyes on the target. They are heading west, right to the airstrip." There was a hint of a smile in Bruno's tone. I felt enormous relief that our plan was falling into place, but that didn't mean the entire operation wasn't extremely risky. When dealing with unhinged men like Aiden, we needed to be smart and cautious.

I texted Diego again with the update.

Once more, his response was instant.

We are ready and waiting.

I swallowed down the nerves I had that this could potentially go bad and realigned my grip on the steering wheel.

Carlo normally drove me, but not when my wife's life was at stake. When Bruno said, "Go," I'd head to my rendezvous point.

For fifteen minutes, I stared through the windshield at nothing, lost in my thoughts. The tension in the car was stifling, both Carlo and I ready to move, until we finally got the word.

"Teams 1, 2, and 3 head out. Team 4 stay on Target 2."

Target 2 was Grace. Target 1 was Faith.

"All teams report back when you reach your position at the airstrip. Team 4 keep us posted on Target 2." Bruno was all business. Not a single member of the team spoke unless they were confirming their assignments.

I put the car in drive and hit the gas pedal.

The airstrip was like any other small airfield. It had a tiny air traffic control tower, a few huge metal hangars where many of the Vegas elite stashed their private planes, and a small concrete building and parking lot where I assumed they dealt with passengers. The best part about the location was it being off the beaten path, not near any highways and surrounded by a seemingly endless expanse of desert hills, cacti, huge tumbleweeds, and not much else. I could tell that the main building had a skeleton crew as there were only a handful of cars parked in the lot.

"Team 2 in place," I announced into my comm.

I waited what felt like an eternity but was really maybe only five minutes before Team 3 announced they were in place. It was Team 1 that we were waiting for. That was Bruno's team. They had been following Faith and Aiden's caravan to the airstrip. I prayed that they hadn't been noticed by his men or intercepted on the ride here. Aiden may have been a piece of garbage, but he was smart and stealthy as a snake with men who were loyal to him. Anything could happen.

We were parked on a small rise about two hundred yards away, surrounded by cactus. As I sat overlooking the buildings from my vantage point, my breath caught when Aiden's first blacked-out SUV pulled into the airport entrance. There were four of them in total. A larger crew than I'd imagined, but not larger than ours with Diego's men. None of whom I could see. For a group of badasses who'd boldly walked into Aiden's hotel earlier this month carrying visible weapons as if they were bulletproof themselves, they were surprisingly good at staying hidden.

Just as I was about to reach out to Diego, he texted me.

We ambush in the hangar.

I pressed my comm. "Diego says we ambush in the hangar," I repeated.

"All teams head to the hangar on foot. Go now!" Bruno barked. "We're close."

Carlo and I pushed open our doors, bulletproof vests hidden under our black clothing as we started to run in the dark toward the plane's location. My heart was in my throat as I watched in shock as Aiden's first SUV tore through the wooden barrier, smashing it into smithereens. They were supposed to go through the front, not the entrance attached to the tarmac that was for airport vehicles only. Then the second SUV drove through, window down, gun pointed at the guard, who had a phone to his ear, likely calling for help. A single gunshot rang out, obliterating the quiet of the night and echoing off the metal buildings as the guard dropped to the ground like a stone.

"Christ above!" I blurted, doubling my efforts, Carlo right at my side. We had not prepared for this.

We made it to a dark space outside the building where a window looked into the large hangar. We could see Aiden's plane being prepped. Carlo and I panted as Aiden's SUVs entered the hangar, the four of them racing in, their tires screeching as they circled the rear of the plane. Some of Aiden's men bolted from the vehicles, and before we could even think to intercept, chaos ensued.

Diego's men alighted from every nook and cranny, guns blazing.

Shots were fired as the rest of Aiden's guards got out and tried to take cover behind their open car doors. Men called out to one another to take positions. I moved to enter the fray when Carlo held me back and shook his head, pointing at his comm.

Bruno hollered in my ear. "Wait for my signal," he barked as his vehicle drove directly into the hangar at high speed and crashed into two of Aiden's vehicles. One SUV plowed into an armed guard on Aiden's side, the car flattening him against the metal wall.

A male voice boomed through the air as a woman screeched at the top of her lungs.

Faith.

I pushed Carlo off and ran to the door and pulled it open. Instantly I was seized by a guy wearing a beat-up leather vest and jeans with face tattoos and slick black hair. He hauled me behind some large metal shelves filled with equipment and put his finger to his mouth in a shushing gesture. Then he crouched, lifted his gun, and disappeared back into the fray, taking out a man that had gotten close to us. The man fell to the ground in a bloody heap, a blackened hole in the center of his forehead.

Carlo gripped my shoulder, and we both focused on the shootout going down. I looked past the shelves, desperate to find a glimpse of Faith. And, like a beacon of light, her quiet strength drew me to her. She was lying on her side, her body splayed on the ground near the steps to the plane. Just as I caught sight of her, the plane's engines came to life.

"No!" I yelled uselessly. There was no way in hell I was going to let Faith get on the plane.

Staying low, I rounded the shelves and ran as fast as I could, dodging fallen men as the sound of bullets popped all around me. I was desperate to get to my wife and was about thirty feet away when a hulking form tackled me to the ground, his gun skittering across the concrete. Before I could get my bearings, I was punched in the face once, then again, my cheek splitting open.

I fought the brute, the two of us exchanging punches until I heaved with all my strength, pushing the solid weight off me. Which was when the man reached for the pistol he'd dropped when he tackled me. We both scrambled for the gun, me jumping on his back and holding him down with everything I had in me. He arched violently, knocking me off and stretching his fingers, about to reach the weapon.

A jean-clad man with a bloody eye snatched the gun and point-blank shot Aiden's man in the head.

"*¡Vamos, hombre!*" *Go, man,* he yelled at me.

I scrambled to my feet and raced over to Faith. She was facing the other way, so when I put my hands to her body, she screamed bloody murder.

"Faith, it's me. I have to get you out of here!" I yelled.

Tears streaked down her cheeks as her pretty blue eyes locked on me as if I was the holy grail, her every dream and wish come true.

"I knew you'd come," she sputtered as I curled my arms around her knees and her back, ready to carry her. But when my hands touched hers, she cried out in pain.

"Fuck, I'm sorry." As quickly as I could, I pulled out the switchblade I carried and cut the tie at her arms and then her feet. "Can you run?"

"I'll try," she sobbed and reached for my hand.

A bullet sailed right between us, and her eyes widened in fear, her lips trembling.

"We have to go, now!" I demanded, hauling her up. Hand in hand, we ran to where Carlo was still hiding, waving us over.

The second I got her behind the shelves, I forced her to the ground. Shots were still firing off, and I worried that we'd reached the limits of our luck.

"I think it's safer if we stay right here." I shielded Faith with my body, holding her directly in front of me, her knees up against her chest, where she was cradling her arm protectively.

"Did he hurt you?" I growled, low and menacing.

"Broken wrist and finger," she stated hurriedly. "Where's Grace? They're going to leave her in the desert."

"We have a team on it now. They'll get to her," I promised, even though it might be too late when they did find her. But we couldn't worry about that now. We had to get out of here and to somewhere safe as soon as possible.

Suddenly, the engines of the plane roared louder. I turned my head to peek through the shelves, where I caught a horrifying sight. Aiden, guarded by a circle of his men, ran full tilt up the stairs to the plane, a couple disappearing inside with him and slamming the door shut. He'd left the rest behind as sacrifices who continued to shoot at Diego's men.

"That motherfucker!" I screamed and moved to stand and wade in, but Faith clung to me.

"No, please. He'll kill you," she begged. "I can't lose you now that I have you back."

I held her tightly and watched as both Diego's men and Bruno's took out every last man standing. One by one, they fell in a gruesome showdown the likes of which I would relive in my nightmares for years to come. All while Aiden's plane, struck by several bullet holes, rolled out of the hangar, hit the tarmac, and jetted toward the runway.

Faith trembled, her body convulsing with the sound of every gunshot while I held her close, wrapped tight within my embrace.

When it became silent, Bruno's voice called out. "It's

over!" His words bounced off the metal walls. Slowly I stood and helped Faith up. Cuddled at my side, we rounded our hiding spot with Carlo and met Bruno and the rest of the men in the center.

"Where's Diego?" I scanned the bodies on the ground, noting all of the men I could see were wearing black suits. None of them in jeans like Diego's men or cargos and black tees like Bruno's.

Bruno lifted his chin toward the large opening where the plane had departed.

Diego was there, standing feet spread wide, arms crossed over his chest like the mafia boss he was. His gaze was locked on the plane racing down the runway.

"He got away!" Faith screeched, tearing from my side and running to the entrance. Her shoulders slumped in defeat at the sight before us. I followed her, as did all the men who had made it through tonight.

"He's never going to stop," she croaked.

I wrapped my arms around her from behind and pressed my face to her neck, breathing her in, reminding myself that she was in fact alive and standing before me.

Diego stepped in front of us, reached out, and lifted Faith's chin gently. His steely dark gaze took in her tear-stained, bruised face as he wiped away a new tear.

"*No, hermosa. No se escapó.*" *No, beautiful, he did not escape.* He let her go and then gestured to where the plane had just lifted off, nose pointed toward the Heavens. "Watch," Diego said in English and then winked.

We all took in the view as the plane soared, reaching high over the barren desert.

Diego grinned as he slipped his hand into his back pocket, pulled out a small, nondescript cell phone, and pressed a series of buttons.

"*La venganza es mía,*" Diego said. His men behind him yelled the same phrase into the night as though it were a battle cry, fists and guns pointing up.

"What does that mean?" Faith asked.

Diego looked at her, smiled wickedly, and said, "Revenge is mine." Then he pressed a single final button on his phone as he stared at the sky.

Aiden's plane *exploded* into an enormous fiery ball of brilliant reds, oranges, and the deepest black.

Just like his soul.

"May you rot in hell forever, Aiden Bradford," I whispered, smiling as I held my wife close, watching the pieces of the plane fall to the desert floor like a cleansing summer rain.

"It's over," Faith murmured in awe. "It's really over."

"Yes, my love. It's over."

Episode 114

Just Us

OPAL

Noah dragged a line of kisses along my neck suggestively as he used a key card to enter our hotel room.

"Close your eyes, poppet," he requested.

I bit down on my bottom lip, anticipation of what the evening's activities might entail sending shivers of excitement down my spine. I trembled within my husband's arms.

"Don't be afraid…" he reassured me.

"I'm not afraid." I cut him off. "I'm excited."

He chuckled warmly against my neck, placed a heated kiss to the ball of my shoulder, and then nudged me forward. "Keep your eyes closed until I say."

"Bossy already," I teased.

He hummed low in his throat, and I could feel the vibrations from his chest through the delicate satin of my wedding dress at my back.

I followed with my eyes closed as he led me into the hotel room slowly. We stopped, and I held my breath for a long moment. A subtle warmth graced my skin as if from a distant heat source. The scent of flowers perfumed the air, making it seem as though we were out in a sun-filled garden. My very skin tingled as I stood patiently, awaiting his next instruction.

Noah's fingers trailed from my biceps down to my hands in a featherlight caress that made me gasp for air. He interlaced our fingers and pressed his front to my back fully, crossing both of our arms over my waist in a comforting embrace.

"Now open them," he murmured, his chin resting in the space between my shoulder and neck.

I opened my eyes to a million flickering flames and an endless array of roses. Cream-colored candles twinkled atop every available surface, intermingled with dozens if not hundreds of white and pale-pink roses.

My mouth dropped open as I took in the extravagant display.

I focused on the large dining table. Candles in varying heights ran down the center, intermingled with beautiful roses. Two dome-covered dishes sat side by side. And at the opposite end of the table was a two-tiered wedding cake, complete with a little wedding topper of a ceramic couple. An ice bucket rested at an angle to the dinner plates with not one but two bottles of champagne and a pair of crystal flutes beside it.

Noah let me go, and I spun in a slow circle, taking in the enormous beauty of the entire room filled to the brim with flickering candles and stunning roses. It was the most romantic thing I'd ever seen.

When I'd completed my turn, I stopped and faced Noah. I wrapped my arms around his neck and smiled widely, my eyes pricking with happy tears.

"Do you like it?" he asked, rather shyly.

I shook my head. "No. I love it. It's incredible. There aren't words for this beauty."

Noah cupped my cheek. "No, you're by far the most beautiful thing in the room." He dipped his head and took my mouth in a slow, luxurious kiss.

Just as I thought he was going to take it further, he pulled away. I stood still as he went over to the bar top, also covered in lights and flowers, and grabbed a small remote. He clicked a series of buttons, and classical music filtered through the room. Noah put the remote down and held out his hand.

"Dance with me?" he asked.

"I'd like nothing more." I placed my hand within his. I didn't exactly know how to dance, but I'd seen enough people dancing in movies to get the gist.

He grinned wickedly and tugged me close.

"Our first dance as husband and wife," he murmured, his cheek resting against mine.

"It's my first dance ever," I confided, my feet feeling light as air while he twirled me.

He pulled back and looked deeply into my eyes. "I'm happy to be your first."

"Soon you'll be my first *everything*," I responded, my cheeks heating with the bold admission.

His dark brown eyes flared with desire as he offered the sexiest wolfish grin yet. "And the honor will be mine, Opal." He tipped my chin up and kissed me softly while we swayed to Chopin's *Nocturne, Opus 9, Number 2*. I'd heard this piece a thousand times and loved it, but in that moment, the song became part of my history. Connected to the first time I'd ever danced with a man. That man being my husband. On our wedding night.

I couldn't have asked for more.

Noah had truly given me the best day and night of my life, and it wasn't even over yet.

We danced for a short while, content to just be with one another, our bodies connected, our hearts beating in tandem as the third or possibly the fourth song finished.

"You must be hungry," Noah stated, gesturing to the table.

I nodded and sighed dreamily, not caring about food, just living in the blissful moment.

"Come." He patted my bum and led me over to the table.

"Now, I have it on good authority what your absolute favorite dishes are, but you'll have to correct me if I've gotten it wrong." He smirked.

I pursed my lips and snickered under my breath. He couldn't possibly have my favorite food. Not because it was impossible to get, but because it would be so ridiculously silly paired with all the luxuries we'd experienced. The hotel, the wedding, our designer attire, the room filled with thousands of dollars' worth of flowers, and yet...

Noah lifted the domed lid off the first plate, and I was shocked to find a delicious-looking, perfectly cooked pepperoni pizza.

I burst into laughter, not believing my eyes.

"But wait, there's more!" he announced with a flourish, snatching the lid off the second plate, where two giant cheeseburgers sat surrounded by a plethora of crisp french fries.

"You didn't! We're having pizza and cheeseburgers for our wedding dinner!" I clapped and couldn't help but bounce up and down on the toes of my sexy stilettos.

"Ruby told me those two things were your favorites. What's a wedding without having your absolute favorites?"

"Noah!" I squealed and plowed into him, wrapping my arms around his broad form and hugging tightly. "Thank you!"

He chuckled and hugged me back, kissing the top of my forehead. "I'm glad you are pleased. Let's eat."

I spun around and grabbed a thick french fry first, biting into it. After spending days on end eating proper British food at the estate, having a night with my absolute favorite American dishes was such a treat.

Noah pulled out one of the chairs, and I plopped down unceremoniously, my entire being focused on the food and my grumbling belly.

The second I sat, I reached for one of the empty plates and loaded one of the burgers right onto it. Then I snagged a slice of pizza and took a monster-sized bite right away. The cheesy goodness hit my tastebuds, and I moaned in pure delight.

Noah laughed as he sat down, loaded his plate, and then reached for the champagne. I was already three bites into the best burger I'd ever had when he handed me a flute filled with the golden bubbly liquid.

I wiped my mouth and held the glass aloft, waiting for him to speak.

"To us." He smiled, his entire focus on me. "May we live each and every day of our marriage to the absolute fullest." He gently tapped his glass with mine.

"To us," I repeated, never losing his gaze as we sipped our first toast as husband and wife.

My hands shook as I pulled out the pins in my hair, letting my long, dark locks fall down my back. I stared at myself in the mirror's reflection. I'd taken off my wedding gown and hung it in the closet. When I did so, I found a stunningly elegant slip of lingerie hanging with a note attached to the hanger.

For the wedding night.
Have fun.
Liza

We'd finished dinner, cut the cake, and danced around the beautiful room until my feet ached. At the first sign I was tiring, Noah had scooped me up and brought me into the bedroom. More candles flickered and danced along the dressers and end tables. Rose petals dotted the surface of the bed and the floor prettily. It had been the most romantic night of my life.

And here I trembled, viewing myself in the mirror while hiding out in the bathroom. What I saw was the sexiest, most elegant version of myself ever.

I looked like a mature, beautiful woman. But I felt like a scared little girl.

"You've got this, Opal." I fluffed my hair and pursed my lips, trying to find an expression that seemed sexy and alluring.

I failed.

I'd never be sultry and sexy like my sister Ruby. Originally, that was the type of woman Noah had wanted. But what he'd gotten was me. A brainy over-thinker who would never walk into a room and turn heads.

"And yet he married you, Opal. Planned this entire day and evening for you," I reminded myself, feeling my confidence come back bit by bit.

I turned to the side and took a gander at my shape. I had good boobs. A nice, firm handful. My skin, however, was amazing. A natural cinnamon color that contrasted magnificently against the dark espresso tint of my hair and the cream nightie. I was tall with long, toned legs and rounded hips. My booty was high, tight, and with enough oomph to grip.

Still, I was Ruby's opposite in every way. And yet Noah hadn't given even a single hint of his unhappiness with me being here right now instead of her. He seemed genuinely happy to be married to *me*. Eager to take the final step toward consummating our marriage. I didn't think he'd want to be with me intimately if he still carried feelings for her.

I inhaled deeply and nodded at my image. Self-doubt pushed to the back of my mind.

"You want this, Opal. You have to go out and get it. Be brave. Be strong. Be confident."

With my heart pounding wildly, I opened the bathroom door and stood there, backlit by the light. Soft music continued from the living space comingling with the pretty candlelight and flowers, giving everything a dreamy quality.

"Bloody hell, poppet. You are a vision," Noah whispered, swallowing so slowly I was able to watch his Adam's apple bob with the effort.

I walked into the room slowly, my confidence keeping me upright. Noah's gaze traced all over my form from the deep V of the front that gave more than an ample view of my breasts to the high slit that came all the way up to my hip. I purposely bared my leg for his viewing pleasure and gloried in the instant sharp breath he took.

Then it was my turn to take in his appearance. He wore a pair of black silk pajama bottoms that dipped low, highlighting the deep indents of his lower abdominals. His golden chest was bare and toned to perfection. I wanted to run my fingers along the fine expanse of skin, teasing every curve and valley with my fingertips.

"Come here, Opal." His voice was a low timbre that reverberated through my chest and settled hotly between my thighs.

I padded over to where he stood and stopped right in front of him.

"Turn around," he commanded.

I spun so slowly, my breath hitched when his fingers landed on my nape and traced the entire expanse of my spine all the way down between my ass cheeks. His hand instantly went *inside* the fabric at the top of my ass, where he brazenly gripped my flesh right at my crack, and then *lower*, teasing my sex with just the tips of his fingers. His hold was possessive, then suddenly gone as quickly as it had invaded.

I mewled in protest, but he ignored it.

"Keep turning," he rumbled against my neck.

I did as he asked, arousal swimming through my veins, my nerve endings on high alert, anticipating—no, waiting desperately for his next touch.

"You are absolutely gorgeous, Mrs. Pennington," he whispered while hooking the fingers of each hand just under the spaghetti straps of my nightgown.

I licked my lips and lifted my chin. "Thank you, Mr. Pennington."

"I think this nightgown is lovely, especially against your skin and the golden light, but…"

"But?" I gulped and watched his awed expression change from sweet to savage in an instant.

"But it will look much better on the floor." He leaned forward and nipped my lips as his fingers eased the straps off my shoulders.

The fabric floated down my body like water flowing over a cliff's edge.

I held my breath, my nerves completely shot as my husband dipped his head and his gaze to my bare body.

"As I expected," he whispered with awe in his tone, his breath fanning across my face. "You bared to me is the greatest treasure." He lightly curled his hands around my ribcage, my breasts heaving and swelling as he stared. Then he reached up and traced each nipple with the velvet pad of his thumbs.

I gasped, the tiny sensation feeling like a firework had exploded in my chest. I clenched my legs together as he slowly ran just his fingertips along my breasts as if he was getting acquainted with them personally. He was in his own world, twirling a circle around one tip while pinching the other.

I couldn't help but close my eyes as my entire body heated and gooseflesh rose on my skin. I was on what I thought was sensation overload when one of his hands pressed flat to my abdomen.

"Open your eyes, poppet. Watch me touch you," he encouraged.

I opened my eyes, stared into his, and then looked down. One of his hands was cupping my breast fully, wantonly, his thumb and finger plucking the tightened peak. I felt that touch like a phantom string dangled from my breasts to straight between my legs. I moaned when he pinched a little harder.

"My wife likes it soft and she likes it rough, I see," he murmured, his other hand teasing the skin around my navel.

I shifted my legs and huffed, frantic for him to touch me *there*.

"Eager?" he asked playfully.

Without preamble, I reached out and curled my fingers around the erection tenting his pajamas.

"Fuck!" He hissed, tipping his head back, his muscles flexing deliciously as I worked him up and down.

Emboldened, I rubbed harder, the fabric sliding perfectly against the palm of my hand. Wanting more, I pushed forward and pressed my lips to his chest. His skin smelled like leather mixed with oak, reminding me of the lush woods Ruby and I used to play in back in Mississippi.

Noah curled one arm around my back and the other behind my head before his lips came crushing down over mine.

He kissed me deeply.

He kissed me hard.

He kissed me with intent.

Then surprisingly, his hands came down and cupped my booty, and he lifted me up and into his arms. I circled his waist with my legs and hung on. Gently he eased me down to the bed and ripped his mouth away, panting, his eyes dark pools of pure lust. He hovered over my form, his gaze tracing my body once more.

I felt beautiful. Absolutely gorgeous lying naked under my husband.

"Make love to me." I reached out and cupped his cheeks.

Noah pushed up to his knees where he removed his pajama bottoms and tossed them over his head, grinning. I smiled as I took in his masculine form. The man was so virile with his length standing proud, erect, and beautifully formed.

"I want this to be good for you, Opal. I need for your first time to be just right. I want it to be perfect," he confided, his voice filled with uncertainty for the first time since we'd met.

I smiled and reached out for him. He came willingly, pressing his bare chest to mine. I hummed contentedly at the contact, wrapping my arms around his shoulders, tunneling my fingers into his hair.

"Look at me?" I asked.

He lifted his head, and his worried expression tore into my heart.

"Noah, I choose you. No matter what came before or what is to come tomorrow, I choose you." I cupped his jaw and ran my thumb over his bottom lip.

"Would you have chosen to give me this gift if I hadn't coerced you into marrying me?" His tone was ravaged with guilt. Something I hadn't expected coming from the confident and normally cocky man.

I smiled softly and wrapped my legs around his lower body until I heard him groan, his cock wedged between us, proving his desire for me.

"You didn't coerce me. I'm here of my own free will. And more so, I'm happy to be right here with you. Today has been the absolute best day of my life. There has been none better. And I experienced that with you, Noah. The man I married. My husband. And I'm asking you to show me what it can be like. To be connected physically with the man I chose."

He tucked his face to my neck, and we held one another for a few minutes before his mouth started to work against the skin there, sending pleasurable tingles everywhere.

I sighed happily, rubbing the warm skin of his back and shoulders and rotating my hips.

"I'm going to make you come so many times, Opal, you'll never want to leave me." Then he adjusted his weight, centered his cock at my opening, and slowly inched all the way inside until there was no he and I.

Just...us.

Episode 115

Happy Endings

RUBY

"There you are, darling." Nile approached me from behind, his arms wrapping around my waist, his chin resting against my shoulder. "How are you this morning?" he asked and pressed a kiss to my neck.

"I'm perfect." I sighed contentedly, watching the boats coast along the water from our balcony while wearing a fluffy hotel robe and nothing else.

"I can finally agree with that statement, my love," he rumbled against my skin. "Especially after two nights ago, and yesterday, and last night." He chuckled. "I'm surprised you're even awake."

I grinned, snapshots of the weekend's events flickering across my mind like a kaleidoscope of colorful moments I'd never forget.

"Couldn't sleep. Not when I'm this happy," I admitted, then turned and wrapped my arms around his neck. "I've honestly never been this content or peaceful…" I shook my head. "Ever."

He smiled sweetly, brushed his nose along mine, and then

kissed me. He tasted of mint and man.

I pulled back and glared. "Hey, no fair!" I chastised playfully. "You brushed your teeth."

He grinned. "Guilty. As much as I'd like to stay here in bed with my beautiful mate, I have something I want to share with you just outside of Eastbourne before we head home to Oxshott. It's one of my favorite places in the entire world. Would you like to journey out and see it?"

My heart swelled. "I want to share anything with you, Nile. *Everything.* After what you did for me this weekend…for *us*… I owe you so much, and I plan to spend years showing my appreciation." I swallowed down the emotion clogging my throat.

Nile cupped my cheeks. "This weekend was for us. Me and you. No one else. Our secret."

I tunneled my fingers into the messy waves of his hair. "Are you happy?" I asked, knowing what we'd done had been a direct response to the tawdry article that came out about me being a stripper.

Nile looked me straight in the eyes, his gaze never wavering. "Ruby, as I stated on Friday night, our lives together started over in that moment. Nothing is going to change that. Not our formal wedding this coming weekend, not the governess and her worrisome overtures, not my twin, your sister, nor the bloody press. You and I made a choice Friday night, and we did so with pure hearts and open minds, right?"

"Right," I whispered, needing to hear his feelings out loud. "Thank you."

He smirked. "For what?"

"Being everything I could have ever hoped for in a man. In a husband." I flattened my ear to his chest to listen to his heartbeat.

He rubbed my back and pressed his chin to the top of my head. "Shower fun, then off to see the Seven Sisters."

"The Seven Sisters?" I queried as he took my hand and led me back through our huge suite to the enormous bathroom.

"Who are these sisters?"

"Not who…what," he noted cryptically. "Last one in the shower leaves without a happy ending," he taunted.

"Oh no you don't!" I pushed past him, flung off the robe, and was in the shower before he could even remove his pajama bottoms.

"Bloody hell. Looks like I'll have to make you come again. Bollocks!" he snapped playfully.

I burst into laughter, dipped my head back, and let the water soak my hair and my body.

After a very pleasurable shower complete with "happy endings" for both of us, Nile piled us and our suitcases into his sleek Aston Martin. After driving a short distance, he parked and got out of the car as eager as a five-year-old might before heading into Disneyworld. He opened my door and pulled on my hand. Once my feet hit the pebbled ground, I was glad he'd encouraged me to wear jeans and tennis shoes. It was only the second time I'd seen Nile in denim. Paired now with a thick cable-knit sweater…oh, boy. Both items looked magnificent on him.

Nile held my hand as we passed a sign that said Welcome to Seaford Head Local Nature Reserve. I followed along quietly as I observed how his body language changed from excited little kid to pensive and thoughtful.

"You okay?" I asked.

He nodded and looked out over the ocean as we walked a well-worn path.

"Just thinking about the last time I was here. It was with my parents on our tenth birthday, about six months before they died."

I squeezed his hand in support.

"We would come every year to see the Seven Sisters. My mom loved them. Believed there was something magical about this place. And for some reason, after this weekend, after everything we've been through, I needed to share this piece of myself and my history with you."

I covered our hands with my free one. "I'm glad you did."

His lips flattened, and he took a deep, calming breath. "You ready?"

I shrugged. "You tell me," I chuckled.

We walked down a bit farther and came around a bend in the path that brought us to a rocky beach.

Nile gestured with a chin lift to look behind me.

I was unprepared for what I would see.

An enormous white wall of rock rose stories high above the beach. The sun glinted off the white cliffside in sparkling bursts of light. "What makes the entire mountain white?" I asked, awe filling me with wonder.

"It's actually chalk, a form of limestone that continues to erode from the waves." He tugged my hand, and we carried on with our walk along the shore.

"Why is it called the Seven Sisters?" I asked, never taking my eyes away from the stunning natural wonder.

"There are seven hills and valleys that make up the natural cliffs. Beautiful, isn't it," he said whimsically.

I nodded, letting him have his moment. I could sense that he wanted to get something off his chest. After what we'd shared this weekend, it was my duty to help him through any painful moments he may have had.

"I wasn't able to come here after we lost my mother and father. It was too raw. Hurt too deeply."

"That's understandable. Especially if this was a family tradition."

"It was. And for years, our granddad wanted to bring us

here to relive some of the memories we shared with them, but I just couldn't. And Noah didn't push for it either. I think we both attached this particular place to the time in our lives when we truly felt that family bond. After losing them, the idea of coming here brought up too many painful feelings. Feelings we weren't ready for."

"And now?" I swung his hand and focused on him. He was so handsome with the sun's morning light capturing his profile, the wind blowing his short hair all over. He was free in a way I hadn't seen until today.

"Now I have you to share things with. You to build family traditions with. But that doesn't mean I want to forget what I had or what they gave us growing up. It's just now that I have you, I'm ready to relive that time in my life. Because I know you'll be there to support me through it."

I tugged his hand and pulled him into a hug. I held on tightly. "I love this place. I'm honored that you wanted to share this piece of your history, of something special you had with your parents. I think we should come here often. And if you want to share some of your experiences, I'd love to hear them."

"And who knows, maybe one day we'll bring our children here," he murmured as if what he'd said wasn't similar to him heaving a giant boulder right off the tallest peak and having it crash to the beach below.

"Our children?" I croaked.

He grinned and shrugged. "Maybe. I always thought I might have a child or two," he said, then bent over, picked up a rock, and tossed it into the ocean.

My eyebrows rose to the Heavens as I allowed my brain to decipher all that he'd shared. "And the three-year agreement?" I cleared my throat, feeling as though sand grated along my esophagus.

"Darling, it may have started as an agreement and a contract with a deadline, but after Friday, can you honestly tell me you'll be willing to let me go in three years?" He held his arms out wide.

"To let us go?"

"I-I…I don't know. What I feel right now isn't what I might feel later," I admitted, not knowing what was going on with the man that I was afraid to want a future with. Our contract came with a timeline. One we'd both committed to.

He moved to face me, then cupped my cheeks. "Ruby, I'm in love with you. I don't know when it happened or how as I never intended for love to be part of our deal. All I know is that when I made those promises to you on Friday, I meant every word. I want it all with you, darling. I want anniversaries and trips across the world. I want charity events, movie openings. I want dancing and making love, and yes, I want children with you. Little blue-eyed, blonde-haired beings with the biggest hearts and the kindest souls, exactly like their mother. I want to bring our children here, just like my parents did. Build new memories of this amazing place with my own family one day." He licked his lips. "Ruby, I want you. I want me and you. I want forever."

I opened my mouth and closed it several times, staring into Nile's eyes so deeply I swore I could see his love, his fear, even his loyalty to me and the future he wanted to give me.

Me.

A woman no man had ever looked at and seen something special until the night he bid on me for my hand in marriage. A woman who had been mistreated in every despicable way possible for years and years. A woman who stripped for money and gave lap dances to pay the bills. A woman with a criminally abusive mother who didn't even know who my father was.

"I guess the question is…" His tone was low and ravaged with uncertainty. "Do you love me? Do you want forever with me? I know I can be a right bastard, often cold, a workaholic, cutthroat in business. And sometimes I come off as a narcissistic arsehole, but I'll try to curb that side."

I pressed my hand over his mouth.

"I know you, Nile." I stared deeply into his eyes. "Honey, *I know you*," I reiterated. "And yes, I've fallen in love with you. The workaholic. The genius composer. The meticulous dresser. The dry humor. The love you have for your brother, even though you enjoy competing with him. The sweet side you show the governess when you think no one is watching. The man who put himself out there to win a girl from the wrong side of the train tracks. The gentle lover who gives far more than he takes. I know you, Nile Pennington. And yes, I love you. I want to be married to you. I want to be with you in all things."

He smiled widely, wrapped his arms around my waist, lifted me up and into the air, and then spun in a dizzying circle. The waves crashed and seagulls squawked, but I was too busy to watch as the man I loved was loving me back, kissing me in his favorite place in the entire world.

Just when I thought my weekend couldn't get better, Nile received a call that Opal and Noah were on their way home from Denmark. I couldn't wait to tell my sister everything that had happened.

So when we entered the estate back in Oxshott, Nile teasingly carrying me over the threshold of his home, it was to the sight of Noah and my sister in a full-on lip-lock at the top of the stairs.

"What in the world!" I gasped, covering my mouth.

Nile put me down at the same time Opal ripped her mouth away from Noah's and stared at me with big eyes. "Ruby-Roo, I can explain." She held her hands up.

But it was too late because Nile was already storming toward his brother. As Noah made it down the staircase, his feet barely touching the landing, Nile was right there. He moved so quickly I wasn't able to interfere when his arm went back and shot out, punching Noah right in the face.

Noah's head flew back along with the rest of him, falling against the stairs, his back crashing to the steps in what seemed to be a painful fall.

"Bloody hell, brother!" Noah coughed and rubbed at the blood dripping from under his nose.

"We trusted you!" Nile roared, then lifted his brother up by his armpits and shoved him to the side roughly. Noah's body went sliding along the marble floor as Opal screamed.

"Nile, no! Let him go," I yelled.

Suddenly there was a larger commotion when the governess entered, barking orders to a couple of burly men who looked like they'd been working in the garden. The two men waded into the fight between the brothers as I ran over to Opal and pulled her into my arms.

"Stop, just stop!" Opal cried.

When the staff got the brothers separated, Nile pointed a finger at Noah. "You lied!" he accused. "Swore you wouldn't touch her! She's been through enough, and you took advantage of her!"

"He didn't take advantage of me. I'm not a child, for Christ's sake." Opal moved away from me and went to Noah's side, wrapping her arm around his waist, her free hand going to his face. "You're bleeding." She sucked in a breath through her teeth and prodded at his nose.

Noah snarled and spat blood onto the white marble floor. "I'll be fine."

"No, you won't. I cannot believe you!" Nile glared. "You need to leave, Noah," he demanded.

"Fine. But I'm not leaving without Opal." He lifted his chin, blood still dripping from his nose.

"The hell you are!" I snapped, moving close to Nile so he didn't go after Noah again. The governess led the others back out.

"I'm not leaving without my *wife*!" Noah snarled and hooked his arm around Opal's shoulders possessively.

My entire body went stone cold and stiff as the dead, my mind trying desperately to understand whatever garbage Noah had just spewed.

Nile, however, had no such problem. He looked at his brother, then at Opal. "You married him?"

She looked away and nodded.

"Yeah, she married me yesterday. It was a beautiful ceremony. Sorry we couldn't invite you," Noah growled smugly.

"You got married this weekend?" I stared at Opal with horror.

"It made the most sense," she whispered, her gaze darting from me to Nile and back down at the floor.

"How?" My voice rose an octave. "How in the fuck does you getting married to Noah make any sense?" I completely lost my cool and moved to lunge for Noah, but Nile hooked me around the waist and yanked me back. "I'll kill you myself!" I shrieked.

Opal raised her hands between us and stood in front of Noah as though she was his shield. That had me kicking my feet and snarling with the need to scratch Noah's eyes out with my fingernails.

"Now you can be free, Ruby. I did it for you. For us."

"You got married for me?" I screeched, my mind spinning in a thousand directions. "Are you joking?"

"No! I did what you were about to do this very weekend. Marry a Pennington you barely know. Only this time, it was me taking the brunt of our troubles on my shoulders for once. Me taking one for Team Dawson."

I shook my head. "This can't be happening." I turned around and put my hands to Nile's chest. "Honey, tell me this isn't happening," I begged.

"We'll get it annulled," Nile barked. "My lawyers will have the paperwork ready by morning."

God, I loved this man.

I closed my eyes and nodded.

"I'm not getting my marriage annulled," Opal announced.

I spun around so fast I felt sick. "You will."

"I won't. Now that I'm married to Noah, you don't have to marry Nile. We'll have all the money we need. Don't you see? I did this for you, Ruby. I did this because I love you." Tears fell down her cheeks. "And more than that, I wanted to marry Noah. We're good together."

Noah kept Opal close then looked Nile dead in the face. "We are good together, poppet," he agreed before glaring at Nile. "I win, brother." He grinned like the wolf that had just kidnapped Red Riding Hood and made her his wife. "The governing interest is mine."

Nile inhaled sharply and shook his head calmly before going over to the satchel he'd dropped when we entered the house and saw them kissing. He rifled through one of the deep pockets until he pulled out a piece of paper.

He walked back over to us and handed Noah the document.

"What is this?" Noah scanned the item.

"No, you don't win, brother. I won the love of my life and the interest." Nile's shoulders slumped as he reached for my hand. "Come, darling, you must be tired."

"What the fuck is this?" Noah sneered.

"It's our wedding certificate," Nile sighed. "We got married on *Friday* in a private ceremony overlooking the ocean in Eastbourne. You got married *Saturday* for nothing. You've ruined our relationship..."—his gaze moved to Opal's and then to mine—"and strained that of my wife and her sister. Congratulations. You do win, brother. You win at being the biggest arsehole I've ever known."

Episode 116

Team Goodall

DAKOTA

I woke with the sun and the need to vomit.

I bolted out of bed, my stomach seizing painfully. The second I reached the toilet, I was heaving like I had every day since finding out I was pregnant. It still blew my mind that there was a tiny human growing inside of me. A little being who was going to be equal parts Sutton and me. I hoped for a boy. When Sutton was not being bossy and gruff, he was actually pretty gentle and sweet. I wanted our child to have his personality and confidence with my passion.

I flushed the toilet and stood weakly, only to find my husband standing there holding a damp cloth. His eyes were sleepy, while the rest of his face hollered *concerned*.

"I'm okay." I cut him off before he could speak and snagged the cloth to wipe my face. "Your mom told us the morning sickness is completely normal. And I kept dinner down last night. It's an improvement." I patted his warm, bare chest as I moved promptly to the sink and loaded my toothbrush with paste.

I went to town on my teeth as he cuddled me from behind, his arms wrapping around my waist gently. He rested his scruffy chin against my shoulder and neck.

"It pains me to see you sick like this," he admitted, his voice a gravelly rumble.

I leaned over, spit, rinsed, and wiped my mouth with a towel. "I know, but it's not supposed to last forever. Think of it this way. As long as I'm sick, we know our baby is doing just fine, right? The pregnancy is progressing. If I felt nothing, maybe that would be a cause for concern."

"That does make me feel a little better in a weird way. Still, that doesn't change the fact that you're going to see Doc Blevins first thing Monday. I've already called their office. Our appointment is at eight a.m."

I rolled my eyes but leaned back against his solid form. "Okay, honey. I'll be there with bells on."

"We'll both be there. I plan on going to every appointment."

I compressed my lips as I stared at his serious expression in the mirror. "Really?"

He huffed. "Yeah, really. My wife is pregnant with our first child. I want to be there for everything." He covered my stomach with his hand. "We're a team. Me, you, and our little one. Team Goodall."

"Team Goodall," I murmured. "I like the sound of that."

Sutton kissed my neck and gave me a light hug from behind before rubbing my belly. "Let's put some food back in so you can throw it up an hour or two from now." He sighed.

"As long as it's not meat."

"Baby needs protein," he countered.

I shrugged as I watched his fine ass walk into the closet. "Baby says meat is a no-go. Eggs are protein," I reminded him, then grimaced at the thought. "Scratch that. Peanut butter is protein. Ohhh, that actually sounds good."

His laughter filled the air. "My girls want a peanut butter

sammi, eh?"

"First of all, we don't know if it's a girl. And second..." I smacked my chops. "Peanut butter sounds awesome. With a banana. Oh, yum! I seriously am salivating for a banana dipped in peanut butter."

"Darlin', we don't have any bananas," he said while pulling on a pair of jeans. He blindly reached out and grabbed the top shirt on a stack of folded, multi-colored T-shirts. He didn't even care which one it was as long as it did the job of covering his beautiful body. This one was an olive green that did amazing things for his eyes.

Then I remembered my situation prior to ogling my husband.

We didn't have any bananas.

It felt like a fucking travesty.

What the hell was wrong with me? I slumped against the vanity, feeling pissy all of a sudden.

Sutton came over to me and curled his fingers around my nape, bringing his head closer to mine. "I'm going to pop on over to Ma's and see about a banana. Though you need to get showered and dressed and head over to your old place to help your sister."

My eyes widened as if I'd just been tased.

"Holy shit! Savvy's getting married today! Freakin' hell!" I dashed into the closet. "I took a shower last night. I'm good. Let me just throw on some clothes real quick, then grab my dress and shoes, and I'll go with you."

"Baby, you have to eat. Food for you and our little one, then you can go help your sister."

I ripped off the shirt he'd worn yesterday, the one I wore to bed last night, and stood glaring, my hands on my hips, my breasts bare.

"Don't call me baby! Especially when you're being annoying," I snarled and reached for a pair of yoga pants.

His eyes dipped down to my breasts and lower, going over

every inch of my body. Then he licked his lips and rubbed a hand over his jaw. I could practically feel that scrape of his morning beard grating along the tender skin of my inner thighs instead of his palm as he looked his fill.

I held back a whimper and shivered as he continued to stare blatantly.

"New plan." His voice was even deeper. "I fuck you. I feed you. I take you to your sister."

My hands shook as I trembled with anticipation. When he spoke like that, my lady bits listened. I clenched my thighs together, and he grinned, his hand going to his button and popping it open. Next he ripped his T-shirt over his head and tossed it aside.

"What is it about closets for us?" I whispered, need flooding my tone.

He fell to his knees, curled his fingers around my hips, and pressed his nose to the apex of my thighs. He inhaled deeply along the thin fabric of my panties before he covered the cotton with his mouth. I cried out as he sucked my flesh through the cloth. I gripped his hair and ground my sex against him wantonly.

That was all it took before he ripped my underwear down my thighs and buried his face between them.

I held on to one of the shelves as he ate. I shifted my legs to give him better access, but he simply grunted, lifted one of my thighs, and placed it over his shoulder. Then he sank his tongue deep. I lifted up on to my toes, the incredible sensation spearing through me with every flick of his magical tongue. He held on tightly to my hips, licking and sucking with wild abandon as I kept one hand on the back of his head, the other on the shelf.

He was voracious in his need, the wet noises he made sounding like an animal tasting Heaven for the first time.

Before long, I was racing to the finish line, sweat beading along my skin, Sutton's fingers digging into my curves greedily, his mouth never letting up. I rocked my hips wildly against his face, desperate to climax. A warm heat flooded my core and spread through me as my muscles tightened and the pleasure climbed to the peak and locked into place.

I inhaled sharply as it came over me. It was massive. Huge. A volcano erupting, hot lava flooding out in every direction. I lost myself to the pleasure, humping his face as though I were riding Marigold at a full gallop.

I arched against him and came *hard.*

When the pleasure finished coasting through my veins, I dropped my leg back to the floor. Then I shoved at his chest until he was sprawled out on his back, mouth and chin soaked with my essence.

Fuck, that was hot.

Filthy, fucking hot, and I wanted more.

Quickly, I unzipped his pants. His impressive erection already attempting to escape his boxer briefs. I pulled out his swollen cock, straddled his hips, centered him just right, and slammed down.

We both convulsed against the intense pleasure.

"Fuck me!" Sutton roared, arching his head and neck back.

"That's exactly what I plan to do, cowboy." I reached for his hands at my hips and held them there. "Now lie back and enjoy the ride." Without further discussion, I bounced on my husband's cock like I couldn't get enough, because I couldn't. I wanted him as deep as he could possibly go. My hormones were all over the place, and all I needed was him embedded within me. And I wanted to come, and come some more.

"Fuck yeah," I breathed, plunging up and down, my mind on nothing but the pleasure soaring through my every last nerve ending. It was as if the very surface of my skin was heated, sprinkled with sensation, tingling with bliss. I was one big ball of pleasure that just kept building into this abundant mountain of pure need.

"I never want to stop fucking you. I never want to stop

fucking you," I chanted, then lifted my hands to my breasts and squeezed them roughly. Pleasure tore through my chest, making me dizzy.

Sutton's eyes were filled with lust as he watched my every move. "Christ, I'm a lucky sum bitch!" He bucked his hips and snarled. "Ride that, baby. Ride my cock hard," he encouraged, pounding up and holding me down, grinding his pelvis against my clit perfectly.

I lost my breath, and my vision blurred, but I didn't lose my mojo to ride.

Sutton groaned. "Come, baby. Come on my cock. Squeeze my fucking dick with that sweet pussy." He let go of my hip with one hand and swirled his thumb right where I needed. It was like pressing the eject button on my orgasm.

My entire body stiffened, my chest constricted, my breath caught, and the walls of my sex locked around his length in a fist-like grip.

"Fuccccckkkkkk," Sutton hissed as I cried out in tandem with him.

We continued to glide in and out of one another until every last inch of pleasure faded and left me boneless. I flopped on top of him, our slick chests sticking together as I caught my breath.

Sutton wrapped his arms around me in a sweaty, gross hug, but I didn't care because I felt happier than I'd felt in a long time. Lying on the closet floor after two amazing orgasms, my husband blissed out because I'd fucked him good. Our baby growing in my womb, and my little sister about to become the most beautiful bride ever.

Who knew life could be this fantastic once you ferreted out all the shit? That shit being my father and the family drama between the Goodalls and the McAllisters. Now we just needed to get Savannah married off, find Jarod's stupid ass, lock him up in jail, and rebuild my farm. Then we'd welcome our baby into the world. Team Goodall, he'd said.

Team Goodall indeed.

"You dead up there?" Sutton chuckled, his chest moving my entire body even though we were still intimately connected.

"Death by orgasm," I mumbled dreamily. "Sounds like a good way to go."

His jovial laughter shifted my hair, and I begrudgingly sat up, our chests making a sticky slurping sound as we parted.

"Guess I'll be needing that shower after all." I grinned wickedly, leaned over, and took his mouth in a deep, reaffirming kiss.

He was such a good kisser. Hell, he was good at everything.

"Looks like I'll be joining you." He snickered.

"If that happens, we'll never make it to Savannah, and she's probably already freaking out. It's her wedding day, remember?"

He cupped my face, his thumb tracing my cheek. "How did I ever get so lucky?" he whispered.

"That you married a woman who knew how to fuck?" I teased.

He closed his eyes and then shook his head. "No. Well, maybe." He smirked, but then his expression became serious. "I love you, Dakota. I love you not only because you know how to ride your cowboy, or that you let loose when I get my hands and mouth on you. I love you because I've wanted this life since I was a teenager and saw the pretty neighbor girl riding a horse. That day I imagined a life where you and I were together. Making a home. Building a family. Working the land side by side. And here you are," he said with complete awe in every word.

I dipped my head and kissed him with my eyes open. He watched as I pecked his lips repeatedly. "Here I am."

"Are you happy to be here, Dakota? Truly?" He threaded his fingers through my hair, cradling my head as though I was the most precious thing, while our bodies were still connected.

I traced his lips with the tip of my index finger. "There is no place I'd rather be than here with you. Making a home.

Having this baby. Rebuilding the land to what it could be. It's all I ever wanted for myself too. I just never knew it would be you who I would love. You who would hold my heart in your hand. You who would give me everything I could have ever dreamed of. I love you, Sutton."

"Team Goodall, baby."

"Team Goodall all the way," I agreed with a much longer, wetter kiss that made my lady bits take notice once more. I clenched around his soft length within me, gauging his interest.

"Again?" His eyes widened, and his eyebrows rose.

I grinned. "Don't look at me. Your DNA is making me a horn dog." I sat up and pointed at my belly where our baby was growing.

"Well, hallelujah. I'll be thanking the Lord for the extra miracle." He laughed while he clapped his arm around my back and one under my bum.

His cock slid from me as he hauled me up and off the closet floor and straight into the shower. He set me down gently and got the water going.

We didn't pick up where we'd left off in the closet, because I needed to get to Savvy, but we did take some handsy liberties washing one another. Once showered, he dried me off, we got dressed, and I grabbed my gown and shoes. He took me to the side of our house where I hadn't realized a good-sized shed sat off in the distance. There in the center of the space was a riding lawn mower, some horse-related items, tools, and a shiny blue quad off to the right.

"We'll have to pick you up one," he said as he slung a leg over the quad, flicked it on, and revved it a few times. "Get on, Dakota." He gestured to the back.

"But I want to drive," I pouted.

He ducked his head and grinned, his shoulders shaking with the effort. "Next time, darlin'."

I stomped over to the machine, hiked my leg over, and looped an arm around his waist. "Giddy up!" I encouraged.

Sutton laughed heartily as he U-turned around a well-worn path I was seeing for the first time. Looked like the Goodalls had thought of everything. Instead of heading to his parents' place, we scooted on toward my land.

When we pulled up to the farmhouse, Savvy was already waiting, hands over her chest, foot tapping rapidly. Every bone in her body said she was pissed way the hell off.

"Where have you been?" she snapped as I got off the quad.

Sutton steadied my hip as I bent down and kissed him, scratching my nails over his jaw. "I'd really like that banana and peanut butter," I said, dead serious.

He snuck another kiss. "I got you, baby."

"Don't call me baby," I warned and narrowed my eyes.

"Don't be cute and I won't call you baby," he rumbled and sucked on my bottom lip, then smacked my ass. "Have fun. See you in a bit."

I smiled widely and stomped up the stairs. "What's the matter? It's literally hours before the wedding. We've got tons of time to get ready."

"I can't find Mom's pearls." Her eyes filled with tears. "I looked everywhere. They're not here." She hiccupped.

"That's because I have them." I dropped the bag with my shoes in it, bent over, dug around, then pulled out the small jewelry box I'd found when I went through our mother's things in the attic.

Savvy took the box with shaking hands. Inside were Mom's pearls and her wedding ring. I still didn't know what we were going to do with that, but I surely didn't want it. I figured that sucker was cursed and should be tossed in the river.

Savannah ran her fingers over the pearls as though they were a delicate family heirloom. Technically, since our mother wasn't of this Earth anymore, they kind of were.

I covered my sister's hands. "I'm glad you're going to wear them. Mom would be so proud of you, Savvy. You're going to make the most beautiful bride."

Savannah sat down on the top stair, and I sat with her, sensing she needed to talk.

"Do you think I'm making the right decision after everything that's happened?"

I tilted my head and put my hand over hers. "What I think isn't important. You're about to make the biggest decision of your life. Even bigger than entering the auction. You're choosing to love and share your life with someone else, maybe *forever.* That means something."

"Does it mean something to you? And Sutton?" she asked.

"It means everything," I stated instantly.

We stayed on the porch, holding hands and looking out over the land for a good fifteen minutes until I heard the sound of the quad once more. My husband rolled up and handed me a brown paper bag.

I took the bag, then peeked inside. There was a banana and a small clear tub loaded with peanut butter. I beamed at my husband.

Sutton tipped his hat, winked, and then sped off without another word.

"Definitely means everything. Come on, let's get you ready to get married."

Episode 117

Savannah & Erik's Wedding Part 1

SAVANNAH

While Dakota munched on her banana, coating it heavily with peanut butter, I stared out the window of my childhood bedroom. Besides the barn having burned down, nothing much had changed in the years I was in college. The landscape pretty much stayed the same. Wildflowers ran along one side of the land, and the cattle dotted the greens as far as the eye could see. It was beautiful. Always had been. It was where I'd grown up. Where I'd planned to grow old and raise a family with Jarod.

Now here I stood in the most perfect wedding gown ready to marry Erik Johansen. A man I'd never in my wildest dreams imagined I'd marry. He represented an entirely new future. One I'd begun to want with my every breath. Erik had shown me strength, kindness, compassion, heart, and true love. Did it happen fast? Hell, yes. Much faster than I would have thought possible for a man and a woman who'd met just a month ago. Except when I looked at Dakota and Sutton, who'd done the very same thing. They may have had a feisty, almost combative relationship, but it was obvious just watching them interact they were an unbelievably good pairing.

A perfect match.

Erik had quickly woven his way into my heart, planted roots, and made a home. I felt him there, supporting me…loving me. I'd thought what I had with Jarod was true love. I was wrong. He'd built our relationship on half-truths and lies in order to get me to fall for him. Perhaps that's why it wasn't hard to leave him when I'd gone away to school. A part of me somehow knew he wasn't my match. Maybe it was also why I'd waited until we were eighteen to cross that intimate boundary after years of being together? Especially when compared to the fact that I'd given myself to Erik within mere weeks.

There truly was no comparison when I evaluated my feelings for the two men.

What I had with Erik was the stuff of fairy tales. A remarkable meeting of two souls, stuck inside the bodies of two people who were meant to be together. Meant to become one whole. I knew that fact with every fiber of my being. And still, I was hesitant to walk down that aisle.

The hair at the back of my neck stood on edge. I worried my lip with my teeth, my mind running a million miles a minute.

Something was off. Today just didn't *feel* right. As if a dark cloud was looming on the sunniest of days.

"*Å herregud, du er vakker!* You are beautiful, Savannah," came Irene's voice as she entered the bedroom.

I pressed my hands to the intricate lace detail of my dress, down the sheer parts of the bodice, and along my hips. My hourglass frame was highlighted well, the dress tight at the bodice and waist then flaring out at the hips in a big, loose skirt. The saleswoman had called the dress bohemian chic. The spaghetti-style strap making it feel delicate and feminine. The fabric nipped in at the waist, the lace falling in a scallop pattern toward my feet. There were wide, almost see-through sections at the hips and closer to the floor in the large flowing skirt offering a texture to it. The tulle overlay stretched out, giving the back a train-like appearance. It was absolutely perfect for a ranch wedding.

"Thank you. I mean *tusen takk*," I responded in Norwegian while I swished the dress from side to side and preened at Irene's compliment.

She walked over and handed me a small leather box.

"For me?" I asked.

Irene nodded. "I wore this at my wedding to Henrik. You don't have to wear it." Her gaze took in my long red hair that was currently curled but left down around my shoulders. "But I'd like you to have it."

I opened the lid as she held the base and found a stunning hair comb fashioned from three large flowers about the size of a nickel each. The petals were brushed pearls with crystals sprouting like baby's breath around each flower. The leaves were a shiny silver and gold mixture that added a subtle, unique flair. The artistry of the piece was breathtaking.

"I'd love to wear it, if you'd help me put it on?" My cheeks heated, and I'm sure they were a startling pink.

Irene smiled so widely her eyes sparkled with joy. "I'd love to, *min datter*." I'd learned that *min datter* meant *my daughter*, and my heart practically exploded every time she referred to me as such. It made me feel special, filling a hole in my heart I didn't know I'd had until her.

I missed my mom. Especially today of all days.

She should have been here, sharing these one-of-a-kind moments with me, and she wasn't. My father had broken her down so badly that she didn't feel her life was worth living. And now here I stood, with someone else's mother being so kind and loving…

I sniffed against the tears threatening, moved to my small vanity, and sat down in the chair. Irene took out the comb and set the box on the table. "Hold this, please." She handed me the family heirloom. I traced its surface with the tip of my finger.

"It's remarkable," I breathed.

Irene stood straighter, her chest lifting with what I assumed was pride. Then she moved behind me and pulled a good-size lock of hair at each side of my head just above my ear. She paired those locks at the back, twisted them into a small swirl, and reached for the comb. I handed it to her and waited patiently as she centered it, then inserted it into my hair. The final look pulled my hair away from my face, giving me an ethereal quality that fit the entire vibe wonderfully.

She pointed to the hair spray, and she moved with me as I reached for it and passed it back to her. For a couple minutes she maneuvered the comb into whatever position she felt was just right, and then sprayed the living heck out of my hair, ensuring the look would last.

"All done!" she announced with glee.

I grabbed my small, handheld mirror and turned around to see the back. As I expected, she'd done a magnificent job of weaving the comb into my hair, leaving the rest to cascade down the open back of the dress.

"It's perfect!" I grinned, then bit down on my bottom lip. "I love it."

She clapped. "I am honored you wish to wear it on this day. Henrik and I are so happy you are joining our family," she gushed, and then pulled me into a deep hug.

I held her tightly, needing to feel that motherly love in the hopes it could chase away the dark and foreboding feeling I couldn't quite shake.

Right then, Dakota entered, her face pale as a ghost, her hand over her belly. At some point, she must have left the room during my pondering, and I hadn't even noticed.

Poor thing was so sick. I too wished she'd already gone to see the doctor, but I was sure that she and Sutton had it handled and would be going this coming Monday.

"You okay, Kota?"

She rubbed her stomach. "Right as rain," she lied and sat gently on the bed as if too much movement might send her racing back to the bathroom.

I took in her attire as she sat scanning her phone. Her gown was perfect for her. A summery, mauve-toned peach color that looked fantastic against her tan skin. It also had spaghetti straps with a triangle top and cinched-in waist. The fabric fell in loose, swishy waves all the way to the floor with a slit in the front clear up to mid-thigh. She looked sexy and sweet even though I knew she felt like garbage due to the morning sickness. I still couldn't believe my sister was going to have a baby. In all my future planning, I'd never envisioned her having children. Being the ball-busting ranch manager that took no shit from anyone? Absolutely. A mother to little ones? Not so much.

However, I genuinely enjoyed seeing this side of her and would miss her terribly when we left for our new lives in Norway. As Erik promised, though, we'd get a house near here so we could live in both places. Being close whenever we chose. I knew I'd need at least until the baby came to be away from everything here, to forget and forgive myself for not seeing through Jarod's lies. It was embarrassing to say the least, but more than anything, knowing I'd been a pawn in his twisted game was gut-wrenching.

There was a light knock on the door.

"Come in," I called out.

Linda, Sutton's mother, peeked her head in, her eyes widening when she saw me. "We're ready when you are, darlin'," she said, sounding exactly like her son.

"It's showtime!" Dakota said, perking up.

I went over to the long mirror and double-checked my dress, hair, and makeup. I looked amazing. The prettiest I ever had in my entire life. Dakota came up behind me with Mom's pearls.

"Looks like you forgot these." She winked, then reached

her arms around me with the necklace. I held my hair away from my neck as she secured the small string of pearls. They landed just under the slight hollow at the center of my clavicle. I curled a finger around them, attempting to feel Mom's presence.

"I'm going to go find Henrik! See you both soon!" Irene stated as she made her exit.

"You are the most gorgeous bride I've ever seen, Savvy." My sister wrapped her arm around my waist and hugged me from behind, our gazes locked in the mirror's reflection. "Are you ready?"

I nodded. "I'm definitely ready to marry Erik, but I can't shake the feeling that something is off. Jarod hasn't been found, and I'm worried he's going to ruin everything." I shared my fears.

"The Sheriff, his deputies, and friends of the Goodalls are patrolling the property keeping an eye out for anything suspicious. If he tries to sneak his way in, someone is going to spot him." She squeezed me tighter.

I put my arm over hers and nodded. "Yeah, you're right."

"Is it cold feet?" she asked.

I shrugged. "Maybe a little. We've only known one another a month. Though I've never loved anyone or felt anything as intensely as I do for Erik. He's my person, Kota. This I know for sure."

Dakota smiled widely. "Sutton told me I was his person too. He used that exact wording. Maybe it's a sign we are where we're supposed to be." She lifted her hand and ran her fingers along the pearls. "Mom would love this. You marrying a good man who wants nothing more than to give you an amazing life. She'd be beside herself, Savvy."

"You think?" My voice cracked.

"I know." She nodded. "And I'm so damn proud of you. Going after what you dream of. Putting yourself on the line for our little family. For land you didn't even want. I'm sorry you felt you had to subject yourself to the auction when you weren't as invested."

"I did it for you," I shyly whispered my biggest secret. "You love the land. I love you. And you deserved it. I watched you for years do nothing but learn everything you could about ranching, the horses, the cattle, running a farm, all of it. You shine so bright when you're working here. Perhaps I wanted to shine with you."

"Savvy, you shine all on your own. So bright it hurts my eyes sometimes to even look at you." She rested her chin against my shoulder and grinned. "We sure are a pair, huh? Doing everything we can for love."

I chuckled.

"I think us entering the auction, you finding Erik, and Sutton finding me were the best things that could have happened to either of us. We may have twisted our lives inside out and upside down, but we weren't really living before. We were going through the motions. Now we can live for us. Focus on the things we genuinely want for ourselves. And we've got two amazing men to love and support us along the way. You can't put a value on that; it's too damn high."

We stared at one another for a couple long minutes, knowing that after this moment, our lives would never be the same.

They already weren't. We had both changed since entering the auction. Two new versions of ourselves that I found I quite liked.

"Let's get you to your hubby-to-be. I'm sure he's shitting bricks right about now waiting for you to walk down that aisle."

"You're probably right." I laughed and nodded, then took my sister's hand. "Thank you for being here. For being my sister. I love you so much, Kota."

"I love you too." She interlaced our fingers and led me out of my room.

Waiting out front of our farmhouse was a shiny black

limousine and a driver who stood with his hands clasped in front of him. But that's not what surprised me. Next to the limo was our mother's horse Marigold, now Dakota's, and one of my stallions. They were both saddled and tied to the porch. Both horses were sleek and glinting in the sun's early light. Both had satin ribbons tied in their manes in neat pretty bows and flowers running along their reins.

"What's this?" I pointed at the car and then the horses.

Dakota smirked. "Well, Madam Alana sent her limo to drive us around to the Goodall land. Very fancy. Very bougie."

"And the horses?" I pressed my lips together, trying not to laugh.

Dakota grinned. "That was all me. I thought you'd rather ride in style. Something more your speed. Figured you might like to take one last ride with your big sis. Maybe head on over to the Goodall ranch and see a man about a wedding," she joked.

"Damn right I do." I approached Marigold and ran my hand down her nose in greeting. She snuffled, allowing me to pet her briefly, then shifted her head and stomped her feet. Marigold was as sassy as Dakota. The two were made for one another.

"Oh hush, ya big baby!" My sister teased her horse, went right to her face, and kissed the tip of her nose. Marigold rubbed her face along Dakota's neck sweetly.

"I see how it is, Mari!" I called out and approached my favorite stallion, Blackie. "Hey ya, boy. You sure are looking mighty fine with your hair braided." He moved his head up and down good-naturedly. Blackie was our biggest boy at just over sixteen hands tall, but also had the sweetest temperament. I'd miss him when I left. I'd miss all of my horse babies when I moved to Norway.

Blackie stood still as a statue as I maneuvered my dress and hefted up and onto the saddle. Dakota fiddled with my gown, spreading out the bottom like a blanket over the horse's body so it didn't get squashed. Then she stood back, pulled her phone out of a secret pocket in her dress, and snapped a picture of me.

"You are the most perfect bride!" She snapped a few more.

"Come on, Kota. Let's go! I'm getting excited now."

She grinned, hiked up her dress, and flew up and onto her horse like the expert rider she was. "People are going to trip when we ride up on horses, but we McAllister sisters dare to be different." She cackled, then prodded the horse with her legs. "Yaw, Marigold!" she called out, and the horse bolted forward.

"Yaw!" I repeated the same process, and we were off. Two sisters riding like the wind in wedding attire heading to the most important event of my life.

I couldn't wait.

Today I would marry the love of my life.

What I didn't notice, and wouldn't until my entire world imploded, was the lone figure staring out the attic window of my childhood home, his face a mask of fury and rage. A shiny pistol clutched in his hand.

Episode 118

Savannah & Erik's Wedding Part 2

ERIK

The Goodall barn had been transformed into a rustic meets country chic wedding and reception space. Edison bulbs illuminated the rafters while twinkle lights wrapped each wooden column, adding to the soft, cozy glow. In between the strings of bulbs were large swaths of cream-colored fabric giving an added element of whimsy. Directly in the center hung a crystal chandelier. I had no idea how the Goodall family had fashioned something so elegant in such a short amount of time, but they did. Round tables had been set up on each side of the large, open interior, leaving a wide aisle down the center cutting between them for the wedding party to walk. At the end was a homemade arbor lavishly decorated in a variety of peach roses, pink carnations, and other wildflowers that I believed grew on the property.

We'd decided to hold the wedding ceremony in the barn instead of out in the wildflower field as Savannah had suggested. The threat Jarod Talley posed was too much for my heart to bear.

If we were out in the open, anything could happen. I felt much safer having our ceremony inside, and Savannah had agreed.

My soon-to-be wife was logical, thoughtful, and put others' needs before her own. I planned on turning those tables throughout our lifetime together. Making sure she was the center of my world and ensuring she knew she held that place in my heart.

So far, everything today had gone exactly as planned. I'd made love to Savannah just this morning. Having her body laid out in a bed was a true gift. Our coupling in the trees yesterday was monumental and life-changing but not nearly enough. I wanted to soak my soul in our love. Spend hours upon hours glorying in her body and the blessing of finding my other half. But we had time for all of that. We had a lifetime to look forward to.

I planned to whisk her away for a month-long honeymoon. We'd start in Paris, the city of love, and work our way through the United Kingdom, Germany, Denmark, Sweden, and then home to Norway. Only instead of going to my parents' estate, we'd make our final destination my home in Oslo. I figured that would give Savannah time to adjust to being a married couple and her new life in Norway while she figured out what she wanted to do in the future. Whatever that looked like.

For one thing, I planned to suggest that Savannah finish her coursework toward her degree. I'd learned that she'd wanted to be a large animal veterinarian. There was no reason she couldn't be exactly that wherever we made our home. I'd happily buy her a building she could make her own and would work with her to open and manage her first business. I'd been through the process what felt like a thousand times and had endless resources to make the experience a good one for her. Whatever she wanted to do with her time and intellect, I wanted to support. If that was being a stay-at-home wife and maybe mother one day, I'd happily agree to that plan too. More than anything, I wanted Savannah to know and understand that the sky was the limit for her. For us.

Our future started today.

As two halves of one whole.

Mr. and Mrs. Johansen.

I sure enjoyed the idea of having a wife to love and cherish. Someone who would be there for me through all the highs and lows of life. And in turn, I looked forward to being a husband. To loving and supporting my wife in all things. Just like my parents. They'd taught me what a beautiful marriage looked like, and I knew that with Savannah by my side, I would be the happiest man alive.

I just wished she'd hurry up and make her appearance.

Our guests had started to arrive thirty minutes ago. Strangers filled the seats around tables that had been decorated by Madam Alana and Christophe Toussaint. They'd done an incredible job transforming boring dinner tables into something magical. The flatware was gold, and the plates sat on something circular that looked like woven straw. White plates sat on top of that, with a shiny rose gold-colored napkin. An intricate gold ring held the cloth in a pretty fan shape on top of the plate. Floral centerpieces matched the wedding arbor. Candles and uniquely colored wine and drinking glasses completed the look.

Sweat beaded along my hairline as I stared at the large square opening people were still filing through and taking their seats. No sign of my bride just yet.

I patted the sides of my hair, making sure there weren't stray pieces poking out. I'd pulled the length of my long hair into what my mother told me was a handsome hairstyle, one I thought Americans referred to as a man bun. Whether that was a good or bad description I didn't know, nor did I care. As long as my *elskede* liked it, that was all that mattered.

"Relax, brother. She's going to be here soon. People are still arriving," my best man Jack whispered as he knocked my shoulder with his.

I inhaled deeply and let it out slowly, taking in every guest. "I don't know most of these people. I should have just put her on my jet and married her back home where I feel she's safest."

Jack clapped me on the shoulder and squeezed. "I understand the concern, but the authorities said they've got eyes on the property. The Goodalls have people at the gate checking off the guests by name to ensure they were invited. This place looks incredible, and we're going to have a great time." He gripped my shoulder with intent, which forced me to turn sideways and look into his dark eyes.

"What?" I huffed.

He chuckled and smiled. "It's your wedding day. I'm happy for you, brother."

I closed my eyes and nodded. "Thank you, Jack. You've been a constant in my life, a true brother by choice, and I'll never take that for granted. Thank you for holding down the fort while I went off the rails these past couple years. And for keeping my parents sane. I know you lost Troy in that accident, and for a long time you lost me too, and for that I'm sorry."

"But you're back." He clapped me again. "And we have Savannah to thank for that. My new sister."

I nodded. "Yes, we have a lot to thank Savannah for. Next, we'll need to find you the right woman."

He smirked. "Already have a plan for that." He smirked playfully.

I frowned and cocked my head. "What's that supposed to mean. You have a plan?"

"I'm joining the next auction, brother. I'm going to find me my very own Savannah so I too can live happily ever after."

"You're kidding?" I gasped, shock making my mouth fall open.

He bit into his bottom lip and grinned wildly. "Already spoke to your Madam Alana."

"She's definitely not *mine* in any sense of the word. I…I, I don't know what to say." I snorted and raised my hand to cup him behind the neck, where I squeezed warmly. "I'm happy for you. It worked for me; it could work for you."

"That's what I'm counting on. Oh, look." Jack lifted his chin as the music started playing. He squinted and focused on the entrance. "Something's heading this way in the distance."

While we'd talked quietly, I hadn't realized that all of the guests were seated properly, each facing the center aisle. Jack and I stood on the small riser off to one side at the back of the barn as instructed by Linda Goodall aka the Boss. That woman was worth her weight in gold. She'd taken on the role of wedding planner and made magic happen in a short amount of time. I made a mental note to send an extravagant thank you gift once Savannah and I were settled into our new lives.

The officiant I'd been introduced to early this morning approached the riser wearing a tidy, old-fashioned brown suit with a peach tie. The effort to match the colors of the wedding was considerate. He stepped up and took his position in the center under the arbor, Bible held within his hands.

I could hear a couple of horses galloping and looked out through the entrance toward the sound. Just past the fence line were two horses I recognized. Both headed our direction. Two redheads, one strawberry blonde wearing a burnt orange and pink dress was riding a light-colored horse, while my flaming redhead Savannah was atop a pitch-black stallion. The women were effervescent. Their bodies rolling with the moving beasts in perfect symmetry. Their hair cascaded behind them in the breeze looking like flames.

My breath caught in my throat as they made their way to the barn, slowing the horses as they stopped just in front of the doorway. Everyone oohed and ahhed at the display except Sutton, who was at the front table smacking his knee while laughing jovially and shaking his head.

"Only my wife would pull a stunt like this," Sutton murmured to his parents, who grinned and smiled happily.

Dakota slipped off her horse and handed the reins to Duke Goodall Junior, who in turn handed her a bouquet of flowers. Without a hitch, Dakota slowly started walking down the aisle to the music. She was smiling and winked at me when she made it to the riser, then stepped up and took her position as witness for my bride.

And then there was Savannah.

She slid off her horse as though she'd done it a thousand times, the bottom half of her dress falling at her feet and spreading out perfectly. She took the flowers Junior handed her, and he took the reins. Then her gaze met mine, and I lost myself. Everything else slipped away. The guests, the music, the lights, the barn—everything ceased to exist but my Savannah.

Her skin glowed a pearlescent white along her shoulders, neck, and face. All except her rosy cheeks. Her mouth was a soft, shimmery pink I couldn't wait to kiss. The entire room stood up as she took the first step toward me. She smiled widely, her eyes never leaving mine as she walked the aisle. Her dress graced her form in delicate lace and see-through sections that hinted at the sultry and sexy woman beneath but was demure in a way that left specifics to one's imagination. I had an excellent imagination.

She was absolutely stunning.

My every dream come true.

I held my hand out when she got to the riser, and she placed her cool one within it, allowing me to help steady her.

"You look magnificent, *elskede*. I am honored you have chosen me to be your husband this day." I lifted her hand to my lips and kissed her knuckles.

Savannah preened, her cheeks going even darker as she squeezed my hand. "You're so handsome," she whispered shyly, pressing her lips together, glancing down and back up at me demurely, smiling as she did so.

My bride was happy to be standing before me.

My heart beat so hard I thought it might explode with the overwhelming joy coursing through my every pore. I closed my eyes for a moment, catching my breath, and then opened them to see she was still there. My every wish was standing before me, about to become mine, as I was about to become hers.

That's when it happened.

The sound of a gunshot blasted through the room.

I reached for Savannah's hands, and we both ducked.

The crowd screamed, and another shot popped, crackling through the air like lightning striking.

"Stay calm or I start shooting all of you!" Came the voice of a male who'd just slid from behind several stacked hay bales in the back corner where I recalled there was a tack room. That tack room also had a door to the outside. One of Sutton's friends had been monitoring that doorway just to be safe. Fear for that man's condition stole down my back in a spine-aching shiver.

The room went deadly silent as I clutched at Savannah. "Get behind me!" I tried to maneuver her.

"No way. He wants to hurt you, not me," she spat, and stood up boldly, a tigress ready to defend her mate. "Jarod, please, don't do this," she stated in a firm, unflinching tone.

"Don't do this? What am I doing, Savannah? Fighting for what's mine!" he snarled.

"Sutton," Dakota called out, her voice angry but seeming direct and unafraid.

Her husband moved to reach behind his back where he had a concealed weapon.

"Don't even think about it, Goodall," Jarod barked. "You don't want to see what happens if you do," he warned.

Sutton lifted his hands up in supplication. "You're the boss."

"You're damn right." He waved the gun around, his face contorted in fury.

Savannah stepped in front of me. I put my hands to her hips and moved my face near her ear. "Get. Behind. Me," I growled and shifted her the best I could to the side, but she wiggled out of my hold, stepping forward a few feet to gain Jarod's attention.

"Touch her again and I shoot your fucking mother." Jarod pointed a gun toward the back of my mother's head. She was sitting next to my father, Sutton, and his parents. His gun was in the perfect position to end her life instantly. Her beloved face was ghostly white and blankly staring over the table, tears falling down her cheeks. My stomach sank and tightened painfully.

I ground my teeth and held up my hands, trying to show him he was in charge. That didn't stop the terror from sizzling through my veins and making my hands tremble. The man was unhinged, a wild card. No one knew what he was capable of, but what I did know was that he needed to feel like he was the authority figure.

Near the entrance to the barn, I could see one of the deputy sheriffs, who was wearing a suit instead of his uniform so he blended in, starting to creep toward the side, staying in the shadows. If we could just keep Jarod talking, the deputy could overtake him.

"Jarod, this is not the way. You need to put that gun down so we can talk this through," Savannah attempted once more.

"The time for words is over, Savannah," he grated through his teeth. "You did that. And anything that happens today is your fault!" He sneered and shook his head, shifting the gun to her.

"No, please, Jarod." Dakota tried to get his attention off Savannah, but it didn't work. His entire focus was on my bride.

"I did *everything* for you. Everything. Worked for shit money at the hands of an abuser every day for years. Why? For the promise of owning the McAllister land. For the promise of a pretty wife who would give me good, strong sons. For the promise of your beautiful warm body in my bed every night. For the love and pride of my family, who never thought I'd amount to anything but being a poor ranch hand." His gun hand shook as his chest rose and fell with his rage. "And what did you do?" He roared the last part. "You went away to school, lost interest in the man who was devoted to you, and left me for some foreigner with more money than God!" he snarled, spittle dripping down his curled lips.

"I'm sorry, Jarod. At the time, I did what I had to do." She held her hands up, her words soft, carrying no hint of malice or anger. She kept her cool, focused on the situation, and was doing her best to talk the maniac down. I was in awe of her for the second time today.

"You ruined everything! You took away my dream," Jarod hollered. "Everything I worked for, gone. All because you wanted an upgrade. Well, Savannah, you can't always get what you want. You taught me that," he growled. "Lesson learned. Now it's time for you to learn a lesson."

He shifted the gun from Savannah and pointed it right at me. I held my hands up and looked him dead in the eye. Looking for any shred of decency that might have been left in the man that Savannah once loved.

I found none.

Jarod Talley stood staring me down, his nostrils flared, his gaze a deathly glare. Then he smiled wickedly and pulled the trigger.

A thundering crack split the air as the gun went off.

Then it was as if everything happened in slow motion.

"No!" I heard Savannah scream though it sounded more like, "Nooooooooooooo," in a warbled, robotic voice.

Savannah's expression was horrified as she turned around and lunged for me.

Her beautiful body jolted and convulsed in mid-air, eyes going wide and shocked, blood spurting out from her chest right before something sharp penetrated my left side just over my heart.

Savannah crashed into me, her blood mixing with mine as our chests slammed together, and we both went down.

Behind us, more gunshots were fired. And then everything went eerily quiet.

Episode 119

Savannah & Erik's Wedding Part 3

SAVANNAH

Agony shredded through my right shoulder as I crashed into Erik. His eyes widened with horror and then pain as we fell backward onto the riser. His large frame cushioned my form as I slammed on top of him. Blood poured from my body, coating us both as I wailed, easing to a hip next to him.

The room exploded into screams as a series of gunshots crackled through the air. I flung my upper half over Erik, trying to cover his frame with my own.

He wasn't moving.

My entire body went ice cold as I sat up, gritting my teeth, pushing through the pain, needing to help the man I loved. His chest rose and fell, but he wasn't conscious. Blood soaked his chest from a hole above his heart. I pressed my palm over the wound as hard as I could.

Dakota was at my side in an instant, clutching a hand over the back of my shoulder.

"Savvy, you've been shot," she cried.

I didn't care. The pain of being shot was nothing compared to the sight of Erik's unconscious form.

"Erik, honey." I cupped his cheek with my bloody hand then realized that was a bad idea as more blood coated us both. "No! No...no...no...no!" I pressed once more over his still-beating heart and screeched. "We need help!"

My sister now had both of her hands on me in a vise, one in back, one in front. "Sutton, help!" she yelled. "The bullet went through Savvy and into Eric!"

Within seconds, there were people surrounding us. Sutton pressed his hand on top of mine to staunch the flow of blood coming from Erik.

"Baby, wake up. Please, show me your eyes," I cried, my gaze scanning for even the slightest movement.

His eyes fluttered.

"Erik! Please!" I sobbed, tears tracking down my cheeks.

He groaned and licked his lips, then opened his eyes. His gaze set upon mine. I held my breath, my entire focus on his beloved face.

"*Elskede*," he murmured with reverence.

His *beloved*.

He'd called me that since the very beginning. After everything, I now truly knew how cherished I was by this man.

"Yes, I'm here. I'm right here. We're getting help!" I choked out.

He closed his eyes.

"No! Stay with me, Erik!" I pleaded desperately.

He opened those golden eyes, filled with pain and then pure love as he looked at me. One of his hands reached out and cupped my jaw. His thumb swept lightly across my cheekbone.

"*Jeg elsker deg*, Savannah," he whispered. *I love you.* Then his eyes closed, and his body went limp.

His chest stopped moving.

"No! I love you too! Please, someone!" I shrieked.

At some point, I was bodily pulled away from Erik,

watching in misery as a flurry of people tended to *my* beloved. My sister still holding both of her hands to my wounds. She was pressing so hard my vision started to blur and blacken around the edges, or maybe that was the wound itself. I started to pray out loud, begging God to save the man I loved.

"Please, God, please!"

"Shhhh, Savvy, you're going to be okay. Erik's being helped by the paramedics now. Calm down and breathe."

I lifted my head and stared at my sister's familiar, treasured face. "Is he dead?" I gulped.

She shook her head. "They're doing everything they can."

I reached up and clenched her wrist. "Is he dead?" I repeated, my teeth starting to chatter.

"No, honey. He's strong. Have faith." She leaned her head down and kissed the top of my hair.

A commotion from close by caught my attention, and I turned my head to see Jarod on his back, his shirt ripped open, and tons of blood-soaked gauze over his belly as two paramedics tended to what looked like a gunshot wound to the abdomen. One of them did compressions on his chest, and then his body suddenly jerked up, appearing to have been shocked.

A cold numbness flooded my veins, and I shivered uncontrollably. I looked away, not giving Jarod even a second more of my energy. Erik was loaded onto a long board and lifted into the air. That's when everything went black.

I woke to a small, cool hand in mine, a weight across my hips, another weight against my ribcage, and a ton of bricks pressing down on my right shoulder.

I opened my eyes to find my sister's head pressed to my side, her arm across my hips. She was snoring, deep purple smudges under her eyes.

The hand in mine tightened, and I shifted my gaze to see Irene's teary eyes and a wide smile. "Welcome back, *datter.*"

"Erik?" I rasped.

"He's still in surgery," Irene said. "From what we understand, the bullet just missed his heart and didn't exit the body. He lost a lot of blood. The doctors took him right into surgery, but they all seemed very hopeful. We haven't heard anything more, but they assured us they would come here the moment they had news." She held my hand tighter. "You came out of surgery first. They woke you in recovery and then gave you meds that put you back to sleep and brought you here."

I didn't remember being woken the first time.

Irene continued with her update. "The bullet went right through your shoulder, clean in and out. They said you were extremely lucky. It will be a painful few weeks of recuperation, but they don't suspect you'll have any issues with mobility after physical therapy."

I nodded, not really caring about me. I wanted to hear about Erik. I wanted him to be okay.

God, please let him pull through this. I've just found him. We haven't even started our lives together.

Tears filled my eyes and slid down my cheeks.

"Oh, lovely, it will be okay. My son is strong, and he has something very beautiful to live for. He will pull through. Of this, I have no doubt," she stated with such confidence I wanted more than anything to believe her.

Except, the other pessimistic side of me knew that Dakota and I had not been dealt the easiest of hands in our lives. Especially when it came to relationships. Erik was my chance at true happiness. Real love. I just hoped God or the Universe saw it fit to let me keep him.

I let go of Irene's hand with a tight smile and then wove

my fingers into my sister's soft strawberry locks. Dakota snuffled and sighed deeply. She was exhausted. The pregnancy was doing a number on her.

"How long have I been out?" I asked, not taking my eyes off my precious big sis.

"Many hours. She's not left your side since the minute they put you in a room."

I noted my sister was no longer in her bridesmaid dress, but a pair of scrubs and an enormous sportscoat.

"Did anyone else get hurt?" I whispered, my heartbeat spiking as I played with my sister's hair. Needing to touch the only other person in the world I loved down to my soul. Half of my heart was hers and would always be hers. The other half owned by a man who was currently in surgery.

Irene sniffed and wiped at her tears. Henrik stood behind her, hands to her shoulders in support as he spoke. "The attacker was shot in the stomach by the undercover deputy right before Sutton tackled him. He got off a few shots that went into the ceiling of the barn as he collapsed, but no one else was hurt."

I nodded as my eyes got heavy and harder to keep open. Everyone was okay. I was alive. My sister was here with me unharmed. Irene and Henrik were watching over us. And Erik was being tended to. I blinked several times, trying to stay awake but the dreamy, drug-induced escape was too much to ignore.

The next time I awoke was in the middle of the night, my sister lying on a cot propped next to my bed. Sutton's long body was draped in a hospital chair, his head resting against the wall, face up to the ceiling, his eyes closed, his arms crossed over his body. But that wasn't the best part. No, the best was that when I turned my head to the side, I could see Erik lying in the other hospital bed, his face relaxed in sleep. If he was here recovering, that meant he was alive, and someone had pulled some major strings to have us placed in a shared room.

With everyone I loved the most of all resting in the same room, I smiled and stared at his handsome face until I couldn't any longer and closed my eyes.

"*Elskede*," I heard murmured sometime in the middle of the night.

The sound of my love's voice had me coming to consciousness instantly. I snapped open my eyes and was greeted by the most amazing sight. Erik smiling, his eyes open.

"You're here," I whispered.

"I will never leave you." He sighed and then closed his eyes, his chest lifting and falling in a regular rhythm. I stared at that rhythm until I fell back asleep.

This went on for a couple days. Until finally, the medical team reduced my pain medication. They did not, however, do the same for Erik as he'd sustained a more serious injury. Still, the doctors assured us that we were on the mend and would eventually make full recoveries. That was all I needed to hear.

Sharing a room had been Duke Goodall and Henrik's idea. Apparently, they'd spoken to the hospital president and promised to make a hefty donation to the hospital if they did what they could to put us together. Since both of our surgeries had gone fantastically, and it wasn't necessary for either of us to be in the ICU, they'd allowed the pairing. The hospital thankfully wasn't at full capacity, making it a lot easier to maneuver such a request.

The next day, I was able to get up and around. My entire shoulder hurt to kingdom come, but I preferred to sit in the chair next to Erik's bed as he slept. Which is where I was resting when the sound of heavy boots clomped near our room. I glanced over just as Sheriff Hammond knocked on the door.

He smiled warmly at me. "May I come in?"

I'd known this part was coming, and I wasn't looking forward to it. No one had told me what became of Jarod after I'd learned he'd suffered a gunshot, and I didn't ask. Mostly because I didn't care. I wanted nothing to do with the man, and as soon as we could, Erik and I would be on his jet back to Norway, getting as far away from it all as possible.

I tapped on Erik's hand. His eyes opened, and he groaned but shook his head, coming to.

"We have company, honey." I gestured to the door.

Erik shifted with his good arm and pressed the button to raise the back of his hospital bed to a sitting position. When he was done, I took his hand and then focused on the Sheriff.

"What can we do for you, Sheriff?" I asked.

"Nuthin' much, ma'am. We already have several witness accounts of the events, not to mention my deputy, who provided his written statement. I just wanted to update you personally on things as they stand, seeing as both of you were targeted by Mr. Talley."

I winced hearing Jarod's last name. The man had been

someone I'd loved and thought I'd spend my life with. Knowing what type of person he hid, and hearing and seeing the things he'd done, I felt like a complete and utter fool.

"Did he survive his wounds?" Erik asked.

The Sheriff nodded. "Not without severe repercussions, though. Doctors are certain he'll be unable to walk ever again. The bullet affected his spine. Not to mention the likelihood of a lifetime sentence in prison."

"It's the least he deserves," Erik bit out.

"Yeah. He's being taken care of, and you don't have anything further to worry about," the Sheriff confirmed.

I tried to smile but couldn't find the energy. Instead, I just pressed my lips together and nodded.

"Also, you know your father accepted a deal with the DA. Well, he pled guilty in court yesterday, and the judge sentenced him to six years in prison, not five like we assumed. Turns out she didn't like how many offenses he had on his record prior to the attack on Dakota, so she added a year to his sentence. He signed over the land to your sister. Wanted you to know that it's all over. The reign of hell you and Dakota have suffered is history."

"Thank you for letting us know," Erik stated flatly.

"I'll leave you to it then." Sheriff Hammond gave a small nod and left our room.

"At least it's done," I whispered. "I can't wait to go home."

Erik's brows furrowed. "To the ranch?"

I jerked my head back and pouted. "No, to Norway."

That had him grinning wide, his eyes sparkling with happiness. "Me too, *elskede*. Me too."

"I heard that!" My sister snapped as she entered the room, Sutton hot on her heels.

She wore a pair of yoga pants, a tank, and an oversized men's flannel, the ends flopping past her hands. I smiled at seeing her sassiness for the first time in days. Most of our visits had been her calmly talking to me about anything and everything because I liked hearing her voice.

"How was the doctor's visit?" I asked, feeling a light airiness caress my heart and mind for the first time in many days. Things were finally looking up.

"Well, we know why I'm sick as the dickens," she growled and glared at her husband.

I glanced at Sutton, who was standing tall, the brightest and biggest smile on his face. He positively glowed with pride and joy.

"What's going on? Why are you so sick? Is the baby okay?" I asked.

Sutton nodded and grinned like a loon.

Dakota shook her head and crossed her arms, while she stared her husband down. "It's your fault!" she griped.

He chuckled. "If you say so. And it's *awesome*," he breathed as though nothing in the world could be better or funnier.

"Um, hello! Two healing people over here being left out of the punch line," I reminded them.

Erik gripped my hand as we waited.

Dakota turned back around, shoved a hand through her hair, and shifted the wild strands.

"What's wrong?" I stared to worry the longer she stared, spitting mad.

"The bastard knocked me up with twins!" she bitched, pointing at her stomach.

Sutton burst into laughter so hard he bent over, clutching his stomach.

"One surprise pregnancy wasn't enough," Dakota griped. "Oh no. Not for big man Sutton Goodall. He had to go and knock me up with not one, but *two* babies!"

My mouth fell open in shock. Erik squeezed my hand and chuckled.

"Two?" I whispered in awe.

Dakota nodded her head and tapped her foot. "Now what the hell am I going to do with two babies at one time! I can barely believe we're having one child."

"Baby…" Sutton cooed.

"Don't call me baby, you punk!" she snapped instantly. "You've already done enough in that department now, haven't you?" Then her face contorted into a mess of emotions and the waterworks started. "Savvy…" Her voice broke. "Two is going to be so hard."

I stood up, opened my good arm, and she slowly walked straight into my chest, her face tucking to my neck, her tears wetting my skin. I embraced her the best I could and leaned against Erik's bed for support.

"You're going to be fine. You have help," I reminded her.

"But you're leaving." She sobbed even harder, her small frame shaking and trembling.

"We'll be here when the babies come. Right, honey?" I glanced over my shoulder, planning to give Erik a silent nudge with my expression if needed.

"Absolutely. Whatever you desire," he agreed without me having to make any effort.

My goodness, how I'd come to love that man. Every minute seemed to add to our connection.

I held onto my sister, whispering platitudes to her the same way she'd done for me when I was at my worst over the years. She clung to me as she sniffled and calmed herself.

"It can't be Sutton's fault." Erik's brows pinched together. "I thought twins happened when the mother released two eggs or the mother's egg split into two after the fact, creating identical twins?" Erik asked unhelpfully.

Sutton slapped his knees, laughing his ass off even harder.

Dakota stiffened, slowly pulled back, and looked me dead in the face, tears still tracking down her cheeks. "You sure you want to marry that man?" she asked, wicked sarcasm flowing to the surface through her tears.

I grinned. "Yes. Yes, I do."

Sutton finally got a handle on his laughter and put his

hands to his wife's shoulders and turned her around. "It's going to be okay, darlin'. You've got me and my family, your sister and the Johansens. Our children will be loved and well taken care of."

"It's scary," she admitted and slumped against him, her cheek to his chest.

"Some of the best things in life are the scariest to wade through. But look at us, and your sister and Erik. We've all been through hell, and right now, all I see are clear skies and a bright future filled with love and family."

She pouted. "You're right. Ugh, I hate admitting that. Feels like sandpaper and gunk on my tongue." She smacked her chops with playful disgust.

I eased onto Erik's bed and slid my body along his good side, resting my head to his chest. "That will be us one day," I sighed happily.

He curled his arm around me. "I can't wait to see you pregnant with our child one day. All good things ahead of us, Savannah. All good things."

Episode 120

Let Them Eat Cake

FAITH

"Detective, I told you everything I know. I'm not sure what more you want me say." I sat cradling my broken, splinted wrist and finger while Joel held court in the seat next to me, unspeaking. His frustration was palpable. We wanted to be at The Alexandra to meet our girls when the helicopter brought them back from California, not sitting in a grimy Las Vegas police station.

"Go over it with me again," Detective Fink requested, his head down, scribbling details onto a notepad. He was an average-sized man who wore a mismatched suit, was clean shaven, and had kind eyes. He genuinely wanted to get to the bottom of what had happened, and I purposely wasn't providing all the details.

I'd learned the hard way the devil was always in the details. And between me, Joel, Diego, and Bruno, we'd come up with an acceptable version of events that would fit the timeline and take the investigation away from us, keeping it where it needed to be, on Aiden Bradford—may he never rest in peace.

"This is absurd and bordering on harassment. My wife gets kidnapped and beaten, and you're interrogating her as though she's the criminal and not the victim. It's untoward. We agreed in good faith to speak with the authorities without a lawyer present because we have nothing to hide. I'm beginning to believe we may need to call for legal counsel if you continue to barrage my wife with questions that lead nowhere. She's dealt with enough."

"I apologize, Mr. and Mrs. Castellanos. I mean no ill will, but a lot of people lost their lives at that airfield, and your wife seems to be one of the only people who made it out alive."

Faith sighed. "I told you. I got a text with an image of my sister being tortured. I provided you with that image and the text. I snuck out of the hotel and took a taxi to the meeting place, which was the drive-in."

"And how again did Joel know where you'd be?" he asked for what felt like the millionth time.

"I'm not an idiot. I knew Aiden was a criminal and planned to hurt me and my family if he didn't get what he wanted. My entire focus was on saving Grace. Since Joel knew I was constantly at risk, we had agreed I should have a tracking device attached to my phone. I knew the second Aiden got me in the car he'd take my phone and destroy it, which is what he did. I purposely removed the tracker beforehand and put it in my hair. That way when Joel figured out I was gone, he could find me. Which he did, out in the desert about three miles from the airport where I'd escaped."

"And how exactly did you escape again?" Fink queried.

I let out an irritated breath, repeating the same story I'd told ten times already. "After I got in the car at the drive-in, Aiden blindfolded me. We drove for a while. I was then tied to a chair in some type of metal room. He strangled me. He slapped me. He broke my finger. Then when he left me alone to tend to business or whatever nefarious shit he was into, I worked one of my wrists free. Upon his return, I attacked him with the chair I was tied to. That's when he overpowered me, sending the chair in one direction and me in the other. My wrist snapped." I held up my splinted arm and finger. The swelling needed to go down before I underwent surgery to repair it. That would be happening later. "I'd passed out from the pain. I had no idea there would be a full-on war happening in the airplane hangar."

"And who was battling it out?"

I shrugged. "A bunch of bad guys, I assume. Someone that Aiden must have pissed off. How am I supposed to know his evil dealings? Until Joel, I'd been off his radar. It wasn't until I came to Las Vegas to get married that he found me and started messing with my family, as you well know," I snapped. "He burned down my father's restaurant to get to me. He threatened Joel with hurting our family, which is why you received notice when I went missing and Joel got word about Aiden's guys planning to raid the resort. You wouldn't have any of those men in custody if it weren't for my husband going above and beyond to assist your investigation."

Joel scooted his chair closer to mine and put his arm around my shoulders protectively. He knew I was out of it, mentally fried, and emotionally strung out. I just wanted to see Grace, who Joel's team had found, the girls, and our parents. For now, I had to be okay with the fact that Grace was currently receiving private treatment from one of Joel's connections. Promptly after that, she'd admit herself to a detox and rehabilitation facility for a year. Something she'd agreed to. An expense we were happy to cover in the hopes it would give my sister a new beginning.

Diego had made it very clear he would be taking over Aiden's warehouse and everything that went with it. This was fine with Joel because he wanted no part of the illegal drugs or cash that I'd seen being managed inside it.

"And how did you escape again?" Detective Fink circled back.

Joel growled under his breath, making it known he'd hit his limit.

I sighed. "I'll tell you one more time, and then I need to see my girls. They're freaked out that their mother has gone missing, and you're keeping me from them. Which frankly, is really fuckin' uncool," I bit out.

"I'm sorry, Mrs. Castellanos. This is a massive situation. Dozens of men associated with Aiden Bradford are lying dead on an airfield. A few airport employees too. Not to mention that the airplane Mr. Bradford was on exploded over the desert."

"That has nothing to do with me!" I complained.

"If you would be so kind to give us a final rundown of your escape…" he reiterated.

"Fine," I hissed. "Aiden dragged me out of the car kicking and screaming, then tossed me by the foot of the airplane. Shots were firing everywhere. I was sure I was going to die. But I also realized after a couple minutes that I was alone. No one was focused on the kidnapped woman. I inched my way across the floor as shots were flying across the room. Men were hollering and yelling. I kept my head down and my focus on getting the hell out of there. When I got closer to one of the shelves, someone pulled me up from behind. I was sure it was Aiden, but it was some guy wearing a mask. I begged him to let me go. He nodded and led me to a door. He opened it, and I was free. That's when I ran straight into the night. I knew that if I could get to the fence line of the airport, I could find an exit, which is what I did. I didn't stop running until I saw headlights. Around that time is when I heard the airplane lift off and then suddenly the sky lit up like 4th of July, because the plane *exploded*. The car that stopped for me was Joel and his driver. That's all I know. Now I'm tired, I'm hungry. I'm scared out of my fucking mind!" My voice rose to an unhinged level.

Detective Fink lifted his hand in a gesture of supplication. "I got it all. Thank you for your time, Mrs. Castellanos. I'm thankful that you escaped such a harrowing experience."

Joel stood and helped me up. "If there isn't anything more, you know where we can be reached," he clipped.

"Thank you. If we have further questions, I'll call. Please don't leave town for the next few days just to be safe."

With that parting request, Joel led me out of the police station and into a waiting blacked-out SUV.

I snuggled instantly against Joel's side.

For several minutes, there was nothing said between us. The day's events—hell, the past week—had been out of control.

Joel kept me close and pressed his lips to my temple. "Rest, my love. We'll be home soon."

Eight weeks later...

It took another few weeks in Las Vegas before we made it home to Greece. In that time, I had surgery on my wrist and helped Grace get settled in her program. My finger had been set, and I was given a cast that not only went to the tips of my fingers but all the way up past my elbow to keep things stable. I had to wear it for seven weeks.

That time passed, and I just had it removed yesterday. The wrist and finger still felt weird without the added weight of the cast, but I was happy as could be to have it off.

"Mommy! Mimi-Mommy!" two little voices screeched with glee as they came running through the back door. Penny had taken straight to calling me Mommy the second I returned from Aiden. Eden still called me Mimi but had now added the

Mommy, so I was Mimi-Mommy. I figured over time the Mimi would fall away, and I'd just be Mommy to both my daughters.

I turned around to face the back door, where I'd been standing by the concrete divider that surrounded our home in Santorini and overlooked the magnificent sea. It was my absolutely favorite place to think.

The girls raced to my side, both hugging a leg and looking up at me with their peachy, joy-filled faces. "We have a surprise!" They vibrated with excitement as I saw a shadow shift over their bodies. I glanced up and lost my breath.

There stood my father, his arms spread wide. "*Cara mia,*" he breathed.

Tears filled my eyes. "Dad?" I gulped, shifting my girls before I dashed into his arms. "Dad!" I breathed, his familiar Old Spice scent invading my senses as I held him tightly.

"My Faith," he murmured against the crown of my head. "I missed you."

"I missed you too, Dad. You're here? You said you'd think about it but then...nothing. I thought maybe because of Grace..."

He shook his head. "No. You and Eden are where I need to be. Now that Grace is set up, I felt it was time for a big change."

I swallowed against the excitement threatening to crush me if he didn't say what I was hoping he'd say.

"Big change?" I tilted my head back and looked into the most familiar face I'd ever known. My beloved father's. My rock. My anchor to who I'd been before Aiden.

"I'm home, *carina.* Joel has helped me move to Santorini." He grinned huge.

"Really?" I squeaked, afraid to get too excited.

"Really, my love." Joel came up from behind my father, and I bolted out of my dad's embrace and plowed into my husband's.

"Baby, it's all I ever wanted..." I whispered against his

neck.

"I know." He hummed against my skin. "We have more news, come inside. Let's get a drink and celebrate Robert's move to Greece and the plans we discussed while you healed."

"You both are too much!" I hooked my elbow with my father's and my husband's as we made our way inside.

Olympia was already hard at work in the kitchen making drinks and putting together appetizers. I'd learned rather quickly she adored having guests. The woman was social to the extreme. If someone walked by outside and she knew them, she'd invite them in for a drink and a bite to eat. It was almost pathological niceness. Since I'd never had any friends, I enjoyed meeting and getting to know new people. Still, I was hesitant. Maybe a little post-traumatic stress from my time on the run.

I was dealing with my past with weekly therapy visits and late-night chats with Joel about what came before, and that was a positive change. Both counseling and Joel were helping me feel secure and safe in my new life. It didn't take away the myriad of nightmares I had, but once I woke, I would realize I was in bed with my husband, my girls were safe, I was safe, and Aiden was dead. It became almost a routine for Joel. Me waking up, freaking out, and him providing unending love and support. Usually I'd get up, check on the girls, and inspect the locks on the doors and windows—something he would walk with me to do so I wasn't scared. Last, we'd talk through the dream and lingering fear until either he made love to me or I fell asleep talking.

Overall, it was working. I was healing inside and out, one day at a time. I still had a long way to go, but I had hope and a future to look forward to. Having my father in Greece would be another massive thread woven into the larger whole of the patchwork that represented my healing.

"Okay, tell me everything!" I begged, taking one of the drinks Olympia handed me.

My father took one as well, but instead of simply saying

thank you, he smiled at Olympia, took a sip, and then gushed on and on about how good it was. How excellent she was in the kitchen. How he couldn't wait to taste more of her food.

I glanced at Joel, whose lips twitched knowingly.

Olympia's cheeks flushed a pretty pink, revealing how much she enjoyed my father's attention.

New goal. Matchmaker. Hook up my dad and Olympia.

Thoughts of this were running rampant through my mind until my father and Joel laid everything out about my father's move. Apparently, Joel had scouted a great location for a new startup. One that had been a restaurant before and already had a fully renovated kitchen. Unfortunately, one of the owners had a family member pass on, and they moved to another country. This meant they were ripe to sell the space right away. Which Joel, being Joel, decided to jump on. He'd called my father, told him the idea, and my dad asked him to pull the trigger on buying the space. My father then paid Joel back with the money the insurance company had paid out for his old place. And bonus, the new space had a one-room apartment above it, so he'd also have a place to live.

"You guys have been keeping this secret forever!" I grouched while smiling.

"We didn't want you to get your hopes up if it fell through, *carina*," my father said. "Now that it's real, I was thinking, I sure could use a partner. Someone to manage the day to day, help me get it set up, decorated, the bar choices. You know I'll have my hands full with the menu and the cooking…"

"I'd love nothing more…" I breathed, completely gobsmacked. A new adventure had just presented itself. One that would bring me joy and fill me with even more purpose. I could see us now. Father and daughter, running a family-owned business together. The girls could come learn right by the master in the kitchen. Grow up learning about the industry just as I had.

"Excellent, because we visit there tomorrow." My father

nodded, already in the business headspace.

I grinned as Joel stood. "Faith, may I speak with you privately for a moment?"

I got up and put my hand over my father's. "I'm so glad you're here, Dad. And I'm truly excited about this new opportunity to work by your side."

"Me too, *carina*, me too."

I followed Joel into our bedroom and waited while he closed the door. Instead of coming straight to me, he went to his nightstand and pulled out a small black box.

"Now that you are free from the dreaded cast, I have something for you," he announced.

My shoulders fell, and I frowned. I'd expected this to come at some point. I mean, we were married. Most people gloried in wearing a wedding ring. And Joel was absolutely the type of man who would want his wife to have a big sparkly ring that said to the world I was taken. I was that person too, only I missed *my ring*. The one Aiden had stolen from me when he broke my finger.

It had been special. It had been perfect. It had been mine.

It had represented Joel's undying love.

"Why the sad face?" My husband approached, his handsome face marred by an expression of concern.

"Because I know you're going to give me a ring and it will be spectacular, but it won't be *mine*, and I'm still brokenhearted over it. I want the one you slid on my finger on the most magical day of my entire life," I pouted, feeling stupid for admitting how upset I was over a material item.

He opened the box and presented me with its contents.

"You mean this one?" he smirked.

I stared in disbelief at *my ring* nestled within black velvet. "What? How? No way!" I reached for the precious vintage teardrop ring Joel had given me.

"Diego." He laughed out loud. "Our friend said he found the ring hidden in a drawer in the warehouse. He recognized it from our wedding. He gave it to me when you were undergoing surgery. I've held on to it in order to give it to you when the time was right. I think today, with your father making our home his home, is the perfect time."

He reached for my hand and slid the stunning ring on my finger. He then leaned down and kissed it where it sat.

My heart could have exploded from the overwhelming bliss detonating like little fireworks all through me.

"In sickness and in health. Forever and ever, Faith," Joel vowed low in his throat.

"I love you, Joel. I love our girls. I love our home. I love our life. Thank you. Thank you for doing exactly what you said you would do from the very beginning. You've given me the most beautiful life possible. I've never been happier." I allowed the tears to fall.

He kissed me then, slow and deep and for a very long time. So long we were bombarded by our daughters, who burst through our bedroom door. I swear those two together were tiny sticks of dynamite.

"*Yia-Yia* says we can have cake because we're celebrating!" Penny announced as though the edict had come down from the Pope himself.

"Cake, cake, cake!" Eden hollered, always seeming to be Penny's cheerleader in all things.

"What do you say? We check Eden's levels and then…cake?" I hugged my husband around the waist and kissed his neck.

"Absolutely!" He lifted my left hand, placed another kiss over my wedding ring, and nodded. "Life is good, and we have much to celebrate. Let them eat cake."

Episode 121

Never Again

OPAL

"I ruined everything." Noah slumped into the lone chair in the room I'd been staying in at the Oxshott estate. He rubbed his hands over his face with finality. "You married me for nothing."

You married me for nothing.

The statement wove its way through my heart and pierced it true, almost as if it was Cupid's own mighty arrow.

"Is that what you think? After what we shared?" I did not allow the frustration in my voice to soften. If he was going to downplay our wedding and subsequent intimacy as being ruined, I sure as hell was going to combat those thoughts and hope to high Heaven they weren't his true feelings. A lot of people said things they didn't mean when they were shoved up against a wall with no window for escape.

Noah opened his eyes and frowned. "You don't?"

I shook my head and went over to my husband, falling to my knees before him. I placed my hands on his thighs and stared patiently at him.

His expression crumbled before me as he clutched the

sides of my neck gently, bent over, and pressed his forehead to mine. "I don't deserve you."

My heart squeezed. "No, you don't, but you were doing a damn fine job of working toward that effort prior to us arriving here. Wouldn't you agree?"

He gave a half-hearted huff. "You married me. Let me make love to you..." His voice sounded pained.

"Multiple times, I might add." I reminded him of the beauty we'd had this past weekend.

"And I lost. You must be so disappointed in me. I'm bloody *furious* with myself," he grated with sharp bursts of air that fanned my face.

"What exactly did you lose? Ruby? More money that you don't need? More work devoted to the family business when your own holdings are far more successful?" I tried to express how much none of those things mattered now. We had each other, and I wasn't going to let him beat himself up for not winning some stupid competition he'd had with his twin.

He groaned and palmed my cheeks. "You deserve better, Opal. The best. And I'm not it."

"I made my choice, Noah," I reminded him. "I'm not going back on it."

"I wouldn't blame you if you did," he sighed, fully defeated.

I shifted out of our huddle and used his knees for leverage to stand. He instantly curled his hands around my hips as though he was loathe to let me go any farther. He needn't have worried, because I lifted a knee and put it to the side of his thigh, centered my weight, and did the same on the other side, straddling his lap. There I sat, my hands to his shoulders.

He looped his arms around me then stared into my eyes as though I held all the answers.

"I don't care that you didn't win governing interest in your family's business. I don't care that you lost a bet to your brother. What I do care about is you watering down all that occurred between us this weekend. Do you want to get our marriage annulled as your brother suggested?"

His expression was stricken while his eyes widened in shock. Noah gripped my hips possessively as if on instinct.

"Fuck no!" he barked, disgust coating his tone. "You are the *only* thing that is worth anything in my life right now. You, poppet, are what I fear losing. Having your husband fail you so miserably…" He choked back his emotions and swallowed as though attempting and failing to get his bearings. "Hurting your relationship with your sister. Everything went to Hell. Nothing happened as I planned, and I…"

I placed my fingers over his lips to quiet him. "None of it matters. You and I have our deal. We have what we have, and I'm committed to that. I want it. I want you."

"Even now?" His voice was low and hopeful.

I smiled softly. "Even now. I want Sunday mornings in bed with you teaching me everything there is to know about intimacy and passion. I want wild adventures. Fancy dinners out where I have to wear one of the ridiculously expensive dresses Liza has chosen for me. I want to go to school while you go to work and us both have someone we care about to come home to. I want to be your plus one at charity events and your club grand openings. I want to travel the world with you. Is it love?" I shrugged. "Maybe it could be. It feels like a start. An incredible one, and I'm not ready to give that up because you didn't win some asinine bet you made with your twin."

He pressed his face directly between my breasts. "Are you sure it isn't love?" he murmured against my chest.

I chuckled as I ran my fingers through his hair. "Perhaps one day, but it doesn't have to be right now. There's no rush. What we've shared is better than anything I've ever had in my entire life. I'm happy moving forward as planned. Excited, even."

He groaned against my chest and snuffled around until he found the globe of one of my breasts. He placed a warm, loving kiss there. My nipples stiffened as they seemed to do when Noah was being playfully sexy. I encouraged his head up with a tap to his jaw.

Eyes the color of hot chocolate on a cold day peered up at me. His emotions were all over the place. I could see he was fully wallowing in self-pity.

"You need to speak to your brother while I apologize to my sister," I suggested.

He snarled. "Apologize? What for? You didn't do anything wrong."

"That's not why I'm apologizing. Ruby and me, we have a pact. One that cannot be broken by man or time. Before you and Nile, it had only ever been us. I haven't begun to scratch the surface of sharing the sacrifices my sister has made for me in the past, nor have I given you much of my upbringing. That will come naturally between husband and wife. But none of it changes the fact that I owe Ruby an explanation at the very least and an apology for not discussing my plans with her. She's done nothing but live for me since I was born. I know if the situations were reversed, I'd be brokenhearted and feel adrift."

"She did the same bloody thing to you!" he clapped back.

I shook my head. "Not exactly. I always knew she was marrying Nile. She made it very clear she was falling for him and excited about marrying him. They just did it a week early in a private ceremony that was just for them. Was it a surprise? Sure. But it wasn't because they were trying to put one over on us, like we did. You heard Nile's response. He won the love of his life. When they came in, he was carrying her over the threshold of his home. They were beaming with love and happiness."

"And we weren't?" he griped.

I pressed my lips together and tried not to smile at his churlish behavior. "We're in the first phases of lust and passion. They are *in love*. Real love. The kind that spans far more than a three-year contract. I can see it in every freckle on my sister's face. In the way she looks at him as though the sky might fall if he weren't there to hold it up for her. Even their body language. How she leans into Nile. How they touch constantly."

"I want to touch you constantly," he murmured, his fingers tightening their grip on my hips.

That made me chuckle. "And I adore that you do because I'm all about it. Still, that doesn't change what we did. I could have talked to Ruby about the plan and given her the choice. That's what I should have done from the very beginning, but it's not what happened. And I wouldn't change it." I ran my fingers through his silky hair. "Though I am sad it upset her, I'm not sorry I married you. I'm sorry about the way I hid it from her. That's not who we are to one another, and I need to cop to the choices I made."

"Do you think you'll be able to work through it?" he asked, legitimate concern making his voice seem strained.

I cupped his clean-shaven jaw. "Absolutely. Ruby loves me down to her cellular makeup. She'd never forsake me. Not ever. It's the one true thing I have in life. Ruby's love."

"And me. You have me, Opal." His gaze locked to mine. "You have me," he repeated it, sounding more like a vow than a statement.

"For the next three years, you're damn right, I do." I grinned.

"And maybe more?" he asked almost shyly, his eyebrows rising with the question.

I shrugged. "Only time will tell."

"True," he sighed.

"You ready to make amends?" I asked, tracing his bottom lip with my thumb.

He nodded. "With you by my side, I can handle just about anything. Even my pompous, tight-assed, stick-in-the-mud brother."

I laughed as I removed myself from his lap and held out my hand. "I don't think you should start your brotherly chat by calling him names."

Noah hooked his arm around my shoulders and brought me close. "No, you're probably right. My wife, the smart one." He chuckled, and hearing that sound helped relax me. He was coming around. We'd fix the rift between all of us.

I nudged his rib with a pointed finger. "Don't you forget it, buster."

"Oh, I won't," he teased, almost back to his jovial self as we exited the bedroom and headed for the living room.

Nile was sitting in a lounge chair, a tumbler filled with an amber liquid dangling from his fingers. Ruby was not by his side. He was looking out the window at the dreary day as though in contemplation. A man who might very well have felt the weight of the entire Pennington name on his shoulders. What he needed to realize was he had Noah. He didn't need to handle everything himself.

He had family.

People who cared.

And that family had doubled by adding Ruby and me to the mix. Ideally, that should have meant more arms to carry the burden. Though I suspected, like Ruby, Nile was used to carrying the brunt of the family's needs, or in his case, their vast fortune and reputation. It would take more than platitudes to get him to see we could be one big team.

Noah cleared his throat, gathering Nile's attention.

Nile's jaw clenched, his lips flattening into a grim line.

"Are you ready to talk? Hear my side of things?" Noah stated with such confidence and grace, I wanted to kiss him.

Since our public display of affection was what started this fiasco, I refrained.

Nile stretched a hand out to the chair opposite him, his expression flat, giving nothing away.

Just as Noah was about to take a seat, the governess entered the room. "Ms. Dawson, you have a call from a Deputy Higgins. He claims it's urgent."

I frowned and glanced at Noah. "You two talk. I'll be back."

"You sure? I can come with you…" Noah offered, and it made my heart swell with affection.

"I'm okay. Don't worry. Make amends with your brother." I shooed him away and followed the governess to a phone located in what I could only call a study, though it had more feminine touches than the entire estate did.

"Just pick up the phone and press the glowing button and you'll be connected. Take your time, dear." Ms. Bancroft gestured to the desk.

When I sat down in the chair, the sight that greeted me was an array of picture frames. Each one included a moment in time of both Noah and Nile. One was of two widely grinning children of only a few years old. Another of them both with gangly preteen limbs clad in what looked like soccer outfits or *football*, as they called it here in England. A picture of what must have been the twins with their parents. And one last image was of the two of them, the governess standing between them. All three of them were in cocktail attire. A shy smile I'd never seen adorned her lips. Noah grinning wide, his natural boyishness coming through the photo, whereas Nile had a slight smile, showing he did have a softer side but didn't like showing it.

I smiled and then realized I'd been sitting staring at the photos and not taking the call. I hurriedly picked up the receiver and pressed the button.

"Um, hello, this is Ms. Dawson." *Technically*, I thought to myself. Though I hoped to change it immediately. I wanted nothing more than to get rid of my mother's last name. Since she didn't know who our fathers were, both Ruby and I had been given her last name. One I planned to replace with Pennington soon.

"Ms. Dawson, this is Deputy Higgins of Glory Springs Police Department. You may remember me?" An image of the man who'd interviewed me flashed before my eyes as he continued. "I'm calling regarding your case against a Ms. Clarissa Dawson."

"My mother, yes." I compressed my lips together, wishing I could just put all of this behind me and move on with my life once and for all.

"Well, Ms. Dawson, I'm happy to say we found her. She's in county lockup and off the streets."

Unbelievable joy raced through my entire body, forcing gooseflesh to rise along my skin. "Really?" My voice shook as I swallowed against the sudden dryness in my throat.

"Yes, ma'am," he confirmed. "And she'll be going away for a long time. Not only did she commit crimes against you, but she was also caught in an attempted convenience store burglary. We've got her on camera shooting at the clerk. That's another count of attempted manslaughter. Thankfully, the kid ducked, or she'd have taken away a kind, sixteen-year-old high school track star with a straight-A average and his sights set on college. Add those charges to yours, and she'll likely be doing life in prison. Best-case scenario for her is twenty years per attempt. That's forty years total for you and the kid, not to mention the two burglaries, which will add a good five to ten on top of that."

Forty years plus five to ten. My mother was forty-two now. Had both me and Ruby very young. That meant she'd be upwards of eighty to ninety years old upon her release. If she lived that long.

"So it's done. She's not going to be able to hurt me or my sister ever again," I breathed, my heart pounding so hard I had to cover it with my hand.

"Depends on what she pleads. If she pleads guilty on all counts, she may get a little leeway. She didn't kill anyone, but that would just mean she'd maybe get a bit shorter sentence, or the possibility of an earlier parole for good behavior. We won't know until things progress, but I'll be sure to keep you informed."

"Thank you, Deputy Higgins. I—I appreciate your call and your candor."

"Take care of yourself, Ms. Dawson. We'll be in touch."

"Yes, of course. Thank you." I hung up the phone and sat there in complete awe for all of three seconds. Until my entire soul exploded with energy, and I got up and raced out of the study, past the two men who were deep in conversation, up the stairs, and headed in the direction of my sister.

"Ruby!" I screeched so loudly the volume hurt my ears. I didn't care. "Ruby!" I cried out while opening every door on the other side of the estate trying to find my sister. I had no idea which room was theirs.

"Bloody hell, Opal!" Noah arrived next to me out of nowhere, bent over, breathing frantically as he'd apparently run to catch up. "What the fuck happened?" His eyes were pleading and scared.

I looked him straight in the face and screamed my sister's name at the top of my lungs. "Ruby!"

A door flung open from farther down the hall. Out came my sister wearing a neon yellow tank and a pair of bright pink booty shorts. Her hair a wild mess from sleep.

She plowed into me, her arms wrapping around me fully. "What's wrong? Are you okay?" She started to run her hands down my face and arms until she realized I wasn't hurt. "Opal, you're scaring the bejesus out of me," she exclaimed.

"Life…" I whispered.

"Life?" she asked desperately, her gaze a mask of confusion. "I don't understand."

"She's going away for life." The tears filled my eyes so fast I could only see a blurry form that semi-looked like my sister's shape.

"Who is? Dammit, Opal! Speak to me." Her demand broke me out of the shocked haze.

"Mom," I whispered.

"Mom's going away for life?" she asked while a pair of warm, large hands cupped my shoulders giving me additional support. *Noah.*

I nodded. "The authorities called. They have her in custody. She tried to shoot a teenager while robbing a convenience store," I croaked, just now realizing that my mother had almost killed a kid. Bile rose from my empty stomach, burning my throat as I breathed through the discomfort.

Ruby covered her mouth as Nile appeared behind his wife. His arm sliding around her belly where he pressed her back to his front.

"She's going to prison for life?" Ruby reiterated as if she needed to hear it again in order to believe it.

I smiled widely as the tears fell. My soul sighing in relief. And that's what it was. Bone-deep relief and gratitude that it was finally over. Our mother's reign of terror couldn't hurt us or anyone else, not ever again.

"It's done," I murmured in awe. "She can never hurt us again."

Ruby slid out of her husband's arms and pulled me into her embrace. I hugged her so hard I didn't know where she began and I ended. We were both sobbing balls of emotions as we clung to one another.

"I'm sorry I hurt you," I cried harder.

"I'm sorry you felt you couldn't come to me," she returned.

I trembled in her arms. "No, it's my fault. I should have told you. I love you so much I just wanted to be the *one*. I wanted to be the one who saved you. Saved us."

Ruby pulled back and cupped my cheeks, wiping my tears with her thumbs.

"Don't you see?" She shook her head. "All these years, you did save me. Without you, I had nothing to live for. Every day, you were there for me, showing me unconditional love. It kept me from ending it all. *You kept me alive, Opal.* I'm here because you *loved* me more than I *hated* her and what she allowed those men to do to me. I wanted to end it all so many times, but I could never leave you. Not ever." Her bottom lip quivered as she stared into my eyes, making me see the truth in her words.

"I love you, Ruby. And I'm happy you found love in Nile. I want you to have everything you ever dreamed of."

Ruby smiled wide and brought me into another bone-crushing hug. "And I want the same for you."

We hugged and dried our tears, wiping at the streaks along our cheeks.

It was all over.

"She can never hurt us again," Ruby said with finality.

"Never again."

Episode 122

A Pennington Affair

RUBY

"How do I look?" I faced the governess as I exited the master bathroom in my wedding gown. She didn't need to know it was technically the second time I'd worn it, but it still gave me a thrill knowing that Nile and I had gotten married privately. A secret shared by two.

Just for us.

Not for my sister, his brother, the silly inheritance rule, the people in his societal circles, or even the governess.

Nile and I had married for love.

The memory made my heart pitter-patter as I faced the governess.

"You look like a proper British bride," she answered while she approached with the veil. I hadn't worn it to my real ceremony, and I didn't want to wear it at this one. I glanced at the veil sourly and pressed my hand against the perfect updo the hairstylist had magically crafted.

The governess tilted her head. "No veil?" she asked as though I actually had a choice.

"I'd prefer it without." I lifted my chin and stood as straight as I could muster against her scrutiny.

I'd learned Eudora Bancroft appreciated manners, grit, stoicism, loyalty, and strength above all things. If I was to get my way, I'd need to stand strong.

Her lips twitched. "An excellent decision, my dear, as I have something far better to offer," she mused. I waited patiently as she went to the bed, where she'd placed a black velvet box about the size of a square dinner plate. She grabbed it then stood directly before me, holding it aloft in her arms.

"Well, go on. Open it. Don't be shy." Her tone was direct but tinged with anticipation.

I reached out as if the box had a coiled snake hiding within it.

She chuckled under her breath, something I found shocking as she rarely showed amusement.

I lifted the small latch and gasped at what was inside.

A diamond tiara.

My mouth fell open as I stared at the sparkling and twinkling jewels. It was a complex swirling design of white gold or platinum in the subtle shape of leaves with teardrop-shaped diamonds sprinkled throughout. At the tallest point in the center, two wavelike swirls curved out and then in, and a large aquamarine teardrop gem sat perfectly between them. It was magnificent and unlike anything I'd seen before.

"This was worn by my best friend, Nicola, on the day she married her soulmate, James Pennington. He purchased it for her as a wedding present. Instead of wearing the veil that had been handcrafted for her nuptials, she wore this with pride." She smiled.

I reached out and traced the line of the tiara, watching the light cast rainbows in every direction.

"Nicola loved to combat societal norms and pave her own path. I see that personality trait in you, my dear, but you hide it often. Always wanting to do what's expected or best for everyone else. That too is a wonderful trait. However, remember that no matter who claims to have your best interest at heart, you always have freedom of choice. Even from a stodgy, formal, British mum or *governess,* as my boys like to call me."

I grinned. "You know that Nile loves you beyond all others. My being with him will never take that away." I wanted her to know that I had no intention of coming between her and Nile.

Ms. Bancroft reached within the velvet box and removed the tiara, setting the box on the bed before she turned back to me. She lifted the tiara and placed it lightly on my head.

"I know my place in my boys' hearts, but I also know there is room enough within them to love a woman of their own choosing and the children who may come from that union. That's all I've ever wished for them." She adjusted the tiara, weaving the ends into my hairstyle so that the sides didn't show, only the jeweled front.

For a couple minutes, I allowed the governess to fiddle with my hair. This was something that my own mother should have been doing on my behalf, but that wasn't my life. Since I'd arrived in England, Ms. Bancroft had been more attentive to me and my needs than anyone outside of Madam Alana and my sister. She'd shown me the path of a Pennington woman and what was expected. She might have been icy in her teachings, but she had never been cruel. Had never called me names or made me feel stupid. She'd provided me with the tools and lessons I would need to succeed in this life with a man of Nile's stature and reputation. I didn't want to be an embarrassment, especially to the man I loved. The governess had made sure I would fit in. Well, to the best of her ability, anyway.

The rest was on me.

As she finished and went to move away, I grabbed her hands with both of mine.

"Thank you, Ms. Bancroft. Thank you for sharing your

knowledge. Being patient with me. Taking the time to educate me on your world. I feel better prepared to be the Mrs. Pennington people will expect..." I glanced away. "Even with my sordid history."

She patted my hand. "I've taken care of that, as you know." And she had.

Pennington to Wed a Stripper was old news. The newspaper now reported on how Nile was basically a modern-day prince who'd saved Cinderella, aka *me,* the stripper, from my wicked mother and handed me a new life. The story wasn't altogether untrue, but it wasn't factual either. I couldn't have cared less. As long as Nile's reputation was solid, I'd go along with any story they wanted to tell. And apparently, the press had eaten up that spin, and we became the little darlings of England's rich and famous. The story was doubly successful when it came out that Noah had married Opal, my sister. Twin brothers marrying sisters... The paparazzi had been enchanted.

I squeezed Ms. Bancroft's hand. "I'll be a good wife to him," I vowed as her steely gaze met mine.

"I have no doubt," she admitted, which was probably the nicest thing she'd said to me to date.

Shockingly, she pulled me into her arms for a quick embrace. She patted my back stiffly. "You're a beautiful bride, Ruby, and I believe you will make my Nile happy. I wish you endless years together."

While I was hugging the governess, Opal entered with the champagne I'd asked her to pilfer a half hour ago. Her lipstick was smudged, and her hair looked ruffled.

"Whoa. Call the press! It's a miracle!" Opal teased.

The governess pulled away, narrowed her teary eyes, and glared at my sister.

Opal waved flippantly. "Oh, relax. Your secret soft side is safe with me. I won't tell anyone."

"Be sure that you don't," she huffed. "I'll leave you to it. I'm going to check on my boys. Do not be late. A Pennington arrives exactly on time," she warned.

I rolled my eyes. "Yes, Ms. Bancroft," I said primly, the same way children did to their teacher in elementary school.

When she left, Opal dashed over to me. "Holy shit, Ruby! That tiara is *everything*," she exclaimed.

I smiled hugely, turned around, and looked at myself in the mirror. "It's pretty fabulous. It was a gift from Nile's father, James, to his mother, Nicola, on their wedding day. I'll make sure to protect it and keep it safe for our children one day."

Opal jerked her head. "Children? Wow. You have definitely changed."

I shrugged. "The love of a good man will do that for you, I guess. And I see you must have taken a detour with the champagne." I tapped the corner of my mouth, referencing her smudged lips.

"Whatever do you mean?" she asked coyly, grabbing my tube of lipstick and adjusting hers in the mirror. The wicked grin she had plastered to her face was admission enough.

"Mmm-hmm. The smudged lipstick and messy hair gave it away. Making out with your husband while running errands." I tsked.

Opal snorted. "I can't keep my hands off him," she gushed happily, sounding her age for once. "It's like Noah opened up this carnal side to me, and I just want to experience it all."

"So he's been good to you, um, in the bedroom?" I thought back to the Eyes Wide Open club and the kinky things they did there. A club he owned and attended, as far as I knew. And Opal was new to personal sexual experiences. I knew for a fact that when she'd arrived, she was still a virgin. I also knew by the new confidence she presented lately that the virgin ship had sailed.

She nodded. "Ruby, he's been super patient and gentle with me. And not so gentle when warranted," she snickered playfully. "Um, how about you, though? I know sex and intimacy have been hard for you since, well, our past."

My breath caught as I let the familiar pain of my past roll through me and then out like an ocean wave. It couldn't hurt me here, while in this beautiful dress, wearing a tiara befitting a princess. To these people, to my Nile, I was worthy of all this and more. He'd made me see my value, and I was working toward believing it with each new day.

"I'm happy for you, Opal. You deserve a man who will take his time. Let you unfold like the flower you are." I smiled softly. "And Nile is better than I ever expected or ever dared to wish for in bed, and in the day-to-day stuff."

"Really? He seems kind but also so serious," Opal said while busying herself pouring champagne for us.

"He is serious. Direct. And very straightforward. I appreciate it so much." I fiddled with my hair, making sure the tiara stayed. "The best part of his personality is that I always know exactly where I stand with him. I never have to guess what he's thinking or feeling. It's such a relief. He simply loves me for me."

"You both seem genuinely happy. That's all I ever wanted for you, Ruby-Roo."

"We both deserve it, and we both have it." I took the glass and lifted it between us. She copied my gesture. "May the Dawson sisters live happily ever after."

"I think you mean…may the *Pennington* sisters live happily ever after." She winked.

We both laughed, clinked our glasses, and drank the bubbly golden liquid.

Our futures had never looked brighter.

NILE

My brother stood at my side while I watched Opal walk down the aisle.

"Bloody hell, my wife is a stunner," Noah gloated.

He wasn't wrong. Opal was a genuine beauty with her dark hair, tawny skin, and doe eyes. She had a gentle, elegant innocence about her that I knew called to my brother's wild side. The past week had proven to both Ruby and me that they were in fact rather good for one another. They enjoyed one another's company tremendously and doubly enjoyed bickering about the smallest things.

My Ruby was the opposite. She was calm, patient, and introspective, much like me. When she wanted to be with me, she made it known through her body language and desire to share space. Often during the week, she'd wander into my studio with a book or a journal. Recently, we'd booked her a therapist to discuss her past and the things that had led up to this point in her life. That therapist encouraged her to journal her thoughts. More often than not, those thoughts would lead her to me. Searching out the security I gave her by merely existing as she wrote down her feelings and experiences.

The process had been cathartic for us both. I had no idea that simply having Ruby in my workspace would allow me to unlock another creative cavern within myself I didn't know existed. The ideas came and went so rapidly I was barely keeping up with the motivation and drive burning at my fingertips each day. So much so that I was currently composing a piece that I truly felt was my life's best work. A piece I planned to dedicate to my wife and our love. Something I wouldn't give away to the world. It would be hers...ours.

My wedding gift to her.

I was musing about the best time to share it with my Ruby when the music changed, announcing the bride. The sound filtered through the speakers into the garden, where the governess had set up the festivities. There were big tents keeping the lushly decorated tables dry in case of unexpected rain as could happen at any time in England. Though the sky currently was a pristine blue without a cloud in sight. But that wasn't what stole my attention.

That was all Ruby.

Standing at the end of the satin-covered white aisle, looking as magnificent as she had the day we'd done this very thing in private, was my Ruby. Though there was one thing different about my beautiful wife, and that was the sparkling tiara that adorned her head. My heart stopped, and my throat dried as I realized what she was wearing.

Mum's tiara.

My mother's prized possession sat atop my wife's head just like it had thirty years ago on my mother's when she wed my father.

My gaze slid to the governess. Her lips were set in a clever, barely there smile.

I mouthed, "Thank you."

As cool as ever, she dipped her chin once, then focused on the bride.

Not long after my parents passed, the governess had placed that tiara in a glass case in our library. It had sat there on display ever since. Always visible. Keeping their memory alive for us all.

And there it was, on my wife's head as she walked down an aisle to marry me for the second time, wearing something my mother would have loved sharing on this day.

Noah gasped and put his hand to my shoulder, emotion flooding through our connection at the sight.

"Mum's tiara..." he breathed, squeezing my shoulder in support. "She'd be honored, brother mine."

I cleared my throat and wiped my cheek, finding it wet from the single tear I'd shed while my mother's love sat atop my heart as I watched my bride approach. Mum would have been thrilled with my choice. Ruby was everything I never knew

I needed but no longer wanted to live without.

I broke the rules and stepped down from the riser, meeting my bride halfway and escorting her at my side, where she should always be. Ruby didn't mind, simply pressing closer, her head to my shoulder as if today were any other.

Then we stood shoulder to shoulder as we declared our love and commitment for the second time.

When the ceremony was over and we'd had our dance, shared cake, and carried on with all the pomp and circumstance the governess had planned, I invited my brother and his wife to a small table in the corner.

There was an important matter that could wait no longer.

As requested, Opal and Noah took their seats. I held out another for my wife and waited while she sat before taking the seat next to her.

I quietly reached for the unopened bottle of champagne on the table and uncorked it. While I poured each of us a glass, Noah eased back in his chair, his wife clinging to his side rather drunkenly. Ruby was no better off. Her hands kept straying to my thighs, my chest, whatever she could touch and tease. Turned out the Dawson sisters were handsy when they had a few drinks. Much to both Noah's and my delight.

I lifted my chin, gaining the attention of our family lawyer, who had been waiting for my signal. Landry nodded, excused himself from his table, and approached.

"What's going on?" Noah asked after having caught the exchange. "You asked us over for a private family discussion and now our lawyer is to be present?"

I smirked as my wife played with my fingers, not paying attention to anything in her boozy, joyful haze. I couldn't wait to get her away and on to our official honeymoon. I wanted bikini-clad Ruby and an ocean, and nothing else for at least two solid weeks. We needed the time alone to not only be together but to learn more about one another, have fun, make memories. But I couldn't leave with such a heavy weight clinging to my subconscious like an unwanted anchor.

"Everything is amended as requested, Nile," Landry interrupted. "And congratulations again...to you both," our attorney said to me and then gestured to Noah and Opal.

"Thank you, Landry. I've got this covered. Please enjoy yourself," I said politely, expressing my desire for him to leave without having to say it outright.

"What's this about?" Opal asked, sipping the champagne before we could toast officially.

Noah looked at his wife with warm affection before scrutinizing me.

"I've made a decision about our family investments," I announced, reaching for two of the glasses. I handed one to Noah and one to my wife. I took the last one and held it before me but did not drink. "Noah, we made a silly and harmful bet between us. Something I believe we both learned a very strong lesson from."

Noah nodded, his expression wary. He needn't have been. I was ending the asinine situation between us once and for all.

"There was some fine print on the contract that neither of us realized. When we had our debacle last week..."

"You mean when you punched me in the face for kissing my wife," Noah goaded playfully, not even a single hint of ire within his tone.

"Mmm, yes. We've made our apologizes and have come to a healthy and rather happy place with our wives, would you not agree?" I asked.

"Things absolutely worked out as they were supposed to," Noah confirmed while wrapping his arm around Opal and bringing her closer to his side.

"With our renewed faith in one another and our better halves at our sides, I thought it prudent to review the contract grandfather left one more time. As I stated, we didn't read the fine print. There was a clause mixed in with the legalese that stated if both parties were willing to share *equal* interest, the initial terms of marriage could be terminated. Meaning, if the two of us agreed to forfeit the additional percentage and instead, govern together fifty-fifty, we would both take ownership immediately."

Noah burst into laughter. "You're bloody kidding!"

Opal's mouth fell open as Ruby leaned over and snuggled against my neck. "Basically, you've both been jerks to one another, and you didn't even need to." She snort-laughed.

I chuckled. "Too right, my love."

"So what you're saying is that you've had these documents amended by our lawyer so that we own equal shares in the family holdings?" Noah pressed.

I leaned back and nodded. "Our family investments should stay equally in the family, wouldn't you agree?"

Noah picked up a napkin on the table and tossed it at me. "Yes, I agree, you dodgy fucker! Always the knight who comes to save the day." He shook his head while smiling.

I reached into my pocket and pulled out the key to my brother's prized Ferrari. He was like a magpie to a shiny object, practically salivating at the sight.

"I may have saved the day…" I wrapped my fist around his keys with a flourish. "But I'm keeping the car." I grinned wickedly, stood, and tugged my wife's hand. "Come, Mrs. Pennington. Let's dance."

"You right bastard!" My brother laughed as I pocketed the keys once more and pulled Ruby into my embrace.

Now that we'd settled any bad blood with our siblings, it was time we enjoyed our second wedding.

Episode 123

What Real Life Looks Like

SUTTON

Three months later...

The light in the den was still on when I entered the house after an intense day helping one of our heifers give birth. The mama had been struggling somethin' fierce, so we ended up having to put her in the calving pen to help the delivery process. It happened more often with first-timers than we liked, but in the end we had a healthy baby calf and a tuckered-out but alive mama.

Overall, a good day.

Seeing that light on in the den meant Dakota was burning the midnight oil. Something she did a lot. Especially when she had bad dreams. Those were the worst. Seeing as I'd left her asleep in bed when I got the call to help with the cow, I didn't expect her to be up. Maybe hoped was more like it.

I stripped down to my skivvies in the mudroom as my boots, jeans, and shirt were filthy. I tossed both into the washing machine along with the load of colored clothing that needed washing and sent that sucker spinning. There was a pair of plaid pajama pants folded on top of the dryer, as though she'd known I'd need something to change into when I got back.

I made my way through our home headed for her office. Dakota's head was down, a finger on a page running through numbers. She said doing the inventory calmed her. I would have called bullshit on that particular activity if it didn't actually work. On those nights when the babies were making it hard for her to sleep, or she had massive heartburn or was plagued by one of her nightmares, I could always find her down here working on something mundane.

My wife had an unbeatable work ethic. The headway she'd already made on the McAllister side of things was phenomenal. Within the next year or so, she'd have the ranch running as well as any of our fully profitable locations.

As I approached, her head lifted, and the sweetest smile spread across her lips. I gloried in that look. The gentle affection it provided. It was a look I'd only ever seen her give me. It was mine, and I adored it.

"Hey, how did it go?" she asked, a teeny worry line appearing between her brows.

"Good. Baby and Mama are safe and sound. We had to use the chute, but I'm sure her next calving experience will be easier."

She nodded and then focused back on her work.

"You couldn't sleep?" I asked, leaning against the desk.

She shook her head. "Something was nagging me. Turned out the new manager ordered the wrong amount of feed for next cycle, and it was throwing off my numbers."

"Ah. But of course you figured it out."

Dakota sighed and rubbed at her temples. "I shouldn't have to. She should know better." She sighed.

Since it was her legacy, I'd wanted Dakota to be able to run her ranch however felt right. So we'd found a person who'd come highly recommended to be the new ranch manager. The woman had barely begun to work with Dakota, and already my wife was finding reasons to be mad.

"It's an honest mistake and easily fixable. Right?"

She narrowed her gaze. "Remember who you sleep next to and whose side you are supposed to be on," Dakota grumbled.

I chuckled and took her hand. "Come on. I've got something I want to show you."

She begrudgingly stood, her bump half-showing from the small tank top that was threatening to rip at the seams. Dakota hated shopping. A fascinating fact. She'd rather stretch all her normal-sized clothing to fit the melon-sized bump she was sporting than buy clothing that fit. At first, I thought it was hilarious and rather cute. Now I could see the woman needed maternity clothing desperately. But to her it was a want, not a need. What Dakota thought she needed was work, food, and sex. Since we were leaving for Norway tomorrow to attend Savannah and Erik's rescheduled wedding, I'd get my ma and Erik's mother on the case. At least the twins hadn't changed our sex life. We were as adventurous and spontaneous as ever. Just that morning, I'd bent her over the table in the tack room until we both were fulfilled.

I nudged her around the desk, turned off the light as we left the room, and led her up the stairs. Instead of turning right at the top where our room was, we went to the left.

"Ugh, don't bring me into the empty nursery. I'm not ready to deal with the fact that I have nothing prepared. I promise, honey, I'll get on it when things are more settled with the ranch." This was a phrase I'd heard ad nauseum over the past few weeks.

I massaged her tense shoulders as we shuffled forward. "This isn't all on you. I'm the father, remember," I teased. "Besides, I got something for them."

That had her stopping in front of the door and turning around to face me. "You bought something for the girls?" her voice rose with a hint of mushy and sappy tacked on.

"Baby, you've been so busy with the McAllister ranch I wanted to take a little pressure off. So me and Ma…" I rubbed at the back of my neck, feeling the tension creep up as uncertainty for what I'd done filled my mind.

What if she hated it?

Her eyebrows rose. "You and Linda did what?" She crossed her arms over her chest defensively.

One thing about my wife—she liked doing things herself. To her exact decree too. But the woman needed help.

I reached for her arms and forced her to unfold them. I played with her fingers, then brought them to my lips, where I kissed them. "You've been so busy, and I thought since these are also my children, I'd get a jump on the nursery."

Her mouth dropped open, and that special "just for Sutton smile" made a second appearance. "If there are two cribs fully put together in there, I am going to fall to my knees and suck you off so good you will see stars," she vowed on a weighty breath.

I burst into laughter but also started to get hard at the visual.

"Open the door, Dakota." I lifted my chin toward it.

She sucked her bottom lip between her teeth. "Okay. Just sayin'… Good things come to those who buy cribs…"

I held my breath as she opened the door.

Dakota entered and gasped, her hands going to her mouth as she slowly spun in a circle, taking it all in.

I'd painted the walls a pale, soothing lavender. My mother had found eyelet lace curtains for the windows, and we'd hung those along with blinds. Against the far wall were two matching white wooden cribs. Inside were quilts handmade by my mother that had dancing sheep on them. Above each crib were wooden letters that Savannah, Erik, Irene, and Henrik had painted and sent as a gift for the twins.

The first crib had *Scarlett* in a rainbow shape over it. The second crib had *Daisy*.

These were the names we'd chosen for our girls. S and D just like us. One would be named Scarlett Savannah after her sister. And the second, Daisy Amberlynn after her great-grandmother who'd started it all. If we ever had a boy, I was going to want Duke in the name. Full stop. She'd agreed as long as if we had girls, she'd get to recognize the women in her family. Honestly, I was surprised she didn't want to use Carol, after her mother, but there were still some hard feelings and emotions she was working through when it came to her mother, and I was A-okay with that.

In the corner was a plush rocking chair my brother, Junior, and sister, Bonnie, had gone in on and secretly delivered while Dakota was at the other property today. There was a matching dresser and diaper-changing station that still needed to be filled, but the bulk of the furniture items were here.

"This is…" She spun around, her eyes filled with tears. "It's so perfect, Sutton, I can't…" She sobbed into her hands. The tears were a regular occurrence as she got farther along in her pregnancy, so I didn't get upset at seeing them right away. "They are going to love having you as their daddy," she carried on, a weepy mess.

I pulled her into my arms and held her while she cried. "And they are going to be the luckiest girls in the world having you as their mama. You really like it? We didn't do too much?" I asked. It was something Savannah had worried about when I told her I was going to surprise her by having the nursery put together. She'd been afraid that Dakota would want to do it herself, but my wife was beyond busy. And there was still plenty to do. Clothing, bathing gear, all the things babies needed like diapers, rash cream, and whatever else was on that list Doc Blevins gave us at our last appointment.

Dakota shook her head and wiped her tears with a soft chuckle. "Not at all. I'm so damn relieved. I mean, with planning to be in Norway for a couple weeks. And with training the new manager… It was starting to become a lot. This is… It's wonderful." She cupped my cheeks. "Truly a blessing. Thank you." She reached up and kissed me.

I smiled against her lips, then pulled back, looping her around the waist, kind of excited to do a show and tell. "Okay, the chair is a gift from Junior and Bonnie. The cribs are the ones we picked out online, as you can tell."

"Mmm-hmm." She went over to one of them. "And the quilts?"

"Made by a very excited soon-to-be-grandma." I grinned.

"They're super cute. I like the look, and the colors are exactly what I would have picked." She ran her hand over the fluffy comforter as if testing its softness.

"We'll still need to get all the clothing, bathing, and other stuff, but I wanted you to have something you could come sit in and connect to our girls when you are feeling overwhelmed."

"I love it. And I love you even more for doing it," she gushed.

I came up behind her and wrapped my hands around her stomach, holding her and our daughters within my arms. It was a position I'd been doing a lot. Feeling my wife pressed to my chest and our babies within my hands was unreal. The most beautiful feeling came over me every time I did it.

"There is literally nothing in this world that I love more than you and our girls. Nothing, baby," I whispered against her ear.

"Don't call me baby." She chuckled. "Pretty soon you're going to have a couple babies of your own!"

"Can't wait. As long as they look exactly like my gorgeous wife but have Auntie Savvy's attitude, I'll be just fine."

Dakota smacked my hand. "Hey! Take that back!"

I let her go and backed away playfully. "Make me!" I hollered and then bolted to our bedroom.

"I'm going to get you!" she threatened.

"God willing!" I yelled back, laughing.

DAKOTA

The next day...

Sutton's hand splayed over my bump for the seventeen millionth time. Even the tiniest bit of turbulence had the man reaching for his children. It was incredibly sweet and a bit annoying how much he touched the bump. I mean, I got it to some extent. I too was constantly rubbing my belly like a genie in a bottle about to grant me three wishes, but the man had zero boundaries when it came to me. That only got worse once my belly started to show, which was really early on since there were two of them invading the small space.

All I'd been able to focus on was when the awesome second trimester feeling was going to hit. I was still a mess. Endless hormonal mood swings, an adversity to meat, and of course, the never-ending fatigue. I was told by Doc Blevins once I was in the second trimester, things should lighten up.

Liar.

Every last person who told me things would get easier after a few months was full of shit. I was technically entering week seventeen, and being pregnant sucked. At least I wasn't vomiting every hour anymore. Now it was usually once a day, which felt like a major reprieve. Yay, me.

I shoved my husband's hand off my bump dramatically.

He snickered and instead moved it to my thigh.

I lifted my tablet and scanned the newest budget increase on the rebuild of the barn. I frowned as I noted another hundred thousand dollars had been added.

"What's this?" I pointed at the line item. "An extra hundred thousand for what?"

Sutton took the device and reviewed the astronomical charge. He'd been with me every step of the way as I rebuilt all that had been lost to my father's ill management over the years and thanks to Jarod's destruction.

"Dakota, you may have a mental block on this, but the person you slated to handle the breeding, that being Savannah, is not coming back to the ranch. And you haven't earmarked any funds for your sister's role that she will no longer be coming home from college to fill. Not to mention, you haven't replaced Jarod's position."

I groaned and lifted my hand in a stop-speaking gesture. "Don't even mention his name."

Linda pretended to be engrossed in her book from where she sat on the long leather couch. Duke Senior chortled and then covered his mouth and promptly stared out the airplane window when his wife chastised him by smacking his knee.

It had been generous of Erik to send his private plane to pick us up in Montana and take us all the way to Norway for the wedding, but I'd have preferred being alone with my husband. Once that thought filtered through my irritation, I immediately tossed it out like the crummy, hormone-induced irrationality that it was. Linda and Duke Senior had been nothing but incredibly loving and helpful since everything that happened on their farm. And they were devoted to hearing every morsel of information about their granddaughters soon to enter our world.

"Darlin', we need the help to get ahead of the season," Sutton rightly assessed.

I let myself slump deeper into the comfy leather chair. "It's just a lot of money. Every time I look at the budget, it keeps growing and growing. I know you said we're in this together, but it's..." I sighed and rubbed a circle around the spot where one of the babies was pushing against my insides uncomfortably.

Sutton took my hand, brought it up to his mouth, and pressed his lips there. "We have the money." He put his hand over the sore spot I'd been manipulating and rubbed it in glorious wide circles. Whichever baby that had been shifting moved again into a more comfortable position at the gentle prodding by their father. The discomfort eased entirely.

I shook my head. "*You* have the money. I'm just your charity case," I grumbled.

"Not true. If it wasn't a good investment, we wouldn't be investing. But since Savannah has written off any ownership, this is something you and I can build together. For our girls." He reminded me of the ultimate goal.

A legacy for our girls.

I swear he used our children as his way to get anything and everything. It worked, too. I clicked off the tablet, sighed, and tilted my head to his shoulder.

"What else is bothering you?" he asked.

"Savannah is getting married," I admitted.

"Yes, and we've known this was coming for months. Since the auction." He dipped his voice to a lower timbre on the word "auction." He'd admitted it to his mother once before, but she'd kind of let it go as though it were a joke, and we didn't feel it important to correct her. We were married. We were in love. We were having twins. How we got together didn't really matter anymore.

"What if…" I swallowed down the ball of fear wedged in my throat. "What if something happens?"

"Dakota, nothin' is going to happen. Get that thought out of your head right now. Everything is back to normal. No more shootouts, drunken fathers, or burning buildings."

"True. I mean, things have been super quiet…"

He nodded. "And that's exactly how it's going to stay."

"What if my maid-of-honor dress doesn't fit? I'm a whale

now."

"I'm sure the seamstress took into account you'd be over four months pregnant with twins."

"Yeah, but it could be tight," I grouched.

"Don't make problems where there aren't any. It's going to be a beautiful wedding. And besides, you'll get to see all the couples again from Las Vegas." He said *couples,* but what he meant was the *candidates* that we had been keeping in touch with since we met. Even Memphis and Jade were supposed to be there, all expenses paid, courtesy of Savannah's insanely rich hubby-to-be.

"It will be nice to see everyone. I just… I want everything to go smoothly. After last time…" I shivered, thinking back to watching my sister get shot, that bullet going through her and into Erik.

Sutton turned to the side in his chair. "I understand that things might be a little scary after what all of us went through, but let's do our best to focus on what this is supposed to be, okay? And that is a happy occasion. Two people who genuinely love one another starting their lives together. Two people you care about deeply."

I smiled and stared into his handsome face. His green eyes were dazzling against his tanned skin. His hair was swept out of his eyes sans the ever-present cowboy hat he wore on the ranch, giving me an unencumbered view.

"I love you, Sutton Goodall. Thank you for being everything I never knew I needed, but exactly what I could ever want."

He pressed his forehead to mine. "I love you too, Dakota Goodall. Thank you for being the dream girl I always wanted since the day I laid eyes on you."

"You're such a sap!" I teased, running my fingers over his jawline scruff.

"Only when it comes to you," he murmured and then took my mouth in a sweet kiss.

"This is your captain speaking," came the announcement through the cabin speakers. "In about thirty minutes, we'll prepare for landing in Oslo, Norway, where the temperature is a cool sixty degrees. Should be a wonderful Norwegian day."

I covered my bump with my hands and spun a circle around them. "All right, girls. Time to see Auntie Savvy get married!"

Sutton covered my hand, and I leaned deeper into his side. His warmth and love seeped into my soul and soothed me completely. With Sutton by my side, everything would always work out as it was supposed to.

Episode 124

Epilogue

SAVANNAH

Four months since the auction…

The dress was perfect. Perfectly me. Unlike the wedding dress I'd worn on the Goodall farm, the one that had reminded me of my mother, this dress…it was all me.

I stared at myself in the mirror and swayed from side to side, watching the silky fabric glide along my curves beautifully. The dress essentially covered me up from shoulders to toes. The top half had long sleeves and came all the way up to the neck. It was a unique crocheted lace style that created a see-through pattern that was breathable, but also included a very intricate design that spoke to me. The gown nipped in at the waist, accentuating my hourglass figure but flared out into a long, loose skirt that hit the floor. I'd chosen a dress that was created by a Scandinavian designer named Sadoni, who was known for the whimsical, feminine style that allowed brides the flexibility to move and be comfortable on one of the most important days of their lives.

Even though it was the end of summer in Norway, which

meant the weather had cooled dramatically, I was determined to marry Erik outside in nature.

We'd chosen a venue that not only included a restaurant with incredible cuisine cooked by world-renowned chefs, but the outside had a large grassy open section that overlooked Oslo. It was known to be the exact location of where Edvard Munch had stood when he painted *The Scream*, a piece of art that was very close to me and my future husband. We didn't have frills or a homemade arbor like before, but what we had was just right for us.

A view.

A meaningful memory.

And a great meal paired with lovely music, Johansen brews, and all of the people who meant something to us.

We didn't need or want for anything more.

My sister bustled into the room wearing a soft seafoam-green dress. It had this super cool twist in between the breasts that accentuated her new, pregnancy-enhanced boobs. The fabric tucked right under her chest in an empire design with the rest falling away loosely like mine.

"Savvy! Look at my boobs. They are huge! Aren't they smokin' hot?" She cupped her assets as if they could disappear at any moment. "At least there's one good side to being a portable cocoon!" She put her hands at the top and bottom of her bump. "Check me out. I look awesome. And I was so worried it would suck!" She continued blathering on until she realized I was fully dressed, then she stopped, her mouth fell open, and tears filled her eyes.

"You look…" Her breath fell away as she sniffed and wiped her cheeks. "I've never seen anything prettier in my whole life," Dakota gushed. "Jesus, why am I crying all the damn time? I swear these girls are turning me into a wuss."

I laughed and pulled her into my arms. "Thank you. And you do look amazing in that dress. I'm thrilled you like it."

She pushed her head back. "Sutton liked it so much we had

to take it for a ride before we got here. Sorry I'm a little late." She grinned devilishly, proving she wasn't sorry in the slightest.

That made me snort. "Glad to be of service."

"All joking aside... How are you?" Her gaze pierced mine in that knowing way only my sister's could.

I pressed my lips together. "Maybe a little scared. But not of marrying Erik. We had a counseling session just last night. Talked out our fears. Which is why we decided instead of the traditional bride walking down the aisle alone or with her dad, I'm going to walk down with Erik. We're taking every step in this new life together. Being afraid together. Taking chances together. All of it...together."

"I think what you're doing is inspiring. It's very you and Erik. That's all that matters today. It's your day. And just so you know, Faith's husband Joel is crazy protective. He puts the term alpha-male to shame. I thought Sutton was, especially since the twins, but..." She shook her head. "Not even in the same realm of protective. The man sent his security adviser and a team of guards early this morning. A *team*. As in like twenty men scouting every possible hiding place and taking up positions all over the property to report the comings and goings at all times. They look like FBI agents but cooler...and hotter." Dakota snickered.

"Yeah, Faith warned me that Joel was still reeling from their fiasco with her ex. Did you happen to get all the back history? She confided in us about being on the run before the auction and having been connected to a bad man, but apparently, there was some type of explosion and a warehouse shootout."

Dakota made a hissing sound. "After what happened to us on the farm, I feel it's best not to bring it up and just be cool with the extra hired security."

I nodded. "It actually makes me feel better knowing there are people here to make sure nothing happens."

Dakota perked up. "Good! Now let's get you in Mom's pearls and Irene's hair comb, and you'll be set to wed a Viking."

"Oh my God. He's not a Viking!" I couldn't help but laugh

at the continued comparison my poor Erik received.

"If it walks like a Viking. Talks like a Viking. Has hair like a Viking. Looks like a Viking. He's a dang Viking!" she continued teasing.

"Whatever." I rolled my eyes but found I was a lot calmer now that Dakota was here and had confirmed the extra security. I'd have to thank Joel and Faith for the support.

Dakota fixed my hair, helped me with our momma's pearls, and off we went to the venue.

When we arrived, we were bustled into a waiting room by Irene and Madam Alana.

"Oh, *cheri*! You look *magnifique*!" Madam Alana stated, then air-kissed both my cheeks.

"It's so good to see you again…under, well, better circumstances. Thank you for coming all the way to Norway."

"I wouldn't miss it!" Alana assured me. "I adore weddings and, unfortunately, this last group of candidates was sneaky with marriages." Her red-painted lips twitched with mirth.

There was a knock on the door, and Sutton pushed his way through. "The guests are getting rowdy. They've already tapped into the booze." He hooked a thumb behind him.

"Doesn't bother me. I could use a drink!" I admitted, my nerves making me jittery.

"Oh, I shall get us champagne!" Madam Alana tutted. "Be back in a minute."

Sutton went straight to my sister and cupped her bump as though it were a basketball, but his gaze was all on her. Constantly assessing if she needed anything or being right there when her gaze might drift to the side, her mind conjuring up bad memories. It happened to me too. The therapist assured us it would come less and less as we continued to heal and lived without anything traumatic happening.

"How you doin', darlin'?" Sutton cooed in that cowboy way that would make any cowgirl take notice.

"Wishing I could partake of the champagne too," she

pouted.

"You know, we could do a big shindig wedding if you'd like? After the babies come," he offered sweetly.

She made a gagging sound. "You think I want to go through marrying you again?"

"Well, yeah?" he answered, a boyish smile taking over his expression.

"You're delusional," she retorted.

"And you're beautiful." He leaned forward and kissed her. "Think about it."

She hummed. "Okay, I thought about it. No freakin' way. I hate weddings." Then her eyes widened, and she looked at me. "Except this one, of course." She tried to cover up her faux pas shamelessly.

Both Sutton and I laughed.

"Ugh, I have to pee," Dakota griped and curved her hands around her belly.

"Again?" I asked.

She glared. "Just you wait, sister. Your time will come," she threatened, rubbing her stomach.

"I'll take you," Sutton offered, looping his arm with hers.

"I can take myself to the bathroom. I'm not an invalid!" she bitched as he led her out of the room.

Irene turned to me and grabbed my hands. "I'm so glad we are here together on this day. I know what you and Erik went through was extremely traumatic and difficult. It was for all of us. But you've come through that dark tunnel and are now on the other side. I wish you and my son the happiest days ahead."

I pulled her into a hug. "Thank you, Irene. I'm ready. Cancel the champagne from Madam Alana and go ahead and ask Erik to come in and have the event planner get everyone seated. Once that's done, notify Dakota she can walk down the aisle with Jack."

She placed her hand on my cheek. "As you wish, *datter.*"

Daughter.

I inhaled fully and allowed that gift to permeate my soul. I was someone's daughter again. Someone who cared about me and wanted the best on my behalf. I loved it.

For a few minutes, I stood silently and just breathed. Allowing any fears to dwindle and fall away. The air changed as I heard the door open.

Erik gasped as I opened my eyes.

"I didn't think it was possible for your beauty to surpass the moment we admitted our love for one another, but I was wrong. You in that dress, about to be mine for eternity... Today you are the most stunning I have ever seen you."

I smiled so widely my cheeks hurt.

He wore a three-piece sand-colored tuxedo with a white dress shirt underneath. The vest highlighted his naturally trim waist and broad shoulders. His tie was a soft seafoam green that matched the new color scheme I'd chosen, which included the pale green mixed liberally with fall colors.

"You look good enough to eat." I smiled demurely, my cheeks heating as I thought back to how we'd started our morning—me spending a lot of time between his thighs before he flipped me over and rode me hard from behind.

"*Elskede*, you have already eaten me today. You'll need to save some dessert for later." He tsked playfully while his gaze heated from a golden hazel to a darker burnt umber color.

I held my breath as he lifted his hand.

"Are you ready to become Mrs. Savannah Johansen?"

I put my hand between his exactly as the music signaled it was time. "I've never been more ready for anything in my life."

MADAM ALANA

The Johansen wedding ceremony was magical. The gorgeous couple never took their eyes off one another from the moment they approached the edge of the aisle that overlooked all of Oslo. Jade Lee sat to my right with Memphis next to her. Behind us was the Pennington clan, squabbling and bickering like little chicks at my back. I had to shush them twice, much to Nile's amusement. He was not the problem. As it turned out, Ruby and Opal had never been to a wedding prior to their own, so they had no idea what to expect. They oohed and aahed at literally everything and whispered commentary regarding each verse from the bride's and groom's vows. It was rather comical and endearing how excited they were to be there.

I simply enjoyed Ruby and Opal. They were refreshingly genuine. Not something I found common in women with the kind of money these two had come into by marrying a Pennington twin. Though I knew the sisters wouldn't allow money to change who they were. After learning their history, I'd wanted to be part of their future growth. Plus, it was nice to have a group of women to turn to. I'd spent little time with the other candidates I'd helped in the past. Of course, I did check-ups to make sure everything was copacetic and each person was following through on their agreement, but most of the time, the personal relationship or connection I had with each of them fizzled out. Not so with this group. They were different. Every last one of them.

When the happy couple was announced as husband and wife, the attendees were led to an opulent reception space. Fall flowers in orange, red, yellow, peach, and brown filled the center of each table. Glowing tealights graced the room, giving a warm hum to the space. Lilting classical music played in the background, making a guest feel comfortable to sit down, have a drink, and chat intimately with the others at the table while the wedding party got settled. Which was what everyone did.

I spied Faith and Joel, their adorable little girls each clinging to one of their parents' hands as they were led to a large circular table in the back corner. Joel's mother and Faith's father followed them and sat down. A hunky, strapping young man took a position in the corner, standing like a sentinel, his eyes scanning the room. I glanced around and noted there were many men in black suits taking up positions across the perimeter. I smiled and shook my head. Joel Castellanos took no chances with his loved ones. I had to admit I was curious about everything that had occurred with them. All I could get out of Faith was that it was bad, it was over, and they were safe and happy in Greece. To calm my own fretful heart, I had requested a meeting with them to ensure Faith was indeed safe. She seemed happy, but with all the security, I would make a house visit to Santorini to double-check.

What happened to my Celine would not happen to any of my candidates.

Christophe reached forward and grabbed one of the open bottles of champagne on the table. "*Un verre, mon amour?*" *A drink, my love?* my husband asked.

"*Oui.*" *Yes.*

Memphis and Jade approached my table and pulled out two chairs. "Mind if we sit with you?" he asked.

I held out my hand. "Not at all."

Memphis offered Jade a seat, then took one of his own. Christophe poured Jade a drink, but Memphis shook his head. "Never had a taste for champagne. I'm going to go grab a beer." He lifted his chin to the other side of the room, where an open bar sat. "Anyone want anything?"

The three of us declined.

When Memphis left, I turned to Jade. "I'm sorry to hear you will not be joining us in the next auction in a few days."

Jade lifted her chin. "I've thought about it. I don't want to be married."

"You don't need to get married right now. You have plenty

of years, darling."

She shook her head. "No. I mean I *never* want to get married. I like being alone. I want to live my life the way I choose, not how a man wants me to live it. Or worse, how my parents expect me to live it."

I read between the lines of what she wasn't saying. "What would you like to do?" I asked.

"I want to be like you."

"*Moi?*" I put a hand to my chest in surprise.

"Yeah. A badass boss bitch. You do what you want. Make tons of money. Run your own business. Travel all over the world seeing whatever you want. You're gorgeous and banging a hot Frenchman."

Christophe chuckled and sipped his champagne, poorly pretending he wasn't listening.

"You just said you didn't want to marry." I reminded her of her own words.

"I don't. I want the hot Frenchman without the marriage certificate. Hell, I want ten hot Frenchmen throughout my life. I do not want kids. I want to be the master of my own destiny and am willing to work for it."

"Then why don't you? I know your family. You have means. You can do whatever you wish." I attempted to be delicate when referencing someone's wealth.

"My parents have means. A lot of means and bigger sway than you can imagine." She crossed her arms in defense. "I'm an Ivy League graduate, and no one will hire me because my father scares them off. He wants me to get married, have a dozen children, and be a good Korean wife like my mother. All of my sisters and brothers have had arranged marriages. It's why I attempted the auction in the first place. I thought perhaps I could get married on my own terms. And at least if I married rich, they couldn't say anything. I just…I couldn't go through with it."

Christophe nudged my shoulder and gave me a pointed look. Just that morning we'd discussed how overwhelmed with bidders I was becoming. I didn't have the time to research and secure as many candidates as my clientele desired. My business was growing astronomically. I needed help.

"Come work for me," I offered. "Be my protégé. Learn the business, and over time, as you grow and make profitable connections, I'll allow you to buy interest in The Marriage Auction."

Her mouth parted in shock before it turned into a smile. "Really?"

"Let's discuss more on the plane ride back to Las Vegas." I held out my hand.

Jade gripped it hard and shook it like a man would. I lifted my flute, and she did the same. We clinked our glasses and gave one another secret smirks. Having someone smart and capable like Jade to assist with the workload was exactly what I needed.

Memphis came back with Jack Larsen in tow, both of them holding large mugs of frosty beer.

The two men took their seats, and Jack's mercurial gaze drifted to mine.

"So, gentlemen, are the two of you ready for the next auction?" I asked.

Memphis and Jack simultaneously said, "Yes."

Memphis swung his head to the side, clearly shocked. "You're going to be a candidate?" he wrongly assumed.

Jack laughed and shook his head good-naturedly. "No. A bidder."

"Shoot, man. You have to find me a Black Queen with legs that don't quit when you're on the other side. Urge her to bid on me. Do a me a solid." He grinned, making him even more handsome. "I'm counting on you, brother."

Jack laughed heartily. "I'll do my best. As long as the Madam here has a sweet lady like Savannah up for bidding on, may both of us be happy men come next week."

"I heard that!" Memphis jovially clapped Jack on the back.

The festivities continued, and the night was filled with love, laughter, a great deal of beer and spirits, music, and couples sneaking kisses and happy sighs when they thought no one was looking. It was my favorite part of a wedding. When things just happened naturally. People making one-of-a-kind memories with their loved ones.

Savannah and Erik made their way over to our table. I reached out for her hand to inspect the ring. It was a brilliant, very large, sparkling heart-shaped diamond.

"Isn't it just perfect?" Savanah stared at the ring Erik had chosen in complete awe.

"It represents my heart being carried within your small hand." Erik had said those words when they'd exchanged vows at the ceremony. Now I knew better what that meant, and it was unbelievably romantic.

Tears pricked at my eyes as I took in the ring's splendor. "There is none better to represent your love," I agreed.

"We just wanted to thank you personally. For everything. Without you, none of this would have ever been possible. I hope you are always part of our lives," Savannah rushed to say and then hugged me tightly.

"I want that too." I clung to the lovely girl, breathing in her gratitude and letting it fill my heart so I was ready for the next group of candidates.

Something told me this next group would be the most gratifying experience yet.

One by one, I approached each of my candidates and bidders, giving and receiving hugs along with promises to keep in touch regularly. And I would. These men and women had become a meaningful part of my life. A part I didn't want to ever let go.

Christophe, Jack, Memphis, Jade, and I left that very next morning on a private jet headed back to Las Vegas.

It was time for the next Marriage Auction.

Episode 124B

Down the Road (Bonus 2nd Epilogue)

Eight and a half months since the auction…

SAVANNAH

"No, move it a bit to the right, honey." I shook my head even though my husband couldn't see it from where he was holding the massive portrait above the mantle.

"*Elskede*, if you keep me holding this picture another ten minutes above my head, after I've already positioned it around the house many times, at your request I might add… you're going to owe more than a blow job. I'm thinking sex, anywhere I want, whenever I want, no questions asked." He turned his head and gave me one of his lust-filled, I-want-to-fuck-you-right-now looks.

I had to clench my legs together. My husband knew how to make love. He could also fuck like a god, and I couldn't pick which I preferred. I just knew that anything he wanted, I was all in.

His lips tipped into a sultry smile, his gaze noticing my

flushed cheeks and the way I bit into my bottom lip as I imagined all the things he could conjure up sexually.

"Deal!" I cocked a brow and put a hand to my hip. "Now move it a little to the right." I reminded him of my request.

His nostrils flared, and he grumbled in mock-frustration.

"You know I'm good for it," I teased.

"That's it. I'm hanging it," he barked, resting the framed image on the mantle as he bent to his tools.

I stared at the image. It was of our wedding in Norway. I was snuggled into Erik's side, one arm around his back, the other in front, my hand over his heart. Both his arms were around me. My pregnant sister was at my other side, Sutton standing behind her looking dapper in his suit, his hands curled around their unborn babies, a proud, shit-eating expression plastered to his face. The Goodalls were standing next to Dakota, Linda and Duke Senior smiling sweetly. Erik's parents stood next to him, his parents in a cuddle much like our own, grinning happily. Jack was standing at Henrik's shoulder smirking, looking suave in his tuxedo.

"Yeah, it's perfect, honey," I whispered, joy in my tone as I remembered how amazing our real wedding had been. The most magical day ever.

My husband's lips twitched as he took hammer and nail to the wall above the fireplace and mantle. We were decorating our new home we'd purchased in Sandee, Montana, as we waited for *the call*. I double-checked my phone was on, the ringer on the highest volume just in case.

"Nothing on your phone, right?" I asked Erik for the millionth time today.

"*Ya,*" he mumbled, not checking his phone physically, which irked me.

Dakota was already in week thirty-four of her gestation. And for a woman carrying twins, the doctors had told us the babies could come at any time. I was determined to be ready the very second she called. The hounds of Hell couldn't keep me from being there for my sister when she brought my nieces into the world.

My nieces.

I was going to officially be an aunt. I'd already had one of the rooms set up in our new home as a children's room with a set of bunk beds. I also had two Pack-N-Play contraptions that doubled as a playpen but also as a sleeping space if Dakota and Sutton wanted a night alone. When Erik and I were here in the States, it was important to me that our extended family feel comfortable staying with us. Most specifically my nieces.

Since Dakota would need a lot of help with the girls and the farm, Erik and I had decided to live a full year in Montana with regular planned visits home to Norway. We also had a room set up for Irene and Henrik, who planned to come stay for the holidays. Since the fiasco on the Goodall ranch, Erik's parents had become close to Dakota's new family and enjoyed spending time together. They acted as if they'd been best friends for years not months.

Erik hung the wedding portrait centered over the mantle, then flicked the switch that made our fireplace blaze to life instantly.

"It's awesome." I smiled, enjoying everything about making this second home something special.

He came over to me and wrapped his arms around me from behind. His bearded chin rested against my neck. "Best day of my life...marrying my soulmate." His voice was a low, sultry rasp against the shell of my ear. Shivers skated down my spine as I leaned into him, covering his arms with my own.

"I loved watching you check off that final item on your bucket list." I sighed and leaned against him fully.

"Speaking of..." He reached into his back pocket, pulled out his wallet, and removed the battered, folded up, yellow piece of paper he'd carried around with him since the accident.

I watched silently, my throat clogged with emotion as he opened it, and together we scanned the list of things he'd completed. So many adventures he'd been on alone. None of those things healing the ache of what he'd lost.

"None of these had made me feel whole after the accident and losing Troy," he admitted. "Nothing but finding and marrying you," he growled, accenting it by tightening his hold on me. But he wasn't done. "My soulmate put all the broken pieces of me back together," he whispered. "Thank you, Savannah." He placed a warm kiss over my neck right where my pulse beat rapidly. "My *elskede*."

My beloved.

"I think it's time. No more bucket list. Just living life the best way we know how. Together. With love." I took the paper from between his fingers and walked over to the fireplace. "You ready?"

"Do it." His voice was a guttural rasp.

I nodded and slowly set the piece of paper over one of the hot logs.

His past hurts and the talisman he'd clung to caught fire around the edges, burning straight through to the center until there was nothing left but ash.

"I love you." I stared at my husband, so damn proud of him my heart was filled to bursting.

His gaze met mine, and he smiled. The haunted broken pieces within him were healed, mended by my love for him.

"*Jeg elsker deg,*" he said in his native tongue. Roughly those complex words meant: *You are my life. You are my reason for existing.*

For an eon, we stared at one another, completely caught up in the intensity of what we shared.

My phone blared from my back pocket, and I scrambled to answer. "It's Dakota," I breathed and clicked on the speaker phone.

"The babies are coming!" she announced.

Erik and I both grinned and jumped into action.

DAKOTA

"I swear on all things holy, Sutton, if you breathe on me one more time, I'm going to punch you right in the face," I threatened. His coffee breath was making me gag as another intense contraction rolled through me.

"Woman, shut your kisser and push already. Quit your bitchin' and bring my girls into this world!" he fired back, his arm holding my thigh all the way back to my armpit.

"Both of you, calm down," Savannah cooed softly, her presence in the birthing room a welcome reprieve from the havoc wracking my body.

"Savvy, just put me out of my misery. I can't do this." I gulped as the excruciating band of rippling pressure squeezed so tightly it was as if a bear trap had clamped around my entire abdomen and shredded me from the inside out. Blackness clung to the edges of my vision. "I love you, Sutton, you motherfucking asshole. Take care of our babies if I don't make it," I whispered as the darkness surged.

"Damn you, Dakota. You are not bailing on us! Get it together. I believe in you." A pair of lips pressed next to my ear. "You can do it, baby. Just one more push and Scarlett will make her appearance."

"Don't call me baby," I griped tiredly. "I can't. It's too much," I sobbed, hot tears tracking down my cheeks.

"You can and you will." Savannah held my other leg back.

I was being split in two.

"It's time. One hard push, Dakota, and we'll see Baby A's little face!" the doctor urged, doing something gross between my legs like massaging and stretching the skin around one of the twins' heads.

"Do it for me, darlin'. Do it for our girls. Come on. Be strong. Our daughters are counting on you."

Our daughters.

Something clicked inside me at remembering these girls needed me. I was their *mother*. It was my job to push everything else aside and fight.

For them.

A kernel of strength grew from the center of my chest and spread out, until it was invading every single one of my nerve endings with the need to fight, to win this battle and come out the victor. I inhaled a full breath as my entire body convulsed with shooting pain. Savannah and Sutton gripped my legs, holding them back as far as they would go as I bore down, pushing with all my might. With every ounce of strength I could muster, I pushed. There was an explosion of extreme pressure and then… unbelievable relief.

That relief did not last.

"Baby A is out!" The doctor sucked something out of the baby's mouth, and a couple nurses rushed to wipe away the birthing gunk. Suddenly a little wail pierced the air.

"Scarlett," I gasped, reaching my arms out. Before I could take hold of my daughter, my body turned against me once more, the pain ramping up to an unbearable level, stealing my breath.

"Fuck!" My head fell back, the weight too heavy for me to hold up. Sutton and Savannah whispered something sweet to me as they held my legs back for round two.

In a haze, I birthed Daisy. Her cries rippled through the air, making her anger known for all to hear. Those little lungs didn't stop until they placed her at my breast, where she snuffled around, found the target, and latched on angrily. Well, I knew which girl would end up like her mama.

Scarlett, however, was more docile, taking a bit more time

to casually latch and find her way toward nursing.

Things moved at the speed of light coming in and out of focus once the babies arrived. I didn't care. All I knew was I'd survived, and my daughters were curled in my arms, their daddy watching over all three of us.

Savannah kissed my forehead. "They're more than beautiful. Good job, Kota. I'm going to leave you four to bond."

"Wait," I said, and she stopped, her bright blue eyes shimmering with unshed tears.

"We just wanted you to know...this one—" I gestured my chin to the baby with shocking red wispy curls all over her crown. "Her name is Scarlett Savannah."

My sister's hands flew up to her face, where she covered her mouth, a shocked sob muffled behind them.

I smiled and gestured to my girl with the straight, blondish hair like mine. "This is Daisy Amberlynn," I whispered, letting my own tears fall.

"Kota," Savannah croaked. "I..."

"They're named after the strongest women I know," I whispered, meaning every word. "Congratulations, Auntie," I added.

"I'm honored. Congratulations, Mommy." She beamed, then slowly backed away and left the room, leaving me and my husband to bond with our daughters.

"Dakota, I have never been more impressed with another person in my life. You are incredible, darlin'. Thank you for making me a father. I will try to never let you or our girls down." He pressed his forehead to mine as we stared at our girls nursing.

"Just love them with your whole heart. That's all they need," I murmured and meant it.

Love was all Savannah and I had ever wanted and needed growing up, and we had it in each other. We also had it in the men we'd chosen to share our lives with. And now all that love would be shared with our girls.

"Well, they already own my heart, right alongside their beautiful momma." Sutton kissed my temple. "Now we just need to try for a brother who can keep them safe and protected."

I rolled my eyes. "I just went through literal Hell, and you're already wanting to do it again?" I griped.

My husband chuckled, loving to rile me up, even in the sweet moments.

"Besides, these girls are *sisters*. They don't need a man to protect them because they've got each other," I boasted.

"And their mommy has a wicked right hook." His green eyes twinkled as he rubbed at his jaw playfully, the memory of me punching him after the auction papers were signed filling my mind.

"Damn straight, and don't you forget it." I lowered my voice and tipped my chin up.

"Never," Sutton murmured against my lips as he took my mouth in a soft, languid kiss I'd remember forever.

FAITH

"Dad!" I hollered as I shuffled through the door of our restaurant carrying the freshly baked bread loaves, rolls, and Greek pastries the locals enjoyed. I picked them up before arriving to work every weekday.

"I'm up to my eyeballs in sauce back here," he yelled in return.

I set the bakery box on the long wooden bar that ran along

the entire left side of our space. It was the most perfect setup. When you entered, a hostess—usually Olympia or me—greeted our patrons from a small divider set in the center of the foyer where we had comfy seats for people to wait for a table if they hadn't called for a reservation. The left side was the bar and casual area. The right side more for the fine dining experience.

To say the Greek people of Santorini appreciated an authentic family-owned Italian restaurant was an understatement. We had many regulars who visited every week or two, not to mention eager tourists who wanted to eat something familiar when traveling, such as spaghetti and meatballs and simple pasta with marinara.

Penny and Eden either came to work with me, hung out with their nanny, Olympia's sister—their great aunt—or spent time with Joel or my father. Between a new business and Joel's busy schedule, we made it work. However, we never worked weekends and were closed on Mondays. We had a team of people who my father and I had trained from the beginning. It allowed us to give as much as we could to our business while still keeping a healthy work-life balance.

"Did the wine from the Penningtons arrive?" I called out while separating the baked goods into sections so I could put them away.

"It did," came a familiar accented voice I'd longed to hear for five lonely days.

I spun around just as my husband Joel placed a case of wine on top of the bar.

"You're home," I gasped, my entire body positively aching with joy.

"I am." Joel gifted me one of his patented boyish smirks, and I bolted into action, flying into his arms. "Oomph!" He fell back a step as I plowed into his strong frame, my face tucked to his neck, breathing in his cologne mixed with his own rich essence.

Before he could say a word, my fingers were tunneling

through his hair and tugging at his head so I could get my mouth on him.

He kissed me as though he hadn't seen me in a year when it had only been a five-day work trip to the States.

He'd met with Rhodes Davenport and his new wife, the same architect who had built The Alexandra. Joel had new sister resorts being built at the same time. A monstrous undertaking because they were meant to be twin buildings with entirely different but unique luxuries. The plan was for guests to be able to take advantage of both locations' amenities, depending on their preferences.

Joel nipped my bottom lip and pulled back. "I see you missed me," he teased.

"More than missed. I hate when you travel more than a couple days," I admitted, clinging to my husband's frame as though he might disappear at any moment.

"I dislike being away from you too." He cupped my cheek and ran his thumb and fingertips across my features. He often did this, reminding himself that I was alive and well. I let him because not only was it necessary for his mental health to physically reconnect with me, but having the love of my life trace my features with reverence also made me feel special.

"I'll call one of my staff in so we can have a family night together, just you, me, and our girls." I waggled my eyebrows in a silly manner that had him chuckling.

"Actually, if we could, I would like to discuss a matter that has been on my mind." He took my hands and brought them up to his lips, where he kissed directly over my wedding ring.

"Serious talk?" I queried.

He nodded as he kissed my fingertips, then let them go. He moved to the case of wine and pulled out a bottle. "I could use a drink."

I frowned, nervous energy slipping down the surface of my skin. "Okay, I'll have one with you." I went behind the bar and grabbed two bulbous red wine glasses in one hand and tucked the wine opener in my pocket. When I made it back around, Joel took my free hand and led me to our best table. It was a small, private alcove that had an open view of the clear blue sea beyond.

I handed him the bottle opener and set down the glasses and watched as he opened the wine and poured it into each goblet.

He unbuttoned his suit jacket, likely having driven directly from the airport to here since he wasn't in casual attire. I waited with bated breath as he held the drink aloft.

"To our future. May it be filled with the sound of laughter," he stated mysteriously.

I clinked my glass with his and sipped, never taking my eyes off of him, trying to figure out what it was he wanted to talk about. Anxiety clawed at my mind, but I pushed it down, centering myself in the present as my therapist had taught me.

"Joel, honey, you're freaking me out. What do you want to talk about?" I finally asked, my heart in my throat.

He leaned back, licked his lips, then rubbed his chin nervously. His hands were shaking. A million negative possibilities flashed through my mind.

"Joel...you're scaring me." My voice shook.

"I want a baby," he blurted completely out of nowhere.

"A baby?" I blinked, not having had any idea whatsoever that was the subject he wanted to talk about. Relief poured through my veins as I picked up the drink and gulped a good portion down, washing away the icky concern and anxiety completely.

"I want us to make a baby. I do not want to wait anymore. The girls are getting older..." He continued, planning to convince me when he didn't need to.

"Okay," I said.

"And a baby would be a wonderful representation of our love and what we've overcome and...wait." His brows pinched together. "Did you say okay?"

I smiled so widely my cheeks hurt. "Yes. Okay. Let's make a baby," I agreed. He'd talked about it before the horror that was Aiden and our experience on that airfield. We'd since been in counseling, moved my father to Greece, started a restaurant, and were living a wonderful life with our girls, who had completely settled into being a family.

He ran a hand through his hair and looked up at me sideways, his head cocked, as though he may not have believed me. "Really? I have a whole speech prepared to convince you. I've been working on it the entire time I was away."

I shrugged and sipped at the delicious wine. "I'm sorry. Did you want to share your speech?"

He stood up. "Fuck, no." He buttoned his jacket over what I noted was an impressive erection. Apparently baby talk got him hot and bothered. "I want to make love to my wife and create a child between us." His tone was direct and warm as melted chocolate.

"Now?" I giggled as he hooked me under the arm and helped me to stand abruptly.

"Yes, darling. If your father wasn't here, I'd have you bent over this table, my cock balls deep inside you. Now I must suffer through the ride home." He pressed his lips together almost as though he were pained.

I snorted at his discomfort. "Dad, I'm taking the night off," I hollered. "Call someone in."

"Will do, *cara mia*! Happy homecoming, Joel," we heard him yell from the kitchen.

Joel dragged me out of the restaurant we'd named *Cara Mia* and into the back of a waiting limo.

The second we were in the car, the privacy screen was put up, and I straddled my husband's lap.

"I can't wait to have a child with you," I whispered against his magnificent lips before kissing him deeply.

He fumbled with his jacket button and then with his pants, freeing his hardened length. I'd worn a sundress, so it was nothing at all for Joel to rip the delicate lace of my panties to shreds.

"I can't wait either. Now hop on my cock, darling." He rumbled his request into my ear.

I shivered, and he groaned and arched his head back against the leather as I slid over his weeping tip and plowed down until he bottomed out, my nails digging into his shoulders.

"God, yes," I mewled.

His mouth dragged over my neck as he palmed my breasts and pinched my nipples through my clothing. "Give me what I need, Faith," he demanded, wanting my orgasm before he would chase his own.

The heat built between us as I rode, desperate for release.

We kissed, we whispered filthy praises to one another, and then we both came on a surge of love and lust.

Nine months later, we welcomed our son, Chance Robert Castellanos.

Named as a reminder to us all that everyone deserved a second chance at happiness.

RUBY

"And the Academy Award for Best Musical Score in a major motion picture goes to…"

I held my breath and squeezed my husband's hand.

"Nile Pennington, for *Karma Strikes Back!*"

"I knew it, baby!" I whooped, not being able to contain my glee as I jumped up and threw my arms around my husband in front of the entire audience and cameras.

He cupped the back of my head and boldly, but briefly, kissed me in front of the entire world.

Nile's elation was painted across his stoic face in the subtle flush of his cheeks as he centered his glasses back into place and smiled. He held my hand all the way until just the tips of our fingers touched before he made his way up the glossy black steps of the stage.

The crowd roared with applause.

I stayed standing, not wanting to miss a single word he had to say as he accepted this particular award because I knew how much it meant to him. How much it meant to *us*.

"Thank you. Thank you all." He spoke with confidence. "I hadn't planned on sharing this musical piece with the world. *Karma Strikes Back* was actually a wedding gift to my wife, Ruby." He smiled down at me.

I held my hands clasped together under my chin while I stared at the man I adored and beamed endlessly, tears filling my eyes.

"She believed the piece deserved to be shared with the world, not kept within the privacy of our home." He held up the award. "As usual, she was right." The audience chuckled. "I'm incredibly thankful to the Academy for this award and to the producers on this film for keeping the name I'd given the piece and using it for the movie title. I couldn't have written a better story to go along with my heart's journey more than what has already been nominated for the Best Motion Picture award."

The crowd applauded wildly.

"Alas, there's only one person who deserves this more than me. My wife, Ruby Pennington." He locked his gaze with mine. "Our love story played out in this piece, and the world loved it almost as much as I love you."

He winked.

"Thank you for choosing me, Ruby."

I did choose him, and karma had indeed struck back, giving all of us exactly what we were meant to have. Opal and Noah were happily married and living in London. She was back in school, and Noah was learning more of the family business. They both participated in charity events right alongside Nile and me. The Pennington brothers and now the Pennington sisters were a formidable foursome. A team that put family and one another above anything else.

I lifted a finger to point at my eye, made a heart shape with my hands, and then pointed at the man who owned my soul. "I love you," I mouthed along with my movements.

In reality, it was Nile who had chosen me almost nine months ago when I'd been the one standing on a stage wishing for my life to change.

The Marriage Auction had changed us all in ways we would never fully understand, but if I had to do it all over again, I'd still sign on the dotted line, knowing there was no going back.

The End of The Marriage Auction Season 1.

If you want to read more right away, with pop-ins by your favorite Season 1 characters, you can read Season 2 as it publishes by episode, right now on Kindle Vella.

Want to know how it all started? Read *Madam Alana*, a 1001 Dark Nights novella featuring the owner of The Marriage Auction.

Madam Alana
A Marriage Auction Novella
By Audrey Carlan

From *New York Times* and *USA Today* bestselling author Audrey Carlan comes a new story in her Marriage Auction series...

I run the most elite auction in the world.

Candidates and bidders come from all over the globe hoping to change their lives.

And I deliver.

I'm in the business of bringing couples together in a mutually beneficial and legally binding marriage. The terms are three years for no less than a million dollars a year, not including my commission. Once a pair signs on the dotted line, the contract ensures there is no going back.

Most couples find over time they are a love match, but not all.

Before I took over The Marriage Auction, there wasn't an extensive vetting process. Some candidates were subjected to horrors that haunt my every waking moment.

I vowed to change that. To stand up for those who deserve more and to release them from the wrongs inflicted upon them by circumstance and chance.

What my bidders and candidates don't know is that I understand exactly what they are experiencing.

I wasn't always known as Madam Alana.

Once upon a time, I too was purchased in The Marriage Auction... And this is my story.

Acknowledgments

I can't believe it's done. Every single book has a ton of additional content that I hope each and every one of you enjoyed! This saga has been the most rewarding project of my entire life. I'm incredibly proud of it and I have all of you readers to thank for its success. There aren't words to express my gratitude. Truly. Thank you.

To **Team AC** for being the absolute best group of women I've ever had the pleasure of calling my tribe, my sisterhood, my team. You lift me up and bring me nothing but support, friendship, and love. I could not dream of a better group of incredibly talented and gifted women at my back. I adore every last one of you:

Jeananna Goodall – World's Greatest PA, Emotional Support Guru, Work Wife

Tracey Wilson-Vuolo – Alpha Beta, Disney Freak, Proofer, ADA Expert

Tammy Hamilton-Green – Alpha Beta, Rock Chick, Educational Expert

Elaine Hennig – Alpha Beta, Brazilian Goddess, Medical Expert

Gabby McEachern - Alpha Beta, Dancing Queen, Spanish Expert

Dorothy Bircher – Alpha Beta, Mom Boss, Sensitivity Expert

To **Jeanne De Vita**, how did we make it this far? It seems unbelievable. Thank you for staying the course, being so incredibly flexible, and believing I could do it. Your editing prowess is a wonder I'll never tire of experiencing. You make me a better writer and storyteller.

To **Michael Lee**, you're an amazing part of Team AC. We

love you and hope we can keep you with us for years to come. And thank you for all your "British-isms" I needed to learn as I fumbled through writing twin brothers from England. Your input was spot-on.

To my literary agent, **Amy Tannenbaum** with Jane Rotrosen Agency, *The Marriage Auction* might not have made it here without your encouragement. Thank you for staying by my side all these years.

To **Liz Berry**, **Jillian Stein**, and **MJ Rose** from Blue Box Press, I can't believe we're finally here. Having my name on a Blue Box Press label is nothing short of mind-blowing. Having it on four titles…shocking in the best way possible. I'd wanted to work with you ladies for years. And it has been better than I could have ever dreamed. I'm honored to be part of the family.

About Audrey Carlan

Audrey Carlan is a No. 1 *New York Times*, *USA Today*, and *Wall Street Journal* bestselling author. She writes stories that help the reader find themselves while falling in love. Some of her works include the worldwide phenomenon *Calendar Girl* serial, *Trinity* series, and the *International Guy* series. Her books have been translated into over thirty-five languages across the globe. Recently her bestselling novel *Resisting Roots* was made into a PassionFlix movie.

NEWSLETTER

For new release updates and giveaway news, sign up for Audrey's newsletter: https://audreycarlan.com/sign-up

SOCIAL MEDIA

Audrey loves communicating with her readers. You can follow or contact her on any of the following:
Website: www.audreycarlan.com
Email: audrey.carlanpa@gmail.com
Facebook: https://www.facebook.com/AudreyCarlan/
Twitter: https://twitter.com/AudreyCarlan
Pinterest: https://www.pinterest.com/audreycarlan1/
Instagram: https://www.instagram.com/audreycarlan/
Tik Tok: https://www.tiktok.com/@audreycarlan
Readers Group:
https://www.facebook.com/groups/AudreyCarlanWickedHot Readers/
Book Bub: https://www.bookbub.com/authors/audrey-carlan

Goodreads:
https://www.goodreads.com/author/show/7831156.Audrey_Carlan

Amazon: https://www.amazon.com/Audrey-Carlan/e/B00JAVVG8U/

Discover 1001 Dark Nights Collection Ten

DRAGON LOVER by Donna Grant
A Dragon Kings Novella

KEEPING YOU by Aurora Rose Reynolds
An Until Him/Her Novella

HAPPILY EVER NEVER by Carrie Ann Ryan
A Montgomery Ink Legacy Novella

DESTINED FOR ME by Corinne Michaels
A Come Back for Me/Say You'll Stay Crossover

MADAM ALANA by Audrey Carlan
A Marriage Auction Novella

DIRTY FILTHY BILLIONAIRE by Laurelin Paige
A Dirty Universe Novella

HIDE AND SEEK by Laura Kaye
A Blasphemy Novella

TANGLED WITH YOU by J. Kenner
A Stark Security Novella

TEMPTED by Lexi Blake
A Masters and Mercenaries Novella

THE DANDELION DIARY by Devney Perry
A Maysen Jar Novella

CHERRY LANE by Kristen Proby
A Huckleberry Bay Novella

THE GRAVE ROBBER by Darynda Jones
A Charley Davidson Novella

CRY OF THE BANSHEE by Heather Graham
A Krewe of Hunters Novella

DARKEST NEED by Rachel Van Dyken
A Dark Ones Novella

CHRISTMAS IN CAPE MAY by Jennifer Probst
A Sunshine Sisters Novella

A VAMPIRE'S MATE by Rebecca Zanetti
A Dark Protectors/Rebels Novella

WHERE IT BEGINS by Helena Hunting
A Pucked Novella

Also from Blue Box Press

THE MARRIAGE AUCTION by Audrey Carlan

THE JEWELER OF STOLEN DREAMS by M.J. Rose

SAPPHIRE STORM by Christopher Rice writing as C. Travis
Rice
A Sapphire Cove Novel

ATLAS: THE STORY OF PA SALT by Lucinda Riley and
Harry Whittaker

A SOUL OF ASH AND BLOOD by Jennifer L. Armentrout
A Blood and Ash Novel

START US UP by Lexi Blake
A Park Avenue Promise Novel

LOVE ON THE BYLINE by Xio Axelrod
A Plays and Players Novel

FIGHTING THE PULL by Kristen Ashley
A River Rain Novel

A FIRE IN THE FLESH by Jennifer L. Armentrout
A Flesh and Fire Novel

VISIONS OF FLESH AND BLOOD by Jennifer L.
Armentrout and Rayvn Salvador
A Blood and Ash/Flesh and Fire Compendium

On Behalf of Blue Box Press,

Liz Berry, M.J. Rose, and Jillian Stein would like to thank ~

Steve Berry

Doug Scofield

Benjamin Stein

Kim Guidroz

Tanaka Kangara

Asha Hossain

Chris Graham

Chelle Olson

Kasi Alexander

Jessica Saunders

Stacey Tardif

Jeanne De Vita

Dylan Stockton

Kate Boggs

Richard Blake

and Simon Lipskar

Made in United States
North Haven, CT
06 August 2024

55727497R10212